Previous books by
Ruth Prawer Jhabvala:

NOVELS

Amrita
The Nature of Passion
Esmond in India
The Householder
Get Ready for Battle
A Backward Place
Travelers
Heat and Dust
In Search of Love and Beauty

STORIES

Like Birds, Like Fishes
A Stronger Climate
An Experience of India
How I Became a Holy Mother
Out of India

THREE CONTINENTS

RUTH PRAWER JHABVALA

A FIRESIDE BOOK
PUBLISHED BY SIMON & SCHUSTER INC.
NEW YORK LONDON TORONTO SYDNEY TOKYO

Copyright © 1987 by Ruth Prawer Jhabvala

First Fireside Edition, 1988

Published by the Simon & Schuster Trade Division by
arrangement with William Morrow and Co., Inc.

Simon & Schuster Building
Rockefeller Center
1230 Avenue of the Americas
New York, New York 10020

FIRESIDE and colophon are registered trademarks
of Simon & Schuster Inc.

Designed by Deirdre C. Amthor

Manufactured in the United States of America

1 3 5 7 9 10 8 6 4 2 Pbk.

Library of Congress Cataloging in Publication Data

Jhabvala, Ruth Prawer
Three continents.

"A Fireside Book."
I. Title. II. Title: 3 continents.
PR9499.3.J5T47 1988 823 88-4588

ISBN 0-671-66362-3 Pbk.

For James Ivory and Ismail Merchant

My thanks and deep appreciation to the
John D. and Catherine T. MacArthur Foundation
for their most liberal—and liberating—support.

CONTENTS

1
PROPINQUITY

MICHAEL, my twin brother, and I always wanted something other—better—than we had. Of course people would say that what we had was pretty good, and from a materialistic point of view that would be true. Our family name was well known, both our great-grandfather and our grandfather having held office in Washington; and though our parents were forever complaining that they were completely broke, this was part of their character rather than actual fact—our father because he was always overspending his allowance from the family trust, and our mother because she was afraid someone might ask her for money. They were divorced, and since the age of six, Michael and I lived mostly with our grandparents in the various embassies to which Grandfather was posted. That was how we came to spend some crucial years in the Middle East and then farther East; and it might be from those years that we got our restlessness, or dissatisfaction with what was supposed to be our heritage—that is, with America. Our last year of high school was in the International School in Bangkok and after that we both got into the college traditional to our family, where Michael lasted one semester and I two. Michael got back to the Orient as fast as he could, and then he traveled around and was sometimes in Kathmandu and sometimes in Goa, and then he turned up in Buddh Gaya, and then Gangtok, and back in Kathmandu. I missed him terribly and really didn't know what to do with myself when he was away.

It was during that year that Michael became involved with Crishi and the Rawul and Rani and all of them. He was one of the people who wanted to give his life for them and their cause. It was I who was skeptical at first; that is, when he first brought them to stay with us. It was the summer when I was nineteen—very long ago—and trying to decide whether to go back for my sophomore year or not. I was relieved when Michael called from London to say he was coming home; he was the one person who could help me decide. I wasn't bothered when he said he was bringing some friends—usually his friends just drifted around in the background and didn't get in anyone's way. I mean, in Michael's and my way; no one of them had ever come between us. But I was surprised the way he was so particular about how these new friends were to be entertained. He told me to call Lindsay, our mother, to the phone, and then he gave her very precise instructions, which threw her in a fit. He wanted all the best bedrooms made up, including the big front one where our grandparents slept when they came, and the entire house and grounds to be cleaned up for these friends of his who were apparently very important. I couldn't understand it at all, because Michael usually avoided important people; in fact, he couldn't stand them.

When they arrived, it really was like royalty descending on us. I'm trying to remember who was with them; they had quite an entourage—they never traveled without one—but so much has happened since and there have been so many people coming and going, that I can't remember who was there that first time. Or perhaps I didn't notice the people on the periphery because they were eclipsed by the ones at the center: that is, the Rawul, the Rani, and Crishi. These three made an overwhelming impression, singly and together. A lot of time has passed and what has happened has happened, and it is hard for me to describe how I saw them at first meeting. But I will try to do so as though they were three strangers who played no part in my life.

It is easiest with the Rawul, because my opinion of him, or perhaps I mean my feelings for him, has not changed so much as for the other two. The Rawul's personality was royal and gracious. He *was* royal, he had a kingdom—a very small but very ancient one: the kingdom of Dhoka. The Rawul was tall and stout and imposing, and he usually wore handsome English suits and shoes, and when in town he carried a rolled umbrella just like an English gentleman—which he was, besides everything else, for he was brought up there and went to Harrow and Cambridge. He had English manners and an English accent, but very much softened by his Oriental disposition. One only had to look at his eyes to realize how different he was from English people—for instance, from Manton, our father, and our grandfathers on both sides; it was over two hundred years since their ancestors came to America, but they still had those very Anglo-Saxon eyes, cold and blue like the sea. The Rawul's eyes were not the usual kind of liquid brown that Indians have but were light gray —opalescent almost, in his dark face. I thought of them as mystical; a dreamer's eyes. Of course he *was* a dreamer—of the past, when his ancestors conquered and ruled their desert kingdom, and of the future, when he himself would rule, in his own way. There was nothing selfish or ambitious about him; he was as idealistic as Michael, and probably that was how Michael got involved with them all in the first place. Because he thought that they—like he and I—wanted something better than there was. And in the Rawul's case this was probably true.

The Rawul was Indian, and when I first saw her, I thought the Rani was too. She was dark and voluptuous, and though she usually moved slowly and languorously, she gave an impression of power and energy held in check. She had marvelous teeth, so strong that she could bite and chew anything. I never got it quite clear what nationality she actually was— as I didn't at first with Crishi; but like him, she was a mixture of various strains, partly French, partly Afghan, even a little bit of German. All this made her very beautiful, and she also had these very beautiful clothes and jewels. She was always called the Rani, and it wasn't till later that I realized this was not a title but the name she had adopted. Her real name was Renée.

As for Crishi—it is impossible for me to look back and see him as I did then at the beginning. What I do remember is that I thought I disliked him. I said so to Michael; I said

"He's—." I didn't have to put the adjective; Michael and I
never had to finish sentences with each other, we always knew
what we meant and usually agreed on everything. But that
time Michael didn't agree. He said I didn't understand, and
I said again, "But he's—." Michael wouldn't discuss it any
further; he was very preoccupied and didn't have time for
me—which made me unhappy, because there was so much
I had to say to him. But he was entirely taken up with our
guests and eager that everything should be done for them.
And for once he and Lindsay were in total agreement. Usually, if we brought any guests, Lindsay just simply, as she
said, couldn't be bothered. If we argued with her, she said
"But darling, everything's there, isn't it, what more do they
want?" It was true that everything was there: that is, the big
house and grounds, with lake and springs and woods—Lindsay's whole estate, Propinquity, which had been in her family
since the early years of the century, when they made a fortune
in dry goods. Lindsay was the last survivor of her generation—the others had drunk themselves to death long ago—
and so it was all hers now and Michael's and mine; we were
the only descendants. Although she had other places, like
her apartment in the city and a ranch in Arizona she had
leased out, this was where she liked to be the most; usually
she was alone here with her woman friend, Jean, and neither
of them welcomed visitors. But this time, with these visitors,
Lindsay felt differently. She was excited.

Our visitors *were* exciting—everyone felt that, even I, who
was the only one not pleased to have them there. Around
the exotic trio was a retinue of followers. Although these
must have had pronounced personalities of their own, they
were so completely overshadowed that I can't even remember
who they all were at that time. The Rawul's retinue was constantly changing because there was a lot of rivalry and jealousy among its members, so that they had often to be sent
away and replaced or reshuffled. But they were always the
same type of people—pale, intense, and overworked; all were
young in age but not in spirit, and there was something depressed about them, or maybe I mean repressed. It was hard
to distinguish male and female because they all wore the same
type of light-blue shirts and dark-blue jeans like a uniform;

they were also all rather sexless. At night, at least one of them slept on the floor outside the master bedroom where the Rawul and Rani were. I don't know where the rest of them slept, or how many to a room, but the whole house was filled with people and activity. The phone rang a lot with overseas calls, and there was always a hum of typing and click of Xerox machines that had been installed, and people going around with messages and important faces. It was all very, very different from Lindsay and Jean's usual life in the house, where they stayed mostly in the kitchen and Jean did the cooking as well as the gardening and other outside work. Now their part-time handyman and cleaning woman and some other local people who helped them out had to come full time, and Lindsay's old Austrian cook, Mrs. Schwamm, whom she had been glad to get rid of and retire, was recalled. Jean couldn't stand Mrs. Schwamm and vice versa, but since she was a marvelous cook and the Rawul a gourmet, Jean had to put up with her.

What was it all about? Who were they, and why had they come? I waited for Michael to tell me, but he had no time to tell me anything. "You'll find out," was all he said. I didn't want to emerge from my room and tried to shut out everything that was going on beyond my door. From the first evening, they all gathered under the maple on the side lawn. I saw them from my window, and also I saw that the Rawul was addressing them and everyone sat still and listened, even Lindsay, who was usually very fidgety and got bored very quickly. The only one who was not spellbound was the Rani, who was playing with the bracelets she wore halfway up both arms. She was also the only one who looked around her and up at the house, and when she did that, I got away from the window. I didn't want anyone to think that I was in the least interested. But actually no one seemed to think anything at all—about me, that is; they never saw that I was missing, not even Michael.

On the third day of their arrival, I went to Michael's room early in the morning. It just shows how wrong things were that I had to wait that long to see him alone, for usually when we had been separated, we had so much to communicate that we stayed together all night. But this time Michael hadn't even noticed, and when I came in his room he said "What's the matter?" and I replied "*You* tell me." I turned the key in the door, which we always did to be together, but he said "No don't, someone might want to come in." "Who?" I asked; and then I said "Who are these people?" He was still in bed, but when I wouldn't unlock the door, he got up and did it himself.

His room was the same as mine. Both of us liked bare walls, bare floors, and no curtains, to let in as much light as possible. The only books were those we were currently reading, which he chose for both of us (the ones around this time were Buddhist texts). Any attempts by Lindsay or Jean or anyone to relieve the ascetic atmosphere were defeated. And besides the sameness of our rooms, being with him was like being with myself; and as soon as he got back in bed, I sat in my usual cross-legged, or lotus, position at the end of it, and it was as it always had been between us. He began straight off to answer the questions I hadn't yet asked—he had got as far as, "When I met them in London, Harriet, from that moment, that absolute moment in time—" when there was a knock at the door that wasn't a knock so much as a rap of command: and simultaneously the door was flung open and Crishi came in. I looked not at him but at Michael—I ought to explain that Michael and I often felt as with one body, so the shock that passed through him at that moment seemed also to pass through me. I was startled, for that was the first time I felt it, though later I got used to it, for I had it too whenever Crishi appeared: the same shock—I would say thrill except that word isn't physical enough to express the sensation he induced, as of a live electric wire suddenly coming into contact with an innermost part of one's being.

He had come only to borrow some shaving cream and departed as swiftly as he had entered: just throwing off some obvious sort of crack and a quick smile and glance at Michael and me. I didn't know it then, but this was typical of him— an inane remark on his lips, he could penetrate you with his eyes and his smile in such a way that after he had gone he remained vibrating within you. Michael leaned weakly against his pillow and even shut his eyes for a moment. But when he opened them, he was radiant. He tried to tell me; he said

"This is it, Harriet. *Om*, the real thing," and an outsider might have interpreted this as meaning that Michael was in love. But I knew it was something much more, for that wasn't what Michael and I had been searching for—the *Om*, the real thing—through our restless yearning childhood and growing up.

I didn't ask Michael if he thought I should go back to school. The question was settled: for if he had found what he said he had, going back to school was a very trivial and irrelevant issue. He began to tell me about the Rawul's movement. It was a world movement, involving empires—actual as well as intellectual ones. Well, Michael and I were used to thinking big—we had always done it. While our parents were having marital squabbles and adulterous love affairs and our grandparents were giving diplomatic cocktail parties, he and I were struggling with the concepts of Maya and Nirvana, and how to transcend our own egos. Anything smaller than that, anything on a lower plane, disgusted us. I was used to following Michael's lead, so when he said that the Rawul and Rani and Crishi operated on the highest level possible, I didn't contradict him, although it seemed to me at that time that they were very worldly people. But Michael understood what was on my mind, and he confessed frankly that at first he too had thought that and hadn't taken them seriously enough. In fact, he had got completely the wrong impression—both from Crishi and from the other two.

He had met Crishi first, in Delhi, where they were staying in the same hotel. Michael was as usual alone, and Crishi with a bunch of other people. The hotel was wedged in at the end of an alley, opposite a Hindu temple where they chanted and rang bells at dawn and at dusk. The hotel was a narrow, shaking building; the rooms were on three upper floors, and downstairs, open to the street, was an eating stall that supplied them with meals. Michael's room faced the temple, and when they started up at dawn, it was as if those holy sounds coming over loudspeakers were right in there with him, shaking the walls. He wouldn't have minded that—in fact, he liked it—but he had been kept awake by the noise from Crishi's room, where they were up talking and sometimes fighting or playing flute and guitar till just before the temple bells got going. Michael didn't complain; after all, he hadn't come to India to *sleep*. Sometimes he joined Crishi and his friends in their room. This was as cramped as his own and was painted in the same bright-blue color and had a dim light bulb under a paper shade; it also had the same smell of dirty bedding, cockroaches, and stale food, which they tried to relieve by burning sandalwood incense. Michael had already met some of Crishi's friends, in Kathmandu and Varanasi and other places where they all traveled. He hadn't met Crishi before and liked him at once. Crishi was easy and friendly. He was also stimulating. One reason Michael preferred to travel alone was that others on the same trail often had a depressing effect on him. They would sit around in their hotel rooms or outside tea stalls in the bazaar, swapping information about the cheapest places to stay, or stories of how they had either been cheated by or had outwitted some native trader. Some of them were sick with dangerous and infectious diseases like jaundice or dysentery, and some of them had blown their minds so that you might as well have been sitting with robots, Michael said. He also said that some of them were so stinking dirty, it was difficult to be near them.

But Crishi and his group were different. Crishi kept everyone lively and alert—it wasn't that their conversation was in any way elevating, not at all, it was often quite childish. But everyone had something to say and was eager to say it; or perhaps eager to get his attention—there was always tension in the air, as of rivalry. Crishi himself was absolutely relaxed and didn't seem to encourage one person above another, but lay on the floor cooling his bare chest under the fan. Michael couldn't remember anything particular he ever said or did, except once when he suddenly turned on a German girl, who was sitting as near to him as she could get, and told her, "Phew, get away from me, Ursula—you *stink*." The girl pretended to laugh it off, but later Michael passed her on the stairs, sobbing with her head on her knees. Michael stepped around her without saying anything—not only was it true that she was very dirty, but she was also very pregnant, and this was off-putting to Michael, who hated anything like that, any female manifestations.

Michael never made arrangements to meet people again,

because he knew he always would. They covered vast tracts of the earth, but they traveled within a narrow route of the same sort of cheap hotels, beaches, and campsites, and spent many nights on the floors of airport lounges or bus terminals. It was in some such place that Michael expected to meet Crishi and his gang again someday; but when he did meet him, it was somewhere so entirely different that he didn't recognize him. It was in Berkeley Square, in London; Crishi was emerging from an art dealer's and about to step into a limousine. It was he who recognized Michael; that wasn't difficult because in those days Michael wore the same sort of clothes wherever he was—jeans, *kurta,* steel bangle, and one earring. But Crishi himself was transformed, in a velvet jacket and silk scarf tucked into his shirt. He was cordial to Michael but was in a hurry; he offered him a ride, which Michael refused because he was staying nearby. "Where?" Crishi asked. Michael muttered—he hated it to be known that he was staying at the embassy. But Crishi got it out of him, and also that the ambassador was a family friend, and after that everything else about our family; so then Crishi became cordial in a different way, and he invited Michael to come and visit him; and that was how Michael got involved with them all—that is, with the Rawul and Rani and their entourage, and with their Seventh World movement.

In order to find out more about this movement, I began to join the group under the tree when the Rawul gave his evening talks. It took me some time to get used to his accent. He spoke the way Englishmen themselves no longer speak —in a very upper-class drawly way that made him sound like a stage Englishman. In appearance he was plump and pampered, not a bit like a leader of a new world or redeemer of the old. All the same, these talks under the tree were inspiring. The setting may have had something to do with it— those beautiful summer evenings with the sky gold from the sun melting into it, and behind us the pillared house dark in shadow, and in front of us the lake illuminated by the sunset and reflecting, like an underwater painting, the woods on the opposite bank and the deer that came out to drink. The members of the Rawul's entourage—those pale messengers—sat enthralled, though they must have heard him a thousand times. Their enthusiasm and reverence affected everyone else—Lindsay and Jean and even Mrs. Schwamm, who came out of her kitchen to listen to the Rawul; and when he had finished, she went back and clattered among her pots and pans, muttering "Good heavens, good heavens," in sheer wonder at what she had heard. It was then I realized that everyone—everyone in the world, maybe, and not only Michael and me—would like to have something better than they had, and when it was offered to them, were ready to rise to heights one would not have suspected.

Even Lindsay, our mother—I say "even" because she had never before in her life shown interest in anything except having a good time. When she was young, she had liked to dance and go to parties and sail and ski and whatever else girls like her did. When she got older, she couldn't understand why things weren't fun anymore; and before she met Jean, it had been so tough for her that she had been trying out psychiatrists and psychotherapists and people like that. But with the Rawul everything promised to start again—the fun, that is—and she really liked having those people there and the activity; and there was no doubt that the Rawul and Rani were what she called "nice people." However small his kingdom, the Rawul really was a king—descended, as he explained in his evening talks, from a long line of kings; and the Rani was his consort. Lindsay was fascinated by the Rani—by her wonderful Paris clothes, and her Oriental jewelry, as well as her manner, which was mostly languid and indifferent. She often absented herself from the evening talks, and also from the terrific meals that Mrs. Schwamm cooked with such enthusiasm and the Rawul ate with such relish. The Rani stayed a lot in her room—the master bedroom at the top of the double staircase allotted to her and the Rawul— and when she emerged, she didn't talk much but yawned often as she moved around in that gliding walk of hers, with her full hips oscillating in silk. Her eyes tended to be half closed, which made her look lazy but also as if she were awaiting what was going to happen, biding her time. Crishi's eyes gave the same impression—as of someone, though more a magnificent animal than a person, half asleep and yet at the same time alert, and watching.

Crishi, it was generally understood, was the Rawul and Rani's adopted son. The Rawul may have been old enough to be his father, but the Rani was certainly not more than a few years, at the most eight or ten, older than Crishi. No one ever went to much trouble to explain the relationship of the three of them, so that anyone who cared to speculate on it was free to do so. Crishi spent a lot of time locked up either with both of them, or with the Rani alone, in their bedroom; but of course they did have a great deal to discuss, all sorts of secret matters of high state—after all, they were leading a world movement; that was what was important, not the personal relationship there might or might not be between them.

However, personal relationships did play an enormous part within their entourage. The air around us became charged with strong feelings, emanating from an unlikely source: from the pale, devoted followers. One would have thought that they had too selflessly immersed themselves in their cause, and besides, were too anemic to be the victims of such passions. But as the days passed, it became clear that jealousy and rivalry raged among them. It was a matter of the highest importance who slept outside the master bedroom, who went in and out with messages, who was allowed to carry out the most personal duties. From behind the closed doors of the attic rooms, into which they had been crammed, came sounds of quarreling; sometimes a girl could be seen running up the stairs with a handkerchief pressed to her face; wandering around the grounds, one was very likely to come across a solitary figure seated in tears by the side of the lake, or lying face down under a tree in what used to be the apple orchard. I began to realize that involvement in a higher cause did not so much still the lower passions as stir them up and bring them to a pitch.

Although I was at that time indifferent to the Rawul and Rani, and Crishi, to say nothing of their movement, I was not immune to the tense atmosphere in the house. That was because Michael had become a part of it. He was deeply involved in the movement—he really believed in it; he was also deeply interested in Crishi. Both these states of mind were new in Michael; I had never before seen him anything but detached, calm, his own person totally. It was the way we both tried to be. Although we were twins, we didn't look that much alike—Michael was very fair and I had dark hair—but there must have been some other sort of close resemblance because people always commented on it. Except with each other, neither of us talked much, or laughed very easily; this may partly have been in reaction to our parents, who did a lot of both. People called us aloof—well, we never put ourselves out to make friends, preferring to be either alone or with each other. Certainly neither of us was the type to join a movement or follow a leader of any kind; we would have been the last people to do that. It wasn't that we didn't believe in anything—we did: but it wasn't ever anything you could share with outsiders, only with each other, who thought and felt the same. For us, believing was something you had to do for yourself—find for yourself—test out for yourself—and not be influenced by anything or anyone outside. Perhaps it was a quest for truth, though we never called it that: We didn't call it anything but we knew what we meant. Mostly we knew what it wasn't, and we used the word *neti,* the way other people use the word *phony.* "Oh no, neti," we would tell each other—about a book, a person, a thought, a situation. When something didn't come up to our standard, it was neti: not right, not *Om,* not *Tao,* not the real thing; phony. I would have said straight off that the Rawul's movement and his entourage, if not the Rawul himself, were neti, but for once, for the first time, Michael did not agree with me.

Here I might as well start talking about Crishi. Only where to start? At that time I saw him so differently. I don't suppose I ever did see him really objectively, because even then, at the beginning, when my own feelings weren't involved, Michael's were. Of course Michael had had special friendships before; I was used to that, and it didn't bother me. Although these friendships were usually intense, it was only physically, so that when that was over, it was all over and Michael was himself, and mine, again. But with Crishi I wasn't even sure that it was physical, though they did the usual romantic things, like taking the boat out on the lake by moonlight, or swimming nude by the waterfall, or if anyone had lit a bonfire they would sit by it and poke around in the embers long after

everyone else had gone to bed. But whereas Michael was tense
and trembly, Crishi seemed too in control of himself, and of
Michael, to be much affected; as if he could take it or leave
it, whereas Michael couldn't leave it at all. If at any time
during the day he didn't know exactly where Crishi was, he
would go quite wild and walk around asking everyone, and
sometimes people told him lies to save his feelings. Michael
knew perfectly well—it may have been partly why he was so
desperate—that Crishi was involved with girls in the entourage. And of course there was the Rani, with whom he was
very intimate—neither of them made any secret of that, and
when they presented each other as adopted mother and son,
it was in an indifferent, believe-it-or-not way. Michael himself
tried hard to believe it. Once, when I commented that she
seemed awfully young to be Crishi's mother, Michael got
quite worked up: "Young? She? She's as old as Medusa."
"How old is Medusa?" When Michael frowned at this would-
be joke, I said, trying to sound casual the way I always did
when I mentioned him: "How old is Crishi?" Michael shrugged:
"Obviously years younger than she is. Years and years," he
said fiercely.

It was hard to tell how old Crishi was; and even harder
when you knew everything he had done and everywhere he
had been, so that on calculating you could only wonder "Surely
he can't be *that* old?" He looked, at first sight, quite young.
That may have been because he was so lithe and quick and
always on the go, you could hardly keep up with him the way
he ran around, and always in a terrifically good mood. It was
only when you looked closer and saw the corners of his mouth
and the skin around his eyes—but of course then, at the
beginning, I never did look closer; that came later. And it
was as difficult to make out his nationality as his age. His way
of speech was a strange mixture—sometimes there was a
slight Oriental lilt, and he used the usual international Amer-
icanisms; but his most basic accent was the sort of Cockney
that was fashionable at the time, having supplanted the English
the Rawul had learned to speak at Harrow. His appearance
too was ambiguous: At first sight, he might have been an
Italian or a Spaniard, but then there were his slightly slanted
eyes, his double-jointed fingers, his very slim ankles, and feet

so narrow that he had difficulty getting shoes to fit him.

Besides myself, the other person in the house who wasn't 100 percent enthusiastic about our guests was Jean. In her case, it was mostly jealousy over Lindsay and the quiet, secluded life they had made for themselves. Or rather, Jean had made—she was always very much in charge, and though it was Lindsay's house, she was glad to have someone else look after it. Jean used to run a successful realty business, which she had sold at a good price after deciding to devote herself to Lindsay. She was an excellent businesswoman, hearty and one of the boys in her dealings with the world, but in her private relations she was ultrasensitive and very vulnerable and feminine inside her shapeless unfeminine body. Before they had settled down together as a more or less married couple, she and Lindsay used to have terrible fights. Many of them were about Mrs. Schwamm, who was jealous of Jean's position in the house and treated her as a usurper. In the end, it became obvious that one of them had to go. By then Lindsay had found Jean suited her so well, in both her emotional and her domestic life, that she had no difficulty deciding between them, though Mrs. Schwamm had been her mother's cook and had gone with Lindsay on her marriage because she was so devoted to her. One thing about Lindsay—she appeared to be very dithering, she *was* very dithering, but she never hesitated to get rid of people when necessary. But now of course Mrs. Schwamm was back again and in charge of the kitchen and Jean had to put up with her. And more, much more, she had to put up with Lindsay's interest in the movement in general and the Rani in particular. And just as Michael used to go around wildly, even shamelessly, asking "Where's Crishi?" so Jean could be observed with the same look of anguish on her face, stopping people to ask "Have you seen Lindsay?"

THEN one day Lindsay decided to donate Pro pinquity. She announced this quite casually and in public, in the course of the Rawul's evening talk under the tree. He had been mentioning the various centers of the movement that had already been established. Besides the one in his own kingdom—the cradle of the movement as well as, so we were often told, of civilization—there were centers in Sussex, England, at Fontainebleau outside Paris, on a baronial estate in Holland, and one on Columbus Avenue in New York. And suddenly Lindsay said "Oh, wouldn't it be fun to have one here?" I'm sure she spoke without premeditation—she never did premediate anything, I don't think she was capable of it. With her it was always "wouldn't it be fun to—" and it might be anything like a trip to the city or to fly to a party in Dallas. I suspect that it was her approach to her love affairs, when she first decided to sleep with someone ("wouldn't it be fun to—?"). And it always came out in a bright, little-girl voice, and then, if her suggestion wasn't immediately taken up with enthusiasm, her face would fall and she urged "But why *not*?" That was what happened this time too. When her impulsive offer of the house was received in silence—and it was a very heavy silence—she looked from face to face and said "But why *not*?" in a hurt voice.

No one answered, for differing reasons. The Rawul had flushed with pleasure; but as he was a modest and reticent man, he must have felt it to be indelicate to rush forward and accept such a handsome gift. The Rani played with her bracelets; there was an aloof little smile on her face, and what I noticed most was the way she was refusing to meet anyone's glance. Crishi too was silent, but his eyes flashed like a person who unexpectedly gets something that he wants. He looked around the circle at Michael, and at me. I saw that Michael met his glance; and when Lindsay asked for the third time "But why *not?*" Michael answered her, "Yes why not." And then everyone was looking at me, in their different ways.

From that time on they got to work on me, again in their different ways. Jean started it, maybe because she was the one who felt the strongest. That night she stood waiting for me outside Lindsay's bedroom door; "Come in here," she said. Lindsay was lying with her head buried in the pillows, the way she did when anyone involved her in an argument, not wanting to hear or see anything. Jean said "You're not going to go along with this nonsense, are you, Harriet?" I said "I don't want to." "No I should say not," Jean said grimly. She looked at Lindsay's slender form on the bed. "Turn around," she said. Lindsay didn't stir. I could see that Jean was tempted to grab hold of her and make her turn around. I had witnessed physical fights between them before and had not liked them; so I really wanted to get out. But Jean looked at me with her pathetic dog eyes: "Try and talk some sense into your mother, if you can, Harriet."

Then Lindsay tossed around to face us: "That's all I ever hear from you, Jean. Sense. Good sense. Common sense. I *despise* common sense."

"Listen to her," Jean said to me. "Now we are too mundane for her. She wants to get onto a higher plane: a *world* movement, no less."

"You've been as involved as the rest of us," Lindsay said.

"Involved with who?"

"With *who:* That's all you can ever think of. Everything with you is personal; as if nothing exists beyond your own little ego. You can't—rise."

She made a vague movement with her hand, indicating some lofty height to rise to. It made me laugh—the idea of Lindsay rising. Jean laughed too. Lindsay spoke to both of us in a genuinely hurt voice: "I thought we were all agreed

that it was something extraordinary. And isn't it about time
that there *was* a Fourth World—that all these different ele-
ments got together—I mean us here, with all our—materi-
alism," she said, gesturing at her crowded dressing table, "and
they with their—"

"Oh yes," Jean said. "They're very spiritual. Especially her;
that Rani. With all her spiritual jewelry."

"It's absolutely no use talking to you, Jean Potts. I'm not
going to say another word."

There was something so appealing in the way she clamped
her pretty lips together that Jean couldn't resist sitting beside
her on the edge of the bed. Lindsay went on pouting—but
flirtatiously now, in the reproachful little-girl way that she
knew would get her anything she wanted from Jean; and
Jean, her voice gruff with tenderness, said "I know I'm a
bore."

"You're *not* a bore—but you are *so* stubborn and contrary.
You make me so *mad*. I want us to do everything together,
as a couple, and how can we when you say no to me all the
time."

Jean brought Lindsay's hand up to her lips and turned it
over and kissed her palm. By this time neither of them cared
about me, whether I wanted to donate our house to the
Rawul's movement or not.

And I didn't, not one bit, and it amazed me the way both
Lindsay and Michael were so ready to toss it away. It was not
that it was a beautiful house—it wasn't—but it was one of
the few big houses in the area that was still intact and still
with the original owners. Lindsay's great-grandfather had
built it as a summer house for his Victorian family, which of
course was very large and included a whole establishment of
servants; and then her grandfather had installed things to
suit his life-style, like a squash court and a billiard room, and
had converted the stables into garages; and her father had
built on another wing in what was the latest in modern comfort in the thirties; so architecturally the house was a mess.
The grounds, however, were beautiful. The site was that of
an early nineteenth-century Federal-type house, which the
great-grandfather had torn down to rebuild to his Victorian
taste; but he couldn't ruin the grounds—the magnificent ma-

ples and oaks and elms, which were much older than the
house and as huge, the line of white birches at the edge of
the lake, the lake itself stretching to the wooded shore opposite, the waterfall, the many nooks and arbors with little
dead fountains where Michael and I used to hide, pretending
not to hear the voices calling us in for meals. But Michael no
longer seemed to care about any of it himself, and made me
feel bad for caring as much as I did.

He took me for a midnight row on the lake. We always
did that when we had something very special to discuss. Since
it was our way to commune in silence, these discussions
usually took the form of gliding on the dark water, breaking
up the moonlit reflections scattered over it, one of us row-
ing, the other brushing aside the overhanging branches where
the lake began to flow between narrow overgrown banks on
its way to the river into which it finally merged. We halted
under a willow and lay there, splashing the water around a
bit to see if we could disturb any fish.

Michael said "It's a good idea." I didn't say anything—by
which of course he knew I didn't agree. I hated to disagree
with him, and especially here on this lake where we had spent
such hours of our deepest communings. Nor did I really have
any right to disagree, because the very subject of these communings was that of nonattachment. We both thought to be
absolutely pure you had to be absolutely nonattached, not
wanting anything for yourself—not possessions, not position,
not even the love of another person. Yet here was I, unable
to give away something as ordinary as a house. I felt ashamed;
so that when Michael, in reply to my silence, said "What's
up?" I said "No it's okay. If you really want to." "Well don't
you?" he said, and I knew he was frowning in the dark,
stretched out on one side of the boat while I was on the other.

There was always something dictatorial about Michael in
his relation to me. He was so used to my being in complete
agreement with him that when I was not, he got irritated. In
the past, on the rare occasions when it had happened that I
wasn't 100 percent with him, I would just say "If you want
it, I do." It was true, but he didn't like to hear it: because he
thought agreement had to spring out of inner conviction and
not out of love for another person. So it was useless to argue.

I said "I'm surprised about Lindsay though." Michael laughed. It *was* strange—normally, when you wanted something from Lindsay, she would have very good reasons why she couldn't possibly give it. I knew what was in his mind— if Lindsay of all people was ready for it, surely I wasn't going to fall behind. Well, I didn't say anything, but I agreed. At least, I brought forward no objections, though my heart was full of them—my God, on this beautiful summer night, alone in a boat with him, our house visible in the distance, shining by moonlight through the dark trees: but I didn't stick up for it, because more than anything else, more than any house, I wanted what *he* wanted. That was how it was between us then.

Next morning the Rawul was having breakfast alone in the dining room; when I came down, he lifted the napkin from his lap so he could courteously rise from his chair for me. His mouth was full of Mrs. Schwamm's terrific pancakes, and he could only gesture hospitably toward the sideboard to invite me to help myself: as if it were his house already, I thought. But in a way it was; for when could we ever have had a stately breakfast like this in the dining room, with the silver-topped dishes all polished and laid out on the sideboard? Before his arrival, we used to make do with instant coffee and frozen doughnuts, eaten while perched on a corner of the kitchen table. But the Rawul lived in style, and having a whole entourage with him, he could afford to. They might be called his comrades, his helpers, his followers, but they also functioned very effectively as his servants; so that for the first time in our generation, and even in Lindsay's, there was a staff large enough to run the house as it was meant to be.

I expected him to start getting at me about donating Propinquity, but he was too subtle and too well mannered for that. Also perhaps too shy—for that was also there in his character; he was a shy person who found it difficult to make conversation with people, though out of courtesy he always tried. The one topic he really had a lot to say about was his Seventh World movement—whenever that subject came up, he spoke volubly and with passionate conviction; and even if you felt dubious about the whole thing, you could have no

doubt about his sincerity. There was something fanatical about
him. The whole idea was fanatical; grandiose—but also grand,
on a grand scale: just to think up such an idea and get it
going with what was only a handful of people. But maybe
that's how big movements begin, with one person really believing and then others gathering around him till an organization is formed with more and more people joining it;
because so many, and maybe everyone, wants to have something or someone to believe in.

To begin with, as far as I knew, it was the Rawul who had
this simple but forceful idea of constituting himself the savior
of world civilization. He felt he had excellent credentials, for
he belonged to what he claimed to be one of the oldest tribes
in the world, with a whole genealogy of primeval mythical
figures and historical heroes. Their breeding ground was a
mountainous desert state wedged in a corner of northwest
India—geographically not very promising, but the Rawul
liked to refer to it as the cradle of civilization; and though
their glory had long since departed—he wasn't even entitled
to be called the Rawul anymore—he felt it to be an ideal
source from which to start the whole thing up again, in a
different way and on a different scale. And if he regarded
his little kingdom of Dhoka—in which he still had a little
palace though no income apart from what he had managed
to stow away in foreign bank accounts—as the physical base
of the Seventh World, then he himself was the human one:
combining in his own person an ancient Oriental title and
tradition with a modern Western mind and education. It was
strange that such a modest man as the Rawul could have such
an exalted notion of himself, but it was almost a sort of self-
lessness in him. He didn't want to be a world leader, but he
felt he was born to be—chosen by exterior circumstances
rather than any value he set upon himself.

I was ready to concede that he had a right to our house.
He was a royal person; and so I guess was the Rani, even if
she wasn't of royal origin. Neither was Crishi: but the three
of them, in manner, in appearance, and in expectations, did
constitute a sort of royal family with a suggestion of divine
rights about them. And perhaps slowly I would have begun,
or had already begun, to come around to the idea of making

over our house to their movement. It did seem reasonable that such a house should be put to a purpose rather than just kept for a few people who didn't even live in it properly. I hadn't yet made up my mind that this particular purpose—the Seventh World—was what I would have chosen to donate it to; but since Michael had, and even Lindsay, there was no reason for me to hold back. I went to the place—behind the abandoned apple orchard—where I hid whenever I wanted to think something out, and where only Michael knew to find me; but there I overheard a scene that changed my mind again.

It was between Crishi and one of the followers—Paul, a man older than most of the others, maybe in his thirties. He looked as if he had suffered some bad sickness from which his face and body remained harrowed; he may also have been very poor, for he grabbed at food in the greedy way of someone for whom it hasn't always been there. He liked to join in on any fun that was going, but again in a rather desperate way, and when he laughed, it half sounded like crying. Actually, he looked like a person who had cried a lot to himself but now was dried up. It was his voice I heard from my hiding place—always unmistakable because of the whine in it, which had risen to a pitch. He was pleading with someone—with Crishi. Crishi's voice too would normally have been easy to recognize but it was transformed; not so much in itself, it was still pleasant and light, but in its tone and words, which were foul. The other kept saying "But Crishi, why me, why me?" to which Crishi gave no answer but abuse so vile that I at once got up to show myself. I was enraged to hear such words spoken from one human being to another, and in our house, in my secret hiding place! I was separated from them by a clump of blackberry bushes and, just as I parted it to get through, I saw the other man cover his face with his hands and sink slowly along the trunk of a tree to the ground, sobbing "I can't, I can't." "I'll show you how you can't, shit hole," Crishi said and raised his foot and kicked into Paul's shoulder, making him fall over and lie along the ground. And when he lay there, Crishi kicked him once more and walked away. At first I wanted to run after him, but instead I retreated behind the bushes and buried myself into the overgrown grass, on my stomach, my head pressed into the earth so as not to have to hear or see anything more. After a while I felt ashamed and got up to help the other man; but when I looked at him through the bushes I saw that, though still lying where he had fallen, he was quite happily watching an ant walk up and down a blade of grass, as if nothing particularly bad had happened.

I went at once to tell Michael what I had witnessed. I described the scene in detail and even forced myself to repeat some of the words Crishi had used. Like myself, Michael detested such language—we really had a sort of physical revulsion against it, as against a dirty act; and it may be one of the reasons—among plenty of others—why we never got on well in the schools we went to or made many friends anywhere, because to most people these words don't mean anything; they use them freely and can't understand why we shrink from them. Michael didn't like me to repeat them— "Yes yes all right, I get the idea," he said when I forced them on his attention—but he wasn't as outraged with Crishi as I thought he would be.

"You don't know all of it," he said. He frowned and I think would have liked to drop the subject; but he was very fair-minded and was used to explaining and interpreting everything as carefully to me as to himself, so he went on: "You don't know anything about Paul—what sort of a person he is. Some people have to be treated in a certain way, for their own good and everyone else's, if it's an organization."

An area around my heart grew cold to hear this from Michael. He felt it of course, and he continued: "You have no idea, Harriet, what it's like to keep all this moving. It's fine for the Rawul to sit under a tree and give these discourses, but to make everything *go*, that's all on Crishi, and it's not easy, I can tell you."

I thought that what he was saying only meant that he liked Crishi very much. But when Michael had felt that way about someone in the past, it had never clouded his judgment. On the contrary, when he liked someone, he applied the same stringent standards to them as he did to himself, and to me: sort of welcoming them to his own world. But with Crishi, it seemed to be the other way around—as if he were giving up his own standards for Crishi's. I think he felt it too, that there was some big change in himself; and as any change in him implied a betrayal or at least a negation of what there was between us, he seemed to feel guilty. Anyway, he didn't want to go on talking about it, and I didn't want him to either.

But he soon told Crishi about what I had seen, leaving him to handle my misgivings. That was the sort of situation in which Crishi must have excelled all his life—handling people, allaying suspicion, bringing them around. All his charm was geared to it. So that evening, when I was about to join the others under the tree, he stopped me; and I knew at once what he was going to say and he knew I knew and said it: "Michael wants me to explain to you."

"Explain what?" I said coldly.

"Sometimes I act really nasty. I can be a swine." But his lips twitched, and next moment he was frankly laughing. "I want to talk to you," he said, looking into my face with amusement and lightly spanning my arm with his fingers. When he saw me glancing toward the tree, he said "You've heard the Rawul before and you'll hear him again."

Still holding my arm, he led me away from the tree and toward the porch in front of the house. I could have resisted but to do so—to snatch my arm away—seemed childish, so I went with him and we sat in rocking chairs. I ought to explain that the porch had always been very handsome, but now the gray-and-white marble floor was polished and the white pillars newly painted; and the lawn it faced had been smoothly mown, and at this moment one of the followers was assiduously watering it to keep it emerald green. A house and grounds like ours did need a large staff, no doubt.

"I know you don't think too much of all that," Crishi said, nodding toward the circle under the tree. From this distance, and in a mellow evening light, the scene was dignified and serene. They were all grouped around the Rawul as in a painting of a sage inspiring his disciples with wisdom and high ideals. "He means well, you have to admit," Crishi said.

I said "I do admit"—no doubt sounding very uptight, for he cried out, half laughing and half exasperated: "Oh Jesus, Harriet, you sound just like Michael!"

Well, to me that was a big compliment, but I didn't care

for his familiarity; he even touched my knee—very very lightly, true, but he did touch it, as one laying a claim. I moved it away and he went on: "You've got such lovely principles, both of you, I think it's wonderful." I sat upright and stared straight ahead of me; my hands were folded in my lap. I knew I looked like generations of my own grandmothers, and I also felt like them.

Crishi dropped his voice and spoke more intimately, sharing a secret with me: "But Michael's changing, you must have noticed. He's coming around." When he felt me tense up— "Yes to me, but that's the least of it. . . . To the Rawul and the Seventh World—yes, okay, I know it can sound quite ridiculous—daft," he said, fishing out that word from somewhere in his cultural ragbag. "But don't think it's all phony; all neti." When he used *that* word, I flinched—he could have heard it in our sense only from Michael, who had up till then used it only with me. Crishi said it quite casually, taking possession of it as easily as of our house and everyone in it. "The Rawul really is a ruler and from a dynasty older than any other in the whole world. It's true," he said, stretching his eyes wide open so I could see how honest they were. "He's a direct descendant from the Moon," he added, and his lips twitched, and he kept on looking at me, encouraging me to smile if I wanted to; and when I didn't, he went on smiling himself—maybe at me as well as at the Rawul. But he changed his tone: "I like it that you're skeptical, Harriet. I wish more people were, instead of being so keen to throw themselves into the action. It's a responsibility when they do that. I don't mean Michael, of course."

All the time his eyes were searching me out—as to what I was thinking, but also in another way, in a quite frankly sexual way. Only strangely it was this latter that was impersonal— it was how he instinctively looked at any girl or woman; whereas the other was much more directed at me, Harriet: what *I* was thinking and feeling.

"It's really nice having Michael with us. He has a good personality. I'm not saying the others don't—they all do really, including Paul. Paul? You know who you saw me with yesterday? Heard me with?" He laughed ruefully, and for a moment put one hand over his eyes. Then he looked at me, biting his lip: "I have this horrible foul temper making me do things. It's a liability to me and a shock to other people." He sounded so contrite that I began to feel I had maybe overreacted.

If I had known him better—or, at that time, liked him better—I could have told him that it was hardly the first ugly fight I had witnessed. I had grown up with scenes between my parents—when I was very small and they were still together, and later each time they met. Now they didn't meet anymore. Whenever I wanted to see Manton, I made a trip to the city without telling Lindsay. I did it the day after my conversation with Crishi. I wanted to tell Manton about all the new developments and also about Michael and Lindsay wanting to donate Propinquity. After another, very short marriage of his had ended, Manton had given up his place in the city and gone to live in a hotel suite. This really suited his life-style much better, and he didn't get married again but had different girlfriends.

The principal one at that time was Barbara. She was my age but had more in common with my father than me. They both liked the same sort of good time and were always going out somewhere to have fun. That day they were going to a premiere where everyone had to come dressed in 1920s clothes; I guess that was the period of the film. When I arrived, Manton was out and Barbara was trying on her dress, which didn't suit her at all and she knew it. She was a big blond girl, very healthy and wholesome and beautiful, and she spilled out of the skinny little sheath into which she had tried to squeeze herself. "What'll I do?" she asked me. She meant about the costume, but Barbara was always asking me what to do, mostly about herself and her life; she didn't have many people to talk to, and was always glad when I showed up. With me helping her, she struggled out of her costume, and she tied a loose robe around herself, which suited her much better—physically and psychologically, because whenever she got me on my own, she liked to be entirely relaxed and talk about every kind of intimate thing. She had taken off her bra too and was naked under her robe. She got on to the usual subject, how Manton wouldn't marry her and how she was afraid of losing him because she was so dumb. "I know

I am, Harriet," she said; her lovely big baby eyes filled with
tears, and I said for the thousandth time, "You're *not.*" And
it was true: She wasn't half as dumb as many people who
think themselves very smart; and besides, she was really good
for Manton, and I hoped he would stick with her. She truly
loved him and looked up to him, the way I used to.

When Manton came back, she got all nervous because of
not being ready. But with me there, he took no notice of her;
instead he went into his father-daughter act he liked to think
we had. And I suppose we did have it—we were certainly
fond of each other, but it was not in a parent-and-child way.
Or if it was, it was the other way around and he was the
child, though I can't say I ever really saw myself as his
parent—I guess his girlfriends like Barbara filled that role,
even if they didn't know it but thought they were looking up
to him. That was what Manton needed from women, to be
mothered and to be admired, the way he had got used to
from his own mother and, even more, from Sonya, his step-
mother.

"Harriet, let me look at you!" He always said that and
always went into the traditional Daddy-looking-over-daugh-
ter routine, holding me at arm's length to beam at me with
pride and pleasure. At the same time he was looking me over
quite sharply. Of course he was desperate about the way I
dressed—or rather, didn't dress—and the most he could hope
for was that my skin hadn't broken out, or some other thing
that might not do him credit. For a daughter was not exempt
from the function of his other women of doing him credit:
Manton would not have kept company with a frump. He
sighed as usually on letting me go and said "Why don't you
let Barbara take you to some of her places, it's the one thing
she knows about." When he turned his attention toward her,
she at once began to babble the way she did when she was
nervous—how she was just getting ready, wouldn't be a second, that she and I got talking and she absolutely forgot the
time, which was unforgivably stupid of her. The more she
went on the more irritated he got, of course, and then she
got more nervous, positively jumpy and crazy, and they were
back in their vicious circle.

I felt sorry for her and mad at him. I knew how he could

be: If you showed the least weakness or nervousness he would take advantage of it (I guess that made him a natural bully, though there was another side to him). But I hadn't come there to listen in on their difficult relationship. I wanted to tell him about Lindsay and Propinquity—to ask his advice maybe, or just to have someone close with whom to talk about it. And as soon as Barbara had gone to squeeze herself back in her outfit, I did tell him. He was *outraged*. He couldn't believe his ears. He knew Lindsay was crazy but this beat everything. Not that he cared a damn about the house—in fact, he hated it, for being ugly—but the idea of giving it away, giving away his children's heritage, and on such a whim and for such a cause: He was *speechless*, he said. I must say, his reaction seemed to me very sane and natural; I felt justified, confirmed in my own common sense while everyone else appeared to have taken leave of theirs. When Manton was angry, his color rose high and his eyes glittered cold and blue. He looked what he was perhaps meant to be: a soldier, colonizer, man of action—quite magnificent really, and formidable. At that moment poor Barbara came in, in her ridiculous little short frock, and all his manly anger turned on her: "Do you really seriously believe," he said, very slowly and drawling like an Englishman, "that I would be seen out dead with you in that ludicrous getup?" I could see her plump knees knocking together as she hastened to agree with him that she looked terrible. "Go and take it off," he interrupted her. "We're not going." She pleaded for a bit, then burst into tears—not for herself but for him, for spoiling his evening. And in fact this would have been considered unforgivable, if he hadn't already changed his own plans; but he had—my news had stirred him up, and he decided that he would drive me back to the country to see what was going on. Barbara was allowed to come and sat in the back, talking away happily.

Here was a further complication in the house, and to explain it, I should say something of Manton's relation to the rest of us. There is no need to talk about Manton and Lindsay: the less said there the better. And Manton and Michael—there was not much to be said there either, except that Manton was not cut out to be anyone's father and especially not Michael's. Over the years they had learned to tolerate each other, which they did mainly by never seeing each other. Then there was Manton and Mrs. Schwamm—he was simply delighted to hear she was back, not only because she was such a terrific cook but because they had this thing about adoring one another. Manton was the type to make himself tremendously popular with any domestic staff, and they were always eager to do something extra for him; and that was how it was with him and Mrs. Schwamm—whom he alone was allowed to call Else, or even Elsie. Finally, Manton and Jean—well, that was better than one would have thought possible, considering how he was this very sexy man whose women had to be women, and she was what she was. But I think they were useful to each other. Jean kept Lindsay completely out of his hair, while he had put Lindsay off men forever—so Lindsay herself said, and in fact, on the very rare occasions when he was around, Lindsay simply clung to Jean, as for protection against him.

So Manton entered this arena—only to be thrown at once because everything had changed beyond his recognition. I had tried to tell him something about the Rawul and his party, but it wasn't possible to get across the fact of their influence: of how they had taken complete possession of the house and everyone in it. And Manton himself was at once drawn into the new dispensation. It happened just as soon as he saw the Rani and was bowled over by her. She was used to that—people being bowled over by her—and knew exactly how to handle him. She wasn't flirtatious as much as friendly; that is, she held him at a distance by giving him her respectful attention; but she was this phenomenally beautiful woman, so that while she puffed him up with her respect, she brought him down with her aloofness. I wasn't sure why she took even that much trouble with him; she didn't with anybody else. Maybe she thought he could be useful in getting me to donate the house; and of course Manton was a very handsome and attractive man, always had been—I mean, it was what he was, it was the essence of his personality.

Barbara's reaction to the scene was unexpected. She was upset about Manton and the Rani, but that wasn't all of it: She hated everything else too—I would never have thought that sweet, soft Barbara could hate anything or anyone, but

my God she did. It was awful for her when Manton decided
he had to stay; he told her to go back to New York and pack
some of his clothes and bring them up, and when she began
to fuss, he said "Well you can bring yours too"; but that was
the only concession he would make. When she tried to argue,
he said "I've never heard such selfish nonsense"—pointing
out that he had been called to help decide whether his son
and daughter should give up their house, and how generous
it was of him to allow her to be in on this family affair. She
found she had no choice—if she wanted to stay with him,
that is, and she did; but she was horribly upset, both before
driving to the city to get their clothes and after she came
back. I found her in tears in her bedroom—she had to sleep
separately from Manton because he got onto this high horse
of how it wasn't proper for her to share his bed in his wife's
house and with his children present. I felt sorry for her, and
also that it was mostly my fault that they were here—they
had been all right in New York, living in their hotel and
going to costume balls.

Michael came in on me while I was with Barbara in her
room. This was constantly happening all over the house,
people looking for each other in each other's rooms, everyone
with something important, and usually intimate, to say. Barbara was lying on the bed crying, and I was sitting beside
her. This room suited her well—it was as fluffy and fair as
she was, with ruffled curtains and flouncy chair covers and
an ivory carpet with pink roses on it. Barbara was never very
articulate, and besides crying couldn't really explain herself.
When Michael and I tried to comfort her, she said "It's not
only Manton and her." Here she burst into a new flood of
tears; she cried like a child and her face went puffy like a
child's. "It's all of it," she said, when she could speak again.
"All of them. You don't know," she said. Michael and I looked
at each other across her. If Barbara implied she knew something that he and I didn't, it must be true because usually
she was very self-deprecating. Barbara's background and experience were quite different from what one might have
expected: Looking at her, knowing her, one would think she
came from some nice family in Connecticut, but in fact her
mother was a movie star and Barbara had spent her early

years in Hollywood and on film sets in places like Morocco or Rome. And now what she tried to explain to Michael and me was that the atmosphere in the house—I suppose she meant the way everyone was so intensely involved with everyone else—was like it used to be around her mother and her associates when they were all locked up with each other on location. And just as she had got this out, there was a brief and very authoritarian knock on the door, which opened immediately afterward—I didn't have to turn around; I could tell by the shock passing through Michael that it was Crishi. "Oh there you are," said Crishi, enfolding the three of us in his smile.

An instant change came over Barbara. She had been lying there in a heap, making no attempt to hide her tears, but now she shot up on her bed and sat very upright, arranging her dress to cover her thighs and knees. She held her head high, and though her cheeks were still wet and swollen, she put a prim, distant, disapproving look on her face, like a matron with an uninvited, undesired guest. I was amazed— I didn't think she could be like that; I had never seen her with anyone she disliked. Crishi felt it immediately, and he moderated his smile and said he hoped he wasn't in the way, or anything? He looked from one to the other and especially warmly at Barbara, who became more prim. Then Crishi raised one slender finger at Michael, meaning one moment, very politely, but also meaning come here, now. And Michael went at once; without one glance at me or Barbara, he obeyed as he would a master's call. When they had gone, Barbara said "He's the worst, Harriet. No," she said as though I had contradicted her, "he's a bad person." I didn't think he was a bad person, on the contrary; but I guess I still didn't feel strongly enough one way or the other to stick up for him with Barbara.

I must have wiped out the incident with Paul; or allowed myself to put a different interpretation on it—at any rate, I no longer held it against Crishi. I hadn't seen Paul around for some time, and assumed he was gone wherever it was Crishi wanted to send him. I didn't ask about him; it wasn't important enough. And they were always coming and going, all the followers—there were so many of them and so many different missions they had to fulfill and different centers to liaison with. I was used to seeing them tramping up and down the stairs, but it was a shock to Manton. In his day, if there was a crowd in the house, it was one that had come for a dance or a party. "What are they—hippies?" he asked me, hippies being the latest thing he had heard of. But Manton was adaptable, and it took him no time to get used to them —or rather, fail to notice them, the way he never had difficulty ignoring people he didn't need. As in a restaurant, he would make a point of being terribly friendly with the waiter who served him and the maître d' who gave him a good table, but everyone else might as well be plants and stones. It would be untrue to say he was a snob because it had nothing to do with class, only with whether a person impinged on his life or not. So he would brush past the "hippies" on the stairs, genuinely not seeing them; and would sit for hours with Else Schwamm in the kitchen, telling her how he was falling in love with the Rani, and what should he do about it; and she, without for one second interrupting the kneading and rolling of her pastry, face red, arms pumping, would give him the benefit of her life's experience, the two of them convinced that it was the most important topic in the world.

The rest of us knew better. I say "us," including myself, for I was now in a position where I wanted to believe—that is, believe with Michael that it was all for some high purpose, and not with Barbara that it was a fraud. I knew Michael wouldn't have been taken in by a fraud. He had spent too much time—all his life practically, and mine—examining truth and faith and every other fundamental principle. He wouldn't compromise any of that on account of his own feelings—for Crishi, that is. He had been in love before, and whereas it may have made him suspend his quest for a while, it had never led him away from it. And it couldn't be so now, when he felt more strongly than I had ever seen him do before. I believed in him, which was how I was ready to believe in everything else.

It was being made clear to me that we were very fortunate to have been chosen as one of the spearheads of the movement. The Rawul's followers felt it strongly—that they were pioneers, leaders of a mission, apostles or whatever; and this was brought home to me one day in a quarrel I had with one of the girls over the use of a bathroom. The bathroom was mine—anyway, the one adjoining my room—and while I had accepted the fact that the Rawul and his party had more or less taken over everywhere else, I continued to think of this one room and bathroom as exclusively my own. But once when I tried to go in, I found the door locked. I wasn't pleased but I had lived enough in dorms to take it philosophically and just wait. Whoever was inside didn't come out and didn't come out, till finally I banged on the door and yelled a bit. A yell came back—it was one of the girls and she was very rude, so I banged some more and was very rude to her, and we had this shouting match through the door. When she came out at last, she was livid; she was holding a book, which she must have been reading in there. She waved it in my face—it was the Dhammapada, and I understood that it was very bad to disturb anyone in the reading of that. I calmed down and said that there were plenty of bathrooms in the house without her having to come in here to use mine. As soon as I uttered the word *mine*, I realized I had made a mistake. I had played into her hands and she could take off from there, about possessiveness and ego and all the rest of it. It so happened I agreed with her, though under the circumstances I couldn't say so; and anyway, she didn't give me a chance to—she just went on and on. She was a very thin, pale girl, who looked as if she were suffering from amoebic dysentery; but if she was physically debilitated, mentally she was very fierce—that is, in her convictions. She asked me did I have any idea what it meant that this house had been chosen, and we with it? In case I didn't, she explained that, whatever we might have been before, we now had to live up to the responsibility of our position. By the time she finished, she seemed to have mellowed toward me and to be really on my side; she even pressed my arm to show me she knew how difficult it was to live up to something greater than oneself.

WE all continued to attend the Rawul's evening talks, which were getting to be like a family get-together with the same internal strains and the same sense of cohesion, of not being able to get out even if one wanted to. But now the Rawul said the time had come to reach outward—after all, we were not a private group, a personal club, but were there to reform the world. The Rawul could make these sort of statements absolutely without blinking, because they were so utterly serious to him; he really felt himself to be on this mission. Up till now, he had what he called "reached outward" only through the mail—that was what most of the activity in the house was about, getting publicity material together to send to government agencies in Washington, the U.N., the press, to schools, sponsors, donors, foundations, and generally responsible citizens. The Rawul now called for more direct contact with the outside world. It was the way they had operated previous campaigns—in England, Holland, and India so far—and had no doubt that it would work here too. The first step was to be a big party on the grounds of Propinquity for people from the town and from the adjacent houses—a sort of open house, like Lindsay's family traditionally had on July Fourth. And in fact it was the July Fourth weekend that was chosen for this opening campaign.

I had doubts about it from the first, which I told Michael. He disagreed with me—we disagreed often nowadays; it made

me sad, but he didn't seem to notice. He said everybody used
to love Grandmother's parties and was eager to come—all
sorts of different people, the bank manager and the real
estate agent, the families from the big houses, the plumber,
Grandmother's favorite butcher, the package-store people,
the garage owner—it was the event of the season for the
neighborhood. Yes, I said, but hadn't he noticed the neighborhood had changed: For one thing, it was much poorer;
the rail service to the nearest town had been discontinued,
the yellow-frame houses with white porches and hanging
plants had been taken over by families on welfare, and the
big houses had either been torn down or bought up and
restored as weekend homes by lawyers and decorators from
the city. And quite apart from the neighborhood changing,
what about us? Didn't he think, I asked Michael, that we—
he and I, Lindsay and Jean, Manton and Barbara—were
quite a change from our grandparents? Michael brushed me
aside. He said I was proving his point—of course the neighborhood had changed; We had changed, two generations had
passed, and didn't I see that it was the moment for a real, a
conscious change? In fact, for a new world movement to
cohere this changed society in a new way? Michael was getting
to be as persuasive as the Rawul.

In the years when Lindsay and Jean were alone in the
house, living mostly in the kitchen, it seemed to rain almost
all summer. But I never remember a wet July Fourth weekend when Grandmother had her open house, and this time
too, for the Rawul, the weather held. Yes, the weather, the
grounds, the house, these were all unchanged from our
grandparents' time, all glorious. And, just as in their time,
the preparations for the party started days ahead and involved the whole household. The Rani and Crishi were in
charge. Both were very good at giving orders and getting
things done; they might have sounded a bit ruthless when it
came to the followers, but they could be very tactful, as with
the local tradesmen, who would later be guests at the party,
and with Mrs. Schwamm. It was an achievement to get her
to hand over her kitchen to the general maneuver and to
participate in it. She outdid herself in the creation of Vien-
nese tidbits, while the Rani supervised the preparations of

various kinds of kebabs and fritters with exotic fillings—not quite Indian but a sort of mixture, like the Rani herself. It was very different from Grandmother's hot dogs, spare ribs, and potato salad; but so were the Oriental rugs and bolsters spread on the lawns from her garden furniture; and most different of all were the principal hosts.

These were undoubtedly the Rawul, the Rani, and Crishi. Even though the family who owned Propinquity—after all, we hadn't yet signed it over—were still there, the three of them completely overshadowed us. The Rawul had exchanged his English suit for white leggings worn under a high-collared coat of white silk and jeweled buttons. Stout and handsome, he looked what he was—an Indian prince. The Rani wore a kind of Parisian adaptation of the North Indian costume of long shirt over trousers, in heavy silk with elaborate gold embroidery over her bosom. The two of them did not move around among the guests; it was left to Crishi, lithe as a ballet dancer in velvet pants and silk shirt, to lead them up to the royal couple, who generated, besides their glamour, grace and benevolence.

The Rawul considered the occasion a great success, achieving everything he had aimed for. As he had explained to me one morning, when he and I had again been alone at the breakfast table, what he especially valued in using our house as his headquarters was that it placed him right at the heart of American society, at the very center of those traditions he wished to merge with his own. He was right, in a way. The guests who came to his Fourth of July party were the inheritors of those traditions—the interior decorators who had bought up and refurbished the big houses, and the antique dealers who sold and resold their contents. There were the traditional local people, like the Pickles family, who had lived here for over two hundred years and had once been prosperous tenant farmers. Nowadays they proliferated in a variety of jobs as cashiers at Shopwell and counter hands at Dunkin' Donuts; and there was Mrs. Pickles, who cleaned some of the big houses, including ours, and had eight children, of whom six had emigrated to jobs in California and Florida, leaving only the younger two, one of whom was deaf and dumb and the other slightly retarded.

Mrs. Pickles herself came, dressed very smartly in a pastel-colored pants suit; other guests included Ernest and Robert, who had bought the van Kuypen estate; and Tom and Stanislav, who ran a mail-order business from the Old Mill; and Henry and Lucy Rabin, whose antique business in their restored historic house could be visited by appointment only; and jolly Mr. McKimberley, who gave out loans at the bank; and the painter Kenneth Lyon and his friend Jerry; the poet Meriel Pitts; the two potters Pete Davidson and Jenny Fine; and many others who milled around the grounds and around the shining figures of our royal family. These three cast their radiance on all alike; and to them everyone probably was alike—not individuals but the populace who were there to be won over to the Rawul's cause. This was certainly how the Rawul regarded his guests, as he beamed on them. One could be less sure of the Rani and Crishi, for while they too beamed, they were not as open as the Rawul, and it was not possible to guess what they were really thinking.

In their way, Lindsay and Manton were almost as royal as those three—in the sense of as remote. Lindsay never particularized anyone either; she chattered away or was silent, as it suited her. Since she never looked at or thought of anyone except herself, it didn't matter to her whether she was addressing Mrs. Pickles, Mr. McKimberley, or Meriel Pitts; she spoke to each in the same way—that is, in the girlish tone and idiom she had used with her mother's guests. And Manton too did not discriminate as to the recipients of his social manner; as on every such occasion, he turned on the tap of his charm and left it running. Michael and I always hated this characteristic in both our parents but realized that it was as natural to them as its opposite was to us. For us, every person we encountered was so individual, made so strong an impact that, far from having too much manner, we had none whatsoever and remained frozen with shyness. I guess that was how we got our reputation of being cold and aloof, arrogant too, and were contrasted unfavorably with our parents, who were, everyone said, so warm and friendly.

I don't know if everybody would have agreed with the Rawul that the party was a great success. He probably never noticed that many things were going on that had nothing to do with his movement but were just our own self-centered emotions. Although everyone, both from the Rawul's family and from ours, was expected to turn out and contribute to the success of the day, there were two among us who wanted nothing to do with it—Barbara and Jean. They didn't even come out of their rooms, except at one point Jean could be seen making her way determinedly through the crowd on the lawn to where Lindsay was in a little group around the Rani. I was alarmed when I saw Jean; and one couldn't help seeing her, she was conspicuously not dressed up for the party but in her everyday jeans and crumpled shirt; and she was frowning too, and looked miserable. I tried to get to her before she could get to Lindsay. Other guests stopped her on the way—the people from the neighborhood who liked her for a decent, nice person. Even now, though obviously overwrought, she was decent and nice and made the right responses to Mrs. Pickles, who told her about someone permanently paralyzed from having been given the wrong injection in the hospital, to Lucy Rabin, who had been successful at an auction with an eighteenth-century pair of fire tongs, and to Mrs. McKimberley, who invited her to join a tour, with picnic lunch, of a newly restored ex-President's house. With all these people Jean did her best, in spite of her swollen eyes, to be her usual caring self—until she got to Lindsay, and then she hissed "Come inside," and gripped her arm.

I saw Lindsay remove her arm—as though it were held not by a person but had got caught accidentally in some thing. Her attention remained stubbornly fixed on the Rani, who was making conversation to the circle that surrounded her. There was this about the Rani's conversation always—it didn't matter what she said; one felt how kind it was of her to say anything when she really didn't have to, when everyone was quite happy just to be near her, within her aura. But there she stood, with her arms folded over her gold-embroidered bosom, talking about—could it be?—yes, about her hairdresser, who apparently was wise and witty though what she reported sounded quite flat. Nevertheless, the Rani was smiling as she quoted him, and everyone else was laughing, obsequiously, as they eagerly listened to her. When Jean asked her to come inside, Lindsay laughed more deliberately, and that made Jean catch hold of her arm again. At that moment, Manton, who was also in the circle around the Rani, looked over at her and, waggling his fingers in greeting, called "Why hello there, Jean—where have you been? We've missed you, darling." He was smiling across at Lindsay and Jean, as if he knew just exactly what was going on and was both anticipating and hoping for some misbehavior.

Lindsay went with Jean as far as the porch, and there she stopped and turned on her: "You leave me alone. Don't you dare come near me. Because I hate you. You'd better know that." She delivered these sentences with the force of body blows, while her icy eyes glared into Jean's face. Jean glared back at her. They were about the same height and age—this somehow made them appear like two little girls who had got into a fight, and one almost expected them to start kicking each other's shins, and pinching. And, in fact, their fights did sometimes have this nursery quality. The first time I saw one, I was appalled; later I got used to them and took no notice, especially as I knew they would make up very soon.

To emphasize her contempt for her friend, Lindsay swung away so violently that the impact accompanied her down the porch steps, making her hips swing, as well as her hair, which she kept long, blond, and young. Jean was left standing there, breathing heavily, frustrated in midfight. I think she would have liked to go running after Lindsay and physically stop her, and it wasn't decorum that prevented her but age: for there is one thing about these sort of fights, these sort of strong emotions—you need to have stamina for them, and Jean obviously didn't. She sank into a chair on the porch, and when I went up to her, I found her panting and swollen with a rush of blood to her face. She asked me to go up to her room for her pills. I went running through the empty house, through the hall and up the stairs—and as always, when it was deserted like this, empty of all its inhabitants, when it was just itself, it was so beautiful, so still and yet breathing with its own accumulated life, that I loved and wanted to keep and possess it forever. However, on my way down, I realized it was not entirely empty, for Barbara appeared at the door of her room, looking tousled and upset. She called to me, but I was in a hurry with Jean's pills.

I sat with Jean after I gave them to her. How could I leave
her? When I touched her, it felt like pulses were pounding
inside her, and for a moment she held her head as if afraid
it might burst. From where we sat we could see the guests
on the lower lawn by the lake, and unfortunately we also had
a good view of the Rani with her circle of admirers, which
Lindsay had rejoined. I tried to get Jean to come inside, but
she wouldn't; she wanted to sit there and continue to watch
Lindsay with the Rani. After a while, she said "Why do we
do this?" She spoke calmly, and I think she was calmer, anyway physically; probably her pills had begun to work. I said
"I don't know why you do it." And I didn't—Jean was a
sensible, intelligent woman, she had had a career and business of her own, everyone liked and respected her; whereas
Lindsay—I don't want to say anything about Lindsay because
she was what she was and perhaps couldn't help it. I knew
other women like her, both of her generation and of my
own—from that class; I mean the one that hadn't had to
work for a living for several generations: utterly, utterly selfish and self-centered and yet with a nervous fervor to improve themselves, literally to become better, which was a sort
of saving grace in them and made people like Jean love them.

Jean said "Don't talk about it. There's nothing left to say;
nothing that I haven't said to myself a hundred times over."
She was right: They always had the same fights; sometimes
Jean packed her bags, but she always unpacked them again,
and Lindsay allowed herself to be coaxed into forgiving her.

"You mustn't agree to give the house, Harriet," Jean suddenly said. She wouldn't look at me—perhaps she was shy
about having to appeal to me, or perhaps she just wanted to
keep her eyes fixed on the Rani's group. "Lindsay's irresponsible—I don't have to tell you how she is—if tomorrow
she feels like turning it over to the circus, she'd do that."
Actually, this was not quite accurate: Lindsay did irresponsible, impulsive things, but they had never before involved
her in giving something of her own away. So there was a
difference.

"She's infatuated," Jean said. "That's all it's about. You
think she cares a hoot about the Seventh World? Or about the
Rawul or any of them except his wife, if that's what she is.

You have to be firm, Harriet; you have to hold out; if you don't agree, there's not a thing they can do about it, she and Michael."

"You think Michael's infatuated too?"

She hesitated, unwilling perhaps to hurt me by talking about anything I might not be aware of. So I went on speaking calmly, to inform her I *was* aware: "I know how he feels about Crishi, but I'm sure it's not the only reason he's willing to give the house. And actually, Jean," I added truthfully, "I'm not all that sure that Lindsay's only reason is the Rani."

"Oh poor Lindsay—as if she could hold two thoughts together in her poor head at the same time; or think beyond the next meal she's going to eat, or the next person she's going to have an affair with." She tried to sneer, but her mouth trembled; I didn't want to continue our conversation.

A figure had detached itself from the crowd on the lower lawn and was approaching the house. It turned out to be Crishi. I hadn't expected him to come and join us on the porch but that was what he did, and it even seemed that he had deliberately come to seek out both or one of us.

"What's up?" he said. He saw at one glance how Jean was feeling and drew up a chair close to her. He scanned her face intimately. "Don't you want to come and see the Rawul hoist the flag? You wouldn't want to miss that, Jean: It's an historic event. And in your house," he said, now raising his smiling eyes to me.

"What flag is he hoisting?" Jean asked—his warm manner drying up her tears.

"What flag? Yours, of course. Isn't it one of your big days today? Independence Day or some big deal like that? I'd think you'd want to do something patriotic. Both of you," he said, glancing at me again—but then looking beyond me, and when I turned around, I saw Barbara had come out of the house and stood there, wearing a short robe. "All three of you," he included her, exuding good cheer to us all.

No one could look as sullen, when she wanted to, as warm, dimpled Barbara; and she wanted to now. She had a fleeting "Hi" for Jean; she disregarded Crishi completely; and she said to me, "Come in for a minute, Harriet. I want to say something."

"Hey! No!" Crishi protested and became very active. He took Jean's hand and made as if to pull her up. He also waved getting-up gestures at me and motioned his hand at Barbara to come on, let's get going: "The Rawul's waiting—he says where are those three daughters of the American Revolution—I can't hoist the flag without them, it wouldn't be proper."

"What flag?"

"Ours," Jean replied; she was wiping her eyes, was amused.

Not so Barbara: "Ours? Our flag? You mean he's actually going to fly the American flag? I can't believe it. Who is he to fly our flag? You wouldn't let him, would you, Harriet? The Stars and Stripes—on the Fourth—in your house? Yours and Lindsay and Michael's house?" She was really sincerely deeply shocked. I was amazed; I had no feelings of that kind and would never have dreamed she had. Now I saw that Jean was beginning to look a bit shamefaced; she too assumed a serious expression and murmured "It's not right."

"It's outrageous," said Barbara.

Crishi lowered his eyes; he bit his lip. "I've put my foot in it. I don't know how but I've done it." He looked up again, from Jean to Barbara and back, appealing to be forgiven for whatever it was he had done wrong.

But Jean, sitting there heavy and blowsy, had begun to look grim; so did Barbara, though pink and disheveled and still wearing her baby-doll robe. Both seemed formidable matrons at that moment, upholders of virtue and tradition: making Crishi, standing between them, elegant and foreign, throw up his hands in a good-natured, giving-up gesture. He turned to me: "You'd better come. Michael wants you." This, spoken straight, was far more personal and intimate than the wanting-to-please tone he had been using; and it put me in his camp immediately—I didn't have to think a moment, didn't have to choose, I simply accompanied him without a glance at Jean and Barbara.

Two flagpoles had been erected between the barns and the lake, and all the guests had assembled there, to watch and to listen to the Rawul's address. Now that everyone was assembled in one spot, they formed a sparse and straggly group: probably because the grounds were so large, with the lawns and tall trees; and the old barns, almost as tall as the trees; and the lake with the sky reflected in it, making both sky and water seem twice as deep and full of light. It turned out there were two flags to be hoisted—the Stars and Stripes, and the flag of the Fourth World. Before the ceremony the Rawul gave a little address, which wasn't in content different from what he said every evening under the tree. He seemed to be very moved—not that he wasn't always moved when he spoke of his Fourth World, his high Idea.

He said it was a great moment in history when the two flags were for the first time to fly together over American soil, for the first time to flutter freely here in the clear pure air of this land of freedom. His audience listened in silence; it was difficult to know how he was being received—they were such a diverse group, it was impossible to think of them as united in anything. Certainly, everyone stood very still—there was no fidgeting, no movement at all anywhere except for the light breeze fluttering around among the tops of the trees. The local people looked solemn the way they were used to looking in church and at other Fourth of July or generally patriotic gatherings. Great principles were nothing new to them. What was surprising to me was the sight of my parents. Not by design, I'm sure, but accidentally, in the forming of the group, they had got next to each other. They both stood very straight—both had fine, tall figures—and with their chins raised, they looked ready to dedicate themselves to something higher than themselves. Their eyes—and these, in spite of everything they had done or left undone, had remained very clear—were fixed on the Rawul; or it may have been on the Rani, who stood a few paces behind him. She too looked solemn—in a practiced way, as though she were used to putting on this expression whenever necessary.

Three followers carrying instruments struck up as the Rawul hoisted the two flags. The music must have sounded strange to everyone except the Rawul's party, for it was a most original mixture of baroque, Oriental, and atonal. Its main purpose was to stir and rouse, and it certainly did that to the three players themselves. I had seen them often but never noticed them much: two young men and a girl, pale, blond, undernourished—I would have said anemic, but there was nothing bloodless in the way they played. One strummed, one blew, one played a kind of drum—all three of them giving it everything they had, pouring themselves into the music as they swayed and swung and bent and rose with it; and when the flags went up the staff, they seemed to go with them—actually rose on tiptoe: until it wasn't possible to go up any farther, and the music stopped in that abrupt way a certain kind of music does, as if recognizing its own limits. Complete silence followed, except for the birds in the trees, which carried on as usual, and everyone looked up to see where the two flags—the Stars and Stripes and the wheel-within-the-diamond of the Fourth World—had taken off in the breeze and flew together side by side. It was the perfect gesture or symbol the Rawul had intended—or would have been if it hadn't been slightly marred by those two unhappy figures in the distance, Jean and Barbara, watching the proceedings from the porch and making them seem dubious.

The flag-raising ceremony was the climax of the party but not the end of it, for the guests stayed on. Perhaps they were reluctant to leave our beautiful house and grounds; or perhaps they were waiting for something more to happen. I had always been aware that our household raised expectations, and that people speculated about us. When I was still quite small and biked over to the farm produce store for their homemade caramels, the old Mrs. Walters who was then in charge of it would keep me talking, trying to extract some information about "your folk up there in the house, your mom and dad," though she knew perfectly well that Manton had moved out years ago. Before he did, in the brief time that he and Lindsay had been together, it was said that what went on at Propinquity outdid the most squalid area of the town, down on Fourth Street, where wives were calling nightly for the police as protection against their husbands, and sometimes for the ambulance as well. After Manton left, there was a lull for a while. The house was empty, and people used to look at it longingly, wanting for it to come alive again. They were only partly satisfied when Lindsay stayed for weekends with different lovers and finally moved in with Jean—none of this was unusual, and interest had begun to shift to some of the other big houses (weird weekend parties had started

up in the Tyler house, now owned by the daughter of a Texas
oilman). But when the Rawul and his group came in, we
moved to center stage again, and our cleaning lady, Mrs.
Pickles, with her inside information became sought after even
by people who had never had much time for the Pickles
family. With this party—at which not only the Rawul and his
retinue were on display but also Lindsay and Jean and Manton and Barbara—we were reinstated as the principal family,
leaving the Texas heiress just simply nowhere, where she
belonged.

But if anyone was waiting for a fight to break out between
Manton and Lindsay, they would have been disappointed. I
think it was not until the ceremony was over that the two of
them discovered they had been standing side by side; instead
of turning their backs on each other as they might have done
under normal circumstances, they exchanged some pleasant
words and even walked away together. I saw Mrs. Pickles
nudge Mrs. Walters of the farm produce store—this was the
daughter-in-law, old Mrs. Walters having been put away in
a home some years ago—to draw her attention to this handsome all-American couple strolling side by side toward the
house, engaged in conversation. I watched them too; I wondered what they could have to say to each other so amiably.
They veered sharply away—away from the house where Jean
and Barbara still stood on the porch, watching them—and
moved off together toward the orchard; but before disappearing in there, Manton turned around and called me, and
when I joined them, he hooked one arm into mine and the
other into Lindsay's, and anyone watching was rewarded by
the sight of this happy family group, father, mother, and
daughter, strolling under the ripening apple trees of their
own orchard.

"I've been telling Lindsay," Manton said to me in the warm
voice he had when at peace with himself and the world. "I
think it's wonderful: the whole thing. And you giving the
house. I'm so proud." He squeezed my arm, and maybe Lindsay's too on the other side.

There had always been moments when I hated Manton,
and this was one of them. They usually occurred when he
was being pompous, smug, putting on an act—maybe I could
only stand him, or I should say love him, when he was being

himself: that is, frankly selfish like a child, but also bewildered and mixed up like a child. Through irritation with him, I announced a decision I hadn't made: "I never said I was giving the house."

"No, but you will," he assured me, as calm, warm, and confident as the director of a bank.

"I haven't decided," I said. I had already disengaged my arm from his, and I wouldn't look at him but down at my own foot digging around in the soil.

"Harriet's being tiresome," Lindsay announced. I saw Manton give her arm a warning squeeze, and he went on talking to me, with perfect understanding: "I think after today we *can* decide."

"Who's we?" I said.

"Baby, you know you asked me to come here. You did consult me, sweet one. And why shouldn't you," he said. "It's what I'm there for: when truly needed. I like to think that." He made his sincere eyes at me; I continued to be irritated and yet involved with him—it was true, I had gone to him, and not for the first time either, when perplexed or in trouble. Though I always wondered afterward why I had gone to him, the fact was he never turned me away but was ready to listen and give his—usually useless—advice. He was, as he said, there.

He went on: "I know it's not easy. I know how you love Propinquity. But it would be a magnificent gesture—and my Lord, how many of us are in a position even once in our lives to make such a gesture? I envy you. Both of you," he said, turning to Lindsay so she wouldn't feel left out. "I wish *I* had something to contribute to such a cause."

But Lindsay's mood had changed. Probably it was the bit about always being there—literally of course it couldn't have been less true—anyway, her back was up. The moment of accord between them was over. She said "If you really want to contribute, you could always sell some stock."

He ignored this with dignity and went on talking to me: "I know my little girl. She doesn't care about owning anything; about owning a house. She'd give it away tomorrow."

"Yes but I might want to give it away tomorrow to an orphanage. Or I might just want to keep it."

"Why?" Lindsay said.

"Because," I said.

It was getting more and more back to normal. We weren't talking about the house but about ourselves—our own shortcomings. It usually happened to me when I was alone with either or both of them—that their inadequacies, as persons and as parents, overwhelmed me.

"*You* want to keep it," Lindsay said, having had time to work herself up. "How do you think *I* feel? Who's spent more time here, you or I? All our vacations—if we weren't by the ocean somewhere, we were always here, my whole childhood, dammit: That means something."

"You were lucky," I said.

"You mean my mother was lucky, that she married my father and not someone like your father—"

"I thought we were going to talk nicely today," Manton put in, still dignified.

"Yes we would, if you hadn't happened to come here bringing Baby Doll."

"*Well*," Manton exhaled. "Is that what's bugging you? Barbara being here?"

"Nothing is, as you put it, *bugging* me. Until this moment I was feeling happy and wonderful. It's not every day that someone like the Rawul comes into your life and makes you want to do something—give up your house, or whatever. I really want to do that, but you make out as if it's just—'oh one of Lindsay's big acts.' Dragging me down; dragging everything down, as usual."

"But why bring in Barbara?" Manton insisted, stamping his foot.

She stamped hers right back at him: "I didn't—you did! And she doesn't even have the decency to try to make herself pleasant but sulks around in her nightclothes, fighting with you. In my house. Under my roof. Naturally, I want to give it away—are you surprised that I'd want to have something better going on in it than you and Barbara?"

"For heaven's sake, what are you talking about, it's the first time we've even been here."

"And the last! And the last!"

"I'm sorry," Manton said to me. "Your mother is hysterical."

He wasn't sorry but rather pleased with himself, for keeping his temper; he wasn't always so successful at it. But I felt sorry for her—she hadn't meant to be this way, she hadn't even meant to say anything about Barbara when she had entered this orchard, still feeling noble from the flag-raising ceremony.

I said to Manton, "I don't know why you always have to get into a fight with her."

"I!" he cried at that and put both his hands on his chest in sincere indignation. All his calm and poise were blown away. "I get in a fight! My Lord, didn't you hear me, I was congratulating her. I was giving her my respect and esteem, and next thing I hear she's running down Barbara!"

Lindsay put her hands on her ears and cried "Don't mention her name in my house!"

Manton moaned, his hands over his eyes as hers were over her ears, and swayed to and fro in his despair.

It was at that moment, unfortunately, that Michael appeared in search of me. He gave one look—of disgust—and told me with his eyes to come away. I must say, I was glad to do so. When we were out of the orchard, he said "Why do you always get yourself into these situations with those two?" I had to laugh because it was true, I did. Michael had never done so. That look of disgust he had given them was, I'm afraid, his characteristic response to our parents, singly or together.

He had no interest in what the row had been about but said: "What shall we do? No one seems to want to go home."

They stood dotted around the lawns, as if waiting for the next event. But nothing further had been planned; it had been assumed that, after the flag-raising ceremony, everyone would leave. No one had done so. The full light of afternoon had faded, trees and house looked softer, melting away into their own shadows. Crishi was coming toward us—smiling, his white shirt fresh and gleaming: "We'll have to organize some party games," he said. I thought he was joking, but not at all. We went in the barn where we collected a pile of old seed bags for a sack race; and then into the house, where Crishi set Mrs. Schwamm to hard-boil eggs for an egg-and-spoon race—she thought it was the funniest thing she had

ever heard; she laughed till she choked. All the guests laughed
too, when invited to participate; but Crishi cajoled, teased,
and gently bullied them; he was the first to get into a seed
bag and hopped up and down to show them how, not a bit
afraid of appearing ridiculous. Led by bold Mr. McKimberley
from the bank, a few of the local people climbed into the
seed bags, laughing at themselves, a bit shamefaced; and
when he had got them going, loudly applauding their skill
and daring, Crishi whispered to me, "We'd better get some
drink into them." Back in the house, I got out Grandmother's
silver punch bowl, and Michael and I and Crishi and Mrs.
Schwamm emptied bottles into it, not much caring what they
were, almost daring each other on as we poured bourbon on
brandy on wine on orange juice on vodka. Mrs. Schwamm
was shrieking "But they'll all be blotto!" in her Austrian
accent—"That's the idea," Crishi said—and she was still
shrieking as she helped us carry bowl and glasses out.

Everyone had joined in the games. Manton and Lindsay
had emerged from the orchard and were watching the Rani,
flushed and full-bosomed, hopping eagerly between Mrs.
Pickles and Mr. McKimberley, all three intent on winning.
When Mrs. Pickles came in first, the Rawul, who sat smilingly
watching from the sidelines, applauded her with his hands
held high in the air, softly clapping and calling out "Bravo."
Mrs. Pickles, scarlet with exertion and pleasure, said she had
always been good at games, didn't know what it was but ask
anyone, when there were games, everyone knew Cindy Pickles
would be first. The Rani cried for a replay—"Revenge!" she
cried—and when they ran again, she did come first, and Mrs.
Pickles said it was her ankle, the old trouble, it had never
been the same since she had twisted it cleaning up in our
attic. We began handing out glasses and inviting everyone to
come and dip into the bowl. The Rani, flushed, panting,
laughing, still in her seed bag, put back her head and drained
her goblet like a warrior queen, before looking around to
see who was playing with her. Both Manton and Lindsay
stood ready to go, and I saw that Jean and Barbara had joined
the crowd. Only the Rawul sat apart, a benevolent spectator,
while everyone else scrambled around and fell over and
laughed and drank more punch. Evening was falling, a pink
light shone in one area of sky, the moon was already faintly

in another; the reflection of the opposite shore was etched
into the lake, an underwater forest gleaming brighter than
the land around it. Crishi decided it was time to change
games—he wanted a three-legged race, and Manton knew
where there were a whole lot of old neckties, up in the attic,
we could use for it. Crishi chose me as his partner and bound
my leg to his with a frayed fraternity necktie that had probably belonged to Lindsay's father. The Rani, though protesting that she was just getting expert in hopping, climbed
out of her seed bag and looked around for a partner. Manton
and Lindsay came forward, but she chose someone from the
town; and now everyone was running around finding partners and race after race was run. But it always happened that
Crishi and I came in first—we were unbeatable, an irresistible
team.

I was getting tired—not physically but in the sense of bored;
besides, I couldn't see Michael, who took no part in the fun.
I asked Crishi, "Where's Michael?" but he didn't hear me,
not even when I said it the second and third time. He didn't
look at me either, not once, although we were tied and running so closely together that we might as well have been one
person. All his attention was fixed on the game; he seemed
to be enjoying it. I began to say "Let me go," and "Let me
go please, Crishi," but he still didn't hear me; and when I
looked into his face, I saw that his eyes, which refused to
meet mine, were hard and cold, and so was the smile of
enjoyment fixed on his face. Although desperate to get away,
I found that, whenever it was our turn to run, I naturally
followed Crishi as if my body obeyed him more than it did
me; and how easily we won each time, our limbs in perfect
accord—we could not help winning, we were just naturally
swifter, fleeter than anyone else. But while physically I was
doing so well, otherwise I was getting more and more
upset—in fact, I was getting almost hysterical, shouting "Let
me go!" as we ran, which made Crishi run faster, with me
forced to follow him. Until finally, when we won again, he
looked around at the others coming up behind us and taunted
them—"What's all this huffing and puffing" (he and I weren't
even out of breath) "I think it's the smoking and drinking
and all the other stuff. . . . Oh you want to go?" he said to
me, as if he had only just heard me. By this time I was yelling

in his ear and hitting his arm with my fist, and to make it
look like part of the fun we were having, he laughed out
loud and bent down to untie my leg from his; and the moment he did that, I sprang away from him and fled—past
the Rawul, who applauded me in the same way he had done
Mrs. Pickles, softly clapping his hands held high in the air
and calling out a smiling "Bravo." I didn't stop running till
I was in the house and was, I felt, safe.

Safe from what and safe from whom? I didn't ask till I was
inside, where it was cool, silent, with lamps lit in the hall and
on the upper landings. Only then did it strike me how stupid
it was to be feeling and to be *fleeing* that way; and only then
did I notice that there were tears coming out of my eyes. I
hate tears—my own, that is—I truly hate and despise them,
and so does Michael; I dashed them away impatiently with
the back of my hand before going into his room. There he
was lying on his bed, reading a book, and I was so overwhelmed with gladness to see him, and to be with him, that
I could say nothing but stood with my back to the door, still
holding the handle, and looking at him. He lowered his
book—some ancient Oriental text, as usual—and said "It all
seems to be going on fine."

"Why aren't you down there?"

"Oh you know."

Of course I knew. Michael never joined in anything—he
was a natural loner; whenever something was going on, pleasant or unpleasant, he disappeared and was to be found reading in his room. We had never managed to get through an
entire family meal without someone saying "Harriet, go and
find Michael," and usually more than once, between soup
and meat course, and then again before dessert.

So it was only natural that he should now ask "Have you
been sent for me?"

"Oh no," I said. "You can stay here; that's all right."

"Are you sure? No one wants me? Crishi's not saying, 'Now
where the hell is that Michael?' " He tried unsuccessfully to
imitate Crishi's very distinctive accent, and smiled tenderly,
as though he could hear Crishi talking.

"No. He's not asking for you."

"Maybe I *should* go down. I mean, with everyone working
so hard."

It was the first time I had heard Michael have any qualms about not joining in. He even laid aside his book and got up to look out the window at what was going on. I joined him there, standing very close behind him as if for protection. But they had stopped playing games. It had turned almost dark outside—deep dusk—and from up here we could make out small shadowy figures moving around on the lower lawn; a dull silver light gleamed from the water and the sky, as from twin mirrors. Someone had taken the boat out on the lake and it floated there as a black speck on the silvered surface. And the two flags hoisted that day hung from the top of their poles, limp in the still air. Michael appeared to be looking at these flags and I at the figures below; usually we felt the same but not now, it seemed.

"Aren't you glad we've got this house?" he said.

"But you're giving it away."

"That's what I mean: glad to have it to give." His face was raised toward the sky; he gave first a sigh—of satisfaction—next a laugh, also of satisfaction.

I saw that some of the figures were beginning to straggle toward the house. I wished they wouldn't; I wanted to stay alone with Michael. I put my hand on his shoulder; this was as far as we ever got touching one another, but it was very intimate between us. Michael didn't like anyone touching him, unless it was lovers, I presume.

"Where are you going this summer, Michael?"

"What? What are you talking about?" He half-turned his head toward me. "You know I'm not going anywhere."

"I just thought if you were, if you'd take me with you."

"What's got into you?" He very slightly moved his shoulder—no more than a twitch, but I took my hand away. I thought he was annoyed because I had asked to be taken with him. Although he did sometimes take me, he certainly didn't want to be asked; that would have meant being tied down, someone making a demand on him. But now it seemed what had irritated him was my suggestion that he was going away somewhere: "You know perfectly well I can't, with everything going on."

I said "What's going on?" His exclamation made me retrieve that a bit: "You mean, the Seventh World and all of that—"

"What else would I mean. You're not being serious, Harriet. And you have to be because it's very serious and important for us. For everyone."

"You mean the whole world?"

"Yes of course I mean the whole world—what do you think it's all about?"

There was silence between us, irritated on his part, sad on mine. The figures were drawing closer—by the dull silver light from the sky I could make out Jean with Lindsay, and at some distance Manton with Barbara. But most of the guests remained on the lower lawn; still no one wanted to go home. There were faint sounds of laughter coming from there, something was going on; I could make out some sort of animal noises—was it hens? cows? I guessed Mr. McKimberley was doing his animal imitations, which were always popular at local gatherings, though it took a few drinks before he could be induced to perform them. The guests had by now dipped freely into the punch bowl and were ready to be taken out of themselves. The night was peaceful, the trees asleep, but the balmy air seemed shot through with expectation and excitement. Or was this only emanating to me from Michael as he leaned against the window, looking at the flags and perhaps also trying to see where Crishi was? Jean and Lindsay had drawn near the house, and I could see that Jean had grabbed hold of Lindsay's arm—no doubt they were having one of their intense scenes.

I said "If the Rawul takes over the house, what's going to happen to Lindsay and Jean?"

"They can stay and work for him. It'll give them something more to think about than fighting with each other."

"They're doing it now," I said, pointing them out to him.

"I don't have to see that. And neither do you." When he was mad at something, Michael literally ground his teeth: "That's why I'm glad this has happened—the Rawul and everything—to get away for once in our lives from all the personal squalor."

But actually Michael had never done anything except get away from it. He had never allowed himself to be involved. When we were children, he saw to it that we had games and secluded places of our own, whether it was here in the house

or in different embassies with our grandparents. Later, when
he grew up, he traveled to faraway places; but even in between these journeys, when he was physically present and
surrounded by his family, he always managed to be engrossed
in something of his own; to absent himself in spirit. He tried
to make me do the same, but I did not have his gift for it.
Michael had never cared what people thought of him and
made no effort to please or placate anyone. Both our parents
were afraid of him; it's a terrible thing to say, but I think
neither of them liked him. Michael was the one subject on
which they were in agreement.

He was pushing up the screen window in order to lean
out: for Crishi had come running across the grounds and
stood under the window to shout up to us. He was asking if
we had any fireworks—"Everyone says there has to be fireworks!" "Do we have any?" Michael turned to me. I said "We
were only expecting everyone for the afternoon. That's all
they were invited for." "Well now we need them. Everyone
wants to stay."

Crishi called for us to come down, but only Michael went.
I decided that for me the party was over; I was tired—it may
have been from having been made to run all those races, but
not only that. I wanted to go and lie down in my room without
turning the light on and to be as alone as possible. But I
didn't even get there—as I was going from Michael's room
to mine, Jean came storming up the stairs. When she saw
me, she said "You can help me carry them, though really I
feel like flushing them down the toilet. The goddamn flipping
fireworks," she said, going into her room.

I followed her. Jean's room was the homeliest and tidiest
in the house. She kept everything just so: her luggage stowed
away on upper shelves, her tortoiseshell brush, comb, and
mirror set, and her Mickey Mouse alarm clock she had since
her college days, winter clothes in polyethylene bags in back
of her closet, and in front her boots and shoes arranged in
rows, the better ones with trees in them. She had boxes of
fireworks on the same shelf as her Christmas tree decorations
and also cartons of old photographs and letters, everything
numbered. As she was getting down the fireworks and handing them to me, she said indignantly, "I told her this is not

what I went and got them for; not for this crowd."

"Then why are you giving them?"

"How many fights can you have," she said dully. "The moment she heard what they wanted—'Oh Jean's got fire-works haven't you Jean, go and get them.' And we'd talked about it, we'd agreed—not this year, not with all these people here. Not after last year."

I tried to remember last year and it took some effort. For me, it had been very dull. Michael hadn't been here—in fact, there was no one except Lindsay and Jean and me. I suppose that was what Jean was remembering. At night the three of us had sat by the lake and Jean had let off these fireworks and at each one Lindsay had exclaimed "Oh Jean *look!*" She clasped her hands and had stars in her eyes. I must have dozed off at one point, and when I woke up, the display was over, and Jean and Lindsay were sitting on the bank with their arms around each other, not talking at all, looking at the moon in the sky and again in the lake.

I helped her pack the boxes in shopping bags and carry them down, but I didn't want to come out with her. I held the door open, so she could get through; just as she was going down the porch steps, the Rani was coming up them. Jean had her back to me so I couldn't see how—if at all—she returned the Rani's greeting, which was very friendly. And the Rani was also very friendly to me as she passed me through the door, and whispered, coming up close, "I have to go to the little girl's room." It was not the first time I had been taken aback by the Rani's simpleness. In fact, almost every time I heard her say anything, it seemed to be banal or naïve. Maybe that was why she rarely spoke at all—because she knew she could not live up to the expectations aroused by her spectacular looks.

I shut the door of my room and was glad to be alone. But after a while I was surprised to hear the Rani calling me—she was opening doors along the landing, trying to find me. When I came out to see what she wanted, she said "Come along—time to join the fun"; she sounded like a games mistress I had had when I was at school in England for a year.

I told her I had a headache and wanted to rest. "Oh poor Harriet," she said, in a voice rich in warmth and sympathy.

She followed me and turned on the light—"So this is your room?" She looked around and noted how little there was to see, how bare it was, on principle; and "Charming," she lied politely.

"Do you mind turning the light out? It's hurting my eyes."

"Oh—" another very warm sound; and she sat down next to me, close by me on the bed, in the dark. "Poor darling," she breathed at me, and touched my brow and gently pressed it with her fingers. It seemed to me that her fingers were transmitting a strange sensation into my brain, but this may have been just my imagination, which was overwhelmed by her physical presence so close to me. She exuded, from inside her heavy silk, a perfume compounded of some costly essence of blossoms and of her own womanliness: This mixture was as potent as those flowering Oriental bushes that come at you in waves of cloying scent and knock out your sense of smell.

However, her conversation continued absolutely banal, and in a tone and language that combined schoolgirl with games mistress: "We've had the most lovely day, Harriet; such fun; such a good time. . . . I'm sorry you have a headache—is this doing you any good? no? should I stop? It must be with all the excitement we've had, and perhaps the sun, running in the sun. I saw you run with Crishi—you were fab, Harriet! Quite a team, aren't you, you two? We should be entering you for the Olympics—just joking, dear; I can be very silly sometimes. . . . Everyone has been so kind, all those nice, nice people down there. Mr. What's-it from the bank, and the sweet lady who comes to clean. And your parents, Harriet: I like them enormously, both of them. And it's a great, great privilege for us to be in an American home, and today is such an important day for you isn't it, historically. We're very proud that you've allowed us to share it with you. It's wonderful to have such good friends," she summed up, "and the whole day's been adorable. . . . I think they're calling us."

"They're calling you."

From all sides down below her name rang out—her name, or was it her title—"Rani! Rani!"—truly, it was like a queen being implored to show herself. And like a queen she stepped to my window—"Rani! Rani!"—it was a chorus, everyone had

taken it up, some seriously, some in fun, or just to join in.
"Aren't they childish," she said, smiling, but at the same time
she did make a gracious gesture with her hand in acknowl-
edgment. And when I joined her at the window, she put her
arm around my shoulders as if I were—I don't know what
—maybe some junior princess, anyway someone to be drawn
forward and drawn in. I stood still—I had no alternative—
I could hardly shake her off with all those people looking up
at us. I didn't see Crishi down below—no wonder, for he was
already in the house, up the stairs, and there he was rapping
on my door and then inside without waiting for an answer.

"Aren't you coming for the fireworks? Everyone's waiting
for you."

"Yes we're just on our way down—we got talking. Girl talk,"
she said with a merry laugh.

"And in the dark," he said, turning on the light. "It must
have been some very intimate secrets."

"Oh but of course. Harriet and I've had a good gossip,
haven't we. Only she's got a headache—no don't look at me.
I didn't give it to her with my chitter-chatter, she had it
before. The poor thing." Again she rubbed her fingertips
over my forehead, only this time I moved away.

I didn't want them in my room. In those few moments,
they seemed already to have taken possession of it—as easily
and completely as of the rest of the house. Crishi picked up
the lump of rock Michael had brought me from Ladakh, but
he must have felt the vibrations coming from me, so he put
it down again; he said "I'm sorry you have a headache," very
sweetly and sympathetically.

I turned away from him; I didn't want to look at him. It
wasn't that I was just sulking—I was really angry with him;
the feelings he had inspired in me during the race hadn't
worn off. He must have been aware of this, for he did not
try to get around me. Instead he said to the Rani: "Do something to your hair." "Oh am I the most awful fright?" She
turned to my mirror and said "Goodness," and was already
pulling pins out, so that glorious dark waves shimmering with
auburn fell over her shoulders and down her back. She took
my comb and used it swiftly and effectively, and in no time
at all she had coiled everything back into her usual perfect

coiffure. Crishi knelt down on the floor and did something to the folds of silk cloth around her ankles, and when he got up, she said "Now how?" He examined her, gave an expert flick to her neckline, and said "Not bad." She tucked her arm in his, ready to go down. "Sure you won't come?" he asked me, but didn't insist. As they stood there arm in arm, both of them full of sympathy for me, hoping I would soon be better, they did look like mother and son rather than anything else. Maybe because he was so slim and youthful-looking, whereas she was almost matronly, and the layer of gold embroidery on the front of her dress made her bosom burgeon even more. And there was something familial in their attitude to each other—his slight air of patronage, and her smiling submission to it like a mother who is terribly proud of her son.

But when they were gone, I thought, Why should I care what or who they are to each other? She had left behind a hair in the comb she had used—I pulled it out to throw away; it was surprisingly thick and strong, more like a piece of wire than a hair. Their lingering presence in my room disturbed me: Actually, it was not so much lingering—that word has something light about it—but more like a cloud heavy with storm and thunder. In fact, it felt so oppressive inside that I thought the weather must have changed; but when I stepped to the window, I found the night to be perfectly balmy and still. The whole party had moved to the edge of the lake in anticipation of the fireworks. I watched from above, looking not so much toward the lake as at the tops of the trees, which seemed to have a veil over them from the softly lit night sky. The first of the rockets came spluttering up, and another and another, popping open and for a moment spreading a little garish color, only to die away very quickly. In contrast, stars and moon, which had appeared dim before, shone with a bright and steady light. Some more fireworks went up—I could hear halfhearted cheering down below—but it was hopeless. Jean's fireworks might have been good enough for a few friends, or for two lovers sitting with their arms around each other by the lake, but they didn't make much of a show at a party, especially not one in celebration of a new world movement. It was a relief when the display was over.

I went down, and found that disappointment with the fireworks had had a bad effect on the party. The local people
were beginning to say they were sorry they had missed the
fireworks at the high school, which were the usual culmination of this day; some of them thought that, if they hurried,
they might still see at least the end of them, so they moved
off to their cars and drove away. Mrs. Pickles whispered to
Mrs. Schwamm to ask if supper was going to be served—
throwing Mrs. Schwamm into a fit of red-faced indignation,
her first that day, which had been an unusually benign one
for her. "Eating and drinking all day like pigs, and now they
ask for supper," she complained to me. Mrs. Pickles then led
off another contingent of local people to the high school,
where homemade lemonade and chocolate-chip cookies were
traditionally served after the fireworks. The remaining guests,
finding that they had overstayed the events of the day, began
to wonder which hosts to thank and say good-bye to. The
obvious ones were the Rawul, Rani, and Crishi—they stood
expectant and smiling, and as fresh as they had been at the
start. They returned thanks more effusive than those they
received, so that the guests felt themselves royally honored;
and it would have been a fine high note for them to leave
on, if they hadn't remembered that there was another set of
hosts to be thanked.

Unfortunately, Lindsay was not as fresh as she had been
at the start of the day. It seemed she had felt shamed by the
inadequacy of the fireworks and was blaming Jean, who fought
back: "But it was *you* told me to get them!"

"How was I to know you bought this crummy lot—oh are
you going? Sweet of you to come—but of course I might have
guessed, you're always so *cheap*, Jean."

The guests backed away, their smiles cooling on their lips.
But here Manton stepped forward as a responsible person,
and they were relieved to shake the hand he held out to them
so warmly: "Wish you could stay—yes wasn't it fun—hope
you'll be with us again soon." Manton had the ability to remember faces and usually to put the right name to them;
and even when he didn't, he compensated with extra cordiality, making the guests feel as good with him as with the
Rawul's contingent. So it happened that they began to go

straight from the latter to Manton—bypassing Lindsay, who
was awkwardly engaged with Jean.

"They would have been fine in Dubuque, Iowa"—which
was where Jean came from, from a very down-home background—"but hardly—goodness!—here at Propinquity. Or
did you do it on purpose, to make me feel an utter fool in
front of my guests?"

Although her complexion, under her crop of gray-brown
hair, had turned ruddier than usual, Jean remained admir-
ably unprovoked. But as Lindsay's voice rose—"I'm sure
you did it on purpose!"—Jean moved closer to her and said
in a low voice, "Have you been—?" Lindsay stepped back,
instinctively averting her face. Lindsay had never been al-
coholic but she did have tendencies that way—it was in her
family—and right from the beginning of their relationship,
Jean had thought it necessary to control her intake. Lindsay
wanted to be controlled; all her life she had been looking for
someone to do just that. But that day she had dipped as freely
as everyone else into the bowl of punch we had prepared, so
now she felt guilty, and instead of wanting to continue her
quarrel with Jean, she was anxious to get away from her.

At once she found an opportunity: Having averted her
face from Jean, she saw Manton bidding his gracious farewell
to the guests. The sight enraged her, and she strode over to
him. She had long slender legs, made for golf courses and
country walking; she didn't go in for either, or any sport,
but when she was indignant, she strode on them with the
energy of a resolute sportswoman. It was in that way she
moved in on Manton and hissed "Get out of my house."

Manton had been brought up as a gentleman and could,
at least for a few minutes, keep his poise. So he went right
on saying "Delighted you could come" to the guest whose
hand he happened to be shaking, even retaining that hand
for a while in extra cordiality, though the embarrassed guest
was straining to get away.

"Right this minute," Lindsay said, not troubling to keep
her voice down, so that the next guest too could hear her.
Two spots of high color had appeared on Manton's cheek-
bones.

I heard Crishi murmur to Michael, "You'd better do some

thing about your parents." Lindsay was really losing her head. Addressing the line of guests waiting to shake Manton's hand, she said "You don't have to thank him, he has no business to be here in the first place." She shook the next hand herself and put on a manner even grander and more effusive than his.

Crishi began skillfully to divert the guests from the Rawul and Rani's line straight to where their cars were parked. Manton and Lindsay were left standing alone, which gave Michael the opportunity to step between them, take an arm of each, and lead them away toward the house. Before they got very far, Jean came up behind them and took charge of Lindsay, leaving Michael to cope with Manton, who was saying "I have never been so insulted in my whole life."

I ran on ahead into the house and told Barbara that Manton might be ready to leave. She got up at once from where she had been lying on the bed and began very quickly and efficiently to pack up her own and Manton's things; and by the time Michael appeared with Manton, she was almost ready.

Manton was saying "For two pins I'd go straight to New York this minute and never come back again. I mean it," and he sounded and looked as if he did—very resolute, with his high color and clear cold eyes.

"I won't be a minute, darling," Barbara said; she had already stepped out of the robe in which she had been lounging around all day and was eagerly getting into her clothes.

"I'd forgotten what your mother was like," Manton was saying to Michael. "She's a madwoman. I feel more sorry than I can say for you two, that you have to live with such a complete lunatic."

"That's all right," Michael said. "We can manage."

"Yes but don't you think I feel a certain responsibility? However much I might like to get out of here and never see the place again, there is the question of my children."

"Ready?" Michael asked Barbara, who nodded; she was swiftly twisting up her long blond hair. Michael took the bag she had packed. "One moment," Manton said. "We have to discuss this."

Michael was not in a mood to discuss anything. Much shorter and lighter than Manton, he moved much faster. Barbara, usually a bit phlegmatic, was also moving fast. I followed behind them with Manton, who was addressing himself to me: "I feel I'm letting you down, baby," he said.

"I'll come to New York. I might stay a few days."

"If you really want me to," he offered, "I could stay. I'll swallow my pride and stay—good Lord, one can do that much for one's children."

By the time we reached the front porch, Barbara had driven the car around and Michael had put their bags in. He held open the door for our father.

"Good-bye, Daddy," I said. "I'll see you soon." I only called him Daddy when I wanted him to feel nice; dignified. And in spite of his scrambled departure, he did look dignified. He sat beside Barbara and turned to us for a last word: "It might look as if I'm running away from the situation, but believe me that is not the case. It's simply that one can take so much and no more. Please make my apologies and farewell to the Rani and Rawul. I hope everyone will understand."

Michael shut the car door. As Barbara drove off, Manton looked back at us with a sorrowful expression. " 'Good-bye, Daddy,' " Michael quoted at me. He could often be cold and contemptuous, and he was so now. He never had any sympathy for Manton; he made no allowances for him at all.

I'm sure Barbara was happy as she drove away with him; and in fact the day ended happily for other people too, so perhaps the Rawul was right and the celebration had been a success. He and the Rani stayed for a long time down by the water where the flags were; they walked up and down there arm in arm—a dynastic couple, an embodiment of traditional matrimony (I didn't know at that time that they weren't married at all). Jean and Lindsay were in the kitchen, where Mrs. Schwamm was fixing a supper for them. It was Jean's belief that quantities of food were the best antidote for Lindsay whenever she had been drinking, while Mrs. Schwamm was at all times happy to feed Lindsay. And Lindsay, relieved to be taken charge of, was calm and obedient and ready to do and eat whatever they wanted her to. Mrs. Schwamm was surveying the events of the day with Teutonic humor, which made Lindsay laugh; and when she laughed, Jean, full of fond love, kissed her cheek and said Lindsay was all better.

And the day ended happily for Michael and me too. Crishi and Michael decided to go for a midnight swim by the waterfall on the outskirts of the property; Michael told me to come along too—he and I often went there; we were the only people who used it except for some Pickles or gardeners' children who had always shared it with us. I would have gone, I wanted to go, but I still had bad feelings about Crishi, so I stayed behind. Awhile after they had left, I was surprised to see Crishi back again. It appeared he had returned for me. When I still wouldn't come, he said "Because of this afternoon." I didn't deny it. "It was just a game, Harriet; a party game." "All the same," I said.

He was silent; he looked down at the ground; he said "What can I say." He sounded rueful, perhaps a bit annoyed but, if so, it was with himself, not me. He didn't apologize; he didn't try to make me change my mind; he didn't look at me but kept his eyes averted. But I *wanted* to go swimming! And it *had* been a party game! I said "Oh all right; let me get a towel." "I'll get it!" He bounced off, bounced back again, he took my hand and pulled me along; he was laughing and skipping, so I had to skip along with him. He appeared so glad and relieved that I felt quite flattered, to have had this effect on him.

Not many people knew about our waterfall. It was down a steep incline, and to get to it, you had to leave your shoes at the top and negotiate a descending series of slippery stones, and at the same time hold aside the branches and bushes overhanging this narrow path. Of course for Michael and me it was easy because we were so used to it. Crishi came behind me and once or twice I had to put out my hand to help him and he took it, but mostly he managed very well by himself. Michael was already in the water, swimming around in the pool formed under the waterfall. It was always dark down here even during the day, and at night the pool was like an underground cavern and Michael a white shape gliding around it. Crishi and I left our clothes on the stones at the side and got in with him. One of the good things about swimming here was that conversation was impossible—the roar of the waterfall drowned out all other sounds as it rushed down the rock in a cascade of foam and spray, which was white by day and silver by night. The three of us swam around in and under the water, and sometimes on our backs, looking up at a few stars flickering there so faintly that only people like us with very good eyes could see them. Crishi, a darker shape than Michael but as slender and swift, seemed to love being underwater, and we never knew when he would be appearing underneath Michael and when underneath me. Michael got out first and sat naked on the stones with his legs drawn up and his arms around them. I saw him look up at the sky and the expression on his raised face was one of utter bliss; the phrase "his streaming countenance" came into my mind. Next moment he was back in the water, and the three of us continued to flit around and beneath one another, our bodies forming patterns that sometimes appeared to intertwine.

THE Rawul wanted to meet our grandparents —that is, our paternal ones, from Manton's side (our grandparents from Lindsay's side were dead—that was how we owned Propinquity and the rest of their property). I couldn't see the point of it myself, but he seemed to think it was important; he wanted to make influential contacts wherever he could. Actually, Grandfather wasn't all that influential anymore, for he had retired several years ago. He was also too preoccupied with his own affairs to have time to spare for anything else. By his affairs I mean the book he was writing about his public career; his moves between his house in town and his place on the Island, with all the books and papers he needed to take, and the clothes and makeup Sonya needed; and Sonya herself. She was his wife now— our grandmother had died several years earlier—but they had been together long before that, and whenever he was sent on a new posting, she used to take a place nearby. In the end she moved right into the residence and they became a ménage à trois, which was useful after Grandmother got sick and needed someone to look after her. By that time Sonya was really like her sister, although they couldn't have been more different—Grandmother was New England, and Sonya some sort of Russian refugee. Sonya was much, much more effusive than Grandmother, and she adored children and had never had any of her own, so Michael and I benefited from that all through these years.

When the Rawul wanted to make contact with Grandfather, Michael and I decided that the best way was through Sonya. Although he had been a diplomat for so many years, there had always been something skeptical and aloof about Grandfather, which made it difficult to approach him; and after his heart attack, it became even more difficult, as though he had withdrawn a little farther from the world. Sonya was the opposite—she must have been in her late sixties by this time (no one knew how old she was), but she was still open to every kind of new enthusiasm, and when we phoned and told her about the Rawul, she gave a gasp and said she *must* meet him. I went with him to the city; I drove the car and he sat in the back so he could spread out and study his papers.

The meeting was an immediate success. Meetings with Sonya always were; she was so eager to be won over that she ran forward most of the way herself: literally, for although their manservant opened the door, Sonya herself came tripping up as fast as she could to welcome us. She was tiny, and the very high heels and high golden hairdo she wore didn't help—she had to stretch up with all her might to get as far as kissing my cheek. Actually, she liked to kiss right on the mouth—it was some Russian custom, I think—but I had long since learned to turn my face aside at the right moment. She had a sumptuous tea ready, with every kind of pastry and cake she must have run out herself to select at Greenberg's, and she wore one of her flowered silk tea gowns that opened deep, deep down into a cleft. Grandfather was summoned from his study, and under her excited fluttering—she appeared actually to be skipping around them—he and the Rawul shook hands and looked each other steadily in the eye like two statesmen. I suppose there was a sort of historic ambience about their meeting—or would have been, if it hadn't happened to take place in Sonya's drawing room. I say Sonya's, for although the house had been given to Grandfather's parents on their wedding in 1898, after her marriage to Grandfather Sonya had managed to make it her own. The original sofas and cabinets and tables and bookcases were still there, but Sonya had overlaid them with her own taste and possessions: with fringed shawls, with rose-and-gold upholstery, and a whole heap of treasures dating from her traveling days around Europe and the Near and Far East and her forays into Madison Avenue antique shops—but all of them, wherever they had come from, marked by a preponderance of gilt and shell-pink ornamentation.

It was an incongruous setting for Grandfather, but he didn't seem to mind. On the contrary, he loved it—no doubt because he loved her so much and was so proud and pleased with her; and all the time she talked and fluttered and fussed around, he watched her with a smile and look you wouldn't think someone like Grandfather could have had for anyone. Without her, I don't suppose he would have had much time for the Rawul and his movement and his inspirational style of speaking. However, he sat there listening patiently, one long leg stretched stiffly out in front of him, and he even took the trouble to nod from time to time as though he were listening, which he probably wasn't but was waiting for the polite moment to return to his study. Sonya was beside herself—everything the Rawul said struck chords in her, and she even claimed that, if she had been clever enough, she would have thought of something like it herself. She said she had always had this intuition—not that she was an intellectual person or educated or anything, but she had traveled and seen a great deal, many many civilizations old and young, and it seemed to her that something like the Rawul's Fourth World was what humanity needed. "Oh wonderful, wonderful, marvelous!" she exclaimed often, clasping her small wrinkled hands with all her rings and squeezing Grandfather's arm to make him respond too. But he only sat there and smiled a little bit at her enthusiasm—except once, when he leaned forward keenly and made the Rawul repeat something he had just said.

This was about Lindsay, Michael, and me donating Propinquity. I was surprised myself to hear the Rawul refer to it so naturally, almost casually. There had been no reference to it for some time, which had been a relief to me, making me hope that the question had been shelved and with it the need for me to decide. But now I learned it *had* been decided—anyway, the Rawul seemed to think so. And when Grandfather heard that, he turned to me and asked "Is that what you're doing, Harriet?"

Grandfather's eyes were the same as Manton's and Michael's: far-seeing seafarer's eyes—though we don't come from seafaring stock at all but from Irish Protestant landowners whose younger sons usually became clergymen or went to India, except for our ancestor, who had come to the American colonies.

I hesitated while Grandfather waited, and the Rawul, smiling politely, also waited for me to confirm his statement. Fortunately Sonya rushed in with "And they say the young are not idealists! Darling, give Sonya a kiss!" She held out her cheek to me and I had to go over and kiss it. I tried to get away with brushing that creamed, rouged, and powdered surface with my lips, but she caught my face between her hands and firmly planted her mouth on mine, which made even Grandfather smile, along with the Rawul.

Sonya and Grandfather usually went to the house on the Island just before the Fourth, but this year they had had to postpone their visit because Grandfather's heart trouble had started up again. Now he said he was feeling perfectly well and was eager to get to the Island, where he loved to be. Only Sonya could have persuaded him to break their journey and pay us a visit at Propinquity; after meeting the Rawul, she could hardly wait to see the rest of the movement. Their reception was organized on a grand scale. The Rawul and Rani, with Crishi just a little way behind them, stood in welcome on the front porch and led them ceremonially into the drawing room. Here refreshments were served while everyone sat stiffly on chairs—the Rawul and Grandfather on the principal chairs on either side of the fireplace, both of them bolt upright as for an official portrait. It was not unlike a state visit, with no conversation at all except for a few platitudes delivered into the glacial silence. Even Sonya knew to keep quiet. The Rawul and Grandfather, both of them born to state visits, easily assumed the formal dignity expected of them.

When it was over, we all reverted to our usual selves—this was something that had always surprised me during Grandfather's embassy days: how quickly everyone became normal again after going through some pompous official ceremony. Sonya tripped excitedly around the house, like one returning to a childhood home, although she hadn't even visited us here all that often. She really was very sentimental. But it wasn't put on; she did feel that way and had tears in her eyes as she hugged everyone—Lindsay, Jean, Mrs. Schwamm—and kissed them on the mouth. Michael was her very special favorite—she claimed that she understood him completely —and she greeted him in what was for her a restrained manner, confining herself to standing on tiptoe and kissing his chin.

She saw at once that Crishi was someone very special too. She stood in front of him, looked up at him, and exhaled a sigh of recognition; perhaps they had met in some previous birth. Sonya was a believer in reincarnation and often came across people she had been close to in other centuries. She held his hand and turned it over a few times and nodded; I don't know whether she was admiring the shape or reading his palm. He took her in his stride, not putting himself out to charm her but just being his usual self. It was the Rawul who made the greatest effort to impress our guests. An hour or two before the usual evening session, he retired to his room, and when he emerged, it was as if he had charged himself with some new and powerful voltage. He had changed into his native dress and looked imposing in a long shiny tunic with jeweled buttons. And what he said that evening was more impressive, poignant, and more personal than his usual address, as if he had thought and felt it all out again from the beginning.

Once again he told us how his family, descending from the moon and passing through a series of semidivine incarnations, had established their earthly kingdom as far as the Caspian Sea on the one hand, and on the other into the Gangetic plains. His own ancestors, after surging as conquerors over Persia, had been driven back into Rajputana, winning and losing various kingdoms until finally cornered in a northwestern fastness of stony desert. Here they had built their fortress on a rock and defended themselves against all invaders so successfully that they were still there today— the oldest surviving kingdom in the world. They were no longer kings except in lineage; modern democracy had caught up with them. He was glad, the Rawul assured us, even proud:

To be part of the modern world meant more to him than all
his ancient titles and privileges. However, he could not escape
from or deny his own lineage—that he was a descendant of
a royal line so long that it reached back beyond antiquity to
divinity: yes, to a time when the gods still walked on this
earth, or rather, when there was not yet any division between
this world and another, higher one. It was a thought that
had haunted him as a child—especially when he climbed to
the roof of the old palace built on a rock, where he truly felt
nearer to heaven than to earth. Such a child would have
different thoughts from other children: A different light
would shine in his eyes—and here he invited us to look into
his eyes. Sonya, who was sitting right by him, did so and
exclaimed at the way the Rawul's light-colored eyes contrasted with his Indian complexion. It came from looking up
so much as a child into the sky, he explained, smiling, half-
deprecating, inviting us to treat it as a joke if we wanted to.
Grandfather said "Hm," but there was no other comment,
only a silence that I believe was rapt.

Whatever it was he had absorbed into himself up there in
the rocky kingdom of the desert did not leave him when he
was sent away to school in England: to Harrow, where his
father and grandfather had gone before him. Remote and
dreamy, he did not prosper in studies, sport, or any other
activity. But already his vision was forming, strengthened
now by his study of history and civilizations. He came to a
conscious realization of everything that lay behind him and
was in him: and it was at that time, as a schoolboy in cold
damp Middlesex, that he came truly to understand his ancient lineage, his own place in the story of Man, and with it,
the responsibility that place conferred on him. Technically,
he was no longer a king; there were no more kings; the world
today didn't want kings. What then did it want? the Rawul
asked us (Grandfather said "Hm" again). It wanted, the
Rawul told him and us, men who were prepared to be kings
in spirit: not to conquer and rule kingdoms but, extracting
what was best in each, to merge them into one great all-
embracing kingdom of this world. This was his dream, he
said. This was what had brought him to our shores, here
into the heart of America: He looked around at all of us—

Lindsay, Jean, Mrs. Schwamm, Michael and me, Sonya and Grandfather—in the hope that we would share his dream and help to bring it to fulfillment. He would not deny that he stood before us as a man with a mission, imposed on him by his birth and kingdom. And if he himself was small and wanting—and he said he was, though he didn't look it at all, tall and plump, shining in silk and jewels—he invited us not to regard him as a person but as a world spirit seeking to express itself; and to look not at but beyond him, not at what he alone but what all of us together could achieve—and here he waved his hand at where the two flags hung side by side over the lake, and everyone looked up at them except Grandfather, who said "Hm" again.

Grandfather was sitting a little apart from the rest of us. We were as usual down on the grass, some cross-legged, some with our knees drawn up, facing the Rawul, who sat on a chair to address us. As a special courtesy to Grandfather and Sonya, two more chairs had been placed at the outskirts of our circle opposite the Rawul. Grandfather made no fuss about occupying his, but Sonya wouldn't dream of it—she at once placed herself in the front of our group and even managed to get into a cross-legged position. Seated thus, her hands folded in her lap, she looked up at the Rawul, ready and eager to be inspired. Grandfather, although directly facing the Rawul and on the same level with him, did not look at, but away from him, across the lake; only sometimes he shot him a quick glance from under his brows, before at once resuming his faraway gaze over the water. The Rawul appeared to be addressing him more than anyone else, but I wasn't at all sure that Grandfather was listening—except for the times he said "Hm," though that too might have been at his own thoughts; he often did that, commenting to himself in his own mind.

Afterward he asked to speak to Michael and me. He came up to Michael's room. It was strange to see him there—I mean, I was used to seeing Grandfather at some great carved desk under the American eagle, not having to perch on the edge of Michael's narrow bed; but there was no chair, only the bare floor where Michael and I sat side by side listening to him. He asked us were we sure about donating Propinquity. Michael said yes at once, but added that I hadn't made up my mind yet. I felt a bit—I don't know, weak or mean-spirited, in the face of his absolute certainty. But it was always like that: Michael strong and certain and looking straight ahead, while I vacillated and saw all sorts of obstacles right and left preventing me from making up my mind. And when Grandfather turned to me, to ask what held me back, there was nothing definite I could say; and Michael spoke up for me, that I still needed time to think. When Grandfather asked him was he sure that he had thought enough, he said of course; and when Grandfather persisted, he became impatient and asked had Grandfather ever known him not to be absolutely certain, and Grandfather had to admit that no, he had not. Then there was a silence between them—not a hostile one, but because Grandfather respected Michael too much to attempt to argue with him. It had been like that ever since Michael was little. Even at that time he had been very definite and decisive in everything he thought and did, and Grandfather treated him as though he were absolutely equal in experience and authority with him. Grandfather loved him very, very much and was proud of him: perhaps also in reaction to Manton, of whom he wasn't proud at all, and I'm afraid he didn't love or even like him either; it was a great relief to him to have a grandson as different from his son as Michael was from Manton.

Grandfather asked me, "If Michael is so sure, why aren't you?"

"I told you," Michael put in, more impatiently. "Harriet's still thinking it out."

Grandfather smiled a bit. He always liked it when Michael was assertive with him; he liked it in general that Michael had an assertive character. He turned to me again: "Even your mother it seems has thought it out." We didn't have to comment on that. We were aware he was speaking ironically, or even cynically. Everyone knew that Lindsay never thought, let alone thought out, but did what she wanted from moment to moment, the same way as Manton. Whenever I heard Grandfather speak about our parents to Sonya—he never mentioned them to anyone else—it was always as "Those two fools," and he could pack an awful lot of expression into it;

if we were nearby, Sonya would say warningly, "*Les enfants,*
darling."

But now Grandfather didn't want to speak about Lindsay
and her motives, or even about Michael's and mine. He
launched off into a sort of soliloquy of his own, sitting there
on Michael's bed and the two of us looking up at him as if
listening to some ancient mariner's tale. Grandfather was in
appearance not unlike an ancient mariner, with his big weath-
ered bulk and his white brows beetling over his keen seafarer's eyes. He had a deep, slow voice that he never had to raise
much, people always being prepared to listen to him attentively. His accent and speech were educated, upper class, but
running underneath the surface was an American sort of
burr that got stronger as he got older and was redolent of
the locality of his childhood. This is more or less what he
said, and it was so unusual for him to speak to us at such
length, and so intimately, that I can still remember it almost
word for word after these many years. There was a special-
occasion feeling among the three of us. I had never before
felt so strongly how he was our grandfather, transmitting to
us his own experience and what he had himself received from
those who had gone before us:

"You could say it's none of my business what you do with
your inheritance from your mother's side of the family. It's
for you to dispose of as you think fit. But I've been thinking
lately about inheritance in general and what it means; what
it entails. I'm aware that nowadays young people, people like
you, Michael and Harriet, prefer to travel light. You prefer
to be rid of those properties, privileges, and responsibilities
that we were taught to take good care of. Well I'm not saying
we're right and you're wrong; no I'm not saying that; I'm
only trying to tell you how it was when I was your age and
my father might be talking to me like I'm talking to you now.
As you know, my father was in the government, as was his
father before him. Public service was expected in our family.
That goes right back to the first Wishwell to come to this
country. Born an Irish soldier, he turned himself into an
American farmer to till this land for his American family—
he married first Augusta Linfield and after her demise her
elder sister Miss Louisa; and when it came time to fight the

British army, he went right back to being a soldier again. Well, when they hanged him for a rebel, it was up to Louisa Wishwell to raise her own and her sister's children, fourteen of them altogether. Nine of them survived and spread all over the country, some as farmers, some as traders, and lawyers, and a preacher too; every kind of trade and profession. I guess we've got family all over, some rich and educated, some plain and poor. Our own branch of Wishwells—and we're the only ones to pronounce it *Witchell*—goes back to Henry, who returned to Concord in the 1830s after an unsuccessful spell of growing oranges in Louisiana. He started his own newspaper, *The Fighter,* and went to jail three times for his radical activities; and once he had to be hidden away by the marshal from an antiabolitionist mob. His sisters and his daughters were not far behind him—we've always had strong women in our family, Harriet, ready to stand up first for the slaves and then what they called the other slaves, that is, their own sex. I don't need to remind you of Harriet Wishwell, the first female president of the Anti-Slavery League, or of Maria Wishwell Knox, the author of *Let Us Be Sea-Captains*! I still remember that other great reformer and suffragette, my great-aunt Harriet Wishwell, who lived up to the age of ninety-eight. It was about her Commodore Dewey said he would rather face the entire Spanish navy than one Harriet Wishwell. These matrons brought up their sons the way the Romans did, and there was never any question in our family of not serving the country in which we had the good fortune to be born. My grandfather, Michael, born 1849, enlisted in the 44th Massachusetts, pretending he was sixteen when he was thirteen, lost a foot at Appomattox, graduated from Harvard College in 1870, set up as a lawyer, made money, bought land, went to Congress, lost an election, made more money, went to the Senate and became secretary of the interior under Teddy Roosevelt. My father, your great-grandfather—more or less the same career except he fought not in the Civil but the Spanish-American war, and in the navy not the army, bought not farmland but urban property and, for himself and his family, the place on the Island. That brings us up to me, and you know all about that."

He was silent for a while, maybe to let Michael and me

recollect what we knew about him. We knew him partly as
our grandfather and partly as a public figure, and in both
aspects he was a sort of monument to us. We also had some
sense of his earlier years, from photographs we had seen—
as a very handsome Harvard undergraduate; as a bridegroom outside Trinity Church with his tall fair bride and
surrounded by his own and Grandmother's family, who looked
just like them, bred from the same stock; as a young con-
gressman in Washington; in Paris on his first international
assignment; windblown on the Island, in white ducks and
yachting cap, having lost an election; with Franklin and Eleanor
Roosevelt at Hyde Park; being entertained by Nehru in New
Delhi as a member of the Peace Commission.

Then Grandfather challenged Michael: "Just tell me why
you want to give the house."

I can't think of two people more different from each other
than Grandfather and Michael: physically for one thing,
Grandfather with his great hulking figure, and Michael slight
and slender; and also in their ideas. And yet they did have
something in common—if only the way they both spoke very
slowly, so that you knew whatever they said came out of their
own deep, careful thinking. Manton was more like Grandfather in appearance, but somehow he had less of Grandfather's air or ambience than Michael. All three of them had
the same seafarer's eyes—except that Michael's seemed not
to be looking outward over limitless oceans but inward, to
whatever oceans lay there.

Grandfather and I waited respectfully for Michael to get
his thoughts together; and when he had done so, this is what
he finally came out with: "I guess I'm impressed with the
whole thing; the whole idea: making a new world based on
everything that is best in previous worlds. It sounds suspect
when you say it straight out like that, but you have to think
of everything that's behind it. All the civilizations, all the
ideals. And the Rawul and everyone with him, they really
believe the way no one else I've ever met does; and as you
both know, I've spent my time looking around for something
I can believe in, and commit myself to it. That's not so easy
nowadays, not so straightforward and plain cut as when you
tell us about the earlier Wishwells. Or maybe it wasn't that

straightforward for them either—how do we know they didn't have the same kind of seeking and inquiring to do before they committed themselves? I'm sure they were serious people who didn't just jump in anywhere; but once they did, they were ready to give everything—a foot at Appomattox, or whatever. So in face of all that, the house doesn't seem such a very big deal, does it." He reflected awhile and we knew he had more to say, and we waited. "Let me put it another way," he said. "When Grandmother used to take me to church sometimes, she gave me a silver dollar for when they came around with the collection. She'd watch me like a hawk to make sure I threw it in, and even then I hung on to it till she had to pinch my arm a bit. I didn't see any sense in throwing that dollar; I knew there were a lot better things I could do with it. But I can't think of anything better I can do with this house than throw it in for the Rawul, and no one has to pinch my arm to make me because I'm ready and willing and glad to do it."

Grandfather waited to hear if there was any more coming, and when there wasn't, he said "And that's all?"

"That's all," Michael said, without stopping to think this time.

"You're sure that's all?"

Michael was sure. Grandfather nodded and appeared satisfied; he believed him. But I'm not sure that I did, as totally and absolutely as I usually believed Michael. Of course I knew him to be completely altruistic and idealistic—but in the present case, weren't there also his feelings for Crishi? I'm not saying they were responsible for his decision, but hadn't they contributed at least something to it? If I had asked him outright, he would have denied it; though not the feelings themselves—he was quite frank and open about those. For me, the fact that he had them, was weakened by them, was not so much a flaw—Michael had no flaws for me—but a mystery in him; as were Grandfather's feelings for Sonya, which were so different from the rest of him. Perhaps Grandfather was thinking about that very same thing, for he remained sitting on the side of Michael's bed with the same sort of soft smile around his hard mouth that he had when he spoke to or of Sonya; and he said in the ruminative way people have when they are speaking to themselves as much as to anyone else: "We all like to think we're in charge of our decisions, but who knows what else there is, what moods and weathers we have that make us do what we do and be what we are: yes, even two Wishwell men like you and me, Michael." He smiled down at us in the same sweet, loving way he had with Sonya, enfolding us. I don't think he could really see us because the room was in shadow, certainly down on the floor where we were, though we could still see his face lit by the twilight coming through Michael's uncurtained windows.

Grandfather also spoke to Lindsay about the house, and this was unfortunate because it upset both of them. It says a lot for Grandfather's sense of duty that he opened the topic with her at all, went out of his way to do so, for usually they avoided speaking to each other beyond the most common and banal generalities, and not even those, if possible. Only to see Lindsay irritated Grandfather, and he couldn't stand to hear her deliver her opinions in her little-girl voice. But he always controlled himself and said nothing either to her or about her, except maybe privately in a sardonic aside to Sonya; but Lindsay of course voiced her opinion of him for anyone to hear. After their interview about the house, I saw Grandfather walk away in grim silence, while she, gasping for breath, uttered indignant half-sentences such as "Can you *imagine*" and "This is *really*" and "I must *say*." She didn't like him for himself, and she detested him for being Manton's father; and nothing could have confirmed her resolution to give away Propinquity more than his suggestion that she should have second thoughts about it. She was so upset that Jean could do nothing for her and had to appeal to Sonya; Lindsay's feelings for—or rather against—Manton's family did not include Sonya, whom she liked. She felt that Sonya understood her, and Sonya said she did—"I understand you, darling, completely," she said, even when Lindsay was what she herself called "just out of my mind," after her interview with Grandfather.

The way Sonya excused or explained Grandfather to Lindsay was to say "But darling what do you expect—he's a Taurus." Sonya herself was a Capricorn, which made her highly idealistic and open to new ideas. She was certainly open to the Rawul and his movement—she ran around the house stirred up and excited, talking to everyone, including the followers, whom the rest of us ignored. She felt that it was the beginning of a new era in our personal history as well as that of mankind; and she and Else Schwamm spent many hours down in the kitchen poring over their tarot cards, of which both were skilled exponents. Sometimes they were joined by the Rani, and when the three of them were huddled together over the kitchen table, it was as if some mysterious rite were taking place in the bowels of the house that would spread an influence over all our lives.

Around this time there were some unpleasant incidents involving the Rawul's followers and some young people of the neighborhood. Although the grounds and the lake were private property, the local boys had always taken it for granted that they could come to fish there in the summer and skate in the winter and for occasional picnics and parties. If they left too many beer cans littered about, Jean would get after them and make a fuss, ending in nothing more than they would have to come help sweep the leaves or cut the grass. But after the Rawul's followers took charge of the maintenance of the house and grounds, they were stricter about trespassing and put up POSTED signs all over the place. The local boys did not feel these applied to them and kept right on coming in, and this led to arguments between them and the followers. The followers were sort of schooled in patience and self-control; but the boys were some of them quite rough, and certainly weren't going to be pushed around, they said, by a bunch of weirdos. They kept right on coming as before, fishing and drinking beer. But one evening two of the followers came out to draw their attention to the POSTED signs; and when the boys laughed at them, they returned with some more followers, so that the boys, greatly outnumbered, had to pack up and leave. A few hours later they returned, with reinforcements; they brought pizzas and six-packs and started a party down by the barns. It was late by then, and many people had gone to sleep but woke up again with all the noise.

Michael and I had been swimming by the waterfall with Crishi. I ought to say that we did this every night and we

stayed there many hours before slowly trailing back to the
house; sometimes we lay down in a field for a while and
looked up at the moon. When we came back that night, we
were surprised to see the lights on in the house and everyone
woken up, with the boys having their party. By that time Jean
had emerged in her robe and slippers and was reading what
she called the riot act to them; but they just invited her to
join them, and one of them put his arms around her and
made her dance with him. She pretended to be angry but
couldn't help laughing; it was all quite good-natured, and
some people in the house had stuck their heads out the windows and were enjoying what was going on.

Michael and I stayed down in the grounds to watch, and
though we joined Jean in making some feeble protests to the
boys, we didn't mean to spoil their fun. Crishi, however, had
gone straight up to the house, and it wasn't long before he
came out again with all the male followers behind him like
an army. And like an army they converged on the boys, and
what followed was unexpected and shocking. The boys didn't
have a chance against the followers, who used what looked
like some very sophisticated techniques on them. It happened
so fast—one moment everyone had been laughing and kidding around and there was music playing, and next thing
there were these horrible thuds and cries of pain and the
grim-faced followers stomping around on the cassette players, the pizzas, and the beer cans. In no time it was over; the
boys had been pushed into their cars and the followers were
cleaning up the mess on the grass. Everyone went back in
the house and soon the lights were out again, and I guess we
were all supposed to be asleep and not thinking about what
had happened.

But we did think about it—I did, and Michael did, and
Michael must have talked about it to Crishi, because by the
time I came to talk to Michael, which was the next morning,
he had already come right around to Crishi's point of view
and explained it to me. I tried to protest—I said I didn't
think the boys had actually been doing anything so bad—but
Michael said it had been a challenge, which had to be faced
and dealt with. Well maybe, I said—but dealt with in that
way? Then Michael said that action has no degree, and either
you do something or you don't do it.

The Rawul was more accommodating—he had to be because he had to deal with Grandfather. I came in on them
at breakfast in the dining room next morning: The Rawul
had as usual heaped his plate from all the silver-covered
dishes on the sideboard, while Grandfather, at the opposite
end of the table, was only stirring a spoon around his cup of
tea. Whenever the two of them were together, they gave the
impression of two potentates conferring on matters of high
state; and like two such potentates, they usually didn't have
to say anything because everything had been said by others
at preliminary discussions, and all that was required of them
was to be there face to face. But this time that was not so;
for while Grandfather did sit there stirring in silence, the
Rawul was talking quite volubly, as one out to convince, and
justify.

If someone else had been saying what he was, I might not
have accepted it. But it was the Rawul talking, whom I knew
to be kind and a gentleman; a kind gentleman. He spoke in
his old-fashioned upper-class accent, stopping every now and
again to take another mouthful of scrambled eggs with kid-
neys; and his voice was soft and so were the graceful gestures
he made with his plump hands, one of them holding a fork.
And he was utterly and absolutely sincere, as was obvious
from the vibrations that came into his voice, and the passionate way he shut his eyes when he spoke of what was most
precious to him: his plan for a new world, a Seventh World,
where all that was best in the other three would come to
fruition. That sounds abstract and unreal, but it wasn't like
that at all when he said it, because it came so deeply out of
him, out of the Rawul in his English suit, eating his breakfast.
It was, as he said, his world view, which he was in the process
of putting into action with whatever means were available to
him. These were not extensive, he admitted; indeed, to the
casual eye they might appear extremely, even ludicrously,
limited: just himself and the Rani and Crishi, and a handful
of followers. But, he asked Grandfather, wasn't that the way
every great world movement had started off—whether it was
religious or, in keeping with our times, secular and political,
a drive by men not toward God but toward other men, toward
humanity? He balled his fist against his heart, as if the weight
of feeling there was heavy and hurting—his feeling for the

humanity he wished to redeem and lead into the paradise of
his Seventh World. Grandfather kept right on stirring his tea
to cool it; his silence was disconcerting, as was the way he
stared at the painting over the Rawul's head—a portrait of
Lindsay's grandfather, who had made his money in the dry-
goods business but here looked more like a Renaissance prince.
The Rawul faltered a bit, and then he had to come down
from the lofty height to which he had risen to a lower level,
to discuss the boys who had been thrown off the property.
And in view of what had gone before, it did seem petty that
this incident had had to be mentioned, let alone justified;
and it was magnanimous of the Rawul to see the boys' point
of view the way he did. He said he knew they meant no harm,
that they thought they were only having a party, but that in
fact and unbeknown to themselves, they *were* doing real harm:
for they were challenging and thereby obstructing the work
of his followers, the global regeneration that had been set in
motion, and no one said the Rawul—and here he did look
less like a kind gentleman and more like a world leader—no
one would ever be allowed to do that.

After the night of the boys' invasion, security measures
were introduced, and though there was no actual boundary
wall, a very definite demarcation line was drawn around Propinquity. Trees along the lake and on the outskirts of the
property had red PATROLLED and POSTED signs stuck to them;
gaps in the hedges were carefully closed with new plantings;
one of the two entrances to the main driveway was barricaded
completely; and at the other a sort of checkpoint was set up
where two followers monitored all entrances and exits. Even
Mrs. Pickles, when she arrived to work next morning, had
to be cleared; she muttered darkly as she pushed her vacuum
cleaner to and fro and packed up and left early, without
having her cup of coffee with Else Schwamm. The same dark
mood was shown by the deliverymen who came on their usual
rounds that day, and the heating people who were checking
our oil supply. They brought news of general indignation in
the neighborhood, for it seemed some of the boys had been
quite badly hurt and their parents were making a complaint
to the police. The Rawul and his party carried on smilingly
with their daily routine; only Crishi was busier than ever that
day, talking a lot on the phone in his easy, persuasive manner

and from time to time roaring off in the convertible he drove to make visits in the neighborhood. I don't know whether it was as a result of his activity, but neither parents nor police appeared at the house on that day or the next; and on the third day there was a beer-and-tacos party at which parents and police mingled in a relaxed way with the people in the house. By that third day Mrs. Pickles too had got over her bad feelings, even though by then there was not only a check-point but a walkie-talkie system by which the followers at the gate called up for clearance to the house. That morning over her coffee with Mrs. Schwamm, Mrs. Pickles expressed her appreciation of the general discipline and order that were now so apparent in our household; and she confided that, speaking for herself and a few others she could mention, and these did not exclude some parents, what had happened to the boys was not altogether undeserved, and maybe it was about time they learned that they couldn't do as they pleased with everyone.

Was I the only one who remained uneasy? What made it worse was that I couldn't talk about it to Michael—couldn't admit to having such feelings because he himself completely approved of what had been done. I couldn't understand it —Michael had always been so much against every kind of outer order and discipline that he couldn't ever stay in a school. He would accept nothing except what came from inside himself; no discipline except self-discipline. Of that he had much more than anyone else I had ever known. Even as a child he used to impose days of fasting on himself, also days of silence and other austerities he knew of; he told no one except me. He would have been the last person to wear any kind of uniform, but he had laid aside his *kurta*, steel bangle, and earring and dressed like the followers in blue shirt and navy jeans. Crishi issued orders to him the same as he did to everyone else, and Michael followed them. He and Crishi were very close—they worked together during the day, supervising the followers on the Xerox machines and tele-printer, and every evening the two of them went to the water-fall. They always expected me to join them, but after the incident with the boys, I no longer wanted to. They didn't press me but went off by themselves while I stayed back, feeling miserable and waiting for them to return. It was very late when they did, and I watched them from my window, walking across the lawn with their towels and wet hair—dreamy and happy, which was the way we always felt when we had swum and afterward lay in the field under the moon. Next morning again I couldn't bring myself to join them, and again they went off by themselves and I felt more miserable than ever. The third night too—this was after the beer-and-tacos party—I had intended to stay behind; but when Crishi said to me, quite casually, over his shoulder almost as he was about to go off with Michael, "Coming, Harriet?" I went to get my towel and hurried after them.

During these days, after his breakfast with the Rawul, Grandfather stayed the entire time in his bedroom. When I went to see him there, I found him propped up in the great four-poster in which our other grandfather had died. Sonya sat beside him on a chair, very wifely and domesticated, with some embroidery in her lap; she smiled at me and said "This big bear isn't feeling so good today."

"Nonsense," said Grandfather; and "We're leaving tomorrow."

"*If* you're better," Sonya said.

"There's nothing wrong with me at all." But he did look sick; his head was laid back against the pillows, as one who is very, very tired. He appeared immensely aged, and grand, with his large head and the tufts of white hair showing where the top button of his pajamas was undone. His hands lay like sculpture on the covering sheet. Sonya laid her own little warm plump hand on one of them and said "Stubborn as a mule, as always"; she looked at me and tried to smile again, but her eyes were scared.

And next day, in spite of her protests, they did leave. Their car, packed with books and luggage, drove up to the porch, and everyone came out to watch their departure. It did not have the stateliness of their arrival, although the Rawul and Rani were both in attendance. In fact, it appeared rather scrambled, as though they were getting away in a hurry; people had to be sent back in the house several times for things Sonya had forgotten to pack. She was crying, and I don't know whether it was because she thought Grandfather wasn't well enough to leave, or because she was sorry to part from her friends new and old. She embraced everyone with the same fervor—that is, all of us as well as the Rawul and Rani and whatever followers were within reach. Grandfather stood a little to one side, as though it were nothing to do with him. I thought he still didn't look well, almost frail in spite of his heavy build; it seemed to me that his clothes had grown too large for him, but perhaps this had been so for a long time and I hadn't noticed it before. The Rawul tried to make a little farewell speech, but with Grandfather remaining grim and withdrawn, it died, and the Rawul was left standing there, smiling and patting one of his hands on the other. While Sonya was still kissing and embracing, Grandfather went down the steps of the porch and settled in the back of the car. He beckoned to me from there, and when I came to the car window, he asked "Where's Michael?"

It was embarrassing, but I had to tell him Michael wasn't there. He had driven with Crishi to the printers to collect a new set of Fourth World literature. If he had known that Grandfather was leaving that morning, he might have postponed his errand; but, as I said, Grandfather left in a hurry—wanting to get to the Island, or just wanting to get away.

"Tell him—" Grandfather began to say to me, and then stopped. His eyes swept up the porch steps, where the Rawul stood smiling with the Rani beside him and some followers behind them. Whatever it was Grandfather had wanted me to tell Michael, he changed his mind and said instead, "Why don't you come to the Island, both of you; come and be with us. I want to see you," he added and stopped looking grim for the first time that morning. He had his hand on the car window and I took it and held it in mine. He smiled at that, and seemed completely to forget about the Rawul and his party standing there. "See that you come now," he said. "Bring Michael; and soon." I said "I'll tell him." "Not just tell him: make him. Make him come home." I couldn't say anything to that; I couldn't promise. I didn't think Michael would want to go to the Island and I didn't think I myself wanted to either. I too felt that we had work to do here, that we had begun to undertake something.

But Grandfather didn't want to know about this. He with-

drew his hand from mine and called to Sonya. Before they
drove off, he said again, "I want to see you there soon"—
but he seemed to have lost interest in me almost as much as
in the others standing on the porch. I guess he was just
looking forward to being on the Island and doing his work
there, writing his book to sum up all his life and what he had
done in it.

BUT Grandfather had a heart attack on the Island and died before we got there. As soon as we had the phone call, Michael and I left for the airfield. Crishi drove us there and chartered a plane to fly us and was both sympathetic and efficient. Michael was very tense and white and silent, and I must have been the same, so it was just as well that Crishi took charge. As we were about to board, he embraced Michael and held him for a moment, and Michael leaned his head against Crishi's shoulder and stood as if he didn't want to leave him. Crishi gently pushed him away, and then he turned to me. I thought—Is he going to embrace me too? and when he didn't, I felt more relieved than anything else.

It was Grandfather's father who had built the house on the Island. At that time—around 1910—there had been only a dozen or so summer homes there, all of them like ours, large and comfortable, to accommodate the big families they had in those days. In the winter the houses had been shut up with a caretaker to look after them, and then it must have been very quiet on the Island, with its one street of stores and the rows of fishermen's houses and the dwellings of retired sea captains. But it had soon become a more popular resort, and the big summer houses were turned into hotels and the sea captains' houses were rented out for the season. Just three of the big houses were still owned by the original families, and not many of us came there regularly. Only

Grandfather had spent as much time there as he could—that is, whenever he was on leave from his missions. It meant a lot to him; it was where he spent his vacations as a boy, and I know he loved the Island very much and would have thought it a good place for him to die in.

He was lying on his bed in his own bedroom. Sonya sat beside him in a little low chair. It wasn't so different from when he had lain on my other grandfather's deathbed, except that now it was his own. He still looked very grand, and his hands were folded in the same sculptured way over the sheet. Sonya, Michael, and I stayed with him through the rest of the day and took turns through the night. Sonya was dissolved in an unending stream of tears; her whole life was visibly melting away. Michael and I were dry-eyed. It wasn't that we didn't feel Grandfather's death but that our own life hadn't gone away with his, as Sonya's had. Staying with him all those hours in the silent room, I studied him, and I know Michael did too. We made ourselves consciously look at death; its complete stillness, its absence of life—which made it a presence; that is, Grandfather was no longer there but Death was. Michael probably contemplated a lot on this subject of presence and absence, being and nonbeing—he had a mind for abstract ideas. I didn't, and soon found myself sliding into other thoughts—the hours were long and slow—and I wondered what they were doing at Propinquity now. Were they under the tree listening to the Rawul, was the Rani laying out her tarot pack with Mrs. Schwamm, did Crishi go to the waterfall on his own or had he taken someone with him?

Michael got on the phone to the people who had to be called: Aunt Harriet, Grandfather's only surviving sister; the attorney; the *Times;* official people in Washington; but what took the most time was trying to locate Manton. It seemed he and Barbara had taken off for Spain somewhere, and after Michael managed to reach him, it took Manton a day and a half to get his plane connections. So it happened that the Rawul and his party got there before him. They did us the courtesy of attending Grandfather's funeral—the Rawul himself, Crishi, and two followers. These latter at once relieved the rest of us of all arrangements—they took over in the same efficient way as they had at Propinquity. By the time Manton finally arrived, the bedrooms in the house had been opened up, and the preparations for the funeral were complete. This was just as well, for Manton was incapable of giving thought to anything except his own grief. He and Grandfather had hardly been on speaking terms for many years, but this was due not to personal animosity—so Manton had once explained to me—but to their being totally different personality types. It did not, Manton told me, detract from his filial feelings in any way, and I must say he proved them now with his abundant tears. He and Sonya rushed into one another's arms, where they clung together; and then Manton went around embracing everyone else including the Rawul and Crishi, so that in a way I was glad Grandfather wasn't there to witness his son's grief for him. Michael stood prudently aside, and when Manton looked around for him, he disappeared. Manton also looked for Lindsay, and when he realized that she hadn't come, he fell around my neck again and thanked God I hadn't taken after my mother but after him and his side of the family.

At the funeral, however, he was controlled and stately. We were not a large group at the graveside—besides the Rawul's party, there was Aunt Harriet, who had flown in from Martha's Vineyard; some local people; an emissary from Washington sent to pay the President's respects; Mr. Pritchett, who was Grandfather's attorney; and Reverend Endicott from the Episcopalian church on the Island. As the principal mourners, Sonya stood between Manton and me, Michael between me and Aunt Harriet. It was more or less as it had been at Grandmother's funeral eight years before. The place was the same—the small maritime cemetery with its very early, very simple graves of fishermen and sailors. It was on slightly higher ground than the rest of the Island, with an unimpeded view, clear above the houses and churches, of an expanse of sky and ocean; and this gave the cemetery the feel of a small craft sailing out into uncharted waters. Michael and I were used to being principal mourners at our grandparents' funerals: Grandfather was the last—besides Grandmother, we had been there for both Lindsay's parents. But I had not felt before as I did now. Perhaps because I was older; perhaps because he had been such a presence—in our lives, as well as in himself. Even last night he had been there, silent and immobile, but still it was he, *his* corpse. Now there was only the sealed coffin being lowered into the deep-dug grave; and the smell of newly turned earth and of the sea; and the sound of the sea and Sonya's sobs and Reverend Endicott saying dust to dust. Grandfather was the dust he spoke of. There was a cramp in my heart, like some hand had caught and squeezed it. Michael felt the same, I'm sure, but he stood as straight and stiff and dry-eyed as I did, watching the coffin go down.

Manton continued being dignified for the rest of the day. He walked away from the graveside with a slow and measured tread, his hands behind his back; the Rawul walked beside him, with the same tread, and his hands also clasped behind him. Just as Grandfather and the Rawul had looked like two statesmen in high conclave, so did Manton and the Rawul. The man from Washington walked behind them, and at the gate of the cemetery they waited for him and took him with them in the front car to return to the house. I don't know what this man's name was, but I knew he was there from the State Department on official business, and it was fitting that he should be. People like him used to turn up on official business at Grandfather's embassies, always with the same blandly relaxed conversation and exactly calculated schedule. They were very different from Grandfather's own friends in government—senators, cabinet members, or other ambassadors—who had hours to spare and smoked cigars and quoted Henry Adams. I wished it could have been one of those who had been sent, but I guess they were too old now or sick or gone altogether, and only the others were left. Grandfather didn't even know this present President, who was a very different style of man from those he had been friendly with, and I suppose we should have been grateful that anyone had been sent. The Rawul certainly felt gratified by the presence of this emissary and addressed many of his remarks to him—not really saying anything but volleying courteous conversational shots to him, which the emissary deftly returned.

The house on the Island had porches all around it, with white wicker armchairs and summery green cushions, and

light and sea air and sea breezes flowed through it from end
to end. The only dark room, wedged between the principal
living room and the pantry, was the dining room, where the
shutters were usually kept closed to keep the heat and glare
out. It was here that we gathered after the funeral for what
turned out to be a sort of ritual meal. This was probably due
to the presence of an official emissary, a clergyman, and an
attorney; and to the Rawul, who conducted himself in a solemn, ceremonial way; and to Aunt Harriet, who, in appearance very much like Grandfather, sat statuesque and stony
silent. But it was Manton who put the final, ritual stamp on
the occasion. He waited until we were all seated; then very
slowly, very deliberately, he went to the head of the table and
drew out Grandfather's chair and, for the first time in his
life, he sat there in Grandfather's place. He looked down the
length of the table and at that moment, surveying his family
and guests, he took on Grandfather's authority. Tall, florid,
every inch a Wishwell, he appeared at last to be in his proper
place.

Sonya sat at the other end of the table. I noticed that she
hesitated before sitting down in what had been, after Grandmother's death, her usual chair, and she gave a quick glance
around as if she thought someone else with a better right
was coming to claim it. When no one did, she quickly hunched
herself up in it, a bowed, bundled, humbled little figure very
different from the vivacious Sonya Grandfather had so loved.
It was harder for her to be here than for anyone else—she
only wanted to be lying on her bed, weeping; but of course
everyone belonging to our family was expected to sit upright
when there was a family occasion to be got through. Aunt
Harriet, in the middle of the table between emissary and
attorney, was the touchstone of this tradition. Tall and craggy
like a male Wishwell, she sat poker stiff in the black silk she
wore for summer funerals. For winter ones she wore black
wool, and for the in-between weather there was her black
crepe. She had attended funerals in every season, having
buried her parents, her other brother and two sisters, two
husbands (Uncle Greg and Uncle Rob), and her son, Cousin
Tom, who had overdosed. In all the years I had known her
she had changed very little, just growing more craggy and

gaunt. I don't think she could hear at all anymore, but it
didn't make any difference since she had never listened but
only delivered her opinions. She was doing it now, and the
attorney, Mr. Pritchett, who knew her well, was nodding respectfully, while the emissary, who didn't, felt called upon to
respond without noticing that it was superfluous. Manton, at
the head of the table, continued to fulfill his function ad-
mirably, both taking up threads of conversation and starting
new ones when necessary. The Rawul gave him full support,
as did clergyman, attorney, and emissary. The only ones who
didn't were Sonya, Michael, and me; we didn't want to be
there, but somewhere else and on our own. As for Crishi, he
played his part and contributed to the conversation when
he had to; but at least twice he caught my eye and gave
the smallest shrug, and then he looked up and seemed to be
imploring the ceiling, "Why do we have to be here? How
much longer?" I think he did the same to Michael, who must
have been glad, as I was, that Crishi was there with us and
knew how we felt.

Manton continued relaxed and assured for the rest of the
day. Together with the Rawul, he took the emissary to his
plane, and both of them warmly shook his hand and conveyed
messages of respect and regard to the President who had
sent him. Manton received condolence callers from the Island
and put them at ease. He conducted the conversation at dinner as he had at lunch. He was respectfully considerate of
Aunt Harriet, reverentially so of Sonya. Sonya too was different. Besides being stricken and tearful, she was apologetic
and anxious not to displease. It was the same air and attitude
she had had when Grandmother was alive, as of a poor relation or a domestic, recalling what I had heard about her
earlier life, in Hong Kong or was it Singapore, where she
had made herself indispensable in rich people's houses.

But next day everything changed. In the morning, we—
that is, the family—gathered in Grandfather's study to hear
Mr. Pritchett read the will. Mr. Pritchett was behind the desk
at which Grandfather had worked on his book. Grandfather's
papers and the volumes he consulted were still piled up on
tables next to it. We had our backs to the windows, but whenever Mr. Pritchett looked up he saw the view—that is, the

ocean—Grandfather had seen whenever he looked up from his papers. Feeling closed in, I turned to glance out at the stretch of beach and the unending ocean with flecks of sailboats on it and of gulls above it. What thoughts had passed through Grandfather's mind as he looked over this view with his eyes the same color as the sea, and some would say, as cold? Aunt Harriet, wearing her hearing aid, was listening keenly to Mr. Pritchett's reading, and sometimes she interrupted him with "Could we have that again, Mr. Pritchett?" And he went back and repeated it in the slow, impartial, careful voice this careful will deserved. Grandfather must have drafted it very meticulously, weighing personal as well as larger considerations, making sure that, apart from some small, fair bequests, nothing went out of the family; that Sonya was financially secure for the rest of her life, and in the place where she felt most comfortable—that is, the house in the city, which was to be hers during her lifetime and Michael's and mine afterward. He didn't leave her this place on the Island because he knew that, without him, she would never come here; he left it to Michael and me, along with the rest of his estate. At that time, to save inheritance tax, people did sometimes pass over their children in favor of their grandchildren, but I don't know if that had been Grandfather's intention. He made no mention of Manton at all. I imagined how, as he wrote these words that Mr. Pritchett was reading, Grandfather had filled himself with the sight of the waves—advancing, breaking, and receding in impartial motion—before writing slowly and what he must have considered impartially: "In passing on to my grandchildren, Michael Samuel Manton Wishwell and Harriet Margaret Maria Wishwell, what has been entrusted to me by my forebears and theirs, I repose my confidence in them that they will act with the discretion, duty, and responsibility their family heritage both demands and deserves."

By the time we left the library, Manton's face was more flushed than usual, but he kept up his dignified behavior. Still the courteous host, he saw off Aunt Harriet and Mr. Pritchett to the ferry; and when Aunt Harriet said to him in her brusque way, "Well, Manton, we don't know what was in his mind, but he must have had good reason," Manton did not say anything, simply held her coat for her to get into, advising her that it might be chilly on the ferry. In saying good-bye to me, Aunt Harriet enfolded me in a hard embrace and in her smell of lozenges, cologne, and the earth she was forever digging in her garden. She pressed me more affectionately than she had ever done before, but I was not surprised. I had already learned from the reading of a previous will—Lindsay's father's, where she and Michael and I got everything—that people's attitude changes both toward the inheritors and the disinherited. That evening, when those of us who remained sat down to dinner, Manton again pulled out Grandfather's chair at the table: Then he hesitated and looked toward Michael, who had already sat down next to Crishi. For a moment it seemed that Manton was offering the place at the head of the table to Michael, as to the person who now had the right to it. But of course Michael had no idea what he meant. So then Manton sat down at the head of the table again, but it was for the last time.

Next day Manton's dignity was shattered. He didn't come down for breakfast, and when I went to look for him, I found him with Sonya in her bedroom. She was sitting up in bed, in her little bed jacket and a hairnet, and she was trying to comfort Manton, who was on his knees by the side of her bed, his head on her eiderdown. She clasped his head and murmured to him, and at the same time tears fell from her own eyes as they must have been falling all night, for her face was stained and swollen with them. She looked like an old, old grieving woman, which of course she was. And Manton, sobbing in her arms, was like a grieving son. "Look, here's darling Harriet," Sonya tried to rally him when I came in, but he kept his face buried, while putting out one hand for me to grasp. I did that, and got up on Sonya's bed and she embraced both of us. It was comforting to be there with her, leaning on her soft warm bosom half-naked under her bed jacket. Yesterday she had had that air of being a dependent, but today it was gone as completely as Manton's calm dignity. But in her case I don't think it was due to the reading of the will but to the strength of her feelings—for Grandfather, and for Manton, and me. She was as truly Grandfather's widow as she had been his wife, and no person and no will could alter that.

It wasn't the fact of the will but its spirit that had laid Manton low. "He didn't love me," he said. "He didn't trust me. And he was right. No he was," he insisted, though we hadn't contradicted him. "He was so different from you, darling," Sonya said. "It happens often with father and son, it's a well-known fact in psychology, there is even a name for it—" She broke off: "But he was so wonderful! Such a wonderful man!" "He was! I'm not saying he wasn't!" Manton shouted; and continued in a deflated voice: "It's me who's not wonderful. Not at all wonderful"; and after a gloomy silence, "Look what I'm doing with Mother's money. I'm again overdrawn, I'm ashamed to say, though how or why I couldn't tell you. I thought when I came into Mother's money everything would change, that I'd be able to manage for the first time in my life, but it's even worse. I guess that means I'm worse. Father was right. Absolutely right." Again he buried his face in Sonya's bedcover, again she did what she could to comfort him.

After a while she wiped her eyes but not successfully, for new tears kept coming. "It's wrong," she said. "I should be laughing and singing with happiness and joy—to have known such a man! And that he should have stooped down to someone so small like myself. Darling Manton, dearest child, if you cry anymore I can't bear it."

"It's not the money," Manton wept from her bedcover.

"I know it's not the money! As if you would have one moment's thought about that as long as I'm here and have a crust of bread to eat." Both knew she was speaking very metaphorically: Grandfather had left her more than a crust, and Manton needed more than that. "But you see, children," she said, and she gathered both of us to her little warm bosom, "what he wanted was that we should look after Manton; that we should keep everything in trust for you, darling, so that you wouldn't spend it all at once with your generous nature. Don't you think so, Harriet dearest? Yes I'm sure that's why he did it like that: for us to take care of it all for Manton."

He raised his face from her bed: He looked not unhopeful. But next moment he shook his head—"That's not what Michael and Harriet want."

"Yes we do," I said quickly, though I must admit I hadn't thought of it that way.

"No. You want to give it away. Like Propinquity."

Well, I hadn't thought of that either, but now that he said it, I couldn't contradict him. And even if I did on my own account, I couldn't speak for Michael.

"I'm not blaming you," Manton said when there had been too long a silence. "It's something you believe in and I admire you for it. And good Lord, I can hardly ask you to believe in me, the way I've carried on. And now there's Barbara," he added gloomily.

"Barbara!" Sonya exclaimed. "We love Barbara!"

"You do? Of course, so do I, but she is awfully young and a bit—she hasn't had that much education, and I don't think she could have taken it if she had—I mean, let's face it, she just isn't bright."

Here I began to protest, and as I defended her, saying every nice thing I could about her, Manton cheered up considerably. He said "Hm. Well. Yes. She *is* a good girl. And quite sensible really. You can't say she hasn't got her head screwed on right."

"You certainly can't," I said.

"Or her heart in the right place. Which is more than you can say about some people. Barbara *wanted* to come—she wanted to be here with us at my father's funeral—whereas your mother," he told me, "his own daughter-in-law, couldn't get her ass over here. Sorry, Sonya. Sorry, Baby H. But I do feel strongly about that." He looked self-righteous, the way he always did when he pointed out Lindsay's shortcomings. "I wish Father could have met Barbara. He'd have liked her, don't you think? Perhaps if he had met her he'd have trusted my judgment more. He'd have known I was no longer the jerk who married Lindsay."

He sighed, and so did Sonya. "When we're young, we think we know it all," she said. "And will we listen to anyone older and wiser? No."

"No," Manton agreed.

"If we like something, at once we have to have it: even if it's poison. And it often is poison."

"Absolutely," Manton said.

"It's a dangerous age. Youth is a dangerous age." But in spite of her tear-swollen face—was it my imagination, or was there just the flicker of a smile, a shadow of remembered happiness? And the same with Manton, while trying to look sage as he agreed with her again.

Suddenly Sonya exclaimed: "Thank God this child is so sensible and wise!" Manton echoed: "Thank God!" It took me a moment to realize they meant me. I was surprised, even laughed a bit. Sensible and wise! When I couldn't make up my mind about anything—like whether to go back to school or not; whether to give away the house or not; even how I felt about people, whether I liked them or not. But there was Manton saying "I don't worry about you at all, Baby H.; anyone unsuitable getting hold of you or anything like that." And Sonya said "Oh no no no—when the time comes, she'll choose someone so beautiful and wonderful—and we'll all be so proud of her and we'll make such a wedding, such a wedding: If only he could be here to see," she said and wept and wept and wept again, although it wasn't only the way people cry at funerals but as they do at weddings too.

Manton and Sonya left for the city next day. Michael and I were ready to leave too, but we were made to feel it would be irresponsible just to walk away from the house that was now ours. It was the Rawul who made us feel that way: not by reproaching us but only asking, in a fatherly manner, what we proposed to do about the house; and when we didn't propose anything, making some suggestions of his own. He seemed very taken with the place and kept walking around it with approval. I guess it was the perfect summer house by the sea—which was what it had been for Grandfather, though never for Michael and me. It had several big living rooms downstairs, surrounded by porches, some of them glassed in to form sun parlors. There were large bedrooms with verandas on the second floor, and another floor with a whole warren of small bedrooms, and an attic divided up into even more and even smaller bedrooms. It was comfortably furnished with worn old family pieces, which had been there since the house was built; some of them had in the meantime become valuable, and there were Grandfather's library and a few collectors' items he kept on his desk, such as Talley-

rand's inkstand. It was because of these probably that the
Rawul and Crishi felt we couldn't just leave everything and
walk away, although that was what had always been done,
with a family from the Island, the Macleods, acting as care-
takers. The Rawul, seeing that Michael and I didn't know
what to do, discreetly took charge. He himself had to get
back to Propinquity, but he arranged for Crishi and the followers to stay behind to look after the place for us and make
some necessary repairs. I also heard them discuss some struc-
tural changes, such as fixing up the top floor, uninhabited
since Grandfather's father's time, when a full domestic force
had lived up there. Crishi didn't trouble Michael and me with
these plans but gave his orders to the followers, who took
over in their usual efficient way.

Crishi loved being there; not inside the house but on the
beach and in the ocean. He walked around in his swimming
trunks and fell into the waves whenever he felt like it; and
afterward he lay on the sand, drying off the drops of water
that glistened all over him. It seemed he stayed outside most
of the night too, for I saw him come in at dawn—tousled,
damp, trailing the towel on which he had fallen asleep. He
slept a good part of the day; when I went walking along the
edge of the ocean, I saw him lying on his stomach in the
shadow of a dune, and when I came back, having walked a
mile or so, he was still there in exactly the same position.
Later, when I went out again, he was gone, and I found him
lying on the black rock, which jutted out into the sea. I walked
past him and kept on walking, on and on, away from the
inhabited part of the Island to where it trailed off to a point.
Then there was only water, and the sucking, lapping sound
of it close by and the dull roar of it in the distance.

On my way back I stopped at the Linton house—the last
on that side of the Island, ours being the last but one. Ever
since I could remember, the Linton house had been deserted:
in fact, abandoned, for it had been built too close to the ocean.
For several years nothing much appeared to be happening
to the empty house; it still stood there in its old-fashioned
modern-architecture geometric style, but there was something eerie about it, for everyone knew it was doomed, with
the ocean encroaching on it. One year the top cantilever

collapsed, and after that the entire front of the house, and now all that was left was the rear wing and the garden and swimming pool. The place had not lost its eerie character—as well as the waves eating away at it, there were the rumors I had heard about what had gone on inside.

Walking past it, I came to the black rock again, and Crishi was still sleeping there, face down. I sat near him and leaned against the rock to rest a bit before returning to the house. The sun was setting, and while that part of the ocean into which it was sinking was burning with fire and color, the rest of the water had grown dim and so had the sky and the dunes and everything else around, smoky blue with dusk. A slight chill had replaced the heat of the day; it ruffled my skin but Crishi kept on sleeping as though he were still drenched in sun. I looked at his naked back and the strange scars I had wondered about before, which appeared so incongruous on the satiny texture of his skin. While I was looking at him, he stirred and quite suddenly he turned from his stomach to lie on his back, and from that position he looked at me, entirely awake and alert. It was strange, the way he always gave this impression of alertness, even though his eyes were dreamy and deep. He smiled at me as he lay there, and his smile was also paradoxical, for while his teeth were white and sharp—one might almost say sharpened—his lips parting over them were silky soft. We didn't speak; he didn't even sit up. I don't know how it happened—I think he gestured to me the way I had seen him do to Michael ("come here, I want you")—gestured and smiled to me; I leaned closer over him, which seemed to be what he wanted, and then he put up one arm and drew me down with my breast touching his naked chest and my lips on his. A swooning sensation came over me, dark, vibrant, and pleasurable, an entirely new sensation for me.

I should mention here that up till that time I had not had much sexual history. I never seemed to be interested the way other girls were, and when they started talking about it, I never cared to listen. I guess that is unnatural, and I know most the girls thought so. I did go out with boys, but I didn't care for any of them and it was always because they wanted it and not I. I felt very remote from them, and it irritated me when they tried to get closer and to make scenes, because I preferred to be alone or with Michael. To oblige them, I let them touch me and all that, and a few times I went quite far—very far, all the way—but only to see what it was like and not really feeling anything and surprised that they felt so much. Sometimes there were older men too, and on the whole I preferred them—they didn't seem to be in such a rush and also knew what they were doing better; but even when I liked them, such as Rob Kemp, my history tutor, I didn't let them get in control of me. There was never any question of that; I just didn't care enough, and on the whole didn't care whether we kept on seeing each other or not. When Rob Kemp's wife, Ann, started to fuss, I thought it would be easier to break off and I couldn't understand Rob's reaction—after all, it was he who had a wife and children and should have wanted to go back to them.

After Crishi had kissed me, he seemed not to want anything more but said it was getting chilly and he was going up to the house to put on a shirt. I was surprised but not sad—no, glad to walk with him to the house; he was holding my hand and swinging it to and fro. Our house had been built some way back from the ocean and quite high up, so unlike the Linton house it had not been endangered in any way but stood as solid as the day it was built. Although the Island was quite populated by now, and the other big houses along the coast were hotels with many summer visitors, our house continued to look solitary. The dunes sloped away from it down to the beach and the only view was of sand and waves and the black rock and the wind blowing through the tufts of dry grass.

Next morning I went walking along the beach again. It was quite early, but I saw Crishi was already lying there, apparently asleep. I resisted sitting beside him but walked on even farther than usual, almost into the town, past all the beaches belonging to the hotels, where children ornamented their sand castles with shells; and on to the public beach, where the lifeguard was, and the changing rooms, and the visitors lying on towels with their suntan oil. When at last I turned back, it had become hot, but the edge of the waves washing over my feet was cool and refreshing. I didn't walk fast, I lingered—I wasn't in any hurry; sometimes, to cool off, I went farther into the water. The nearer I got to where I had seen Crishi, the more I delayed—I wanted yet didn't want to sit by him and put off the decision. When at last I approached him, Michael was there with him, and that was a relief and I didn't hesitate to join them. Crishi was still sleeping, and Michael was looking at his back the way I had done the day before. It was very hot sitting there, for the sun had shifted and with it the shade in which Crishi had sheltered himself. Michael and I didn't move or speak but waited for him to wake up.

When he did, it was in the same way as before—suddenly turning around with his eyes wide open and alert as though he hadn't been sleeping at all. He said "Are you crazy, sitting here in the sun," and he got up and ran across the beach till he was in the shade thrown by the black rock. Michael and I followed, bringing the towel on which he had been lying. By the time we caught up with him, he was already in the water and called to us to join him. The tide was coming in and the waves were high and he was letting himself rise and fall with them. Actually, one was not supposed to swim here but within the area where the lifeguard hoisted a white or red flag to say whether it was safe to swim or not. Crishi didn't know that, or care about it, and we felt embarrassed to tell him; he looked so free and easy bobbing there and would surely have laughed at us for thinking of danger. We followed but didn't catch up with him, for whenever we got near enough, he turned and swam out farther. Michael and I were good swimmers but not spectacular like Crishi, and we didn't feel at ease in the ocean the way we did at the waterfall. The farther out I swam in the ocean—and Crishi was making us swim much farther than we wanted to—the more helpless I felt, not so much against the waves as everything beneath them, all the mysterious unknown dark goings-on there like some vast cosmic unconscious threatening to overwhelm the light of day or reason. But for Crishi the ocean seemed to be his favorite element, and he wasn't being overwhelmed by the tide surging up from God knows where but playing along with it, absolutely at his ease as he swam now on his back, now on his stomach, now tossed high up, now out of sight, but always laughing and calling to us. There came a point where Michael and I could no longer follow him but had to give up; unable to surrender ourselves like Crishi, we were struggling and that left us exhausted and a bit afraid. We had to turn back and wait for him on the shore. He stayed in there, went out even farther, evidently enjoying himself. When at last he swam back—not because he was tired but because we were waiting—he didn't mock or reproach us for not following him but affectionately put an arm around each of us and walked back with us to the black rock, where we lay and dried off, with grains of sand sticking to the salt water on our bodies.

Crishi explained to us that the reason he so loved being here was that he spent years living on the beach in Bombay. What years were those? we wondered, but he wasn't very specific. We gathered that it was when he was a boy and there were other boys also living on the beach and it wasn't too hard to survive. There were coconuts people didn't want to finish eating and leftover grain and flour cakes the hawkers had thrown away, though you had to be careful with that—once a whole family of beggers had died from eating spoiled flour cakes; and the monkey keepers could spare some nuts and bananas, and there were tricks to perform if you were a reasonably good acrobat. Most of the year it was warm enough to sleep out at night on the sand, only during the monsoon you had to find somewhere else. Crishi was very good at diving for coins, he said, and he mostly did that when he moved north to Fatehpur Sikri, where tourists threw them into a tank.

Well, all this seemed a far cry from the almost royal Crishi we knew, with his air of being the crown prince in the Rawul's entourage. Yet somehow it fit, as if this free life by the sea were the ideal boyhood for a future prince, and that it was there that his slim brown supple subtle body was formed; only the scars on it remained unexplained. Michael and I were thrilled by what he told us. It was so remote from our own childhood, in Lindsay's house and Grandfather's embassies, with intervals in Manton's hotel suites. And yet, although we had come by such different routes, sitting there by the black rock we felt very close together; at least Michael and I felt very close to him. Michael, who doesn't say much usually, began quite a long speech about how he felt alienated by an environment of sea and sand, that this was too volatile for him and bright, and what he really liked was a rocky mountain landscape with practically no vegetation but only snow, ice, and caves inside the rock. Crishi laughed at that, and turned to me and asked me what I liked. I had never thought it out but I tried to; and what I came up with was that I liked sitting under a tree after it had been raining, and even with the sun shining, there was a breeze sweeping over the lake with the smells of wet growing things, and when it grew a bit stronger, some remaining drops fell down on me from the leaves of the tree; I said I would be looking at water—not restless water like the sea but a still, sweet body of it like the lake at Propinquity. I guess I talked a lot of nonsense. Anyhow, Crishi didn't hear most of it—he was asleep before long, lying on the sand in the shadow of the black rock with Michael and me looking at each other across him, smiling at each other and feeling happy.

Feeling happy: That was how it was with us during those days on the Island after Grandfather's funeral. It might seem strange that we should be that way when Grandfather had just died, but to us it was perfectly natural—that he was buried here where he so loved to be and at the same time plans were being made for the house he had cherished. We felt vaguely that we were acquitting ourselves well as Grandfather's heirs. Not that we gave much thought to our heritage—for one thing, because at that time we were not concerned with heritage, either as a concept or as property, and also because we were so entirely taken up with Crishi. We spent every minute we could with him—all day, that is —and he was very nice to both of us. I knew he could be impatient and imperious, but he never was at that time; probably because he was so relaxed, sleeping on the sand and swimming in the sea. We stayed outside till it got dark, going in only for the meals the followers prepared for us, and by night time we were so drugged with sun and sea air and, as I said, happiness, that we fell asleep immediately.

One night—a week after Sonya and Manton's departure —I woke up suddenly, as if someone had called me. As a

matter of fact, someone had: Crishi had come into the room
and stood by my bed. I thought oh my God, what shall I do;
my heart beat very fast—I didn't want to sleep with him, not
now, not yet. Also I think I had just been dreaming of him;
anyhow, he had been somewhere in my dream and I felt it
difficult to reconcile that dream figure, which had risen from
inside myself, with the real Crishi. But it seemed all he wanted
was for me to come out on the beach with him. I was relieved
and got up very quickly and slipped on a robe, for I was
naked, which was the way I always slept. We went through
the sleeping house, past Michael's room. I had expected that
we were going to wake up Michael too, but this was not
Crishi's intention. When we got on the beach, he said "Why
don't you take that thing off," meaning my robe. It seemed
a good idea, and I did so and left it lying there. It was very
pleasant to walk that way on the empty beach, where everything shimmered with a pale hidden light from the moonless
sky, or was it from the ocean? In this ghostly seascape we too
were like ghosts—I was white and naked, and Crishi wore
only a pair of pajama trousers, the Indian kind, wide and
white, billowing out from the waist. I might have had difficulty knowing what to talk to him about, but he was fluently
making the sort of conversation a boy is supposed to make
with a girl he is walking out with. In fact, he was quite banal,
telling me what sort of cars he liked to drive.

We walked toward the end of the Island, in the direction
of the Linton house, and when we drew level with it, Crishi
said "Let's go in." I didn't want to, I liked it out here on the
beach, but he said "I've never been in," so we went. It was
eerie—as I said, the front of the house was gone, and you.
couldn't forget that sooner or later the rest would go too, for
there was the pounding sound of the sea that was coming to
get it. We looked in at the window of the long room at the
back, which was still intact. It had been a ballroom, where
they had given parties and dances; though the furniture had
long been removed, some textured panels remained on the
walls, and the ceiling was painted with ogres, angels, and
unicorns. The Lintons had been a young couple about the
same time as Manton and Lindsay, and while at the beginning
their marriage had been happy or, anyway, high-spirited,

later it turned terrible and the Island rang with wild rumors
about them. Finally, Mrs. Linton was found dead in the empty
swimming pool, and Mr. Linton was charged with murdering
her, and though acquitted, he killed himself within a year. I
told Crishi some of this; I didn't know too much. Grandfather
never talked about it, and while the local people and Sonya
did, I wasn't that interested in listening.

There was a terrace outside the ballroom and some steps
leading down to a sort of bower, which enclosed the swimming pool. The high bushes around it were straggly and
overgrown, making the space inside appear like a forest clearing. The empty pool had a cracked mosaic of mermaids, and
the same motif was repeated in a mural behind the bar built
within a niche of the changing rooms, and also on the little
circular dance floor facing it; a rusted music stand still remained, as did some bar stools to perch on. Crishi got up on
one of them and called for a Manhattan with a cherry and
laughed at his own joke. He seemed to like being here—he
said he thought they must have had a pretty good time before
everything went rotten. I wanted to leave, to get back on the
beach, maybe even go home and go to sleep or wake up
Michael.

"What are you scared of?" he asked me, and then "Who
are you scared of?" and then "Is it someone dead or someone
living? Give us a clue," and again laughed as at a good joke
he had made. I shook my head—no, I wasn't scared, I only
wanted not to be in this place. He began to be very nice to
me. We had been sitting side by side without touching—he
didn't even hold my hand as he sometimes did. But now he
let his cool brown fingers rest first on my shoulder and then
slid them down my arm and toward my breast, where he
paused, hesitated, smiled. "Let's have a look at you," he said
and held me at arm's length and commented on my figure
in such a natural way that I couldn't help smiling with him.
He said he guessed it could be called a good figure, if you
liked this particular type, more boy than girl. "Look," he said,
inviting me to study him as he had studied me, "not all that
different, is it." He undid the cord at his waist and let his
pajamas fall, so that I could study his narrow hips and long
thighs. Well, it was true, we were built along the same lines

—the same as Michael too, except that Crishi's penis was very different from Michael's or any others I had seen. It was much longer and also darker, the darkest part of him; though slender, it looked very powerful, like a potent weapon; he had very little pubic hair and was uncircumcised. As my gaze so irresistibly lingered, he put both his hands over it and said I was making him shy; but next moment, not a bit shy, he touched my genitals, quite delicately and inquiringly. We moved together and we kissed, and this too was delicate, though no longer inquiring but affirmative, as it had every right to be, for by this time each tiny nerve in my body was quivering for him. It was long, long, long ago—in another life—but is very easy for me to remember.

He took my hand and led me down the steps of the empty swimming pool. Although the rest of the bower was dark and overgrown, the pool itself was open to the moonless sky, which gazed down into it like another pool—not an empty one but filled with dim shifting clouds. We lay down on the mermaids, and I had hardly time to think "Not here," when he was on top of me, very quick and ruthless. That potent weapon of his lived up to its appearance, and I cried out several times, as I had never done before; and he came much too quick for me, leaving me in tears of disappointment. He was amused and said "Better luck next time"; and to make up for it, he kissed me tenderly all the way down from my neck to my thighs.

When we came out of that bower, I had lost the distaste for the place I had had when we entered. I thought that whatever bad thing had once happened there had been exorcised. We went back to the beach, walking as before by the edge of the water; we were holding hands, and he was swinging mine in his. When we got to the changing rooms and pavilion, Crishi stopped and lay down on the platform there and asked me to lie down too. His body was very warm; we lay side by side, one of his hands was laid on mine, the other toyed with his penis; we both watched him doing this and how it grew bigger, and when it was very big, he took my hand to hold it. It was *hot*. "Like it?" he asked and didn't wait for an answer. He entered me again and was as before, very swift and strong, but this time I came with him and it was the most filling, fulfilling sensation I had ever had. Afterward I was so tired and spent and blissful, I wanted to stay lying there forever, but Crishi remembered he had left his pajamas by the Lintons' swimming pool and asked me to get them. "Not now," I said, unable even to open my eyes, and when he insisted, I said "You go." "Please," he begged in a little-boy voice, "Crishi's so sleepy." He brought his face as close to mine as possible and kissed my nose and eyelids with pursed lips; and "Please," he cajoled in the sweetest way possible, and who could resist him? I got up and ran as fast as I could back to the Linton house and to the deserted swimming pool. There was a rustling or was it a soughing sound in the over-grown foliage—I didn't even wonder what it was but snatched up his pajamas, and clutching them against my chest, I ran back with them. Naked, swift, and unimpeded, I felt exultant and like a woman savage running to her mate. Only when I reached him, he was no longer alone but Michael was with him. I stopped being a woman savage and became Harriet, naked and embarrassed before Michael. He had found my robe where I had dropped it on the beach, and he handed it to me and I was glad to wear it. Michael and I didn't know what to say nor did I know what he felt or thought, which was the first time that had happened between us. Only Crishi was unembarrassed—he got up from the platform, he yawned, he said "Don't you two ever get tired?" He led the way back to the house and Michael went with him, and I walked behind both of them, trailing Crishi's pajamas, which he hadn't re-claimed from me. Some of that night's happiness was abating, but by no means all of it.

I had expected that next day Michael and I would talk about what happened, but the unusual silence continued be-tween us. It wasn't that we were distant with each other but only that we didn't talk about—well, about Crishi. Crishi himself continued to be absolutely natural with both of us, as if nothing at all had occurred. But for me it *had* occurred, and it was like a revolution inside me—a physical one almost, with my heart, my womb, or whatever was the deepest part of me, overturned and in turmoil. I was in a state of the highest excitement, both pleasurable and painful. I looked back on the previous night—carried it inside me—but did not think I could bear another one like it: I mean, I wanted it yet dreaded it. But there was no repetition, for Crishi decided that everything was in order with the house and we could leave. The followers stayed behind to supervise the work being done on the house.

Michael and I spent most of the next week in New York, seeing Mr. Pritchett and Grandfather's accountants and signing all sorts of papers to effect the settlement of the estate. We had been through it all before, after Lindsay's father's death, so we were familiar with the procedure as well as the shift of attitude toward us. I guess Michael and I were very rich now, and what we felt more than anything was the responsibility of our position. We wanted to do everything right and to behave right. Michael was even paler than usual, and he often frowned trying to understand something the accountant told us; and when he had understood it, he made sure that I did too. As always, we were and acted like one person, even though we had not yet spoken of the night on the beach. Manton had gone back to Spain with Barbara, and we stayed in Sonya's house. It had become a very busy household—when Grandfather was there, he always needed a lot of quiet for his work but now all Sonya's friends were coming to call and comfort her. They wept together and stayed for hours and others joined them, and it was rather like a party going on all day, with constant meals being prepared in the kitchen. Sometimes Sonya herself went down there, to make something very special for Michael and me, like her own little Russian tea cakes that she knew we loved.

Crishi called us every evening at the same time, and we both waited for the phone to ring at that time. I restrained myself from running to answer it because I knew how much Michael wanted to; but he always called to me quite soon to pick up the phone in my room, and Crishi talked to both of us. He talked about what the weather was like up there, and what Else Schwamm had been cooking for dinner, and whatever news there was—nothing that he couldn't have said to anyone, except that his voice held something very intimate for us alone, spoken to each of us alone, so that the most banal words were like a secret or a promise; but whether it was the same one for both of us I don't know. He didn't ever say "When are you coming back?" or "I miss you," and at first I assumed that was what he meant, that it was what lay behind his intimate tone. But when he didn't come out with it, I became impatient: I wanted to hear those words, and more than that, I wanted to act on them—that is, go back to Propinquity. Because I missed him terribly, though I was with the people I loved most, with Michael and Sonya and in her house. Perhaps it would be more accurate or more honest to say that it was not so much Crishi I missed as the sensation he had made me undergo that night, first the intense longing in the empty swimming pool, then the pain and bliss on the beach. I tried not to think of it—not to give way to my desire—but by the third night away from him, it was overwhelming. I had to bury my head in my pillow, seeking relief by drowning myself in darkness, while my whole body shuddered in an attempt to reach out toward an unattainable satisfaction. I felt ashamed to be overcome that way but couldn't help myself.

At last our work in the city was done—at least, Michael said it was, or it may have been that he too was very anxious to get back. We left as soon as our last meeting with yet another trust officer was over; Sonya begged us to stay at least till next morning, and while we wanted to be with her, we couldn't. The drive to Propinquity was a familiar one, over the parkway, winding past meadows and hills and new young woods with spindly trees. Everything was green for summer, with sudden flashes of water—estuaries of the river, lakes and reservoirs, or just a little silver pool of rainwater sunk in grass. And the sweet homely names of the places along the way: Cow Pond Lane, Butterfield Farm Road, Pudding Hill—after each one, I thought, We'll talk about it now, meaning the night on the beach, but each time I decided, No, later, and Michael probably decided the same; so we never did get around to it—in fact, we hardly spoke, neither of us wanting to spoil the beautiful drive or the anticipation of our arrival.

It was late when we got there, but Crishi was waiting for us to go swimming by the waterfall. We went straightaway, not bothering to take our things out of the car. We descended the rocky path—we were so used to it, we never had to look where to put our feet though it was dark and very slippery; I kept thinking of the phrase "skipping like lambs," and it

applied both to our bodies and our hearts. That was a wonderful swim we had, the three of us flitting around naked in
the water, Michael and I like two white fish and Crishi slightly
darker. The water gushed down from the rock and drowned
out the noise we were making—a lot that night, for we had
much to talk and to laugh about, as we dived and swam and
circled around one another. When we finished, we didn't
linger as usual in the high meadow but were in a hurry to
get to the house and our rooms. I lay on my bed, damp and
happy and tired from our swim. I felt so confident he would
come that I even fell asleep for a bit; but when I woke up,
it was by myself, for he hadn't come. The strong and shameful
sensation swept over me again, as it had in Sonya's house,
and I thought I couldn't bear it, having to wait anymore; but
I did bear it, and also the thought that the reason he didn't
come was that he was with Michael—I endured that too and
accepted it for the sake of both of them.

Next day I thought that now surely Michael and I would
talk—about the night on the beach as well as about last night
and whether Crishi had gone to Michael. But again we said
nothing, and neither did Crishi—at least not on those two
subjects, though on plenty of others; he had a lot to say that
day and was in a terrific good mood. At night we went to the
waterfall again, and made the same amount of noise, but it
was not so good this time because I felt tense and anxious,
wondering what would happen later. What happened was
that Crishi did come to me—very late, in fact it was the early
hours of the morning, and by that time I thought if he doesn't
come I'll go mad—but no, he came and lay on my bed with
me, and it was a combination of swimming pool and beach:
that is, the first time disappointment, the second time fulfillment. There was a third time too—he was very strong that
night, which made him cruel, but that was part of it, I found.
Next day again no one said anything, and there began a
pattern: After swimming by the waterfall, one night he was
with me and the following night not, and while each time I
expected to ask Michael next day whether he had been with
him, I never did, so I was never sure.

Meanwhile the work of the movement continued in the
house, and everyone except me was very busy. Myself and

Jean—she appeared to be the only other person who was not working for the Rawul. She had even lost her occupation, for the gardening she used to do had been taken over by the followers and on a much larger and more efficient scale. Everything in the house was on such a scale—for instance, Else Schwamm's kitchen: She was still ostensibly in charge, but she had a rostrum of followers to help her prepare an unending succession of meals and snacks. It had become almost a hotel kitchen, for besides the many people living in the house, a whole lot of visitors came for the Rawul. There were leaders of newly formed political or religious groups, ecologists, social activists, free-lance writers and journalists, parapsychologists, spiritualists, scientists and economists with revolutionary theories—every kind of person who felt called upon to change the world and men's minds; and if individually they gave the impression of being lonely cranks, together they made quite an impressive front of alternative opinion. And however poor, solitary, far-out, or even crazy they appeared, the Rawul received them ceremoniously in the front drawing room for a high-level discussion or exchange of fruitful ideas; and as they arrived one by one and were received, orders went down to the kitchen for refreshments to be sent up. And it would have been beneath both the Rawul's dignity and Else Schwamm's if these had not been elaborate and elegantly served. The visitors had good appetites, and some of them seemed not to have eaten well for a long time. All went away satisfied with the refreshments, and with the Rawul himself—his seriousness combined with his courtly manner; and Propinquity, now restored, thanks to the followers, to former grandeur; the order and discipline of the entire household, apparent from the first contact with the gatekeeper and his walkie-talkie and reinforced by the silent obedient figures of the followers in their semiuniforms; and the way everything went with military precision or, as Else Schwamm said with approval, left-right, left-right, one-two, one-two.

The Rawul called Michael and me into the drawing room for what he said was a talk but appeared to be in the nature of an audience. Everything around the Rawul was taking on more formality; I guess it had to be so, to impress the people who came to see him. One follower was stationed outside the drawing room to announce the visitor and another to usher him inside. This procedure was followed even for Michael and me, who lived in the house (and, for that matter, whose house it was). We hadn't been in the drawing room for some time—there was usually some high-level meeting going on in there—and we were surprised by its transformation. In Lindsay's parents' time, the furniture had become shabby, giving the room a comfortable, lived-in feel. Now everything had been refurbished with brocade upholstery, the mahogany and brass had been polished, as had the floor, and my grandparents' ordinary carpet had been changed for an ostentatious Oriental one. The portrait of our great-great-grandfather—a kindly, shrewd trader in a high stock and collar (very different from Lindsay's grandfather, featured as a Renaissance prince over the dining-room sideboard)—had been replaced by one of the Rawul, looking as Orientally colorful as the new carpet.

But the Rawul himself, an impressive, portly figure standing underneath himself in oil, received us more like a father than a political leader or king. And it was with a father's concern that he spoke to us of the future—that is, of his future plans, which he took for granted were ours too. These were long-term and involved a good deal of traveling. He said that with a worldwide movement such as his, it was necessary to plan not months but years ahead. The problem was one of organization, he said: Arrangements had to be made for travel and accommodation, participants notified—no, he didn't want to burden us with too much detail, but if we would care to glance over the schedule compiled for the next three years? Michael said he had seen it—had in fact helped to photocopy it—so it was handed to me, and I saw that the program involved a general meeting followed by a training course in England, the next year a refresher course in India, after that a summer camp at the house on the Island, and in the succeeding fall a series of lectures at Propinquity. Well, said the Rawul, taking the program from me before I had quite finished reading it, there was no need for us to break our young heads over these organizational problems, but he did want to mention that he was thinking along lines of a general transfer to the movement of both Propinquity and the house on the Island, along with some other assets to keep up these properties. Again he apologized—he said we must be sick and tired of lawyers, but it would perhaps be advisable for all concerned to have some sort of signed legalized document before the scheduled meetings on the Island and at Propinquity: It would also, he said, be helpful in solving visa problems for himself and other foreign participants if the association could show financial assets in the U.S. Michael nodded—he seemed fully aware of the problem; but the Rawul wasn't asking for our consent—what he wanted, he said, was to do everything he possibly could for us at this difficult stage of our lives, with Grandfather gone and all our new responsibilities to carry. He wanted us to feel that he was there for us at any time and for any problem, if there was anything whatsoever he could do—"Michael?" he said. "Harriet?" He looked at us both, beamed on us, and then he did something very warm and caring—he put his arms around both our necks to draw us to him and laid our heads against his chest. Even Michael, who so hated being touched, accepted this gesture and let his head rest for a moment on the Rawul's silk coat. He made us feel like orphans who had found a father—not strictly correct, since Manton was still there and so was Lindsay, though perhaps in a parental role the Rawul was right to discount them.

That same day I was surprised to be summoned by the Rani as well. She received me—that is the word, received—in the small and very sunny little room that had been done up as her sitting room. It was as much a sun parlor as anything, and had new wicker furniture and apricot cushions with huge flowers on them, amid which the Rani bloomed as the most opulent flower of all. She patted a footstool close to her chair and said that we had to have a chat. Like the Rawul, she beamed on me, and I expected her to make the same offer of parental protection. But what she said was something quite different. It stunned me, and when I stared at her, she repeated it and smiled and emphasized: "He really wants to, you know." What she had said was that Crishi wanted to marry me.

"He came to my bedroom in the middle of the night," she

reminisced, still smiling. "He woke me up—I said 'Crishi, is this the time to talk, darling,' and he said 'Rani, I *have* to.' So I knew it was serious."

I said "But he could have told me himself."

She laughed outright: "He said he was too shy." She laughed louder, at the absurdity of it. It was absurd—Crishi shy! And on such a topic: and when he had just been with me himself—he must have gone straight from my bedroom to hers. I couldn't help laughing too, so we both did together for a while.

She said "Poor boy, we shouldn't laugh. Because he's really very serious about you, Harriet darling. He says he feels about you as he has never before felt for anyone, dear." She put her finger under my chin to tilt up my face, studying it to see if I was worth so much consideration. She seemed to decide that on the whole yes, while with her other hand she lifted up my hair and rearranged it a little, trying out whether it wouldn't suit me better that way.

"He's a funny boy," she went on, smiling again at the thought of him. "You'd think he is a very bold and dashing type— and he is—if I were to tell you the things he has done—"

"Yes, tell me," I said.

"I will, one day. But today I want to tell you about the other Crishi. The little boy Crishi. The shy little Crishi who came to me last night and said 'Rani, help me.' He can be so sweet, Harriet, I can't tell you. Just irresistible."

She was still playing around with my hair, but I put my hand up and disengaged myself from her.

"He's like my own son to me," she said. "Sometimes I think that's why he's there—why he was sent—to take the place of my own little boy who was taken from me. No I don't want to talk about that now, Harriet," she said, deeply sad. "But I will one day."

When she started playing with my hair again, I let her. At the same time I surreptitiously studied her: Was she really old enough to be Crishi's mother? I was sitting very close to her, beneath her peacock chair. Her skin was absolutely smooth and glowing, peach-colored; her eyes and deep-auburn hair sparkled with health; and the only indication that she was not quite young anymore was a certain fullness of her chin and jawline, hardly yet the beginning of a future double chin.

"One day I'll tell you about him and me and all of us, Harriet. How we found each other. What we are to each other."

"Hadn't you better tell me now?"

She stroked my cheek and smiled at me—on me—very lovingly. "That's not what he asked me to talk to you about. Not at all. Not about him and me but about him and you. A very different story altogether, Harriet dear."

I was beginning to feel smothered. She was too close to me, too large and smooth, too creamy and perfumed: a fleshy flower of too strong a scent. Or was it that my mind was in such turmoil with what she had told me, and hadn't told me, that I had to put some distance between us to allow me to think. I got up abruptly, and the stool she had pulled up for me fell over. I exclaimed "I don't understand this!" and began to pace around the room, which was too small for much pacing and full of little wicker stools and tables to stumble over.

"Oh dear," said the Rani, "I've made a mess of it." Although she was blaming herself, she remained calm and self-possessed: "I put it wrong. It's my fault entirely, Harriet; absolutely." She went on, still relaxed and in command, "I did my best, but you have to admit that it's something very, very difficult to do for another person. It's impossible. He's just put me in an impossible situation, that's all. He should never have asked me."

"But why did he! Why did he ask you!"

"I wish you'd come and sit down."

There was a hint of sharpness in her voice. I hesitated for a moment—why should I obey her? Nevertheless, I did. After all, I did want to go on talking because what she was saying was of such overwhelming interest to me: more interesting than anything that had ever been said to me in all my life.

"That's better," she said, when I picked up the stool and seated myself at her feet again. "You can't shout this sort of thing across a room. It's difficult enough as it is." She fondled me again—my hair, my cheek, my neck; and as the Rawul had been tender as a father, she was so as a mother. And physically, in spite of her youthfulness and beauty, there was something maternal about her; probably it was her abundant bosom, so different from Lindsay's tight little breasts, which

I had inherited. I felt tempted to lay my head on that bosom—perhaps she wanted to tempt me that way, knowing in what great need I was at that point of love and support.

"Do you like him very much?" she suddenly whispered to me. "Very very very much?" And then she did what the Rawul had done earlier—she drew me down to rest against her. It was as if that fleshy flower was enfolding me completely, so that I wanted to fly off like an insect from a trap; but also I wanted to stay and sink down there in all her warmth and softness; and when she whispered again, "Do you? Very much? Tell me how much," I shut my eyes and did sink—or would have if she hadn't pushed me away, smiling a little bit. "Of course you do," she said. "How can you help it?" and gave my cheek a dismissive little slap.

Normally I would have gone straight to Michael and told him about this extraordinary conversation. But the way things were, I didn't. That evening we went swimming by the waterfall—if I had expected Crishi to give me soulful, searching glances, and perhaps part of me did, it didn't happen. Everything was as usual—that is, cheerful and nice. He didn't come that night, perhaps to let me think his—or the Rani's —proposition over. She didn't mention it again, and I hovered around her, hoping she would. I so longed to talk about it, but the way she and Crishi carried on was as though she and I had never spoken. The routine of the house continued in its orderly, disciplined way, with a part to play for everyone—from the Rawul in the drawing room to the watchmen by the gate and Else Schwamm with her helpers in the kitchen. And underneath everything there was the groundswell of emotional tension I had already noticed among the followers—but drowned out for me by our own disturbances: Michael's and mine, Lindsay's and Jean's, the original inhabitants of the house whose lives had been so plowed up and changed by the Rawul and his party.

One could say that the change was good—anyhow, exciting—for everyone except Jean. We might have gained, but she had lost—her position in the house, her life with Lindsay, her contentment, everything. If I had been less absorbed maybe I would have had more sympathy instead of being as irritated with her as everyone else. She struck such a discordant note with her tear-stained face, swollen and middle-aged, and the way she dragged around without occupation; and her constant bickering with Lindsay, or outright fights, so that they lived in a state of exasperation with each other, which made Lindsay hide from her whenever possible. Jean could be seen wandering around the house and grounds searching for her and probably unaware herself that tears were running down her face. It was awful, but as I said, none of us had the time to spare any thought for her.

All my thoughts were concentrated on waiting for Crishi to follow up the Rani's proposal. When he didn't, I began to wonder if he was waiting for me to make the next move: to give him my answer, as it used to be called. I didn't think much about what that answer would be, but only how and when I would be called upon to make it. When I wasn't, I became frantic. He didn't even say anything when he came to my bedroom again—at last—the second night after my talk with the Rani. He carried on as usual, and I have to admit that I was so anxious for this to proceed, that I carried on with him; and it was only afterward, when he was very sleepy—he had rolled away from me and was curled up in a sleeping position—that I asked him: "What's all this the Rani was talking about? Or don't you know?"

"Of course I know," he said, without turning around. I poked my finger in his back; it was firm and smooth and I liked the sensation and did it again. "Ouch," he said. "Don't."

"But you have to say *some*thing."

"What?" he said. "What do you want me to say?" But now he did turn toward me. "Anyway, I thought she'd said it all for me."

"That's another thing: How could you let her? How could you ask her to?"

"Oh but didn't she tell you?" He was lying on his back looking up at me where I sat over him, scanning his face. "Didn't she tell you I was too shy?"

I continued to scan his face—which he kept very serious for as long as possible. When I saw his lips twitching, I said "Oh God, Crishi," and collapsed on top of him. We both laughed and kissed and rolled around together, so I guess that was his way of confirming the Rani's proposal.

Anyhow, I assumed that it *was* confirmed and wondered what the next step would be. Nobody made one; it seemed left to me. I decided that I had to tell Michael and thought this would be very hard, but it turned out not to be so. Michael didn't pretend that he had known all along, but he certainly showed no surprise. He seemed pleased rather than anything else; he said it was a good idea.

"A good idea!" I exclaimed. Since I had never thought of getting married, I had never thought how Michael might react: but certainly not like this.

Unaware that he was disappointing me, he went on calmly: "You don't have to be so torn now, about giving the houses and joining the movement and all of that."

"Joining the movement," I repeated, feeling sad.

"Yes, you'll just be part of it. It'll make it much easier for Crishi."

"Oh is that what you think? That he wants to marry me so he can get hold of everything? . . . What are you saying, Michael?" I knew that consideration was there and might even be uppermost in a lot of people's minds; but I hadn't expected it to be in Michael's.

And of course it wasn't; not in such a crude way. "Be reasonable," he said. "Think for a moment. Stop walking up and down. Come on." When I was calm enough and sitting close by him, he said "Don't you think it's better to marry more than just a person—to marry *for* something, beyond that person?"

"No," I said. "No. No. I don't think so. I'm marrying just a person. Just Crishi."

Michael looked pale and stubborn. There was something he was hiding, didn't want to say. Not that he didn't believe what he said—about marrying beyond a person, for something better and higher, some ideal held in common: Michael did live and think on that level. But not entirely. He wasn't as cold as people thought he was—didn't I know that better than anyone from the feelings he had for me?

I said "If you don't want it, I won't do it. It won't happen." I hadn't expected myself to say that, but I meant it and was going to stick by it. Let Michael decide. It was a relief. But it made him furious: "What do you mean? What do I know about such things or care about them? You know very well

I'll never marry anyone, thank God," he said, gritting his teeth. "So don't involve me."

"Did you think I'd never marry anyone too?"

But it was what both of us had thought. When we were small, I used to say so all the time—how when I grew up, I was going to live with Michael. Later, I no longer said it but still meant it, and I was sure he did too. It was like a promise to each other we had been born with.

Now that was changing, and it was I who was changing it. But I couldn't do so without his consent, and again I asked him for it: "If you don't want it, it won't happen."

He became more exasperated: "But I've said, haven't I, it's a good idea. I want it. I like it!" he shouted.

"Because I'm marrying a movement?"

He gritted his teeth again and came out with "And Crishi."

"You're glad because it's Crishi?" I had never been like that with him—pushing him, making him say things that he didn't want to say but I wanted to hear.

And there was something else I wanted to hear but didn't ask: that question between us—did Crishi go to him on the nights he didn't come to me—remained unspoken. But supposing it was true? Supposing we did share him? It seemed ideal that, if I had to marry, it should be someone we both loved—and in such an intense physical way, which was the one way that had been left out of our love, Michael's and mine.

Perhaps he was thinking along the same lines, because he relaxed suddenly and said "It's okay. It really is."

"What's okay? Joining the movement?"

"Yes that."

"Giving the house?"

"Yes that."

"Crishi?"

"Yes that. There—that's three times yes and no sage ever gives more. Which they call *tyad*," he quoted from one of those old texts he was forever into. He grinned, and I guess if we had been the hugging sort we would have done it. He looked so sweet, with his slightly crooked grin, his seafarer's eyes in his very white face, and his freckled nose: dearer to me than anyone, still, even now.

THE interest that my intended marriage to Crishi might have generated at this time was usurped by a publicity event. The Rawul was very keen on publicity, for he considered it the best way to penetrate into—this is how he put it—the minds of men, the hearts of nations, and the core of the world. Up till now his access to it had been limited to our local paper, some call-in radio programs, and the pamphlets and bulletins that were compiled at Propinquity and sent out around the country. As a result there had been some stir of interest, if not quite on a national level, at least from peripheral publications and from groups and individuals of similar belief in global reform. Each of these stirrings was greeted by the Rawul as a straw in the wind, and as we kept on generating our wind of pamphlets, more and more straws came flying in our direction, so I guess the whole thing was really building up. The Rawul was particularly pleased and satisfied—he had a way of gleefully rubbing his hands when he felt like that—because a free-lance writer and journalist was coming to do an in-depth study of our movement. She was called Anna Sultan, and the Rawul seemed to think she was very famous; none of us had ever heard of her. Her visit was being prepared for as an important event, and one that put my own marriage plans entirely in the shade.

As it turned out, it was lucky that so much trouble had been taken: Anna Sultan was extremely nervous and fussy

—she had to be, because to enable her to function at her best, the greatest possible care had to be taken of her health and general comfort. She was received as only the most important visitors were; and there was no one like the Rawul to make a welcome royal. Unfortunately she was too tired that evening to go through anything social, or to eat the elaborate dinner Mrs. Schwamm had prepared. She had to be immediately shown to her room—the Rani herself did that—and a tray sent in with clear soup, scrambled egg, and a salad without dressing. Lindsay was delegated to carry in the tray, and she did so with the air of proud responsibility that we all brought to our allotted tasks. When she came out, she looked pleased, as one who had acquitted herself honorably; but she was waylaid by Jean, who attacked her furiously: "What are you—their *maid* or something!" Everyone heard her, and some of us came running to see what the matter was.

I was shocked by Jean's appearance. It struck me that it had been several days since anyone had seen her. She must have holed up in her room without bathing or eating; and there was something about her of a wounded animal that had dragged itself out of its lair for a desperate confrontation.

Lindsay, cool and crisp in pale-green linen, and with her good-girl expression, was so shocked by this sudden attack that she was speechless. We all were, and the Rani actually said "I'm speechless." She said this in general, to air her indignation in a dignified way, before addressing Jean in particular: "Don't you think it's rather inconsiderate to make a scene when we have a guest in the house?"

"A guest in the house! More like five hundred guests in the house, and my Lord they've begun to stink like the Chinese fish!" When no one said anything, she yelled "To stink and stink!"

"I'm afraid she's hysterical," the Rani addressed Lindsay. It seemed like a command, and Lindsay obeyed it by stepping up to Jean and slapping her face. The sound of this reverberated and made everyone fall very silent.

"Why did you do that to me?" Jean said in a quiet bewildered voice, as intimate as if the two of them had been alone together.

"You made me," Lindsay said, but a bit desperate.

"And in front of everyone. All these people."

Lindsay began to look around at everyone—maybe for support, or maybe not to have to look at Jean. No one wanted to look at Jean with a red mark on one cheek.

Only the Rani was brisk and commonsensical; she had taken on her aspect of English games mistress: "Well I for one am not going to stand here and watch this kind of bad behavior." She turned and marched off with a determination that made everyone else turn and march with her. They went down the stairs, and only I stayed with Jean on the second-floor landing where this scene had taken place.

I've never been any good at comforting people—it doesn't come natural to me—but I couldn't leave her standing there by herself, disgraced and hurt. As I wondered what I could do to make her feel better, she turned on me: "How could you, Harriet! How could you allow these people—these strangers—to take over your house? Our house? It's like a nightmare," she said, covering her face and shuddering as if she were really seeing one.

And at that moment, for just a moment, I saw it too—could it be, and how had it happened? I stared at the staircase, empty now, down which the Rani had marched with all of them meekly following her. And the Rawul holding court in our drawing room. And the guards at the gate, screening visitors, all of whom were for the Rawul. And the computer, the Xerox machine, and teleprinter in what had been the library. And the helpers in the kitchen endlessly cutting, grinding, and stirring under the direction of Else Schwamm. How had it happened to us, to our scrappy amorphous household, that we had been turned into someone else's organization?

Lindsay came hurrying back up the stairs, glancing over her shoulder as if afraid of being followed. When she reached us on the landing, Jean burst out again: "How could you!" at Lindsay this time.

Lindsay thought she meant the incident of a moment before and began to justify herself for that: "You know perfectly well you deserved it for being horrid"—but she stroked Jean's cheek where she had slapped it and made a sweet kissing

sound at her. "It didn't happen; it never happened," she
assured her, rotating her hand on Jean's cheek.

"I didn't mean that. As if I'd care about that: as if you
couldn't do anything you wanted with me. But the rest of it!
The nightmare of it!" Again she covered her face and shuddered, clinging to Lindsay.

"Sh-sh-sh," Lindsay said, looking around nervously. So did
I. The three of us standing on the second-floor landing were
very exposed—at any moment someone might come and
order us to go away, or send us on some errand. We went
quietly, almost on tiptoe, to the end of the landing, where
Jean's room was, next to Lindsay's, and once inside we locked
the door and felt safer.

Being in Jean's room was like a homecoming—I think
Lindsay felt the same, even though neither of us had been
aware of missing any sense of home. But here we were in
Jean's room with her clunky, homey objects, like the American history dolls—Betsy Ross and Sitting Bull—her aunt had
been famous for carving out of apples, and the photograph
of her grandparents and parents on the porch of their yellow
Victorian house in Dubuque. It was here in Jean's room that
all our birthday presents were opened—Jean had this tradition of hiding them so you had to go seek while she yelled
"Warm!" or "Cold!" or "Brrr—Iceland!" Usually the room
was meticulously tidy, with the green-and-red embroidered
quilt smooth over the bed and handmade doilies under the
vases of the wild flowers she loved to pick on her walks. But
today the bed wasn't even made, and the wild flowers had
crumbled away into dead petals and pollen all over the dresser
and floor.

"Jean Potts, I'm ashamed of you!" Lindsay cried. She threw
herself into an inept effort to straighten the bed, and while
she tugged and pulled at it, she scolded Jean—a complete
role reversal, for usually it was Jean who, rightly, grumbled
about Lindsay's messiness. Lindsay soon gave up on the bed
and started on Jean instead: "You haven't even combed your
hair, and when did you last wash it?" She passed her hand
over Jean's tangled mop of hair, and Jean, utterly delighted,
beaming through her tear-swollen face, caught that hand and
held it against her cheek.

"A big grown-up girl letting herself go like that, what am I to do with you?" Lindsay said, making herself grumble and frown. But next moment Jean grabbed her and playfully pulled her down, while Lindsay was protesting, not too vigorously, "You must be out of your mind." She made a big show of straightening her dress and hair, which Jean had mussed. "Carrying on that way, and in front of Harriet."

"Oh Harriet's seen us before," Jean said. It was true, I had, and I never minded it. There was something bearlike and playful about Jean—she loved to romp and chase Lindsay and roll around on the grass with her. Lindsay shrieked louder than necessary and demanded to be let go, but I think she enjoyed it—and who wouldn't, to have someone so fond and demonstrative. It was certainly a change from her fights with Manton and other, later men friends, who had made Lindsay tense and miserable. But ever since she had been with Jean, she had been much more relaxed and seemed to enjoy the simple, girlish things they did together.

"Why don't we go on a trip?" Jean was hopefully asking her. "We haven't been for so long, and before we know it, the summer'll be gone." That was another of the fun things they did together—threw some stuff in the car and took off across the country. When they were tired of driving, they checked into a motel; Jean had her camping gear, and what she loved most was to get up in the mountains somewhere and pitch their tent and live rough for a few days. It wasn't quite Lindsay's style, but when they came back, sunburned and full of mosquito bites, they had a lot of stories to tell, mostly of misadventures they had enjoyed together, and were very close and affectionate.

But now Lindsay looked cross and said "You know perfectly well we can't leave, with everything going on."

"What's going on?"

"For heaven's sake," Lindsay said, looking more cross.

"What's going on, Harriet?" Jean said.

I thought this was as good an opportunity as any, so I came out with "I guess I'm going to get married," adding maybe overcasually: "to Crishi."

"Harriet Wishwell!"

They both exclaimed at the same moment—Lindsay spun

around toward me in what looked like glad surprise, but the way Jean shouted my name was as if she couldn't and wouldn't believe her ears.

Nothing more was said because I was urgently called for to run an errand for Anna Sultan. Although she had recovered enough to get up occasionally, she still spent much of the time resting in her room. Her bell rang often down in the kitchen—the room-service bells had been restored, for there were people to answer them, which hadn't happened since Lindsay's grandparents' time. Some mornings Anna had to have champagne with her orange juice—by no means every morning, but it did mean that it had to be kept on ice for her, just in case. Then there were the times when she was expecting important calls and everyone was warned to keep the lines open; and she liked to sleep late, so most mornings we were all walking around on tiptoe. She was so delicately balanced that the machinery by which she functioned was easily thrown out of gear. Altogether she was delicate. I had thought that a woman journalist like her would be tough, but she was physically fragile, with small, dainty hands and feet. She was pretty, though not young; maybe in her middle thirties. She behaved like someone who had always been admired a lot, both sexually and for her intellect. The Rawul certainly admired her—for her intellect, that is—and treated her the way she treated herself, as a great virtuoso performer. I don't know what her origins were—she had a very English accent, but there was her name; she had dark hair and eyes and magnolia skin. She had made her reputation with a very daring profile of a Middle Eastern leader who was later executed; it was daring because she had recorded his private along with his public activities, and had not drawn back from chronicling her own affair with him.

The Rani didn't like her. I watched her looking Anna up and down, the way I've seen good-looking women do to each other, and with a face that showed she didn't care for what she saw. But she was scrupulously polite to her and personally made sure that she had all the many things she needed. She also submitted to a long interview with her, as did the Rawul and everyone else Anna summoned. These interviews became the central activity of the house, and everything else was subordinated to them. Anna herself fixed the time, but since it took her ages to get herself together, she usually kept her subject waiting, including the Rawul, who sat there very patiently. But when she did appear and turned on her tape recorder, her tired manner dropped from her completely. She was like a sharp, pecking bird as she chiseled away with her tiny, carefully pointed questions; and when she perched over her little typewriter, she and it seemed to be humming away in perfect coordination as she peck-peck-pecked swiftly on its keys.

She hadn't yet called me to be interviewed, and I didn't expect her to—what could I tell her about the movement of which I was only the most peripheral member? She never seemed to see me, though I appeared in her field of vision often enough, for the Rawul thought it a gracious gesture for me rather than one of the followers to serve her. I was forever carrying in her little drinks and snacks, and she would say "Could I have some more ice in this, thanks," without taking her attention off whatever she was doing. But she did call for Michael to be interviewed. Michael had no hostile feelings toward her—he had no feelings for her at all; he never did for strangers—and was certainly willing to talk to her about the movement. But after a short while he could be seen storming out of her room, with that pale, intense look he had when he was furious. Crishi saw him and was amused; he said "She couldn't have made a pass at him? She wouldn't be that dumb?" I followed Michael to find out what had happened. He said he had been perfectly prepared to talk to her about the movement and its principles, philosophy, and organization, but all she wanted to know about was himself; and when he had clammed up, she became offensive, trying to pry him open by making him angry, so he had got up and left her, stalked away as we had seen him do.

Later that day she asked for me to be interviewed, but I wouldn't and Michael also said I shouldn't. In the meantime, though, she had talked to Crishi and he said I should. She got on very well with Crishi, I ought to have said before. She was always calling for him and he was very good-natured about it and always went, even though sometimes she forgot what she had called him for. She didn't make any secret of

it that he was her favorite person in the house, and once
when I came in with her tray, she waved me away and said
"Not *now,* I'm talking to Crishi." He made a face at me behind
her back, which made me feel better but not really very good.
Another time he and I were with the Rani when a message
came to say Anna wanted him. The Rani turned down her
mouth corners and said "I'm sure she does," but Crishi laughed:
"*Some*one has to chat her up," and the Rani said "And of
course it has to be you." Crishi made the same face at her
he had made at me and went off in the cheerful, brisk way
he went to any job. Anna had of course had long sessions
with Crishi talking into her tape recorder, and I wondered
whether he had told her about his relationship with me. I
mean, he was going to *marry* me—he would surely have at
least mentioned that in such a long interview! But if he did,
she gave no sign of knowing anything about it. In fact, no
one in the house did, except the people I had told and Crishi
and the Rani, and they never mentioned it. Even the Rawul,
it seemed, hadn't been told. I realized that it was to be a secret
engagement, though I didn't see why. *I* was ready to talk
about it; I wanted to.

But I didn't at all want to talk to Anna, and went and hid
where I couldn't be found. There used to be many places to
hide, but now every corner of the house from the attic to the
cellar had something going on in it, and the followers were
also digging, clearing, and planting all over the grounds. But
there was one place I still knew to go to: You followed alongside the brook that ultimately fell into the waterfall, but just
before it did, there was a tiny path so overgrown it was in-
visible, and this ended in a sort of cavelike dell where Michael
and I had once buried a dead raccoon. It was damp in here,
for the sun couldn't reach inside and the dead leaves of many
falls had been rained into the earth where they moldered
and crumbled. The only other person who knew about this
place was Michael, so when I heard the crunch of footsteps,
I was sure it was he and was glad he had come. But it was
Crishi, and the way my heart turned over was very different
from the glow of being glad. He stood looking down at me,
and then sat next to me very close and put his arm around
me. I stayed hunched up, with my face hidden. Suddenly it

began to rain—we could hear it falling on the leaves above us, but it took longer to get to us because we were so sheltered; and when it did, it was filtered through all that green and was damper and colder than only rain. The two of us seemed to be sitting inside a grave, where no sun and also no noise and no pain could ever get to us. When Crishi said "How long do we have to stay here?" I said "Forever," and I put my head against his chest, breathing him in together with the earth and rain. "Great," he said; "really cozy," but he stroked my hair and made no move to go away.

"How did you find me?" I asked.

"Michael told me."

I had a twinge of disappointment. I had imagined that it was his own sure instinct—his lover's instinct—that had brought him to me. And I had not expected that Michael would tell anyone, anyone at all, even Crishi, of any secret place we had between us; any more than I had expected him to tell our use of the word *neti*.

"He wanted me to find you," Crishi said. "He wants you to talk to Anna. . . . No listen, you've got to. There's no two ways about it."

I began to explain to him why I couldn't talk to her. It was the way we were, Michael and I: solitary, and needing to guard ourselves, something within ourselves, which we felt it irreverent to share with anyone; that the way I sat here in this place, shielded even from the sun and no one knowing where I was except Michael, was what I liked best. And the fact that he, Crishi, was here with me and so close to me, the two of us buried and being rained on—this showed how deeply he had entered into me as I had never thought anyone could. It wasn't easy for me to get all this out, and the effort made me concentrate on myself without looking at him; and when I did, I saw he was frowning impatiently. He didn't try to hide it either, and before I had finished talking, he said "Don't be stupid. We need the publicity and anyone who can get it for us, Anna or whoever. I don't know what all the fuss is about. You and Michael both—sometimes I think you are what she says you are." Before I could get to ask what this was, he said "And do we have to go on sitting here in the rain much longer?" We went back in single file, along the

brook with the rain falling into it and on us too. He was
walking in front of me, and he never looked around to see
if I was following, not expecting me to fall back; and I
didn't—part of me may have preferred to stay buried inside
that dell, but even more I wanted to go with him.

Although I submitted to being interviewed by Anna, I didn't
tell her that I was going to marry Crishi. I felt I didn't want
to, and also I couldn't, since no one else thought it worth
mentioning. When the article appeared, the Rawul was pleased,
and although this wasn't till later, when we were in England,
I might as well talk about it here, just to show how someone
from outside saw us at that time. She described Propinquity
very well—she described everything very well; she wasn't a
writer for nothing—but from her account it sounded as if it
had been an organizational headquarters forever; no one
would have guessed that only a short time ago Lindsay and
Jean had lived here on their own, mostly in the kitchen. She
called it a very ugly house, which I guess it was, seen objectively. And seen objectively, probably Michael and I were as
she described us—that is, these nineteen-year-old twins who
hadn't managed to finish their education or ever had to work
or make contact with other people. She described us as self-
centered, self-conscious, uptight, and definitely weird, typical
last-of-the-line scions of a once-prominent and moneymaking
American family. Even physically it seemed we were typical,
pale and slight, and with a faraway self-absorbed look in our
strange eyes. But she didn't waste much space on us, who
were only these peripheral figures around the true center of
the house and movement—that is, the Rawul, Rani, and Crishi. Although she gave an outline of the movement itself, she
presented it mainly as an emanation from these three vital,
life-giving personalities, who had erupted in and transformed our eroded lives.

Of the three, she seemed to have had the most difficulty
interpreting the Rawul. She wrote an account of his royal
ancestry and kingdom, his English education, and his English
accent and manners. She described him as physically soft; it
was true, he was getting very plump, with Else Schwamm's
devoted cooking. She said he gave an impression of compassion—a man who wouldn't hurt a fly; of gentleness, who

wouldn't say boo to a goose; and courtesy, who would never precede a guest out the door, that sort of thing, all true. But she went on to speculate whether these qualities—compassion, gentleness, and courtesy—were those of a potential leader. After some discussion, she decided that there was no reason why they should not be, provided they were held together by one essential quality: She called it first "single-mindedness," and then slipped in the word "fanaticism." If that was there, she wrote, the other qualities were absorbed and used by it; she even speculated that the softer qualities were the ones that most easily turned into ruthlessness. She gave some examples, but I didn't feel that she made her point, or that any of this applied to our Rawul, whom I so often watched at breakfast, pouring syrup overgenerously on his pancakes.

I don't know if Anna was aware of the Rani's hostility, or if she returned it, but it certainly made no difference in how she wrote about her. She admired her: for her beauty, her strength of character, her calm exterior, her organizational skill. She compared her with a whole host of outwardly feminine and inwardly virile Oriental women from Cleopatra to the present. However, she pointed out that the Rani was only partly Oriental, and she gave more information about her than anyone had ever told me. The Rani's mother, part-French and part-German, had married an Afghan and gone to live with him on his family's estate outside Kabul. There was quite a little colony there of foreign women married to rich Afghans, and they entertained each other at coffee and card parties and drove around in chauffeured cars. But after a while—this was when Rani (or Renée, to give her real name) was about three—the monotony and strangeness of a semi-purdah life palled on her mother and she returned to Europe, with Rani. Although she took as much jewelry as possible, their circumstances were not as luxurious as they were used to. Rani made up her mind at an early age to improve them. She was fifteen—so Anna speculated: The one fact the Rani had not been outspoken about was her age—when she married her first husband, a German businessman in his forties. Three or four years later, after a nonamicable divorce, she married an Englishman by whom she had had the little boy she had hinted at to me. Everything I had only guessed at

Anna seemed to know for sure, as though the Rani had been entirely candid with her.

The same was true of Crishi. He had never told me what he told her, and it was only after her article came out—that is, after he and I were married—that I learned all this about him. Not that it would have made any difference. Anyway, it was from the article I discovered that his mother was Assamese; that he too had been married—at eighteen in his case—and had not one but two children. Some of the things he had told me—like living on the beach—he hadn't told her; and vice versa, so that it was only after reading the article that I learned the details of his two prison sentences, one in Tehran for a drug offense and the other in New Delhi for fraud. He told her the second was a frame-up by some characters he had got involved with in his youthful ignorance. These two sentences accounted for four years of his life and the rest were spent in traveling in some very distant places and making his living in various businesses, usually connected with precious gems and art objects. For the past eight years he had been with the Rawul, who had legally adopted him, devoting himself entirely to the movement. He told her he was thirty-four years old—which amazed me, in fact I couldn't believe it, and it wasn't what his passport said either. But then his passport gave his name as Christian Ambasta, and his birthplace as Brussels, which wasn't what he had told either her or me; but it did say, correctly, that he had several scars along his shoulder blades, and one from an abdominal operation.

But I'm jumping ahead and I must mention other things first, principally how we got married. I hadn't thought about our wedding too much, hoping that when Crishi was ready to talk about it, he would. The subject was precipitated at the time of Anna's departure, which, like everything connected with her, went off with the maximum fuss. Although she had stayed with us barely a month, she had come with several suitcases, each one containing something very important that needed special care by the followers carrying them. She agitated and gave contradictory instructions, and when at last everything was stowed away and she was sitting in the car, she found she had forgotten her vitamin pills and someone had to run back for them. "It's too awful," she said, holding her pale forehead with a frail hand. "All this rushing around, it's killing me." And truly one felt it was too much for her and wondered how she survived her continual flying around the world. "Anyway, I'll see you in London," she said to Crishi, who stood with his hand on her open car window; she laid hers on top of it. "Absolutely," he said. "In two weeks." I had such a shock that, before we had even gone back in the house, I said to him "I didn't know you were going to London."

"Well of course, what else?" he said, frowning a bit the way he always did when anyone questioned any plan of his.

I burst out "What about me?"

"You?"

I must have looked pretty stupid—I felt that way—for he started to laugh. "Oh yes," he said. "I forgot about you."

I knew he was teasing me; he liked doing it—that way he was more of a brother than Michael. But I felt confused, and shy, feeling it wasn't up to me to pursue this subject though I wanted to. That night, however, when he came to be with me he did take it up and he did talk more or less seriously, for him. I ought to explain that usually we hardly talked, which was fine because we made so much love together. Only sometimes he was in a chatty mood, on subjects like night spots, rock concerts, cars, LPs—he took an interest in all these things.

But that night, when we were resting, he said "Do you really want to?"

I said "Yes. Yes. Yes."

"Funny," he said; meaning either me, or the fact that I should be so eager to marry him. He drew his finger along my hip bone, which I admit was bony: "Might as well marry Michael," he mused. "How old are you anyway? Are you sure I'm not going to be had up for doing it with a minor? Oh really? I thought it was thirteen." He laughed at my protests. "You'll have to eat and get fat. Don't you know I like voluptuous women? The bigger the better. And this *room*, Harriet."

"What's wrong with it?"

"It's got nothing in it. It's like a cell. Who wants to fuck in a cell? I don't."

I tried to prove to him that he did, but he was in a strange mood. He held me away from him to say: "You sure you want to go through with this? Marrying and all? I'm serious, Harriet. I'm warning you seriously."

And he really was—his face was grave, and he continued to hold me away from him. But what a time and way to warn me: lying naked by me on my bed, at the height of my passion for him, or what I thought was the height, not knowing at the time one could get higher. He must have known how useless it was to say anything to try to hold me back.

No one could, although there were others who tried. There was Jean, who was very forthright, but what she said was ridiculous: If Crishi was the fortune hunter she said he was, he wasn't a very active one, since, far from pressing marriage on me, he never even mentioned it again. His present plans were only for England, where he was to precede the rest of the Rawul's party to make arrangements for the scheduled program. It was I who again had to bring up the subject, and he said, as if it had slipped his mind, "Yes we'd better do something about it before I go." "But that's in two weeks!" "It only takes five minutes," he said in a reasonable voice.

"He's right," Michael said, which was as much interest as he could be expected to take.

As for Lindsay, although she had at first been thrilled, her native caution had reasserted itself, backed up by Jean, and she said "Hadn't we better wait, darling?"

I was frantic! I who had never thought of getting married, who was bored listening to others talk about it, who felt sorry and even a bit contemptuous of Barbara when she carried on about Manton not marrying her—I had become worse than anyone. I appealed to the Rani, who, after all, had brought the proposal but appeared to be in no hurry to have it carried out. "What an anxious bride," she mocked me; I couldn't take offense, for it was true. I called Manton in Europe: "Daddy, I'm getting married!" "Darling daughter! God bless you!" When I said who to, there was a pause before he asked in a much smaller voice, "When?" "Soon. Next week." He began, like Lindsay, "Hadn't you better—" but I didn't let him finish; I hung up. What shall I do, I thought; what *shall* I do. In later years I sometimes remembered my despair at that time and found it almost amusing.

Since the Rawul and his party would soon be shifting their

base of operation to London, they wanted to prepare for the transfer of the properties to the organization. This was not yet possible in the case of the house on the Island, for though almost a year had passed since Grandfather's death, his estate was nowhere near settlement; and besides, Michael and I were still under twenty-one. As for Propinquity, Lindsay had changed her mind. "They're all here anyway," she said, "so what difference would it make?" "And if tomorrow you take it in your head to turn them out?" Michael argued with her. "But I don't want to do that," she replied, her eyes stretched wide in innocent surprise. There was no point arguing with Lindsay; she always had her reasons for doing what she felt like from day to day. She was the most pragmatic person anyone ever knew, and in this as in every other way the exact opposite of Michael, who acted only on principle.

Crishi surprised me by asking me: "Have you told Sonya yet? About us?" When I said no, *he* was surprised: "Don't you think she'd like to know?" He was right. Sonya was the first person to react as people are expected to when told about a marriage. And more—if it is possible to overreact on such a topic, she did it. But that was her nature. She had to hang up on me when I first told her because she was so overcome; but she was back on the line within moments, and after that throughout the day. At night she went to consult a psychic friend of hers, like herself of Russian origin, and very late the same night she called again, trying to suppress her excitement and not to promise too much: but it seemed the friend had had some wonderful intuitions, and wanted more details of the exact date and time of Crishi's and my birth. Crishi knew his to the second—did he really, or did he make it up? He certainly didn't blink while he gave it (the year would have made him twenty-six, which was not what Anna later published). Lindsay vacillated about the hour of my birth—she couldn't remember if it was day or night and didn't want to be reminded—"Can you imagine the state I was in, with two of you?" Jean said "Poor pet." But finally, with some suggestions from Crishi, a definite time was agreed upon and Sonya went back to her friend and called again with an ecstatic result of the matching of our two horoscopes.

SONYA insisted that the wedding should be at her house in the city. She said Grandfather would have wanted it, and we must not deny her that privilege. The only person to protest was the Rawul, who wanted to have it at Propinquity. Our news turned out to be a complete surprise to him, and like Sonya, he was overcome: Those two were the only ones, besides myself, who were 100 percent enthusiastic and affirmative. The Rawul flushed with pleasure; he kissed me, clumsily—in fact, he missed and kissed the air. It was shyness that made him clumsy; although a public figure, he was personally a very shy man. He saw our union as a symbol of the synthesis that was the heart of his movement. It was everything, he said, he could have dreamed of and desired; he went on and on, and Crishi looked distinctly bored, though because it was the Rawul he sat through it patiently. The Rawul was the only person of whom Crishi was respectful—his relationship with the Rani was quite different, and he could be as impatient with her as with others; but never with the Rawul. The Rawul was the first person to inquire about the form of the wedding ceremony. I had assumed, and I guess Sonya and Lindsay and everyone else had too, that someone from St. Thomas's would come and perform it at Sonya's house; but the Rawul said that, just as this union was symbolic of his newly forged movement, so its mode of expression would have to be emancipated from all outworn forms. He himself, he decided, would officiate

—which was all wrong, he smiled, from every point of view, for he was neither a Christian priest nor a Brahmin (he was of the warrior caste) and therefore unqualified to perform any kind of ceremony. No matter, he exclaimed; what he—what we all—were there for was to break every rule and make our own.

Crishi asked me "What about clothes?"

"What clothes?"

"Yours. I told you I'm not marrying a boy. You'd better get some."

He always surprised me. He had taken no interest in the whole thing—didn't care where it was, when it was, even, I sometimes felt, whether it was. But here he was worrying about what I was going to wear and telling me to get a trousseau. I was thrilled—not that I cared about getting clothes, but that he should care.

Manton and Barbara flew back from Spain for the wedding. It is strange the way, once a wedding is decided on, everyone gets excited about the event itself and forgets or suppresses other feelings. If Manton did have other feelings, he said nothing about them but was pleased and proud to be the father of the bride. As for Barbara—the one person who really disliked Crishi—she so adored the idea of a wedding that the actual protagonists didn't matter; or was it that for her, once a person was a bridegroom, he became automatically good? It was Barbara who took me shopping for the clothes Crishi wanted me to have. She enjoyed it tremendously, and I did too—not the actual trying on and buying but to be with her in these mirrored cubicles with little velvet chairs, surrounded by billows of all the clothes she was choosing for me. She went especially overboard on nightgowns and lingerie, neither of which I ever wore, and drowned me in frothy pastel silk things more suitable to her soft fair form than my thin hard one. Once I said "He thinks I'm too skinny." It was the only personal thing I said, about him and me, though Barbara and I were talking constantly—that was what I liked about going shopping with her, all those hours of talking shut up together in the little cubicles with her helping me to dress and undress and studying the effect from all sides. I guess it was like girlfriends are supposed to be with each other, only I had never had one I was intimate with; Barbara was my first. She talked a lot about Manton and herself—she was only twenty-two and everyone said how dumb she was, a real dumb blonde, and it was how she thought of herself too, but she seemed to me quite wise. She said what she appreciated most about Manton was that he was a real person—I stared a bit at that, for it was not the first thing I would have said about him. But Barbara said I would understand what she meant if I knew the sort of people among whom she had grown up—her mother's crowd, including her mother herself, who had been nothing apart from their public success, and when that failed them, they ceased to exist in each other's eyes and in their own. But Manton was always, whatever happened to him from outside, Manton: himself.

The Rani assumed responsibility for my wedding dress. As the Rawul was devising his own ceremony, so the Rani devised her own version of a bridal dress for me. It wasn't Oriental and it wasn't Occidental, it wasn't anything you could characterize, but it was very gorgeous. The material was a South Indian silk with alternating panels of a heavy brocade and was to be worn over white satin trousers gathered at the ankles. It was supposed to fit over the bosom and at the waist, but since I have this tendency to go straight down, it had to be taken in at the one place and out at the other. The Rani herself fitted it on me—it embarrassed me to have this royal woman turn herself into my dressmaker, but she seemed to think nothing of it and worked with professional skill. She didn't talk to me while she was doing this—she couldn't; she had pins in her mouth. When I glanced down at her, I saw that around these pins the lines of her face were very set. She looked as if she were holding herself in, her emotions in, for fear of something in her giving way. The Rani was unhappy. Well, it had nothing to do with me, and I couldn't help her. So we did this—the fitting of my wedding dress—in complete silence, both of us concentrating for all we were worth on the task in hand.

"Render unto Caesar," said the Rawul with a smile, after we had been to City Hall and had everything legally done and signed. But of course the real wedding was in Sonya's house. It was a strange mixture—as was the house itself. Most of the furniture from 1898 was still there, and though there had been many additions and alterations over the years, until Sonya moved in these had all reflected the same tribal taste carried over several generations. Now Sonya's taste prevailed, and it was not good but very expressive of her personality. That was why Grandfather, himself so austere, had happily lived in this ormolu-and-pearl bower, which she had created and had choked up with her lifetime collection of hideous art objects from various continents. Year by year she added to them: Whenever some large package arrived for her, Grandfather had learned to steel himself to the unpacking of one more gilded team of horses carrying a lampshade, or elephant with stomach sliding open for cigars.

The guests assembled in this house for my wedding were very different from previous Wishwell wedding guests. The last couple to have had their marriage reception there were Manton and Lindsay, and their photographs still showed quite a number of Wishwells, including Aunt Harriet, who now-adays attended only funerals. The Wishwells present at my wedding were Michael and I; Manton; and I guess Lindsay could be counted too, although she had reverted to her maiden name and was there with Jean and Else Schwamm. As usual, our party was completely swamped in numbers and promi-nence by the Rawul's. The followers had been brought from Propinquity, with only two left behind for security reasons, and there were some I hadn't seen before from the New York chapter—which I hadn't known existed. But for once it wasn't the Rawul's party who stole the show, or gave the tone to the occasion, it was Sonya. Just as she had made this house her own, so she did the wedding. All her friends came; I had seen many of them before, for they were often there for card parties and séances, but never so many together. Some of them were very, very old, like the one they called the Princess—they said she was of the Yugoslavian royal house though she had lived mostly in Basel and Paris before settling in New York. By now she wasn't anything except this very ancient, very wizened figure, almost bald, propped up in a wheelchair by her nurse, both of them in white sneakers. I'm sure she had no idea what was going on but her friends were very pleased that she had come. Sonya rushed up to her and kissed her on the lips and also kissed the nurse, and all the friends did the same.

Besides the Princess, European aristocracy was represented by a German baroness who had been a skating champion and taken part in the Olympics of fifty years ago, and an Italian countess who had been first a fashion designer and then a Buddhist nun before returning to the world and taking an apartment on Madison and Seventy-third. There was Sonya's Russian friend, the one who had asked for the horoscopes, hinted to be the illegitimate granddaughter of a grand duke, and Sonya's best friend, an American called Dorothy, who was the widow of a very big Hollywood producer. All these ladies, except the Princess, whom her nurse had dressed in a simple checked cotton frock, were there in their outsize jewels and glittery gowns from famous designers of previous decades. Altogether these guests gave an impression of previous decades—especially Dorothy, who seemed to incorporate a different age, with her fabulous clothes and jewels matching her highly volatile manner. But they were all— again except the Princess, who was, as it were, switched off —very highly charged, in spite of their age, and tremendously excited to be at a wedding. And Sonya had seen to it that it was a real wedding—her favorite florist had stifled everything under banks of flowers, her favorite caterer was in attendance with a cohort of waiters already rushing around in white gloves, and a string quartet sat on the landing playing Mendelssohn.

The ceremony took place in the principal drawing room. It had been transformed by the followers, who had removed every bit of furniture, down to Sonya's last set of wise monkeys; they had taken down her hangings, and while they couldn't do anything about her rose damask walls, they had given them a neutral tint with some ugly lighting. On one wall the American flag hung alongside the Rawul's, and in between them the Rawul himself in a tinted photographic portrait. Up to that point—that is, walls, flags, and leader's portrait—the room had been institutionalized; but the floor glowed with a Persian carpet, full of flowering creepers, birds, and tigers, and there was a scattering of smaller rugs blooming with tiny flowers. White sheets had been spread for the guests to sit on and bolsters for them to lean against. Most of these guests were certainly not used to sitting on the floor, and for some of them it must have been very hard to get their old legs into position, but they managed it, and it added to their excitement. Only the Princess was allowed to remain in her chair, which had been wheeled to the front, almost level with where Crishi and I sat facing the Rawul.

The Rawul was sitting on a special little rug of his own under the flags and his portrait. The ceremony he had devised wasn't that different from his evening talks at Propinquity. He said the same sort of things about the transcending of East and West to bring them into a higher synthesis; only here he saw the actual realization of that synthesis in the joining together of Crishi of the East and Harriet of the West: so that our marriage was not only a personal but also an historic celebration. I could hear Sonya sigh out a breathless "Beautiful," and another wave of murmurs emanating from Sonya's friends, who had never heard the Rawul's evening lectures. I, who had heard them, tried to be reverent, but I was too excited to listen properly; and I was nervous because Crishi beside me was getting definitely fidgety. Crishi never cared to sit still for very long, and I suspected his mind was wandering ahead to the arrangements after the ceremony, for though they weren't his responsibility, he did tend to take charge. So I could feel him wishing the Rawul would hurry—only the Rawul was not to be hurried on such an occasion, and especially not with this new audience in their gowns and jewels hanging on his every word.

In front of the Rawul stood a golden vessel, and when he had reached the climax of his speech, he lifted it and said "Let this ancient cup unite your lineage." He explained how, as far back as anyone could remember, it had been in his family—or rather, in his genealogy, for there had been many permutations and crossbreedings since their first descent from the moon. This vessel had crossed deserts and dried-up riverbeds, had been secretly buried, lost for a generation or two, murdered for by sword and poison—it had a lot of history and legend behind it. I could hear Sonya exhale behind me, and Dorothy giving a low, drawn-out *"Gee."* The Rawul joined

our hands around this goblet encrusted with gems and hiero-
glyphics, and we raised it to our lips and looked at each other
across it: and I did feel reverent, because of this being a
marriage and because of loving Crishi so much and drinking
with him from a cup steeped in such horror and beauty. The
wine it contained tasted as though it had come to us across
measureless distances and times and had been kept in places
where wine should not be kept—in fact, it was spoiled. Crishi,
after the tiniest sip, made a face of disgust; I did manage to
take quite a big mouthful till he whispered to me "Ugh—
sick—spit it out." The wine was in my mouth—I was afraid
of laughing and spurting it out, but if I swallowed it, I might
choke on it. It was a dilemma, and I had to solve it on my
own, for all he was doing was silently laughing at me. I gave
one big swallow and got it down and Crishi said to me under
his breath, "Oh, well played, Harriet" in a very English accent,
at which point the Rawul pronounced us man and wife in
the same accent, only with him it was genuine.

At the far end of the room, in the space between two
windows where a cabinet full of porcelain usually stood, was
the same group of musical followers who had played at the
July Fourth flag-hoisting ceremony. On that occasion, Crishi
had given them the signal when to strike up—that is, at the
exact moment when the two flags, the Stars and Stripes and
the Rawul's, began their ascent. Now again it was he who
gave them the signal, and the moment was when he and I
were supposed to be sealing the ceremony by our kiss; but
even as our lips met, his eyes swiveled around and his hand
rose to make the musicians strike up. They did so, on the
same note of jubilation as on the previous occasion. Crishi
sprang away from me—maybe to see that everything was
functioning as he wanted—and it was the last I saw of him
for several hours. Probably it is that way at a wedding—I
mean, your own wedding—that you are parted from those
you want to be with by a crowd of well-wishers surrounding
you and saying things you're too overwrought to hear. I
didn't see Michael either but guessed he had gone to read
somewhere upstairs. The first person to come up to me was
the Rani—not to wish me well; she didn't say anything, only
rearranged the wedding dress she had fitted on me. I had

no time to think of her because I was soon claimed by Sonya and her friends. They led me up to the Princess in her wheel-chair and appeared to regard it as a solemn moment, though neither the Princess nor I knew what it meant. "Lay your head in Highness's lap," Sonya whispered to me. I didn't want to, but realizing it was important, got down on my knees before the wheelchair; there I hesitated, and Sonya had to press my head into the royal lap. There appeared to be noth-ing human within the cotton smock, no lap or legs on which to lay my bridal head, just this little heap of skeletal remains. Someone took the Princess's hand to guide it—she didn't like the situation any more than I did and had to be rebuked by her nurse not to be a silly; her hand was pressed on my head to bless me, and we stayed like that, with me holding my breath and the Princess making whimpering sounds, till they released us.

There was a lot of noise from the followers playing their instruments, and on the landing the string quartet had struck up a medley of old Broadway show tunes. I was surrounded by Sonya's friends, all of them terribly excited, for they loved a wedding; they loved parties in general, and these were not as plentiful for them as they had been—some of the grand dresses had a musty smell to them under the layers of heady old-fashioned perfumes. There was a babble of languages around me, Russian, French, and German, but mostly it was various exotic accents of English, all outshouted by Dorothy in pure American. They held glasses and plates of delicious food, and some of them were so wrought-up, their hands shook so much that they spilled champagne and crumbs down my paneled dress; they brushed me down and Sonya helped them, everyone laughing and crying, and before long I was too. They didn't give me time to look around for Crishi, but I knew that when they had gone, there would be he and I together and married; and it was this thought that was the cause of my laughter and tears, whatever might be theirs.

There had been no talk about where we would spend our first married night together—we could stay here in Sonya's house, or go to some hotel, or drive back to Propinquity. I looked forward to it, whatever it was. The last guests had gone, including the family—Manton and Barbara returned to their hotel, and Lindsay and Jean drove to Propinquity, as did the Rawul and followers. The caterer's men were carrying out their paraphernalia, with Sonya tripping after them, tucking tips into their pockets. I went to the front bedroom next to hers, where I had changed into my wedding dress. Crishi was in the room; he had already taken off his bridegroom's brocade coat and was back in his usual clothes, buttoning up his shirt. The Rani was there too; I was surprised, for I thought she had gone back to Propinquity with the others. But there she was, folding up his bridegroom's coat very carefully, as though it were some prop she was putting away for the next time.

"Oh there you are," Crishi greeted me in the distraught way he had when there were other things on his mind. "You must be dead with all that going on."

"I'm okay."

"Well you're lucky, you can get to sleep straight off. . . . Stop messing with that, Rani, put it away and we'll pick it up in the morning when we get back."

"Get back from where?" I asked.

"It's always like that. Always the same. It's what you have to expect from that bunch of psychos. Now Harriet I have to go. You know that."

"No. No I don't. I don't know that."

I stood at the foot of the bed, straight and stiff so as to keep myself together. They were on either side of the big double bed that Sonya had got ready for us in case we decided to stay. It had a bedspread with a scattering of bowknots on it, and above it—a new fantasy of hers—matching drapery suspended from a Victorian crown of gilt. The Rani was concentrating on the suitcase into which she was packing his coat; she kept her eyes lowered with a modest air, not wishing to interfere between husband and wife. Crishi was so amazed at my tone that he stopped buttoning his shirt and stared at me for a moment before bursting out: "And who do you think is going to go up there and get it all straightened out —if not me?" As usual when he was or pretended to be worked up, his London accent became more pronounced. "You don't think I've had a hard day, you don't think I'm about ready to drop, you don't think all I want is to crash here on this nice soft bed the way you can. But no such luck for me," he ended up bitterly. The Rani felt very sorry for him and looked up from his suitcase and suggested in a gentle voice, "Perhaps I could try to manage by myself."

"Yes you could try," he said with the same bitterness. "But I don't think you're going to get very far. That's the way it is in this outfit—if I don't look after every single dumb stupid thing myself, someone else is sure to get it all balled up. I'm sick of it, I can tell you. But what to do—I'm in it up to here, and fed up with it up to here too. And then to have people pulling at you—no don't go, stay with me, hold my hand— I don't understand you, Harriet. I really don't."

"Oh no no," the Rani intervened between us. "She didn't mean it like that. She knows you have to go."

"Do you know?" Crishi said, looking at me like he dared me to say no. I didn't say no, but I didn't say yes either. I kept my eyes fixed on the beautiful bedspread Sonya had newly bought for us; probably she had put it on the bed herself, with many lovely loving thoughts as she smoothed and patted it all around.

The Rani became very busy. She shut Crishi's suitcase and put it by the door, she looked in the mirror and touched up her hair—"Goodness! What a mess"—she came up to me and kissed me, for the first time that day: "Just go to bed and have a lovely sleep." Her face was no longer unhappy but blooming as usual, as she preceded Crishi out the door. He was following her but turned and came up to me again: "I'll be back; you're not going to get rid of me that easy." He tucked a strand of hair behind my ear and whispered into that ear: "Too bad it's tonight, but it's not exactly like it's the first night, is it. Is it?" he repeated and blew into my ear, tickling it so that I had to smile. Then he was gone, leaving me with that smile on my lips and his breath on my ear, as if these were enough for me on that wedding night.

I sat on the bed and tried to have sensible thoughts. He was right—it wasn't our first night; we had had many before and would have many, many more after. And it was true too that the organization depended largely on him, that nothing went right without him. I also tried to have sensible thoughts about the Rani, who was so closely bound up with him in the work. The Rawul was the apex of the movement, but Crishi and the Rani were the base on which it rested. They were collaborators; they worked together. The Rani was married to the Rawul, Crishi to me, but within the organization, in the work itself, the two of them were closest to each other. This was how it was and might always be. I took off the wedding dress she had given me—or had she only lent it?— and wore one of my new nightgowns. Barbara had selected the one I was to wear tonight, and I put it on though I didn't really feel right in it, with all that lace and frilly stuff.

I couldn't stay alone any longer. I left the room and went into the front bedroom, where Sonya was. I opened the door and found her kneeling by the bed. She had her back to me and could have been a little girl saying her prayers. She too was wearing a nightgown—an even more elaborate one than mine, full of old lace; she had bought it from a friend of hers who ran a very exclusive lingerie business. She didn't hear me come in—my feet were bare, her carpet deep—and wasn't aware of me till I stood beside her. When she raised her face, it was not a little girl's but an old old woman's. Yet the expression on it was a child's, glowing with pure feeling—and the feeling was all for me; she had been praying for me. She pulled me down beside her. I buried my face in the counterpane of the big double bed—a heavy dark austere bed, which Grandfather had first shared with Grandmother and where as a child I had seen them lying side by side like two carved effigies; and afterward I had seen him with Sonya in it, only she had been snuggled up close to him and he held her in his arms like a doll. Now she knelt beside me, praying—fervently, the way she did everything. When she had finished, she got up, and she thanked me for coming in to her—tonight, of all nights: "Only now you must go back to him," she said and kissed me, as was her way, full on the lips.

I left her but couldn't return to the room she had got ready for us. I went up the stairs to the next floor. This was where Michael and I had our rooms when we stayed in the house. Michael! I hadn't seen him all day. He must have been sitting behind me during the ceremony, but when it was over and I turned around, he was gone. I hadn't thought of him since, but that wasn't unusual; I didn't have to think of Michael, he was just there. And when I opened the door of his room, he *was* there—lying on the bed with a book, as always. I was so relieved, so relieved, I had to hold on to the door handle for a moment. He looked up and said "What's that?" He meant my unusual nightgown. I took it off and put on his old robe hanging behind the door. I lay on the opposite end of his bed, looking at him in the lamplight. He moved his feet so I could lie properly. He didn't ask me anything— where Crishi was, or anything. He just lay there reading his usual kind of book. My eyes, fixed on his face, began slowly to close; the Rani was right—I was exhausted and needed to sleep. I woke up once and found Michael asleep too, with the light still on and the book on his chest. I meant to turn it off but was too tired and went back to sleep, my feet touching his shoulder, and his mine.

2
THE FAMILY

MY married life really started in London, and it wasn't what I had expected. Crishi didn't live with me but with the Rawul and Rani in the apartment —or *flat,* as they said in England—below the one where Michael and I were. The building was one of those gloomy old five-story English houses with high ceilings and tall narrow windows that had been one-family houses with many children in them and servants in the basement and the attic; now they had been converted into flats and let out to rich foreigners. The houses overlooked a garden in the center to which everyone living in the square had a key, but all the time we were there it was never warm enough to sit out; anyway, it was usually raining. I spent a lot of time looking out the window at the trees in the rain. I was usually waiting—waiting for Crishi, that is. He would call sometime during the day to tell me when to meet him and where, and this always varied. It was not at all the way it had been at Propinquity, where everything had been so structured, with the followers running the house and the Rawul's visiting hours and his evening lectures that everyone attended. Here there was no regular program, and most of the time I didn't even know where everyone was. Sometimes I found that, when I thought they were in the flat downstairs, they had gone out somewhere. It might be ten o'clock at night before Crishi called and said to come to some restaurant where they were having dinner. We would stay sitting around there till long after midnight, which was all right for me because, having nothing to do except wait, I had slept through a good part of the day. When we all went home, Crishi sometimes came upstairs with me but by no means always, and I never knew if he would yawn at his landing and say "Goodnight, sweetheart," and go into their flat with the Rawul and Rani, or if he would make the extra flight up to mine and Michael's.

I got the impression that they were all—that is, the Rawul, Rani, and Crishi—more relaxed and at home in London than they had been in the U.S. That had been literally a new world for them, but here they were in their own old world. They seemed to have many connections here, unlike in the States, where they had only us and the followers and the rather weird people who were beginning to hear about the movement. In England many more people knew of it, and the Rawul sometimes lunched in the House of Commons with a member of an independent party, or at the Savoy with the leader of a new parliamentary group. Most of the followers I had known were left behind in the U.S. to carry on the work there and to look after Propinquity and the house on the Island. There was a different group of followers in London, and they didn't live with us but in another house, which had been taken for them in Earl's Court. I saw only isolated members when they came to clean our flats. There was also an office, so the movement was really separated from our domestic lives; and that may have been why the Rawul, Rani, and Crishi seemed more like a private family here, living in a big family flat where everything was comfortable and familiar to them.

It was in London that I discovered the Rawul had another wife. No one had mentioned her before but it was not as if she were being kept secret—at least not privately, though officially, as the leader of the movement, he had only one consort, and that was the Rani. But actually, legally, the Bari Rani, as she was called, was his wife; and so as not to get them mixed up, the Rani was actually called by her real name in England, and it was as Renée that I too began to think of her. The Rawul may have gone through some sort of ceremony with her—maybe the same as mine—but he had never divorced the Bari Rani. She too was living in London, not in the same house as ours but one that was almost identical and in an identical square a few streets away. She had three teenage daughters called Priti, Daisy, and Baby, and the four of them came to visit us shortly after our arrival. Crishi had told me that they were very excited about our marriage and couldn't wait to see me. He advised me to wear some of my new clothes; he said they would be very disappointed if I didn't come up to their standard, which was high. As soon as I entered the room, there were these four pairs of eager eyes on me, but next moment they were tactfully lowered, for I had failed to take Crishi's advice. I didn't feel right in those clothes Barbara had bought for me. The visitors themselves were dressed and made up exquisitely—Crishi had told me they spent all their time shopping, and it showed. All four of them were bright and quick, with quick darting eyes and movements and voices. They had brought a lot of highly colored pastries for us, as well as the Rawul's favorite walnut cake. The mother, in her pastel diaphanous sari, was sipping tea out of a porcelain cup, and the girls in their pastel diaphanous dresses were sucking Cokes through straws. At first the four of them looked the same age—but of course with the mother the effect had been achieved artificially, or rather, so well was it done, artistically. She was older than Renée, but it seemed the other way around—maybe because of her chirping manner, the same as her girls'. Renée, placid and full-bosomed, appeared very mature beside her, almost indulgent, with a little smile playing around her lips as she listened to their chatter. The Rawul had added the dignity of a paterfamilias to that of statesman and English gentleman. He wore what is known as a smoking jacket, in midnight-blue velvet, and his girls called him Papa. There he sat relaxing in the bosom of his family—and I guess we *were* a family: The Rawul and Renée were the royal couple, with Crishi as their crown prince; which made me the crown princess, even if it was difficult for me to feel like one; and to complete our Oriental dynasty, there was another royal consort with another set of princesses; and around us, acting as household staff, were the various followers who had come up from the house in Earl's Court to serve our tea. Through the French windows we could see the flag of the Seventh

World, which had been hoisted from the little wrought-iron balcony—not an unusual sight around here, for other national standards proclaiming foreign embassies drooped over the wet and leafy square where English nannies had once wheeled their tow-headed charges in stately prams.

The flag was the cause of the first disagreement I witnessed within our extended family circle, which up till then had appeared to be, considering the circumstances, quite harmonious. From time to time the Rawul went to visit the other household—that is, his wife and children—and whenever he did, he wanted them to fly his flag from their balcony. He even sent over a follower to hoist it. The Bari Rani kept quiet about it for a while, but one day she refused to let the follower on her balcony, so when the Rawul arrived, there was no flag. They must have had a big fight about it because soon the Rawul came back home, looking flushed and uptight. The phone rang and it was the Bari Rani wanting to speak to him, but he wouldn't and sent Renée instead. She tried to be calm and diplomatic, but the Bari Rani slammed the phone down on her, and after a while she rang again, and again the Rawul sent Renée. This went on two or three times and ended in the Bari Rani arriving on our doorstep, in a state. Although so tiny, she looked commanding, and if the Rawul had wanted to evade her, he didn't have a chance. She ignored everyone else, including Renée, and continued her row with him. She told him that he could do what he liked in this house but not in the other one, where she lived with her children. Here the Rawul interrupted her to say that, wherever he happened to be, whether it was in this house or in that, for the duration of his stay it was his territory where his flag had to be displayed. That much respect was owed, he said, to him and his movement. "Oh respect," said the Bari Rani, and she made her eyes glide over Renée, and from there back to him, and then she repeated "Respect," and seemed for the moment to have got off the subject of the flag.

The Rawul, keeping his dignity, went back to it: "It's our emblem and we have to display it wherever we are—literally keep our colors flying."

"And quite apart from anything else," Bari Rani retorted,

"it looks so silly. Poor Daisy, she's dating her first boy (I want to talk to you about that), and when he saw that thing, he just laughed and laughed. She didn't know where to look, she said. She absolutely begged me, 'Please, Mummy, please ask Papa to take it down.' Naturally, it's embarrassing for the child."

"She ought to be proud of her father's colors displayed in his house."

"*His* house? Well, hardly—any more than this one." She half-shut her eyes in an insinuating way and pulled her sari closer around her shoulders. There was a pause—she seemed to be debating whether to go further or not and then decided yes: "I don't think this is quite what Daddy expected when he bought these properties for me. But of course there are other things he didn't expect either, and sometimes I'm almost glad he is no longer here to see everything I have to see." Suddenly she turned to me. I had come downstairs to see if Crishi was there—he wasn't—and had got trapped when she entered and stood between me and the door. I felt even more trapped when she spoke to me: "You'll find out that everything is not what you expected. Perhaps you've found out already. . . . I'm used to it by now but—oh what a pity when young people are disappointed."

I felt as if from behind me the Rawul and Renée were pushing me to answer her. They and I were standing on one side of the room, Bari Rani on the other; so when I said "I'm not disappointed," it was as though I were replying to an adversary.

"Let's hope you never will be," Bari Rani said, not at all like an adversary but sighing as one who wished me well.

"We're here to see to that," said Renée, very energetically, and she came and stood beside me, with her arm laid around my shoulders. Now I felt like a pawn between them, but Bari Rani was not playing—I don't know for whose sake she gave up and turned with a last "Just get that thing out of my house!" and swept from the room.

Renée was indignant: "Coming here, making a scene—and in front of Harriet." She dropped her arm from my shoulder: "I can't think why she should start in on you, unless of course you've been talking to her. Complaining or something." Her indignation was now directed at me, and it was about me she said to the Rawul: "After everything we've given her, and given up for her. Everything we've done to make her welcome. I hope you feel that," she challenged me, narrowing her eyes. "How we've welcomed you with open arms. Like a daughter."

"She *is* a daughter," said the Rawul, shifting from foot to foot in embarrassment.

"Of course she is; who says she's not? My goodness, how much more could we possibly do for her than we've done already!"

Afterward I brooded about what she meant: Was it that they had given me Crishi? If so, even she had to admit that they hadn't given me all that much of him. When he was home, he was mostly with them downstairs while I was upstairs with Michael, if he was there, or usually alone. Even when Crishi came to me at night, by the time I woke up in the morning, he was gone. I argued, I yelled, I fought with him—he smiled, and it was as though he had only to put out one hand and brush me aside. The truth was, he couldn't lose with me. For those few hours he sometimes spent with me, I was willing to put up with all the waiting and frustration. I had no alternative. He had aroused me so completely that the sex he gave me—rationed out to me—was absolutely essential to me. Deprived of it, I was as if without breath and air. Really sometimes I lay there in such an agony of unfulfilled longing, I was fighting for breath. I was hardly a person anymore but just this fearful *need*. It is shaming to write this—to have allowed myself to be so overcome. I was furious with him when he didn't turn up, but when he did I flung myself on him in a fury of desire. I tore at him, I literally did. I was a starved animal and he laughed and liked it. I had no defenses at all—against him, against myself, against this sex. I don't want to say any more. Yes I blame myself but even now, looking back, I can see I couldn't help myself. Sometimes I think it would be better if people could have their full force of sexual desire when they are older and have learned some control to deal with it; but in youth, there is nothing between you and it, so it can become the devouring hunger it was for me at that time.

I wondered often about Michael. I knew Crishi had a strong effect on him—I had seen that current pass through him in Crishi's presence—but I couldn't imagine that he went through the same agonies I did. While I had never been sure whether Crishi went to Michael's room at Propinquity or on the Island, here in London I was sure he didn't. He came up to me for a few hours and then returned to the Rawul and Renée, while Michael remained alone in his room. But they were often together during the day—Michael had become Crishi's closest aide—and they could have gone anywhere and done anything. I don't know. That way Michael was a complete mystery to me. I knew he was homosexual and had met him with boyfriends, but I knew nothing about his true relations with them and with many others I did not meet. For me, in my thoughts, he was always alone—whether he was traveling the way he used to all over the world, or just living in a place and moving around in it: He was alone and aloof, walking with his head held high and not looking right or left, as if nothing concerned him. He looked pure and untouched; yet perhaps he did, like others, spend hours in men's toilets or went to the baths or whatever other places there are. The knowledge of it was there in my consciousness but unconnected with him as he was, not only in his essence but also physically—slender, upright, clean, and fair.

It was a strange time for me in London. Although everyone else was very busy working for the movement, I had nothing to do except wait for those few hours when Crishi came to be with me; if he came, that is. I went around on my own, traveling on the tops of buses, walking through the parks in the rain. I went to museums and looked at pictures and antiquities, and went to see films in multiple cinemas, and when one was finished, I went in another one. I was so crazy with sex at the time, I went to some porno ones too, and that was strange, with all those men in raincoats, sitting very still and concentrated. Altogether London was strange to me—very different from the way I had known it on my previous stays there. The streets, the stores, and especially the museums seemed to be full of tourists, busloads of them with camera equipment and foreign languages I didn't always recognize. Sometimes it seemed to me that the only English people I saw were museum attendants and policemen directing the flow of travelers into the right channels. When I look back on that time it was very often Saturday afternoon with everything in our neighborhood of tall Edwardian houses shut tight, except for a little general store run by an Indian family who kept open late into the night though not many customers came, everyone having gone away for the weekend.

I could always visit the other house, where Bari Rani and the girls lived on a permanent note of high-pitched excitement. Usually they were getting ready to go out, and the baths were running and girls shrieking and charging into each other's bedrooms to exchange articles of clothing, perfumes, and makeup. Sometimes I went along with them, but I contributed nothing to their shopping expeditions, not buying anything for myself and unable to give sound advice on their purchases; nor to their parties, where they never noticed that I wasn't having as fabulous a time as they were. Their phones rang a lot, very often from Bombay, and the Bari Rani would talk for hours and had no difficulty hearing above the noise of the LPs the girls were playing. She often said to me, "We must have a long talk, Harriet," and I think she meant to, but it couldn't happen because she was continually being called away to the phone or to advise on an outfit; or she was fighting with Teresa, the Indian Christian girl they had brought with them, who had been their nanny and now was their companion and help. Teresa had an Indian boyfriend, and so did all the girls. I had difficulty keeping the girls' boyfriends apart because they were all handsome and polite and exquisitely dressed, and fantastic dancers, as were the girls. Everyone talked in a lilting English with Hindi phrases thrown in—they talked constantly but no one had to listen and in fact it all sounded the same, all on one high note, more like singing than talking.

The girls were a few years younger than I—the eldest, Priti, had her seventeenth birthday around this time—and I knew that, like everyone I had gone to school with, they were very interested in sex. They talked and read about it and discussed it, with each other and their friends; but here too I couldn't contribute, for although by this time I thought of nothing else either, it was in a different way. They knew nothing about the kind of sex I was going through, and I didn't want them to know; it was as though I were protecting them. Probably they thought I was frigid, as everyone usually did, and I preferred a hundred times to have them think that than to know the reality. Only Crishi knew the reality, and it amused him no end. "What would Aunt Harriet say?" was his standard crack whenever he involved me in some act he knew about. Aunt Harriet was one of his favorite jokes— he had seen her only that one time at Grandfather's funeral, but he made her into this sort of archetypal figure to which he claimed I would revert. Whenever I hesitated to perform some new thing he wanted me to do, he said "There, see, you've reverted already." He had many Aunt Harriet stories. He said she always had to wear a brooch on her blouse so people could tell which was front Harriet and which was back; and once he came with a very serious face, saying a dead woman had been found and they were about to carry her off to the mortuary when he saw her and cried "No wait stop! That's no corpse, that's my Aunt Harriet." And so on. The frigidity of Anglo-Saxon women was a favorite subject with him, and the more we did at night the more jokes he made by day.

Unable to stay another minute alone in the flat, or cope with the romantic-girl atmosphere in the other house, I would walk miles in the hope of tiring myself out and dropping off to sleep till Crishi came. It was getting into fall, damp and chilly, and though the leaves were still on the trees and still green for the most part, they kept being blown off and lay on the paths and were trodden into mulch. Sometimes I sat on a wet bench in Hyde Park and got even more wet from the leaves dripping down on me. Lonely men wandering by stopped, and some sat with me to talk but I didn't answer them much, so they soon wandered off again, sadder than ever. One man—quite an old man with a hat on that he didn't take off—lay down on the grass near me, and it took me awhile before I realized he was masturbating, so I moved. I thought it was terrible that people, and even old people, should have these sensations, and be tortured by them. Another man must have witnessed this and he followed me and offered to call the police. He said it was disgusting and such

persons must be stopped. I said no it's all right, and walked
faster and he walked faster too, and then it seemed he had
to protect me and wouldn't leave me. He said London was a
very dangerous place, very bad people around, and a girl
like me shouldn't be walking in the park. He said in his own
country no girl ever walked alone, and if she did, she was
picked up by the police and sent back to her family. He didn't
say which his country was but referred to it constantly, so that
practically every sentence started with "In my country . . ."
He was short, muscular, dark in a Middle Eastern way. His
clothes were quite clean and whole but looked as though he
might have bought them secondhand, maybe found them
hanging in a market on a Sunday morning. After a while,
walking with me, he took my hand, very nicely and respectfully, so that I felt I had to leave it there. His hand was very
very warm, even hot, as if the climate of his country were
stored in it. The rain kept on squeezing down the way it does
in London, out of spongy colorless clouds. All around us in
the park were these magnificent tall old trees, and when we
came out there were these magnificent tall old buildings
looming up into the wet air. He kept on talking, about his
country and other general topics, still holding my hand very
respectfully; sometimes he tickled my palm but stopped at
once when he saw I didn't like it. We went down a tube station,
and since he had only enough money for one ticket, I bought
my own. It was a long underground ride, anonymous and
ghostlike, as though I had just died and didn't know where
I was bound for and neither did the other people who got
in and out as the doors slid open at the stations; there was
an unending stream of them, all smelling damp as if in their
grave clothes. I felt completely passive and had stopped noticing that he was holding my hand.

   When we got off and emerged up a long escalator, it was
still raining from the same drained sky and over streets and
streets and streets of identical houses. They were smaller
houses than the ones where we lived, and grimier, and there
were more gaps where some had been torn down and weeds
grew in their foundations. There were also more shops—
laundromats, a few supermarkets, a few very small shops
going out of business and others already gone and boarded

up; every block had at least one Pakistani or Bangladeshi restaurant and a donna-kebab place. We turned in to a doorway beside one of these places and walked up a very dark staircase. On the first landing he stopped and kissed me and his lips were as hot as his hand. He said his name was Salim. There was a dense smell of kebabs and the oil in which they had been fried many times. We walked up one flight more and he unlocked a door and invited me into his room. It was poorly furnished but he kept it nice with a tablecloth and photographs. He had made his bed before going out and there was a blue cotton cover on it. A pair of dark trousers was folded over the only chair. He hung them in the wardrobe so I could sit down. There was an awkward silence, for it was difficult to find anything to say. He had a clock, ticking with a tinny sound, and this seemed the most prominent object in the room except for the wardrobe, which was a very bulky piece of furniture and leaned forward slightly as though about to crash down.

He made tea on a tiny portable stove he had by the open fireplace. The tea was very good, very strong with creamy milk and much sugar and some other taste that may have been cloves. I wished I could have drunk it and said thank you and good-bye, but of course that was not what we had come for on that long underground ride. I looked at the photographs that stood on the tablecloth as on a little altar. There were some old people, some children, some young men in military uniform; when I looked at them, he explained who they were and at the same time he put his hand on my knee. I moved this knee slightly and in my embarrassment asked more questions in fast succession. He answered them and put his hand back on my knee. I picked up a studio photograph of a young man—I thought it was he but he said no, it was his brother. "Dead," he said, and I had hardly made sounds of regret, when he added "Shot." He slid his hand farther up my thigh, and feeling shocked and sorry about his brother, I didn't like to stop him. He leaned forward from the bed and pressed his lips on mine. His chin felt rough and stubbly—he may have shaved in the morning but probably needed to do so at least twice a day. He smelled like a person who tried to keep himself clean but did not have adequate bathing facilities. He was now breathing hard and tried to make me get off the chair and join him on the bed. I said "I must go. My husband's waiting." I'm sure I sounded like Aunt Harriet. If I had had gloves, at this point I would have put them on.

I had forgotten how much stronger men are than women. It wasn't that he was a rough or brutal man—on the contrary—but that his need was great. After all, he was away from his wife, his family, and lived alone in this little room in a rainy city of endless row houses. He even tried to argue with me—he said, quite reasonably, "Then why did you come?" I couldn't say for the tea; I couldn't say anything. I felt I had to go through with it. But anyway there was no choice anymore. Lying under him on the lumpy bed onto which he had thrown me, watching his contorted, sweating face, I stroked his cheek because I felt sorry to have roused him so far. He didn't take long and afterward appeared to feel satisfied and grateful. I also felt grateful—that it was over, for one thing, and for another that I hadn't enjoyed it: not at all, there had been no gratification of any kind for me. I realized that my ravenous need was not that of one physical animal for another but for one particular human being—for Crishi, for my husband, whom I loved.

If only I could have seen him more often! But some days he was only a voice on the other end of the telephone—I didn't even know where he was calling from, and often it sounded like a pay phone. He was always cheerful and charming but always in a hurry, and when I called, desperately sometimes, "Where are you? When am I going to see you?" he would say "I have to go now" and hang up. I was reminded of what I had read about the Lord Krishna, when Michael was in his Indian period: how Krishna had all these girls in love with him but he would tease them, hiding himself from them, just showing a glimpse of himself every now and again to keep them in line, while they would be staggering around day and night calling for him—"Where are you? Can't you see how I'm longing and waiting for you?" All they heard was his laughter from behind some trees, but when they followed it, he was gone.

I SAW a lot of the Lord Krishna during these days because of all the pictures we had, the Indian miniatures. They hung on the walls of the flat upstairs and there were more downstairs, in gold frames, and portfolios of them were kept in drawers. Many of them were scenes of nature and others were interiors, but they were all somehow erotic. New ones kept arriving, and Renée and Crishi pored over them together. Various kinds of people brought them —some of them were followers, who had no interest in the pictures but acted only as couriers. But there were also some Indians, most of them stout and shining all over—their suits shone, their big rings with jewels in them, their oiled hair, their brand-new shoes—and these did have an interest and argued with Renée and Crishi over the date and place of origin of the pictures, and their price. Renée and Crishi usually won these arguments; they seemed to be real experts. I thought at first they were collectors but then discovered that they were dealing too. Besides receiving consignments from India, they visited salesrooms—here in London, or one or both of them would fly to Switzerland or Holland, and once or twice to New York. These trips were always very sudden; I didn't even know they were gone till Crishi called me from Zurich or somewhere, or sometimes he didn't call but was missing for a few days. When he turned up again, I would pounce on him in desperate relief—"Where have you *been*?" and he grinned and said "I'm back now."

They visited various art galleries, but there was a particular one, just off St. James's, they were in all the time. Crishi often called and told me to meet him there. He was usually late, so I spent a good deal of time waiting for him and got to know the pictures really well—they were the kind I was familiar with at home, for the gallery specialized in Indian art. Many of the visitors appeared to know each other, and the gallery was almost like a club; and as in a club, if they didn't know you, they didn't speak to you, so I sat there reading the same catalog over and over, pretending I wasn't hearing the conversations going on literally over my head. There were the usual very superior sort of girls who work in art galleries; and after asking in frigid voices if they could help me, they left me conspicuously alone. It was no better when Crishi finally came, for he knew everyone and had a lot to talk to them about. He never seemed to notice me sitting there waiting till he was ready to go, when suddenly he said "Well are you coming or not?" as if it had been I who had kept him waiting. The only person to take notice of me was the owner of the gallery, who gave me different catalogs to look at when he saw how long I had been reading the same one. In a way, he appeared to be as much an outsider as I was, for whereas everyone else had a lot to say in loud confident voices, he was quiet and withdrawn; when he did speak, he stuttered a bit, but that may just have been his hesitant way of talking. He was a tall, very English Englishman called Rupert.

It was Bari Rani who first told me that Rupert had been Renée's husband. She told me a lot of things, for we did finally have that talk she kept mentioning, at least in part. It wasn't an undisturbed session, for it took place in her house, with the girls running in and out calling to her and to each other and to Teresa, who was pressing their clothes and packing them. They were all going to Bombay for a wedding— it was their second trip since I had known them; they stayed for a few days, did a monstrous lot of shopping, and came back loaded with presents for everyone. Teresa went too, to help with the luggage. It was about Teresa that our talk began, when the Bari Rani confided to me: "They've been trying to get at her—you know, to make her take things. But I said absolutely not." I didn't know what she meant and waited for her to go on. She had to exchange some more shouts with the girls, but she came back to me: "It's something where I've always put my foot down, since the beginning: otherwise they would be on to us too, can you imagine—the girls and myself. And you, Harriet. You'll have to be very firm about that." Here I did have to admit I had no idea what she was talking about. She was astonished: "Oh my goodness," she said and got up and shut the door, which was unprecedented in that house. She came and sat very close to me on her gold sofa: "I should have known," she said. "You're exactly the sort of innocent person they would trap. Trap and use. . . . No, Daisy, I'm talking, shut the door! I said, shut it!" She sat beside me, sighing. I waited and wondered; actually I didn't want to hear too much. "Where to start," she said and was silent a bit longer. I looked down at the floor. I thought, If she says too much, I won't believe her.

She started at the beginning, with her own marriage to the Rawul. "His family wanted him to marry some traditional girl from a royal house, but he chose me. I'm not even saying it was because of Daddy's money—though he did need it, for his movement. I believed in the movement too. I thought it was wonderful. I thought he was wonderful—such an ideal-ist and so clever and educated; and of course a very ancient title and a state of his own and a palace—not that I would spend five minutes in it—it is the most gruesome place, Har-riet, and you must never let them take you there. But Daddy bought us a flat on Malabar Hill and a house at Devlali and these houses in London, so we could be wherever we liked and it was really quite beautiful, Harriet, in the beginning. I'm not saying it was ideal—no marriage is ideal—Baby, did you hear me! I don't want to be disturbed, I'm talking to Harriet, very privately!—there were difficulties naturally, problems, I'll go into that some other time, Harriet, when you've been married longer and will understand better—but it was working out quite all right, till she came. Renée. That's her name—not Rani, not the Rani—she has no right to a title. Just Renée." She had to collect herself a bit before going on: "She came for the pictures and things first. There were others like her who made friends with the royal houses and went from one to the other to see what they could buy up and sell at a big profit in their galleries or at auction. It was all illegal of course, high-class smugglers, that's all they were, but so charming and such nice company, you know how English people can be when they want to. Not that she's English, not properly, though she's married to Rupert—you didn't know that? Oh yes, poor Rupert. I don't think he knows in the least what's going on. No one really knows—not the Rawul, he's much too up there in the clouds—only she knows, she and Crishi." Here she gave me a sideways glance, and I felt we were reaching the point where it was not my business to hear much more. She caught hold of my hand urgently: "Don't let them involve you, you mustn't. They'll use anyone in any way they can—I told you, even Teresa, the stupid girl. She had no idea what they gave her, she thought she was just taking a little package among her bras and panties; that's what they told her. But when I found out, I put a stop to it, once and for all. I was furious. I told Teresa yes, and if the customs had opened your baggage, do you know where you'd be today? In jail where you deserve to be, not to speak of the terrible publicity for us. Let them use their own people, my goodness, there are enough of those poor sick creatures and no one would even miss them if they rotted away in jail for the rest of their lives."

She meant the followers. I'm afraid we all thought about them in that way, as if they were both indistinguishable and dispensable. Here in London the area of Earl's Court where they lived together was in the process of being upgraded. Some of the houses had already been converted into apartments and had window boxes and yellow front doors. Others were boarded up, growing black and derelict as they waited to be refurbished; Crishi had taken one of them for the followers, and the boards were removed from those windows that still had glass in them and the electricity was reconnected. There was the usual copier, teleprinter, two office tables with typewriters on them, and a telephone standing on the floor of what had once been the front drawing room; on the wall hung a duty schedule and the Rawul's official portrait. The followers slept all over the rest of the house, some in beds, some on mattresses on the floor, some in sleeping bags. There were plenty of extra rooms for anyone who wanted to stay there, but only one bathroom was functioning. The kitchen was in the basement, and everyone more or less fended for himself down there—I think because they were all on different diets, many of them being vegetarians but not of the same kind, some eating eggs and others not even taking root vegetables like onions and potatoes. But there were also some who needed a high-protein diet, with lots of underdone meat.

I went to see them sometimes, going there on the tube and walking through many streets identical with theirs. I had already discovered that being in London involved a lot of walking in the rain down long streets of grim and grimy houses. Whenever I arrived, they were busy at their own occupations or preoccupations and had no time for an outsider like me. Yes, it was strange but they did regard me as an outsider. Being married to Crishi evidently didn't count with them; it wasn't a real commitment like the one they had made. From their point of view, they were right. I hadn't given up anything the way they had—I didn't have to live in this bleak house and do every kind of menial work for the movement and its leaders. Here in London they stood at street corners distributing pamphlets announcing the Rawul's meetings, and they went from door to door selling literature like the Rawul's biography, and tapes of his lectures, and pin-on medals with his picture on them. They did everything they were told eagerly, regarding it as important to the movement, and to themselves personally. Why? For what? I couldn't see what was in it for them, except the commitment itself. There was one girl, Debbie, whom I had known at home— she was the one with whom I had had the fight about the bathroom: One day in London I saw her come in soaked through and very dispirited because she hadn't been able to sell her quota of literature though she had tramped around in the rain the whole day. The moment she entered, the phone rang and it was from headquarters—that was the office in Mayfair—saying they needed some people to help Crishi and Renée get a consignment of pamphlets ready to take to the airport. There was no shortage of volunteers, but they let Debbie go because she was so keen, and anyway she was wet already and could hurry over there just as she was.

Debbie was the only one of them ever to ask me for money, and then not for herself—she didn't need it; they had no personal cash but drew out of a central fund. While on the subject of money, I might as well talk about mine. A regular income was paid into my account, but I never used it so the accountant took it out again to reinvest or something. After my marriage, Crishi looked after all that for me, and he did use the income; and because expenses for the movement were so high, he tried to get a bigger allowance out of the trust fund and also some capital. There were a lot of arguments between him and the people looking after the trust, but he told me not to bother about it and I didn't. It happened sometimes, when he asked me to sign something, that Mr. Pritchett had already called me from New York to inquire if I was sure I knew what I was signing; and in case I wasn't, he explained it to me and seemed to suggest I shouldn't, but I always did. Anyhow, when Debbie asked me for money, she said it was for Paul—"You remember Paul?" she said. She described him to me, but I soon interrupted her, for a scene I had removed from my memory arose with him: Crishi in the orchard kicking someone lying on the ground—"Yes, yes," I said to Debbie, to make her stop describing Paul.

"There's this letter from him," she said. It looked like an ordinary envelope with foreign stamps on it, somewhat grimy and creased as if it had traversed difficult terrain, but the return address was a jail in Turkey. "It's the winter that's the most difficult," she said apologetically. "You wouldn't think they'd have such a severe winter, but I guess being so near Russia. . . . He needs to buy blankets and some warm clothes. You can buy anything you want if you've got money but he doesn't have any. Food too, and it does make a difference, I mean to have some proper food inside you instead of what they give you—you can read what he says."

But I didn't—I just wrote a check for her, made out to bearer so she could cash it and send it to him. I didn't ask Debbie too many questions as to why he was there. I remembered how he had pleaded with Crishi, "But why me, why me?" I guess I knew now more or less what that had been about, but all the same next time I saw Crishi, which was the next day, I asked him, "Why's Paul in jail?"

"For being a fool," Crishi answered at once; and when I protested that no one gets put in jail for that, he said "Well they ought to be."

"But he must have done *some*thing."

It wasn't easy to go on insisting this way because I knew that he hated being asked questions about what he considered his business and not mine or anyone else's. Also, he was very good at evasion, and when it looked as though I were going to ask more, he picked up the phone and was soon in an important conversation with someone in Scotland. After that, it turned out there was an appointment he had forgotten about and, very tender and apologetic about having to leave me, he took off.

Still, I would have returned to the subject of Paul—I had made up my mind to, even at the risk of getting Crishi angry or, worse, making him rush off—but I was diverted by something that happened with Michael. He came to tell me he was going away for a couple of days; when I asked where, he answered reluctantly, "To Amsterdam," and when I asked what for, he didn't answer. Crishi would have had no difficulty making up some lie—he would have enjoyed it—but Michael couldn't, and said nothing. I told him about Paul being in jail, and how he must have got there through smuggling for Crishi: I didn't have to use any roundabout ways with Michael—I could let him right into my mind and whatever I was thinking in there. And it seemed Michael knew all about it, had gone through it in his own mind, for he answered at once: "You have to take risks." He had that stubborn look he got when he had struggled with a dilemma and had come out with a decision. Even if it was a wrong one, he would stick by it. His face was more white and bony than ever, and he looked as though he hadn't slept for a couple of nights, going through this struggle with himself. But now he was resolved and nothing I could say would make him reconsider.

While he was away, I was too tense and disturbed to think about much else, and anyway Crishi didn't give me an opportunity to return to the subject of Paul as I had intended. And when Michael came back—and he did come back, still very pale and saying nothing about his trip—I was so relieved

I again forgot about Paul. But in the meantime Crishi had been going through my checkbook as was his habit, and he found the bearer check I had made out to Debbie. When he questioned me about it, I could go right in about Paul again. This time he didn't say Paul was a fool, but that Debbie was to ask me for money and I to give it to her.

I said "But he's freezing and starving and who knows what else."

Crishi wasn't impressed: "He ought to learn how to manage. . . . Anyone can manage in jail if they use their brains, but he doesn't have any. Last time too—he sat through the whole five years, without even trying to get out. Not even *trying*. How dumb can you be? Don't look at me like that, Harriet: Of course I've been in jail and of course I've got out. They caught up with me again, but that was rotten luck. At least I tried. I didn't sit there asking the girls back home to send me money."

Anna's article hadn't come out, with all the new information in it, so what he said was a shock to me. I tried not to show it, but he burst out laughing: "Who'd have thought it —Aunt Harriet married to a con." But at the same time he took me in his arms and kissed my face and neck in the nicest way, to make me feel better. And after some moments of this gentle treatment, I saw it was naïve to be shocked, when people were in jail all over the world and for every kind of reason. I became calm and sensible and asked him what he had been in for, and he said "Political," and looked serious. I nodded; it was natural that he should have been jailed for political reasons—after all, we were a new and revolutionary movement and had to expect opposition from the existing order. I said that to him, I was ready to talk about it, but he was more interested in making love, and we didn't go into it any further.

Although I spent so much time alone and with nothing to do, I can't say I was bored or homesick. They often called me from home—Sonya, Manton, Lindsay—each of them eager to know how I was, worried about me, wanting to hear from me. I had no difficulty assuring them that Michael and I were very well and happy. I was glad to hear from them but never thought of calling them myself. I suppose it is natural to be entirely engrossed in your new life when you are first married, even if it is not what you had anticipated. I lived in a constant state of excitement—principally waiting for Crishi, when he would call me, where he would tell me to go, if he would come upstairs at night or stay down with the Rawul and Renée. Although that was my central preoccupation, there were other new things, other aspects of my new life, I was beginning to learn about. But that too was part of being married, I thought, having to get used to a whole different pattern of life. It wasn't a pattern that became clear to me all at once—really, it never did become entirely clear—but only in jigsaw pieces here and there. I never knew what piece I would find next.

AFTER the Bari Rani told me about Rupert, I took more notice of him whenever I had to wait around in the gallery. It was hard to connect him in any way with Renée, let alone think of him as having been married to her. He looked very English, in his yellow sweater, Harris tweed jacket, and Old Etonian necktie, but there was also something unworldly about him. This may have had to do with his hesitant speech, and his shy smile, and dreamy eyes. He was the co-owner of the gallery but deferred to the girls he employed. These girls had a confident manner and were arrogant toward everyone except one person—Rupert's partner, Nicholas, who was sharp and sarcastic with them, though very deferential with potential clients. Nicholas appeared to be completely in charge, deciding about hanging pictures, giving instructions to the girls, smilingly attentive to everyone who came in, and greeting many of them by their first names and kissing the air near their cheeks. Everyone in the gallery spoke in the same kind of English accent as the Rawul—the kind one doesn't hear too much anymore—only with them it sounded not comic, the way it sometimes did with him, but intimidating.

This was true even of Rupert, who was so shy and hesitant; and of Nicholas, in spite of his fawning deference to anyone who might turn out to want to buy something from him. Probably it wasn't anything personal but the accent itself, which had once rung out over jungles and deserts and many other unlikely places, telling everyone what to do. On the same principle, something intimidating remained in the rows of overwhelming, overbearing buildings, even when these had alien flags hanging from them, or ground floors rented to halal butchers and Bangladeshi restaurants. But to get back to Rupert—the habit of command may have remained in his ancestral accent, but nowhere else in his personality. I watched him once when Renée came into the gallery: how he rose to his feet, how he blushed, how his prominent Adam's apple went up and down under his Old Etonian necktie; and there was the same shock I had seen pass through Michael and had felt pass through me, with Crishi, which I knew to be as undermining to one's personality as an earthquake to the foundations of a building. And truly, as he stood there talking to her, Rupert seemed to be shaking as from the effect of an earthquake. And I thought, My God, why is it like that, why does it happen to us like that, what is it in us that makes it happen?

Renée was her usual self, only maybe a bit more impatient than usual as Rupert stood stuttering and shaking before her. There was a little boy who sometimes came to the gallery and appeared to belong to it. He was very quiet—I mean, for a little boy—but not apparently quiet enough for Renée. When she heard him ask for a Coke in what she considered too loud a voice, she spoke to him sharply. She also spoke sharply to Rupert; she said "If he can't behave properly, you shouldn't bring him here"; Rupert stuttered "No—no—he's all right." "Only brats shout like that," Renée rebuked the boy and Rupert, both crestfallen by now. "And anyway he shouldn't be drinking these things, unless of course you want his teeth to rot and spend a fortune at the dentist."

Although this was the only interest I ever saw her take in the boy, I gathered he was the child she had told me about, whom they had taken away from her. "They," was Rupert, and he hadn't so much taken away as taken charge of him because Renée hadn't the time. That impression was confirmed by Renée herself while we were walking away from the gallery after this encounter. Unlike the pain with which she had mentioned the boy to me before, she spoke in exasperation. She said it was impossible for someone as deeply

involved in the work of the movement as she was to be at
the same time responsible for a child, and that she had had
to make her choice; and that of course for her the work had
to come first. She frowned as she spoke—she was striding
beside me down a wide and elegant street that somehow
suited her personality. It had shipping offices, a Rolls-Royce
showroom, and a soldier-duke, sword in hand, astride a horse.
Renée attracted attention wherever she was, but here she was
striking in a different way from at Propinquity. She dressed
differently—she wore woolen cloaks and wide-brimmed hats
and fine leather boots, so that there was something martial
about her, almost granite, the same as the soldier-duke.

But at home, in the flat she shared with the Rawul and
Crishi, she was as soft and opulent as when I had first known
her; but what I hadn't realized was that Renée was terribly
untidy, squalid even. When she took off her clothes, she
simply dropped them wherever she happened to be. She
stepped out of her luxuriant bath without pulling the plug
to let the water out. When she ate, she liked to pick up bones
and gnaw them, and wipe her hands on whatever was nearest.
Her underclothes, more soiled than one would have thought
possible for someone so outwardly elegant, appeared mys-
teriously in the living rooms as well as her bedroom; so did
flakes of pressed powder and the combings of her rich hair.
She never noticed; nor did the Rawul and Crishi—they didn't
care what happened with their own discarded clothes, or the
wet towels they left on the bathroom floor. When the followers came to clean up, they had to work hard for many hours,
but a day or two later everything was as before. The three
of them were too grand to notice; or maybe they even felt
comfortable—they liked lying around on their unmade beds,
surrounded by crumpled newspapers, opened letters and
telegrams, and the remains of some meal that had been brought
to them on a tray.

The Bari Rani hated this aspect of our lives. "It just shows
what sort of a background she comes from," she said with
that downward turn of the mouth that accompanied most of
her references to Renée. I thought what it showed was that
she had always had servants to look after her, but the Bari
Rani said "No—look at my house, and I've always had servants, not she. You come from a nice family, Harriet—how

can you bear to live like that with them? The number of times I've asked him that," she went on, referring to the Rawul. " 'How can you bear it?' I ask him. Of course he pretends he doesn't know what I'm talking about—what else can he do, poor man." She often said she pitied the Rawul, and I think in a way she did. She firmly believed that Renée had put some spell on him—given him some potion or other—she really believed it.

Bari Rani prided herself on being a modern, cosmopolitan person. She was the daughter of a rich Bombay industrialist and had gone to boarding school in England, with a year at a finishing school in Switzerland. It was there she had met the Rawul, who had come on a skiing holiday. Her family didn't care for the match—Indian royalty was pretty much played out by that time, and the Rawul wasn't very big royalty either, not compared with states like Hyderabad or Jaipur; but in the end her father had given his consent—"Daddy would do anything for me"—and they had had a big wedding in Bombay, and after that had divided their time between Bombay and London. When the Rawul had to go to his state of Dhoka, he usually went without her, because "It is such a backward place, Harriet, no civilized person can stand it."

She told me that it was in Dhoka that he had met Renée. She had come for his collection of paintings, which had been in his family for centuries, although no one, including himself, had ever cared about it. It was rediscovered, and was brought up from the storerooms where it had lain moldering for all those centuries, and Renée arranged to have it taken out of India. She had had a lot of experience getting art objects illegally out of the country—in her own luggage or in that of unsuspecting friends, or in the diplomatic bags of various embassies. "I don't want to say anything bad about her," the Bari Rani said, "but sometimes I think she is just a crook." She also thought that Renée had cheated the Rawul and had made far more than her percentage out of the sale of his paintings. "What would he know about it?" Bari Rani said. "He would be a child in the hands of a person like her"; not to speak of the potion or whatever it was she had administered to him—"It's a *fact*, Harriet"—to bind him to her will.

Because of my own situation, I understood something of

Bari Rani's attitude to her marriage. I didn't like Crishi living
downstairs with Renée any more than Bari Rani liked the
Rawul doing so, but I was willing to put up with it just as
long as I was near and kept seeing him. That was what I
waited for and was there for. At this stage, Bari Rani didn't
care about the movement any more than I did, but we were
bound to it by our feelings as firmly as everyone else was by
their beliefs. And the movement was gathering force day by
day. The Rawul's lectures in various halls were becoming
more popular and plans were made for speaking engage-
ments in other parts of the country, and for weekend courses.
The continuous stream of propaganda issuing from the office
and the Earl's Court house was beginning to have an effect;
and around this time we took what the Rawul said was a giant
step forward when Anna's article appeared in the color magazine of a Sunday paper.

It was just as well that Crishi had told me about being in
jail, or I would have had to learn about it from Anna's article.
He had told me that it was for political reasons, but that was
not what he had told her—maybe because he knew she would
put in some research and discover his record on her own;
whereas I wanted to believe everything he said. There were
other discrepancies in the versions he had given us—for instance, he had told me that his mother was Italian and his
father Assamese, but to her he had told it the other way
around. When I took it up with him, he didn't seem concerned. "Did I tell you that?" he asked. He was so pleased
with the article—they all were—that it didn't matter to him
what it said. It was the first major media exposure the movement had had, and it put him in a very good mood. When
I wouldn't let up about the discrepancies, he said "What's it
matter? As long as people read about us." "Yes but what's
true?" "It's all true." He made innocent eyes at me: "Surely
you don't think I'd tell lies?" He added "I used to, but not
after getting married to a good woman who taught me right."

I was beginning to agree with him that facts didn't matter
in his case. He had such a many-sided personality, and it was
in his nature to show different facets of himself to different
people. He had given Anna a very romantic version of his
first meeting with the Rawul. When he had come out of jail
in New Delhi, after his wrongful confinement there, his plan

was to get to Tehran, where he had friends to help him reestablish himself in business. Since he had no money, his only means of getting there was to hitch rides on trucks and as a ticketless traveler on the railways. One of these free rides had left him somewhat off course in the Rawul's state of Dhoka, and here he prepared to spend the night in a tomb he found on a hill. Anna said that everything in Dhoka was on a hill. It was a very beautiful tomb, or mausoleum, a small octagonal pillared structure open to the winds, which a fourteenth-century ancestor of the Rawul's had built for a Persian poet. Anna even gave the story of how the poet had been on a pilgrimage to Delhi, where the saint Nizamuddin held court; passing through the Rawul's kingdom, he had accepted a slice of watermelon, after which he developed a severe case of dysentery and was dead within twenty-four hours. Crishi didn't know anything about the poet, but he welcomed his tomb and, exhausted from his travels, fell asleep in it immediately. Meanwhile the Rawul was also sleeping—in his palace, on another hill. He was sleeping and dreaming. Here Anna's tone became a bit ironic—she seemed to say, Believe it or not, but anyhow it makes a good story. The Rawul's dream was that a beautiful boy had come to Dhoka and was at that moment lying asleep in the poet's tomb. This boy had been the Rawul's son in several previous incarnations, but not in the present one, where only daughters were born to him. At dawn, before anyone was up, the Rawul made his way through his palace, down the hill, across the town, up another hill, till he came to the tomb; and there he found the beautiful boy.

When the Bari Rani read this account, she was outraged and arrived at our house to brandish the magazine at the Rawul. He didn't know how to defend himself; he too had been puzzled by the publication of the story, for when Anna had questioned him about it, he had smilingly denied it and said it was just one of Crishi's jokes. All the same, she had printed it. "I didn't know you were so disappointed in our girls that you had to go and find a boy in the streets," said the Bari Rani; and the Rawul muttered "It was a misunderstanding." He looked for help to Crishi, who didn't give him any—he was pleased with himself and with the story. Renée was also pleased, but she made some attempt to rescue the

Rawul: "You know what these sort of people are; writers and people; they'll make up anything."

"Oh she made it up? Out of the air?" Bari Rani said. "Someone must have given her some information—because they do have that tomb, on one of those hills—I remember the police raided it and arrested two clerks who had set up a still for illicit liquor. That's the only thing I ever heard about happening in there. And your photograph was terrible," she said to the Rawul. "Those two came out all right, but you look years older."

"No—really?" said the Rawul and took up the magazine. Copies were strewn around the room—hundreds had been ordered. "I don't think so," he said, having studied his photograph and then himself in the mirror over the marble mantel.

"Well I do," said the Bari Rani. "People will say What's happened to your husband, haven't you been looking after him properly? You look very fat too in that picture, but that's because you *are* getting very fat—you'd better watch out and not eat so many sweet things."

"I don't," protested the Rawul. "Only when you and the girls bring all those pastries."

"I thought you like them, that's why we bring them. . . . Yes, and what about my girls? What are they going to tell their friends when they ask about all this nonsense? We'll be a laughingstock from here to Bombay for the rest of our lives. Dreams and beautiful boys asleep, who's ever heard such rubbish and lies."

"But it's what the common reader wants," Crishi said. "Ask Harriet—you liked it, didn't you? There, see, Harriet liked it and she's a very common reader. You have to give them these sort of stories."

"Every movement has to have legends," Renée said. "Look at Christ—look at Mohammed—those are very colorful stories and people have loved them for centuries."

"My goodness!" cried the Bari Rani to her husband. "Christ and Mohammed! I thought you were supposed to be this ultramodern person who didn't believe in religion."

The Rawul shut his eyes and said: "If you ever listened to anyone but yourself you would have heard me say repeatedly that the movement is a religion for a world which has outgrown religion. I'm a rationalist, through and through; a modern man; a leader for modern men, and women of course."

"You don't have to give us any speeches," said the Bari Rani, "we've all heard you, including Harriet, I'm sure, a thousand times—though what she makes of it, poor child, I can't think. *Any* of it," she said—I suppose meaning our complicated family as well as our world movement.

Unlike the rest of us, who pored over Anna's article for days, Michael only glanced at it once and threw it aside. I don't think he bothered to read what she wrote about him and me, how we were these rich uptight American kids. He dismissed everything as gossip. The story of the Rawul's dream didn't disturb him any more than the rest of it; it was all on the same level for him. And he was equally lofty or indifferent toward our unusual family situation. He never commented on the fact that he and I lived upstairs and Crishi with the others downstairs—maybe he considered it quite natural, or maybe it was too trivial for him to think about. I had heard Michael called subhuman and superhuman—strange, spaced-out, and I knew that most people, including our own parents, were uneasy with him. No one understood him, and neither did I, though that never made any difference to my feelings for him. I couldn't understand the way he kept on making these trips to Holland or Switzerland, usually with just a briefcase that Crishi gave him to carry. He accepted that his journeys were necessary for the work of the movement, so he went without question. He probably didn't even bother to ask what was in the briefcase.

He and Crishi were like brothers—well, they were brothers! Crishi had involved Michael in every aspect of the work, including what they called the military exercises. These took place in the Earl's Court house and were carried on in such secrecy that for a long time I didn't know about them. The way I found out was when Michael sprained his wrist and came home with it in a sling. At first he wouldn't tell me what had happened. That didn't surprise me, for whenever he had hurt himself, even when we were very little, he wouldn't let on. It was part of never allowing anyone to see him cry, never feeling in any way sorry for himself, or giving anyone else a chance to. He hated that worse than anything; he was so proud. But he couldn't tell a lie, and when I persisted in asking him about his wrist, he told me he had sprained it during the military exercises. He wasn't aware that I hadn't known about them. "Yes of course we have them," he answered me impatiently; "every day." "Why didn't anyone tell me?" Michael was surprised: "I thought you knew." It never struck him to keep anything secret from me, or that anyone else would want to. He told me quite openly, though not in any detail—Michael wouldn't waste time on detail—that all the followers took part in these exercises, which consisted of classes in various martial arts and learning how to handle weapons. "What weapons?" I asked. "Oh we have some," he said vaguely; "naturally, anyone who is serious about their principles has to know how to defend them. I thought you knew all that, H." "No I didn't." I tried to extract more information, but the most I could get out of him was how there weren't enough weapons to go around, so they had to take turns learning to handle them. They were taught by one of the followers who had been in some army in South America, and Michael himself was in charge of the cache of rifles, which was kept locked in a closet under the stairs. Before he took them out, the doors and windows of the house were shut and blinds drawn against the neighbors. That was all Michael would tell me—it wasn't that he didn't want me to know but that he was tired of talking, which happened quickly with him.

Crishi on the other hand was always ready to explain at great length, to talk as long as I wanted him to, but unlike Michael he wasn't ready to tell me whatever I asked. But when he saw that I had found out something for myself—as with the military exercises—he pretended he thought I had known all along. He did it this time too: "I thought you knew, Harriet," he said—the same words as Michael's but in his case untrue. He went on to reproach me for my ignorance; he said it was dumb of me not to know everyone had to learn self-defense.

"But what about me? Why can't I learn?"

"You!" He was first amused, then shocked—both reactions so exaggerated that he didn't even pretend they were real. He started in on one of his stories about how I would be sent

to a safe place in any situation of danger—"What danger?"
I asked, unheard, anyway unanswered. "Not like in the bad
old days," he went on, making one of his favorite poker faces.
"What they did was light a big fire and threw all their wives
in so they wouldn't be raped by the enemy. Aren't you glad
we're a modern movement? Or would you rather be raped?
You'd enjoy it, bet you anything. I can prove it to you," he
said, ending the conversation in the usual way between us.

Anna's article had opened so many questions for me—had
revealed so much new or contradictory information—that I
felt I had to follow it up. I wrote her a note at the magazine,
but instead of getting an answer from her, I was told by
Crishi, "Anna says you want to see her." He seemed to think
this was perfectly natural and wrote down her address for
me with instructions how to get there; in return he expected
me to accept it as perfectly natural that he and she were
seeing each other. She had given him a time when it was
convenient for her to receive me. She lived in an unexpected
place—in a salubrious suburb and in a large comfortable
family house with several children of school age. Some of
these were at home, entertaining their friends, and one was
practicing the flute. Anna made it clear that she resented
being there: It was a friend's house, and she had had no
alternative but to move in, her own place having been snatched
from her by a rapacious landlord whom she was taking to
court. She went on and on about this—she was the sort of
person for whom her own concerns loomed so large that they
swallowed up everything else. At one point a woman opened
the door without knocking and glared at both of us before
banging it shut again, giving me the impression that Anna
was not only an unhappy guest in the house but an unwel-
come one.

"They're such philistines, you have no idea," said Anna in
real despair. "They have no respect for my work at all—for
any kind of creative work. All they know is stockbroking and
housecleaning. And whenever any of my friends, Crishi or
anyone, comes to see me, they carry on as if I'm running
some sort of massage parlor in here. That's why she came
in, to check up you weren't him. Well of course he comes to
see me," she answered in wide-eyed surprise to a question I

hadn't asked. "He knows I can be useful to him, with publicity and so on—though unfortunately not with money. He's very keen on money," she said, giving me a keen look. I didn't react, and there was a pause before she went on, "When will you be twenty-one?"

"Next June."

"Oh well, that's not so long to wait. . . . I hate living in this house, I hate living in this suburb, and that's the way he hated where he grew up too."

"You wrote he grew up in London."

"Isn't that what he told you? He does have several versions; I wonder which is the one he gave you. But I know mine is correct because I checked up on it, as he knew I would. I called his mother—in Hong Kong, that's where she is now, conveniently far away. What did he tell you she was—an English model or a Burmese princess? He tried both versions out on me before giving me the correct one: She's partly Assamese, partly English—grew up in Calcutta and still has such a sweet Calcutta accent. There's no love lost between those two, I can tell you. All she did was warn me about him."

"About her own son?"

"She said he was a hopeless case; a criminal; a disgrace to her whole family, who had always been very respectable, working on the railways. I asked her about his father's family, but it's rather a dark area. He himself has several fathers to offer—one's an Indonesian jeweler, another an Italian naval officer—which one did he give you? The fact is, I think she's not sure who the father was. There must have been a lot of men. My guess is, she was very attractive—I mean, look at him. . . . She's living with someone now, a younger man, a Chinese wrestler. Well I don't know why you've come to me for information: After all, they're your family, not mine." She gave me a strange look, and then said, seriously puzzled, "Why? That's what I don't understand: why you and that brother of yours had to get mixed up in it. What is it that you want that you haven't already got? It's different for the rest of us—look at me," she said, with a pained expression at the domestic noises surging up to her door. "Not even a decent place of my own but having to put up with people who have absolutely no conception of the peace and privacy I need for my work."

She didn't put up with them much longer, for a few days afterward she moved in with us. Crishi came up one morning to Michael and my flat with a follower whom he instructed to get the third bedroom ready. "For Anna," he said to me; and to the follower: "Get some flowers in. . . . Poor thing," he told me, "we have to be very nice to her to make up for those boring people she's had to stay with." He wasn't in when Anna's luggage began to arrive—all those pieces I had seen at Propinquity, and Anna fussing at the followers who were carrying them. She looked around the flat—well, apparently it would do, if not ideal. She asked me to take away the flowers, since that particular kind gave her an allergy. As soon as she was settled and resting on her bed with pads on her eyes—"You won't make a noise, will you, Harriet? No TV or anything?"—I went in to Michael to see how he felt about our new roomate. As I might have known, he didn't feel anything; he was not disturbed by her. Michael might be alone on a mountain top, or crammed into a temple hostel with hundreds of noisy, reeking, snoring strangers; he was perfectly private everywhere. Anna couldn't impinge on him in the least. I tried to emulate him, but it was not so easy for me.

Anna took over the flat with all her habits and hang-ups, familiar from Propinquity. That didn't bother me too much —but what did was the way she sat at night waiting for Crishi. She even made out that he was coming to see her and not me; as soon as he entered, she called to him from the living room, where she was doing her nails, with a drink and watching television, and asked him where had he been, why was he late. When he left her and came with me, she called after us how selfish we were—we knew perfectly well she suffered from insomnia and how did we think she was going to amuse herself all night? It was true about the insomnia—whenever we woke up we could hear her fiddling with her TV or radio to get different stations or banging around getting more ice or soda for her drink. I would whisper to Crishi, "Why does she have to be here?" and he would say "Oh poor Anna, where else would she go—everyone else threw her out ages ago." There was plenty I could have said in reply but I hardly wanted to waste these hours when he was with me arguing over Anna.

Renée quarreled with Crishi about her—it was the first fight between them I had so far witnessed, and it showed Renée in a different light. It wasn't really a fight, because that takes two, and Crishi was not responding to her. By the time I came in on them, she was not exactly crying, but she had her handkerchief to her mouth and her eyes above them were wide open, as though she were willing them not to shed tears. Her voice, usually so low and lazy, had risen high: "Isn't it enough—don't I have enough to put up with? And now you bring that journalist, or whatever she is."

I wanted to go away, but instead Crishi said he had to be somewhere in a hurry and left her and me alone together. She didn't seem to mind that I saw her in this state. She still didn't allow the tears to fill her eyes, but she laid her head back against the sofa and gave a deep, deep sigh. She said nothing to me, made no confidences.

Anna spent several hours a day with the Rawul, and at night I could hear her transcribing her tapes. I'm not sure what the plan was—whether she was writing a book about him or helping him to write his own. While everything I have described was going on—our involved family and other relationships—he was never for a moment diverted from thinking about and developing his theories. It was at this time that he changed the name of the movement to that by which it has since become known: Transcendental Internationalism. The use of the word *transcendental* was surprising because he had always insisted on being secular and operating entirely within the limits of this world. Now he explained that the boundaries to be transcended were not spiritual but national ones, and all political forms: It was these he wished to pull down and build up anew, just as other movements had aimed at doing within the mind and/or spirit of man. Anna was useful to him, for she drew him out and guided him beyond his founding vision to some sort of statement of practical principles. Practical! Well, it might still have sounded weird to an outsider, but as was pointed out to us over and over, every revolutionary movement started off with the vision of one man who was regarded as a crank by all except a tiny nucleus of believers. I guess we were those believers.

THE RAWUL may have been influenced at this time by his contact with another, earlier movement. Some years ago this had been a worldwide movement, and its leader, Babaji, had been famous—one of the really famous Indian gurus—and had attracted so many followers, and so much money, that he had been able to establish centers in India, England, the U.S., Germany, France, Holland; everywhere. That had been in his heyday. But now he was an old man, and I guess most of his followers were old too, or middle-aged, since he didn't attract younger people anymore. One by one the centers had had to be closed, the movement had shrunk till only this one house in England remained, where he lived with two faithful followers. He was old and sick and eager to return to die in India. The one remaining house was for sale, and Crishi wanted to buy it.

I hadn't realized that he had been negotiating for this property, and only got to know about it when I had a letter from Mr. Pritchett. The mailman threw letters through a slot in the front door downstairs, and they lay there on the mat till someone came to pick them up. There were other tenants in the building, on the floors above us, but Crishi was usually the first one down; he was always expecting, and getting, a lot of mail, and anyway was too impatient to wait for someone to bring it up. But one morning I happened to be the first down. I was on my way out for a walk to get away from Anna, who had a migraine and was making demands for coffee and head massage. I found the day's letters scattered over the doormat and was about to step over them—I never expected any letters; my contacts with home were on the phone—when one of them caught my eye because it had my name on it. The envelope had the title of Mr. Pritchett's firm printed on it and I wasn't terribly interested in the contents, which I knew would be some sort of legal business. Still, I opened and skimmed over it and had just read how Mr. Pritchett was surprised at my lack of response to his previous letters when Crishi came running down the stairs to get the rest of the mail. He said "What have you got there?"

"Crishi, did Mr. Pritchett send me any letters?"

"Oh he's always sending you letters." He was down on the mat, scooping up his mail, and then he stood and flicked through it. "Usually warning you not to sign anything—he's such a tight-assed old fool, I'm just counting the days till you're twenty-one and we can get rid of him. Where were you going? For a walk—in the rain?"

"I'd rather be in the rain than upstairs with Anna."

Crishi laughed—he often said that Anna was there to teach me patience and forbearance—and opened the front door to look out. It was raining, but it was fresh and cool and much more pleasant than inside the tall dark hallway with the black-and-white marble tiles and big gilt mirror that had black spots on it from age and damp. Crishi came out with me, and we sat side by side on the top step, where we were partially sheltered by the doorway. He said "You don't mind, do you, that I've been opening your letters? They were all from that old fool."

I thought for a while—I guess I'm like Michael, and unlike Crishi, that I can't ever respond very quickly; then I said "No I don't mind. But why do you keep wanting to get money from him?"

"But of course I want to get money from him; what do you think—from anyone, from anywhere I can get it." He ground his teeth a bit—a habit of his when charged up about anything; he had these very magnificent teeth, and the effect was always striking.

"Is that why you keep going off to Holland and places? And sending Michael?"

He gave me a sideways look; his teeth were still on edge but he forced himself to smile: "Have you been brooding about that?"

"Yes," I said, quite quickly this time. "I've been scared."

"She's been scared." He took a strand of my hair and tucked it behind my ear. "Well you know you can't live without cash, not if you're in the world-movement business. And someone has to get that cash. Someone has to take risks. . . . Are you getting wet?"

"No." I was—and so was he—but it was that soft English rain, very sweet and cooling. The trees in the square were wrapped in a wet mist, and so were the passersby on this typical English morning—businessmen in business suits under black umbrellas, an Arab with his white robe trailing over the wet pavement and several shrouded women behind him, the milkman in a striped apron clattering in his little van. A policewoman in a trim uniform was going around writing down the license numbers of cars illegally parked around the square.

I said "You'll have Propinquity, and the house on the Island, as soon as we're twenty-one."

He nodded—a bit impatiently, so I felt these two properties were really not a very big deal. And it was true that, whatever they might be for a private person, they didn't count for much within the spectrum of a world movement.

He said "I got this chance for a good investment here, only where's the cash for the down payment—that's why I've been calling the old fool. I don't want you to get into any of this, sweetheart. It's tough enough for you with everything else. All of it," he added. "All of us."

"I don't mind," I said, and I didn't at that moment, sitting in the rain with him.

"I know you don't." He again tucked the strand of hair behind my ear and at the same time looked at me with such tenderness. The milkman came up the steps carrying our milk supply for the day—"A very nasty morning it is," he said but beamed as though the sun were out: I guess we looked pretty romantic, Crishi and I, sitting on the doorstep. And what Crishi was saying was romantic too: "Don't think I don't appreciate you. You being with us and everything."

"But of course I'm with you. I'm your wife, remember?"

"Oh, so you are. . . . Well that makes it even better, that you don't make these demands, wanting to eat me up—"

"I do want to eat you up."

"Only physically," he said. "Not like the others." He put both his arms around me and I stayed there, sheltered though wet. Mr. Pritchett's letter had dropped out of my lap onto the step below, where the rain fell on it and blotted the type, and then it blew off into the street and landed I think in the gutter among the dead leaves.

One day Crishi and the Rawul took me with them to the old guru's house, which they were trying to acquire. It was on the outskirts of London, even farther away than where I had gone to see Anna, and in a more rural type of suburb. The houses were larger, and each one built to someone's personal taste and specification; some were modern, others baronial or Italianate. They had big gardens with flower beds and rosebushes, and beyond the gardens there was a lot of open land, some of it with horses in it where there was a riding school, and some with picturesque streams meandering through what was almost a meadow. But the houses fronted a highway where cars whizzed constantly, along with big vans and trucks and a bus connection to the tube station. The location suited the Rawul because it was near enough to London for people to drive out for his lectures and big enough to accommodate those staying for his weekend courses.

Probably that was why the guru in his day had taken the place, for he too had attracted many visitors and followers whom he had engaged in a round of activities. But that was in the past: Now there was no trace of any kind of activity, or of what had once been a vital movement. If anything, the house resembled a nursing home—a sort of hushed tone, with everything very clean and doing the best to look like home without the nursing. The woman who opened the door for us could have been a head nurse—she looked sturdy and sensible and had brown-and-gray hair neatly bobbed. But she wore a white sari, and she introduced herself as Nina Devi, and another sari-clad woman who came clattering down the stairs as Maya Devi. Where Nina Devi was short, calm, and controlled, Maya Devi was tall, gawky, and excitable.

They showed us around the house, explaining and remin-
iscing as they did so, and often Maya Devi's voice rose so
high that Nina Devi had to shush her and glance warningly
upward, where presumably someone lay sick or resting. There
seemed to be no one else in the house; Nina Devi and Maya
Devi were the only two followers left.

They told us that they had bought the house twenty-five
years ago from the stockbroker who had built it. There were
a few fancy touches outside, including two little turrets stuck
on like stovepipes at the corners, but inside it was totally
conventional and comfortable, with parquet flooring, green
sofa sets, and a pale oak dining-room suite. They described
what had gone on in each room and there was nothing conventional about that: morning and evening meditations in
the front drawing room, daily discourses in the rear drawing
room, discussion groups with buffet refreshments in the dining room; for weekend lectures, the hall had been cleared
of its umbrella and coat stands and packed with collapsible
chairs. Babaji had been very meticulous about arrangements—everything had to be running smoothly and to an
exact schedule: "Who says Indians have no sense of time!"
cried Maya Devi, shrieking a bit so that Nina Devi had to say
"Sh," and glance up again. "He was a wonderful organizer,"
Maya Devi continued in a lowered voice. "Was?" said Nina
Devi. "Is," Maya Devi corrected herself; "I certainly had to
change my ways with him—what they couldn't teach me at
school, I learned here, from him. I was everyone's despair:
such an untidy girl, always sent off to the headmistress for
having ink spots on my uniform. 'Will you *never* learn, Alice?'
Miss Pratt used to say—I was called Alice then—well, when
I became Maya Devi I certainly learned, and double quick! . . .
But that's the way it is, isn't it?" she turned to me. "The only
teacher you can learn from is the one you love." She brought
her face close to mine, with a smile that seemed to know all
about me.

While Nina Devi was demonstrating closets and light fixtures to the other two, Maya Devi took me into a space that
may have been designed for an office but had become a
prayer room. There was a white sheet spread on a mattress
on the floor; a little shrine with a fresh flower garland and

a stick of incense burning; and a picture of what was presumably Babaji. A blind had been lowered over the only window, so it was dark in there, but Babaji glowed on the wall: Perhaps it was his bright-orange robe that made him luminous, or was it his burning eyes? I guess he was the usual kind of Indian guru, and if you believed in him you could see a mystical light in those eyes, and if you didn't, it was just cunning and cleverness. Maya Devi sat cross-legged on the mattress, facing the shrine and the picture, and she invited me to do the same. It would have been impolite to refuse, so we both gazed up at the picture, but I'm sure with different feelings. "You may pray, if you wish," she whispered to me, and did so herself; and when she had finished, she jumped up in a clumsy, coltish way, laughing and looking refreshed.

We followed the others upstairs, where Nina Devi was showing them the bedrooms. There were many of them, large ones on the second floor and a few little poky ones on the third. Maya and Nina Devi occupied two of the little ones, and the others were empty. Yet they were ready for occupancy, waiting for guests, with fresh sheets and bedspreads and bowls of flowers from the garden. The whole house was like that—empty yet ready for life, alive, with the parquet floors newly polished, the windows washed, the vases filled. The movement may have been dead, the disciples departed, but there was still a vital spark somewhere that kept everything going—including the two women, who, though in their fifties, were jolly as girls. They stopped outside one of the bedroom doors; they looked at each other—"Shall we? Should we?" They giggled, and bent down to call coaxingly, tenderly: "May we come in? May we bring you some guests?"

"Yes! Yes! Yes! Yes!"

They giggled again, and enfolded us in their conspiracy, like aunts with a special secret treat. They opened the door, and there was another bedroom with flowers and flowered curtains and a pastel carpet. This was Babaji's room, and he was lying on the big, double, double-mattressed bed: tiny, shrunken, old, and sick, wearing a saffron nightshirt with saffron nightcap on his head. "Yes," he said once more, "who is it?" and he scanned us, narrowing his eyes a little, which gave him a very shrewd look—as if those eyes were not shrewd

enough already, and bright with the vital spark that lit up
his withered form and this room and this house and I guess
the hearts of his two women.

Nina Devi introduced us, and the Rawul stepped forward,
with his hands joined together in the Indian salute. But Babaji
stretched out his two hands, inviting the Rawul to grasp and
shake them; and as the Rawul did so, it was as it had been
when he had greeted Grandfather—historic, momentous, a
meeting of two world figures. The rest of us stood in the
background, an admiring circle of courtiers—that is, Maya
and Nina Devi and I did; Crishi was going around the
room as he had done around the others, checking up on the
fixtures.

"Well now," said Babaji after this handshake. "I want
to hear all about it: all about your world movement!" His
voice was weak but high and shrill, as one used to rallying
spirits. The Rawul's voice in reply was very deep, full of
health and strength: and that was the way he appeared too,
in contrast to the spent figure on the bed. He was murmuring
modestly—praising Babaji's contribution to the world spirit,
deprecating his own. It was a statesman's courtesy, but Babaji
had no time for it—he wasn't listening, he was looking eagerly
past the stout figure of the Rawul, and spying me between
Maya and Nina Devi, he cried out "Who have we here!"

The two women smiled, again like aunts with a treat—but
now the treat was for Babaji as well as me. They pushed me
forward—they even tugged a little at my clothes to make
them fall more prettily. "Closer!" cried Babaji, and gently
their hands propelled me toward him. The Rawul stepped
aside to make room for me by the bed; I wasn't sure what
was expected of me—everyone murmured at me in encouragement, and even Crishi joined us and he too murmured
at me, in fact murmured right into my ear what it was that
was expected of me: so then it was difficult for me not to
laugh—which would have been terrible, with everyone so
reverent.

But it was Babaji who burst out laughing: "Yes! I see!" he
cried in such high glee that everyone else laughed with him,
including me. "Closer," he cried again, and I stepped up
fearlessly, and sat where he patted the side of his bed. And

he was so gentle and sweet with me, talking to me as if there
were no one else in the room, only him and me. He asked
me many questions, the sort one child might ask another—
what's your name? how old are you? where do you live? any
brothers or sisters? When I told him I came from America,
he exclaimed: "America!" as though it were truly a newfound
land; but he was that way with all my answers—everything
I told him was new, unexpected, unprecedented, exciting.
And those bright eyes roved over my face, reading everything
there was to read, taking me in, drinking me in; and in the
end he said "Those two were like you once: When they first
came to me, they were like you." And his eyes wandered
from me to Maya and Nina Devi, who stood there beaming
(but were there tears in Maya Devi's eyes?). Babaji's glance
fell on Crishi, he pointed his finger, he said "Who's that?" I
told him—"My husband," I said—whereupon Babaji's mood
changed, and again like a child, or a very old man, he made
no attempt to disguise it. "I'm tired," he sulked. "You'd
better go."

Nina Devi turned out to be a tough businesswoman—well,
she had to be; she was in charge of whatever funds were left
and had to meet their expenses out of them and see to Babaji's
comforts. She wasn't going to let the house go below its market price, although Crishi tried every way to make a deal.
But since he couldn't for the moment meet her price—and
wouldn't be able to do so till our birthday next June—they
came to a compromise: that for the next few months they
would move up to the top story, while we took over the rest
of the house and its expenses. The Rawul began to give his
weekend courses there, and we usually moved to the house
on Fridays to be ready to receive the twenty or so students
who would be arriving the next morning. Renée came with
us, to help Crishi with the practical arrangements for the
weekend, but she would depart as soon as possible because
she couldn't stand the suburban atmosphere, she said. When
she left, Crishi and I stayed in one of the three attic rooms,
next to Babaji and the women in the other two. The Rawul
slept in what had been Babaji's room—that is, the principal
bedroom—and when she consented to stay, Renée would be
there with him and so would Crishi for at least part of the

night. I always hoped she would leave, though usually there was a fight because she wanted Crishi to go with her. Sometimes he did, sometimes he didn't. Of course I was very happy when he stayed; I loved those nights with him in the little attic room, shushing each other so that Babaji wouldn't hear us.

But Renée was passionately angry when she had to go off on her own, and she stayed angry through the week when we rejoined her in the London flat. She would quarrel with me and say I was keeping Crishi away from his work, and when I pointed out to her that on the contrary his work was with the weekend course, not here with her in London, she would flare up tempestuously. Then she appeared very Oriental, with those flashing eyes full of dark feelings, and I thought of the stories of intrigue and poison and other hidden deeds taking place in the harem. But invariably, after one of her outbursts of hate, she became extra sweet to me, coaxing and loving and giving me little presents—though as she slipped one of her bangles on my arm, I thought of those stories even more. The Bari Rani was constantly warning me against her, hinting at things she knew and I didn't, and working me up to assert my rights; and there were the tensions between her and Renée, older and more intense than those between Renée and me, and these too alternated with periods of affection too cloying to be sincere, and with periods of a sort of relaxed harmony that *was* sincere, born of the mutual interests that keep a family together.

When Crishi did go back with Renée, I was left upstairs with Babaji and Maya and Nina Devi. I was amazed by their cheerfulness—I mean, here they were reduced to living in the attic, after having been the center of a movement much larger than ours. But far from resenting our usurpation, they took an intense interest in everything that went on in the house. When the weekend students arrived on Saturday mornings, Nina and Maya Devi would be hanging over the top banister to watch them. They kept Babaji's door open so that they could report to him everything that was happening, and if they were too slow in doing so, he called out to them impatiently. They thought it a great privilege to attend the Rawul's lectures and discussion groups, and without feeling

entitled to join in, they sat there attentively with their hands
folded in their laps. Nina Devi was always very polite when
she commented on what she had heard. "*So* interesting," she
would say, and added "Fascinating," in case anyone felt she
hadn't said enough. Yet I knew she had her reservations
about the Rawul's movement, which was so different from
their own. It was Maya Devi who sometimes voiced these
reservations—"Yes," she would say, "but there has to be
something more; something else." Nina Devi wouldn't allow
her to say anything further—she didn't feel they had the
right to criticize—but Maya Devi was too impetuous to be
able to keep her strong ideas to herself. She would come into
my room—this was when Crishi had left with Renée—and
sit cross-legged on my bed and talk about the old days, and
Babaji, and everything he had meant to them.

Although theirs had been a religious and transcendent
movement—I guess ours was political and immanent—they
had had a lot of worldly fun. There had always been something to celebrate, like Babaji's birthday or some great date
either in the Hindu calendar or in the history of the movement, which had given them an excuse to perform great feats
of vegetarian cooking and put up banners and garlands and
strings of lights; and always there was music and singing—
such *singing*! Here Babaji, who was listening from his room
next door, would burst into a sample for my benefit: in his
cracked old high voice but with leaps and jumps of joy in it,
and Maya Devi would clutch my arm and whisper "There—
that's what I mean." God knows what he was singing, but it
was uplifting—I mean, it did seem to ascend to some strange
heights I hadn't known about. And perhaps it was an echo
from those heights, or some fragrance of whatever it was that
grew up there, that lingered on in the house and insinuated
itself into the Rawul's teaching.

The Rawul's audience here was different from what it had
been under the tree at Propinquity. For one thing, it was a
paying audience, and the fees were high. I had heard Crishi
and Renée arguing about how high they should be—Renée
protesting that they wouldn't sign up for so much and Crishi
overruling her, saying "They'll pay, they'll pay." He had
been right, but it did mean that the students were eager to

get everything they could out of their weekend, by way of food for thought. In any case, they were very serious people, educated and thoughtful. Most of them were English—it's strange that the largest conglomeration of English people I met in London was in this suburban house that the Rawul had taken over from Babaji. At Propinquity, after the Rawul's lectures, everyone sat silent and inspired, or if any questions were asked, it was usually Lindsay who asked, or Sonya when she had been there, and they hadn't been difficult for the Rawul to answer. But here they were often too technical for him—about forms of government and economic tariffs and that sort of thing, which he didn't know too much about. It was from this time on that we began to have academic types around—Crishi found them, and attracted them to the movement. That was his way—when he needed someone he attracted them, by charming and I guess inspiring them, even people you wouldn't think could be charmed and inspired. Anyway, these experts were there on the dais with the Rawul—an economist, a sociologist, a professor of political science—and after the Rawul had given his address and the questions began, they were there to answer them in a professional way.

This left the Rawul free to concentrate on his own ideas and philosophy, which as I've said were beginning to change. It was now that he first used the term *transcendental internationalism*, and when asked if this had any religious or metaphysical connotation, he would answer something like this:

"No! No, my dear friends! Not that 'other world' the theologians have been fooling us with but *another* world! We too aim to transcend the world—this sorry wanting place of separate nationalities, countries, and continents—but transcending in the sense of transforming it into a new, a stateless, casteless, countryless one: not to leave this earth for heaven but to make heaven on earth, if you'll pardon my use of fairy-tale lingo."

Up to this point, he was more or less saying the same thing as before; but from here on, he lowered his voice, became more questioning, even diffident, as he continued:

"And why is it—I ask myself, I ask you—why is it that men have always used this language? Why have there always been

terms like *heaven,* like *gods,* like *God?* What have we men been
seeking beyond being men? Is it to be something better than
men? To transcend ourselves as we are—to reach new heights
within as well as outside ourselves?"

Crishi was usually too busy to be present at these lectures;
but once when he happened to come in when the Rawul was
talking about being better than men, Crishi asked Renée:
"What's he on about?" She shrugged. I had noticed this about
both of them, Crishi and Renée—they didn't care what the
Rawul said as long as he had an audience to say it to. That
was their business—getting the audience; getting houses and
money; getting the movement going. The actual content of
the movement was left to the Rawul, and he was completely
free to think it out for himself. Although he was surrounded
by so many people—all of us, and the followers, and the
professors, and the students, and Anna and other journalists,
and members of other political groups—there was an aura
of aloneness about him, as though he were still by himself in
the rocky desert of his kingdom, his eyes absorbing the color
of the sky as he looked up at it for inspiration. Maybe it is
so with all world leaders—that ultimately, at the center of
their movement, they are alone and lonely.

I noticed that he often came up to Babaji's little attic room
next to mine. Whenever he had a free moment between
lectures and other activities, he would tap timidly on Babaji's
door. He wasn't always admitted. Babaji would cry out: "Who
is it?" and when the Rawul identified himself, he might say:
"I'm sleeping! Go away!" The Rawul wouldn't argue but would
humbly leave, though often Nina Devi took pity on him and
let him come in her room. There she made cocoa for him
on the little portable stove on which they did all their cooking,
and she explained to him about Babaji, how he could understand and help you even without actually admitting you
into his presence. But sometimes Babaji did admit the Rawul,
and I heard them talking—or rather, Babaji talking: He used
strange terms, like *Adhibhautika,* which he said was the cos-
mological dimension, and *Adhyatmika,* the anthropological dimension; and later I would hear the Rawul use these terms
in his lectures and give his explanations of them.

I have to admit that Babaji was more interested in me than

in the Rawul. He liked it that I was next door to him and often called through the wall to make sure I was there. When Crishi was with me, it was no use trying to keep our sex low-key because Babaji heard every sound—avidly listened for it—and was not above shouting encouragement to us. Often he sang, some pure song of joy, which made Crishi laugh but at the same time grind his teeth. Babaji never called Crishi in to see him the way he did me; when I asked him why not, Babaji said "Oh, I've seen plenty like him." I said "But you've seen plenty like me too." "Oh yes! Plenty!" he cried. "But never enough." He loved nothing better than to tell me about all the girls who had come flocking to him; leaving behind their parents, friends, lovers, husbands, they had followed him around the world, clad in orange saris, sandals, and with his picture on a medal around their necks. And it had been so easy for him, fatally easy. Sitting cross-legged on his bed in his nightshirt and nightcap, he described to me how he had sat on his throne in his audience chamber while new girls were led up to him, one by one. All he had to do was look at them, into them, and at once they threw themselves, literally, at his feet; and he touched them ever so lightly with his peacock fan on their bowed backs, and from that moment on they were his. "It doesn't work anymore," he said, ruefully though not regretfully. "How do you know?" I asked. "It's not working with you," he said; he shut one eye in a roguish way and said "You want to try?" I agreed, and he looked what I guess was deep into me—and he was right—it didn't work. Once he called Maya Devi in to give a demonstration: He asked for his peacock fan and she brought it, and then she prostrated herself by his bed and he touched her with it the way he had described to me. He winked at me over her back, and he and I both laughed; and when she got up, Maya Devi laughed with us but there was such radiance in her face—well, I wondered, would that still be there on my face after Crishi and I had been married for thirty years?

Michael didn't come for the weekend courses but was there during the week, when the rest of us had gone back to the London flat. I had never in my life seen so little of him, or perhaps I mean been so far from him, although we belonged to the same organization and were closest to the same person—that is, Crishi. We no longer looked alike either. In the past, people had often commented on our resemblance, but Nina Devi said to me, "Your brother doesn't look like you at all." Maya Devi confirmed this. They saw Michael quite often when he and the other followers came there during the week for the martial exercises, which they held in this house, it being less conspicuous than the Earl's Court one. They shut the doors and windows and drew the curtains and asked Maya and Nina Devi to stay up in the attic with Babaji and not come out to watch. "We don't want to watch," Maya Devi said with a hint of complaint in her voice, which made Nina Devi say "No dear, we must let them do what *they* think right." "But in this house," Maya Devi said in a more complaining way, "with Babaji here—who would never even wear violent shoes." They explained to me that violent shoes were made from animals killed for their hide, whereas Babaji would wear only those made from animals who had died a natural death. "And do you know where they keep their guns and things?" Maya Devi said. "In the prayer room," she said, choking back her outrage. "No," said Nina Devi, "it's not our prayer room anymore. We pray upstairs." "But it used to be! A sacred place." "Oh—sacred," said Nina Devi. "Any place can be made that if you do something good in it." She smiled to reassure me that the matter was not serious enough for me to worry about it.

But I did mention it to Crishi and Michael—and they both dismissed it, in their different ways. Crishi said "Oh isn't that terrible," clicking his tongue in pity before adding "but then why the hell don't they get out and leave the house to us." "They can't, Crishi," I said. "You know they can't—not till you get the money to pay them." "Oh yes the money," he said. "We're all waiting for the money. Your fault: Why can't you have your birthday now instead of June?" It was useless talking to him.

And for once talking with Michael was useless too. It turned out he hated Babaji—"All that stuff: the incense and the nonviolent shoes and the sublimated sex. It's rotten," he said. "Soft and rotten." His face took on a contorted, harsh expression that I didn't like to see, and he knew I didn't. He defended himself: "They're so fanatical, you have no idea."

"But don't you have to be?" I asked. "If you truly believe in something?" "Of course," he said; "but what you believe in has to be the truth, not made-up lies like theirs." There was no point in arguing with him; he was so proud and sure. Maybe that's why we had begun to look different from each other, for there was nothing I was sure about. If he resembled anyone now, it was the other followers—and not only because he wore the same clothes and had his hair cropped close to his head: It was something in his bearing too, something rigid and trained. This was probably due to the martial exercises they practiced; but how to account for the change in his eyes—no longer the far-seeing seafarer's eyes he had inherited from Grandfather and Manton, but more like the other followers', unblinking and almost blank in deadly certainty.

CRISHI still often called me to meet him in Rupert's gallery, and I dropped in on my own too, to see Rupert. Since discovering he had been married to Renée, I regarded him as a member of our very extended family. The way I felt about this family was that some members of it I liked better than others, but in any case there we all were. I certainly liked Rupert, and even felt a sort of bond with him, maybe because he was the only one besides me who didn't seem to be confident about anything. Even in his gallery he looked as if he didn't know why he was there. I often wondered why he was—he wasn't the type to run any kind of business; and in fact he didn't—he left everything to his partner, Nicholas. There were frequent parties at the gallery, and while everyone was shouting darling at each other, Rupert sort of hovered about, looking apologetic when he took anything off the trays the waiters were carrying around. The gallery was on two floors, one of them a basement with the tiniest little cubbyhole tucked away in it, and this served as Rupert's office. It was a hiding place as much as an office—that was what I used it for during these parties, and sooner or later Rupert would join me. It was there that he told me about Renée and himself and other things he didn't usually talk about. He kept interrupting himself—"Is this boring you?" Sometimes other people would come in to ask about some picture on display, and when he went out with them to look at it, he stood there swaying on his heels, not knowing what to say but too polite not to show interest, till Nicholas came bustling up to rescue both him and the potential buyer.

Rupert had met Renée in India. It had been his first visit, though his family had an association with the country going back to the eighteenth century. He had gone to visit his brother Tom, who had joined a kind of mission there—he was a priest but he didn't work to relieve people's religious needs so much as their physical ones. There were a lot of physical needs in India, Rupert said and fell silent and looked down into his glass reflectively. At this point someone came to ask him about a picture, and I saw him go through his usual routine in front of it, till Nicholas took charge. Rupert certainly knew about the picture, but he was too reticent to air his views. When he came back and it was only me, he talked about it knowledgeably and made me go and see it with him. I had seen hundreds like it—in the gallery and with Indian dealers who brought them to the flat. This one showed a prince in pearls, turban, and silk tunic entertaining his beloved at a picnic, both of them sitting on a carpet with maidens at hand playing musical instruments; in the foreground were tiny delicate dishes and flasks, along with the flowers in the meadow, and in the background a palace that had open doors and windows and all sorts of goings-on inside, and behind that there was a stream and you could see the fish in it and above it blue rain clouds and cranes flying through them. I don't know what it was that made these pictures so erotic, so charged with something exciting and delicious about to happen. Rupert felt it too; and talking about the picture, he told me that it was in just this sort of place and atmosphere—very different from his brother Tom's mission in Meerut—that he had met Renée. He had been invited to a palace in Saurashtra by one of the princes, who had gone to school with him; Renée was there too—she traveled from palace to palace in her search for treasures to buy and sell.

From the moment he met her, Rupert kept on following her around, and she let him. She involved him in her business too, and he helped her get things out of India, either by carrying them himself or through people he knew in various embassies. Although she had many contacts herself, high and not so high, she made him follow up every one of his, and when they returned to England, he introduced her to his friends and acquaintances, even those he hadn't seen in years. She was at that stage of her career when anyone at all might be useful to her. Although they went in and out of India constantly, he did not see as much of his brother Tom as he would have liked because Renée's business kept them so occupied. She was having visa trouble in India as well as residency difficulties in the U.K.—she held the wrong sort of passport from her first marriage—but that was taken care of after she married Rupert. At that time Rupert still had the house in Yorkshire, which had been in his family since the seventeenth century. He could afford to live in only a part of one wing, but had struggled to keep the place, especially as Tom had liked to come there on his leave from India every three years. But Renée could not bear it—it was impossibly cold, lonely, and dreary for her, and far from everywhere she had to be. Not long after their marriage she put it on the market and got a very good price from a Lebanese businessman in need of an English country place. With the proceeds, she bought the gallery and brought Nicholas in to manage it. She had known Nicholas for some time; he too was connected with the art world and he and Renée had sometimes been able to help each other out over some deal. He was energetic, and shrewd, and perfectly able to run the gallery on his own; but after Renée had got together with the Rawul and Crishi and had divorced Rupert, Rupert had involved himself more in the gallery—not because he was its nominal owner but to remain in constant touch with Renée.

Some time after Rupert had told me this at one of the gallery parties, the trouble with the police started—in fact, it started at another party there. Someone who did not look like a guest came to speak with Nicholas. He was not obtrusive, and I don't think anyone else noticed; probably I wouldn't have noticed either if Nicholas had not come into the cubbyhole where Rupert and I had taken refuge. Nicholas, who looked pale and tense, told me to go out—he was very brusque, but Rupert said "Would you mind awfully, Harriet? For a minute?" The man smiled at me and said "If you'll excuse us, miss." They shut the door behind me. I was trapped in

the middle of the party, among these strangers who had such
a lot to say to one another; but as I stood there wedged
between several lively groups shouting across me to each
other, Crishi came up, and looking toward the closed door
of Rupert's office, asked me what was going on in there.
When I told him about the man talking to Rupert and
Nicholas, Crishi signaled to Renée—it had struck me before
how easily, wherever they were and however many people
there were between them, these two managed to communicate with each other. She made her way across to us and he
said something to her I couldn't hear. There were too many
people clamoring for their attention for any discussion between them, but when they were swept apart, they kept up
their secret communication, both of them electrically aware
of the door opening and the man emerging.

He left quietly, raising his hat to me and apologizing for
having taken me away from my friends. Crishi and Renée
came over to me immediately to ask what he had said to me;
then they went into the room with Rupert and Nicholas. I
stayed outside waiting. The party had drawn to its close, only
a few stragglers were left looking around for hosts to say
good-bye to. Crishi and Renée came to the door occasionally
and so did Rupert, though Nicholas, who was usually the
most affable and visible host, stayed inside the office. Soon
the gallery was empty except for me and the caterer's men
packing and cleaning up. There were loud arguments inside
Rupert's office; I could hear Nicholas sounding very shrill
and almost hysterical, but Rupert's voice was as calm as
Crishi's. And when at last they came out, they looked as they
had sounded—Rupert and Crishi as they always were, but
Nicholas seemed to have shrunk in size and authority. His
smooth confidence had gone and he was shouting: "I'm not
responsible! You can't say I am! It's not my responsibility."
Renée and Crishi ignored him—"Ready, Harriet?" Crishi
said to me, as usual, as if it were I who had kept him
waiting—but Rupert was concerned about Nicholas and reassured him: "Of course not, of course you're not; I am."

And that was how it was arranged: Rupert was responsible.
The case built up very slowly, and it was never clear to me
what it was about, and I doubt whether Rupert understood

either. Some years ago there had been a series of major thefts from an Indian museum, and the Indian police, working through Interpol, had traced some of the missing items to Rupert's gallery. Well, it *was* his gallery and he was responsible for what was in it, however it may have got there. And since there was a lot of unpleasant publicity including headlines in the evening papers—like PEER'S SON IN MAJOR INDIAN ART THEFT—it was better that Rupert's name should come up rather than Renée's or Crishi's, which would have been embarrassing for the movement. Crishi was more upset than he wanted anyone to know. Actually, he never did show it when he was upset—only if you knew him well, you would notice him becoming even more cheerful and energetic than usual, with the tiniest frown between his eyebrows and that habit he had of setting his teeth on edge so you couldn't tell if he was smiling or what.

At this time he got in a fight with one of the Indian dealers, whom I guess he held responsible for getting everyone in this trouble. I had seen the man before—at least, I think it was he, although there were several of them looking more or less alike, all plump and brown and middle-aged in tight-fitting suits, with shiny shirts, neckties, and rings. They brought pictures and, with a tender smile, unwrapped them like babies out of linen covers. That was what this man was doing —smiling, delicately unwrapping—when suddenly, without warning, in a tiger's leap, Crishi jumped him. It was a horrible scene, but at the same time a bit comic—the way the expression on the man's face changed, and he cried out the Hindu names of God, several of them, while Crishi was crying out these vile Hindu abuses. Crishi couldn't speak any Indian language well, but he was fluent in the curses, some of which he had taught me for a joke and maybe for excitement, because they all involved female genitals and so on. The man lay on his back on the carpet, his stomach rising like a dome; he begged for mercy, but Crishi didn't have any. There was nothing comic now; I was reminded of the time when I had seen him kicking Paul in the orchard at Propinquity. The Rawul, who couldn't stand violence, had left the room, but Renée watched with her arms folded. I went out too because I didn't want to see what was being done to the man, nor

Crishi doing it. Besides, I had Robi with me, hiding his face against me.

Robi was Renée and Rupert's son, who usually stayed with Rupert. After Rupert was in trouble and kept having to make court appearances and even had to spend some time in prison before bail was granted, Robi was brought to live with us. That was all right, except that he and Renée made each other terribly nervous. She was forever finding fault with him for making too much noise or not eating his food, and when as a result he became very timid in her presence, she accused him of being a dull, dispirited child. She was watching him all the time, couldn't take her eyes off his face; and if she wasn't scolding him, she might suddenly seize him and hold him close to her and kiss him as though devouring him, and that frightened him more than anything. He preferred to be with me, and he slept upstairs too, and I took him to school and brought him home. I enjoyed waiting outside with the mothers to be claimed by him when he came running out in his striped cap and socks. To get away from Renée, we often went to the other house, to the Bari Rani and the girls. He was completely accepted there, like a little brother, and everyone fussed over him, combing his hair, kissing him, making him open his mouth to count his teeth. He ran in and out of the rooms, even when the girls were dressing; and when their friends came, he wouldn't go to bed but fell asleep in a chair in the middle of the party. He was like a little Indian boy—even in appearance, he didn't seem to have got anything from his English father. This hadn't struck me till Bari Rani pointed it out—more than once. She was always returning to the subject, asking whom did I think he looked like. Well actually, though he had Renée's coloring, he didn't look like her either, but it could hardly be expected that a timid frail little boy should resemble such a tigress. "How old is he now?" Bari Rani would ask me—she knew he was six better than I did, for she had been around when he was born. They had already been a sort of family at the time, including Crishi, who had appeared among them some two years before that. Sometimes Bari Rani suggested that he resembled Crishi—although of course, she added, it might be just the coloring, the faintly olive skin of someone partly Oriental.

"Don't you think he's small for his age?" she said. "And with such a tall father—Rupert must be over six feet. Poor Rupert," she ended up. "What have they got him into?"

Robi often fell asleep in my bed, and I would study and study his face—you couldn't say he looked like Crishi and you couldn't say he didn't. But I liked to pretend that he *was* Crishi's—that is, Crishi's and mine. When I told Crishi that, he laughed and said "I hope you're not getting any ideas." But he was very passionate with me during these days. I was beginning to notice that whenever he was particularly worried about anything, he would want to make a tremendous amount of love at night. It was as though he wanted to forget everything and just become this body pouring himself into sex. He came up every night; he never failed me. Robi was asleep by that time, and Crishi would pick him up and take him into another room. He never bothered to do this gently and often Robi woke up and began to cry, the way children do when suddenly awakened. But when he opened his eyes and saw it was Crishi carrying him, he became quiet at once. The truth was, he was afraid of Crishi, even more than of Renée; and I also have to say that I have seen Crishi strike Robi—for almost nothing really. If Robi asked a question during some grown-up conversation, Crishi without hesitation would slap his face, very hard and not at all the way one would slap a child. Robi dared not even cry out and Crishi didn't glance at him, but continued talking as though no interruption had taken place.

Whenever Crishi came upstairs and especially after he began appearing so regularly, Anna made her usual fuss. First she tried to keep him talking with her, using all the delaying tactics she could: and when he left her at last and was with me, she began to play her tapes very loudly, or turned the TV up and laughed ostentatiously at what she saw there. She also woke up Robi and made him sit and watch TV with her and engaged him in long loud conversations—only they weren't conversations—they were monologues to be overheard by us, for she couldn't stand children, had no time for them at all. "How much longer is he going to be here?" she asked me about Robi. It was exactly the same question I asked Crishi about her, while the two of us lay in the dark and she made all the noise she could in the next room. He said not much longer, then he said she had to be there because of her work with the Rawul, then he said, "What difference does it make to you?" Well, I guess it didn't make all that much—after all, he was here with me, in my bed, it was he and I making love while she watched TV.

Renée began to do something she hadn't done before— she came up during the day, when Crishi was not there. Although she had a reason—that is, Robi—she came mostly when Robi was at school, and if he wasn't, she sent him away to another room so that she and I could be alone together. If Anna was there, she ignored her completely; she wanted to be only with me. She came into my room and sat on the bed and sighed and stroked the pillow and turned it around and stroked the other side. She was very gentle with me, and friendly and open. She confided in me—but in a sort of general way: about being a woman, and getting older, and losing so much of what was dearest to you. It was as if she wanted me to pity her. But how could I: someone so strong and beautiful. She said "I don't expect you to understand, Harriet—I wouldn't have understood at your age when I still thought I could have everything I wanted, anytime I wanted it."

I said "I don't think that." And I didn't; and in any case all I wanted was Crishi, and I couldn't have him anytime I wanted—I hardly needed to tell her that.

But she hadn't come up to talk about me. She said "Everyone thinks I'm so strong and can stand anything. I suppose it's because I don't complain and whine and try not to show what I feel. But I do feel," she said and raised her magnificent eyes to me, so that I could see them brimming with emotion. I was standing while she sat on the bed; she tried to make me sit beside her but I wouldn't. As it was, she was too close to me. In addition to her usual overpowering physical effect that filled any room she was in, she was giving out these emotional waves—giving them out deliberately, willing me to feel for her. What was she asking me, what did she want? She was still stroking the pillow, now one side now the other, until, overcome, she flung herself down and buried her face in it. It gave me a strange sensation to see her large figure

on my bed—on our bed, on Crishi's and mine; and then I
realized she was thinking of that—of how he and I were on
this bed together—and it was a torment for her.

When she sat up again, she said "You wouldn't know about
it, Harriet. You've never had to fight for anything but I've
had to, for every single little thing. When you've had to do
that, then you hold on to it, for all you're worth. You just
hold on to it," she said and closed her hand with the long
red wonderful nails into a fist. It sounded like a threat, but
she was smiling at me, and coaxing me again to sit beside
her. When I did, not too close, she began to play with my
hair, which was open and hanging around my shoulders and
down my back. "We belong together, Harriet," she said, smiling, tender as one friend with another. "We all of us need
one another. I need you. . . . Look at you, how you're shrinking from me when I touch you, even this little bit?" She
touched my knee very, very lightly—I didn't exactly shrink,
but I did sort of contract within myself, as if shielding myself.
"You're so closed," she said, in sorrow and not anger. "I've
given you so much—given up so much—and you give me
nothing in return—not even pity, nothing." Her voice had
sunk very low but suddenly she raised it: "Oh I shouldn't be
asking you! I should be too proud to ask you!" She was
holding my hair again, and for a moment I thought she was
tightening her grip on it, to wind it into a rope to drag me
along. But with an effort of self-control, she let go, she got
up and went out of the room, out of the flat. I could hear
her strong tread on the stairs, like a giant walking there.

Shortly after this she came up for the first time at night,
when Crishi was with me. As before, she sat on our bed and
she and Crishi talked in a desultory way. They didn't have
much to say to each other, and I wondered why she had
come. But she didn't go away even when they had run completely out of conversation; and it began to dawn on me that
she didn't mean to leave but to stay with us; and that was
what she had been asking me. Into the silence that had fallen
I said "Oh no." "It'll be all right, sweetheart," Crishi said.
"Really it will." He took me in his arms, but I knew that over
my shoulder he was looking at her; they had already reached
complete accord. It was she who got up from the bed and

turned off the light. We could hear Anna's TV going, and Anna laughing at it too loudly, making sure that we knew she was there. Michael was home too, reading in his room, into which Crishi had carried Robi; so we were all there, and the only one who was asleep was Robi. But although the rest of us were awake and aware, the next day nothing was said by anyone; no, not even by Crishi and me, although I was determined that before the next night I would speak to him and not let it happen again. I took Robi to the Bari Rani, and all that day I wandered around by myself, in various parks, walking and walking under the trees. I felt so hot— heated, burning, a sort of burning sensation inside me, under my skin, so that the rain and breezes passing over me were unable to cool me. The phrase "burning with shame" kept on coming into my mind. It got late and dark, but I wasn't tired and I didn't want to go home. When I did, only Michael was there. I went in his room, and I lay on the other side of his bed with my feet resting against his shoulder, while he went on turning the pages of his book. We didn't speak, but it was not our usual silence of communion. In fact, I felt him willing me not to speak—that is, not to speak of last night. All the time I was tensed away from him, and when the phone rang, I knew it had been in that direction that my senses were strained.

Crishi said "Where have you been? Come quick, we're waiting." Michael and I took a taxi to the restaurant—and there they all were, a big family party, including the other household, the Bari Rani's, who had brought Robi with them. It was the Rawul's favorite Indian restaurant, done up in Edwardian Bombay style, with carved screens and tall palms in golden pots. Our party was in an alcove, at a round table with a pierced brass temple lamp throwing a dappled light over it. They had begun eating, and everyone had a round gold tray with many little gold dishes on it, of curries and condiments. There were already so many of them around the table that it seemed there couldn't be any more room; but they easily fitted in Michael and me, and we slipped into the places they made for us, mine beside Crishi. The girls were coaxing Robi to eat; he sat between Daisy and Priti and each was trying to insert some morsel into his mouth. Crishi did the same for me—he tore off a piece of chapati and scooped some vegetable up in it and coaxed me the way they were doing with Robi; only Crishi was more successful, for I opened my lips to him much sooner; he was pleased and did it again and again, morsel after morsel, and I let him. It was a complete reconciliation between us—or rather, a complete reconciliation for me because it was I who had felt estranged, not he at all. Across from us, Renée sat beside the Rawul, and sometimes she smiled at us in a benevolent, maternal way to see Crishi feeding me; but mostly she was too busy eating, as was the Rawul—both of them Indian-style with their fingers, skillfully and with delicate greed scooping inside the golden bowls. The waiters in turbans and red cummerbunds hovered behind them, ready to refill the bowls. The Bari Rani, on the other side of the Rawul, warned him that he would get too fat, but when a waiter wasn't quick enough, she would herself gesture impatiently toward the Rawul's emptying tray. She also complained about some of the dishes, that there was not enough ginger or too much, and argued with the girls, and scolded Robi for not eating —how would he ever grow, she said and appealed around the table that wasn't he too small for his age, and with such a tall father? It was our usual sort of evening, and it ended in the usual way, with the two households going to their separate establishments. Crishi came to the upstairs flat, and although I had meant to talk to him about the night before, there was no opportunity for it; but I thought, If she comes up again, if she comes up now, I won't let her. But in fact she didn't, not that night nor for several nights after; and when she did come again, they both acted as though it were entirely natural and expected. By the third time, it had become for me if not natural then not as unnatural as that first time; that burning-with-shame sensation also subsided, for what shame could there be when everything was in the dark? During the day no one spoke of it, so it remained as secret as any sexual act, unmentioned rather than unmentionable.

IT was at this time that Manton and Barbara came to London. I hadn't been aware that I had missed them or anyone from home, but when I saw them, I couldn't help it, I burst into tears—of joy, I guess. Barbara was embracing me in welcome; she was so soft and fragrant and familiar, I didn't want to let go of her. I clung to her, and she held me; but she was shocked. She said "But what's the matter, what happened?" for she was not used to me crying—I mean, I never did and if I had to, I made sure no one saw me. But now I couldn't help it. Barbara was the opposite of me—she cried at the drop of a hat, and she wasn't about to lose this opportunity; and Manton was considerably affected to see the two of us weeping away—he put his arms around both of us and also spilled a tear or two. That made me laugh, but they both remained sad and serious. Barbara kept on asking "But what's the matter? Are you ill? What's wrong?" However much I protested that I was fine, that I was well, that I was happy, they didn't believe me. Barbara even wanted to go with me to a doctor because she said I had lost so much weight. I wasn't aware that I had, and I also didn't like her suggestion that what was growing inside me was a sickness and not the flower of my happiness unfolding.

I spent as much time as I could with them. They had established themselves in a suite in one of the more famous London hotels—I thought it was very musty and uncomfortable but they loved it. Barbara adored everything in London, now that she was here with Manton; in the past she had come as part of her mother's entourage and all they had ever done was sit around in their hotel, entertaining movie people and financiers and having interviews and photo sessions, so that they had been too tired to go out and just had room service sent in at midnight. But she and Manton did every kind of London thing, and as soon as I had left Robi at school, I joined them in some museum or shopping in Harrods, or getting Manton's shirts and shoes made. Sometimes I brought Robi with me—he was no trouble and they liked him, although Manton would look at him and ask me: "Whose is he?" I told him several times, but he never seemed to understand; maybe it was too complicated. They also found our household arrangements very complicated. Everyone wanted to do what was proper, so they came to visit us in the flat downstairs—I didn't tell them about upstairs but let them believe that Crishi and I stayed downstairs with the Rawul and Renée, which was strange to them but not as strange as the truth might have been. They joined us at the Indian restaurant and met the other household, but that evening wasn't a success. Manton and Barbara looked and felt very odd in the middle of our family. They didn't merge at all the way the rest of us did but sat there upright and uncomfortable on the brocade settees. Besides, neither of them could stand Indian food—it made them sick to their stomachs next day.

There were Barbara's feelings about Crishi that she had expressed to me before our marriage, and though she never spoke of him after it, I knew very well how she felt. So did he, and he never tried to charm or change her in any way, but simply accepted her antipathy, almost as though he were used to certain people disliking him and there was nothing he could or would do about it. I tried to be equally indifferent—but it was difficult for me never to speak with Barbara about him, when we spoke about everything else. If his name came up during our conversations—and it inevitably did since he was what he was to me, that is, the central fact of my life—Barbara wouldn't look at me and fell silent, afraid of what she might say, or remembering what she had said in the past. But I was longing to tell her that I was entirely happy, especially when she started in again about me looking ill. I laughed when she said that and told her, "Just because I'm not fat like you." All the same, I did look at myself more carefully in the mirror when I was alone in the flat upstairs. I couldn't make out any change—I had always been thin and with a tendency to shadows under my eyes, ever since I was fourteen; Michael and I both.

They didn't have to tell me Michael had changed; I could see that for myself. He made Manton and Barbara very uncomfortable whenever they met him. But this happened rarely, for Michael was always elsewhere—with the followers in the house in Earl's Court, at Babaji's house, in the Mayfair office, or on an overnight trip somewhere on the continent of Europe. He was completely involved in the work of the movement and had even less time for his father than before. But it turned out that, besides having a vacation in London with Barbara, Manton was here to speak to us on two matters of family concern. One of these he left it to Barbara to tell me, over a favorite occasion of hers—English afternoon tea in their hotel. Here she and I sat on seats that were covered in buttoned velvet but had straight backs to make you sit upright while the waiters filed past to serve you from their trays. Each alcove held a group of foreign guests, everyone on their best behavior, backs straight, conversation subdued, some of the women in formal little hats, everyone attentive to the waiters, who, though foreign themselves, kept to the strict routine of an English nursery tea. "Isn't it adorable," Barbara said over her anchovy-paste sandwich; and then she told me that she was pregnant and that she and Manton were planning to be married. It was not a place to display strong emotion—the waiters came around with their silver teapots, demanding decision among India, China, and Earl Grey—and Barbara and I sat there, pressing each other's hands under the table. Her hand was as plump and warm as the rest of her; demure in her afternoon dress, she exuded a wholesome bliss. Manton joined us, and he too—my poor disinherited father, florid with self-indulgence—somehow appeared wholesome, perching on a little chair by the side of our table, attentive and gentlemanly to both of us, full of uxorious care. There was an authority about him that the waiters recognized at once, making us a favored group. "Have you told her?" beamed Manton. Oh he was so proud—principally of himself, who was going to be a husband and father again, and of Barbara, and of me, the married daughter. It seemed as if we—that is, the Wishwells, now including soft, fair, pregnant Barbara—were in the process of reacquiring a status that had been slipping away from us.

Yes, Manton had changed. In his fifties, with Michael and me grown up, he had had to wait all this time before he could enter into the authority of his age, his status, and his own impressive physical presence. His head no longer turned automatically after every good-looking woman; even Renée, I was glad to see, did not affect him. In fact, he didn't care to be with her—or with any of the rest of the family. After the first courtesy call in the downstairs flat and the courtesy dinner in the Indian restaurant, Manton and Barbara didn't visit us again. I was the only link between what I was beginning to think of as two camps. But then Manton said he wanted to see and talk to Michael. I said "If you mean about Barbara's baby, I've told him." I had, though with no reaction from Michael. But still Manton insisted and asked me to bring Michael to his London club. That wasn't easy: Michael disliked and never entered Manton's club in New York, of which the London one was the reciprocal and the prototype. But the hotel would have been just as bad, or any other place that Manton frequented; and the places Michael went would have been impossible for Manton, so there was really no place where they could both meet and be comfortable.

Manton was seated in his club armchair under some ancient portrait and was being served his drink by an ancient club waiter, whom he made a great thing of knowing by name. Comfortable and at ease in these surroundings, Manton was inclined to be expansive and was beginning to speak, as Grandfather had once spoken to us, about our family and ancestry. But Michael didn't let him get far: "What's all this about?" he interrupted him.

His question surprised me. I hadn't thought it had been about anything except that Manton wanted to be with us here in his club—which *was* like the New York one, only older and smaller and shabbier, as though the people at home, in copying it, couldn't restrain themselves from outdoing it. But I was wrong and Michael was right: Manton did have something in particular he wanted to say to us—about the house on the Island; and Propinquity; and our money; and I guess everything we owned. In doing so, he set himself up as a bad example. He said how he had never cared about any of it; certainly when he was our age, he had never given it a thought; and here he had to say how he admired us and was proud of us—Michael had tensed up horribly and before long he said again: "What's all this about?"

But Manton was launched and couldn't be brought up short. "When I remember what I was at your age, all I can say to you is, never look to me as an example. Look instead to my father; your grandfather. Not that he was as totally one hundred percent perfect as he would have liked everyone to believe; he had his little fling here and there too, and more than a little, as we all know. But as they say, *de mortuis nihil nisi bonum*, nothing mean about our dear departed—yes if you please, Eric," he said to the solicitous waiter, handing him his glass, "and two more tomato juices over there." When Michael shook his head—"One more tomato juice, with nothing alas in it. . . . I want you to meet two wonderful young people, Eric; and you will never guess who they are: my own son and daughter, I'm proud to say, yes indeed, my own dear kids."

"Very pleased to meet you, I'm sure," said Eric—and seemed intrigued, looking at us from under his brows, as shaggy and old as those of practically all the club members. He, as well as other waiters and the porter, had already scrutinized us on our arrival, to make sure we were with someone and not a couple of anarchists come to blow the place up. "I think I see the resemblance, sir," he lied, lowering his eyes away from us—put out no doubt by Michael's fierce stare.

"Do you, Eric? Well then you see more and further than other folk do. No these two fine young people are an entirely different kettle of fish. They have their act together—only a saying, Eric, just the way we quaintly put it, it doesn't mean they're acrobats or some kind of performers, no no no ha ha ha, far from it, don't be misled by their unusual appear-

ance. Are you sure you won't have anything more?" he asked
Michael. "A lemonade? Or how about a plain old club soda
—we can do one of those, can't we Eric?"

"I'm about ready to leave," Michael warned, and Eric went
about his business.

"Sit down, Michael, I have many more things to say. Serious
things, you'll be surprised to hear: not just any old Manton
chatter. I'm sure everyone has heard enough of that; yes
everyone has heard enough of the old Manton; we're all,
including myself, fed up to the teeth with him. But I'll tell
you something that'll make you sit up and it is this: The old
Manton is dead, he is no longer with us."

"Is he drunk or something?" Michael asked me.

"On only two of these?" Manton said. "You underestimate
me, dear boy, but then you always have. You remind me, in
the most unfortunate way, of my father; your grandfather.
He had the same knack of making me feel a heel." Eric
returned with his drink and Manton started in on it at once.
But when he put it down, his mood had changed. He was
silent for a while; eyes downcast; and then hand over eyes:
"I know you won't believe me, and you have every right not
to, but I truly have turned over a new leaf. At last."

"Harriet told me about your getting married and a baby
and all of that."

"Yes all of that; all of that." Manton was still subdued. "I
know what you want to tell me; what you have every right
to tell me: that all this should have been done twenty years
ago; when you two were born. That was the time to turn over
a new leaf, to get myself together and be a proper father for
you two."

Michael said "Oh hell really."

"Oh hell really indeed! And it is, I know, psychological hell
for children not to have proper parents. There I sinned
against you even before you were born—in choosing your
mother. But that's a different story altogether. Only you must
do me justice in this one thing—I didn't as it were pick her
off the streets. Lindsay—whatever she is, and unfortunately
we all know what—but there's a couple of generations of
money there that's not going to do you any harm at all. Not
to speak of Propinquity. But let's for a moment do that: speak

of Propinquity. Yes yes yes I know," he raised a hand to ward off the interruption we didn't make, "I have no right to say anything about Propinquity: any more than I have a right to say anything about the house on the Island or any other Wishwell property. No legal right whatsoever, though perhaps some other kind of right. Say shut up and get out right now, if you want to."

Michael didn't tell him that, but he did say: "We've been over all that before, with Grandfather. He asked us the exact same thing you're working around to: if we're sure we want to do what we're going to do with all of it. And we'll tell you what we told him: Yes we are sure. Okay? Does that take care of it?"

It *was* what he had told Grandfather—but in such a different way. At that time, sitting on the floor of his cell-like room at Propinquity, Michael had been very, very slow and reflective, deep-thinking. Now he was as brisk as Crishi; even his way of speaking had changed, and he no longer had to think an hour before bringing out the thought it had taken him two hours to formulate. It was all there, all formulated. He was dead certain.

Manton too was trying to change, but he was only in the beginning stages, and Michael's certainty left him floundering; and a bit sad and defeated-looking. "Yes," he said, "I suppose you have your ideas and principles. I've never had too many of those, and it's too late to start having them now. What a pity. What a pity, I mean, for Barbara and— well, the new generation of Wishwells. . . . Barbara wants to get married in church, in a white dress, with bridesmaids and all of it. We're going to look for a place to live. We're sick of hotels. Somewhere in the country, or by the ocean. With a lot of scenery; a lot of rooms too. Space. For the baby. And for you two, whenever you want to come there, which we hope will be very often. We'll have Thanksgiving, Christmas, the whole bit. We'll start again, as a family."

I said "What about my family? Don't forget I've got married too."

"No I'm not forgetting that," Manton said, looking down into his empty glass. There was a silence in which I was afraid he was going to say something bad about Crishi.

He may have wanted to; but there was a tactfulness in Manton, a reticence—not unlike the atmosphere of this club we were in. Maybe that was why he fitted in so well here, looked so much in his natural element. It was Michael who was, and looked, out of it; and it was Michael who broke up the tactful atmosphere. "All this is completely pointless," he said in a voice too harsh and loud for the place. "Whatever you're trying to say, you can't shake Harriet and me out of doing what is right."

"Oh God yes," Manton said hopelessly. "Doing what is right."

He left it at that, said no more; and anyway, it was impossible to keep Michael any longer. The whole conversation—Manton's plea—left him tense and furious; and although he didn't talk about it with me, he may have done so with Crishi. The two of them were so often together, had so much business together, that they had a lot of opportunity to talk—more than Crishi and I had. He may even have told him the same day, as soon as we left the club. Crishi said nothing to me that night, but he did the next morning when, as usual, I took Robi to school. In good weather Robi and I liked to walk across the park; but today we had to take a cab because of the rain. As so often when it rained, there were no cabs to be had. We were standing at the corner, quite wet, looking up and down the street, with Robi shielding his head with his schoolbag, when Crishi arrived—maybe by accident, or more likely having watched for us to leave. He asked "Why are you standing in the rain?" When I said there were no cabs, he said "What nonsense," and at that moment one came around the corner and stopped exactly where we stood. It was one of those things that happened around Crishi—a melting away of minor obstacles—so that when with him one almost expected and relied on it. He got in with us and rode with us to school; and after we dropped off Robi, I told the driver to go to Manton and Barbara's hotel. But when we drew up outside, Crishi said to the driver, "No, we've changed our mind," and we drove on. I protested, I said that Manton and Barbara were waiting for me, but Crishi said "Let's go for a drive," and he leaned forward to give a new direction. It was pleasant, driving enclosed in the high dark roomy upholstered London taxi. Drops of water slid down the glass,

blurring the people on the wet pavements as they struggled
with their umbrellas and avoided being splashed from the
road; the trees lining the mall and stretching farther into the
parks had melted away into mist and so had Buckingham
Palace and stone-white Queen Victoria. Crishi held my hand
in his. He said "Manton and Barbara don't like me."

"If they don't, it's too late, isn't it. Is that why you didn't
want me to stop?"

"Do you believe it? What's on their mind?" Feeling me try
to withdraw my hand from his, he held it tighter. I didn't
struggle; I liked it. At the same time I didn't like what he
was saying, and wouldn't answer him; and so we rode along.

"In a way it's true," he said at last, slowly as out of deep
thought. "I wouldn't have married you without it—without
the money—I'd have wanted to but it wouldn't have worked
out. You understand that?"

I said I did. I knew he needed to have it, that the movement
depended on the funds he and Renée could raise; and as the
movement grew, so did their need for money. He had spoken
to me about this before—even quite bitterly—how the Rawul
could afford to soar into the heights of his abstract philosophy
while he and Renée had to stay down below and do whatever
had to be done.

But today he said more; he said yes, he needed money for
the movement—but also for himself; because it was so unbearable not to have it. I said "That's what Renée says too."

"Yes she too." He continued to hold my hand securely.
"It's a tie between us, between her and me. But between you
and me, I love it that you *don't* know, and never have."

"Is that why you never tell me anything?"

"I've told you a lot." His teeth were on edge in what may
have been snarl or smile. "Or you've found it out from Anna.
She told you about my mother."

"You never did."

"I try to forget her."

I could understand that because there had been times when
I tried to forget Lindsay. But when I told him that, he laughed.
He seemed to think it funny to hear any comparison between
my mother and his.

We were driving through the park, which was absolutely

empty of people, with the trees dripping heavily and leaves dropping from them in wind and rain. I said "I must go back. I told Manton and Barbara I'd be there by ten." I didn't want to go back, though.

"My mother was ever so pretty," Crishi said. "That's why I like pretty women such a lot. No, you could be too—you could, in your Aunt Harriet way—if you'd just—" He picked up my hair, piled it on top of my head, ran his hand over the nape of my neck. "She was tiny—she'd come up to your shoulder maybe, no more. She had this beautiful skin, you can't believe it, how soft it was and nice. She loved dressing up in new outfits. Dressing up and going out. What she'd do is, there was this girlfriend she had who was an usherette at the local Odeon. She'd drop me off with her and I'd stay till they closed down after the last show. I saw a lot of movies and ate a lot of chocolate bars and stuff. It was perfect."

"Where was this?"

"I'll take you there one day. We had this little house in London, in Woolwich—a council house—I don't know how she managed to get it but people did do things for her. I suppose being so pretty and poor with this little boy—me. Now she's old and fat and lives in Hong Kong with a Chinese wrestler. She looks quite Chinese herself. Well she's partly Assamese—do you think my eyes are slanting? They are, aren't they, a bit. When she was mad at me, she'd call me 'Chinese devil.' I could drive her mad, I tell you." He laughed—outright, with pleasure, not his usual snarl. "She'd chase me down the street with the bread knife, all the neighbors watching. I didn't mind it—I thought it was a lark—but afterward she'd feel so ashamed she'd cry her eyes out and then she'd be mad at me all over again. I was the man in her life," he said, proud and amused. "Then she married that Portugese salesman and we moved to Goa. That's when I kept running away and at first she'd have me brought back by the police but then she didn't bother anymore. She was glad I was gone."

I guessed that was when it had all started: the beach in Bombay; the traveling with strangers; the jails. I didn't ask him and he didn't tell me but it was all part of him, like the mysterious scars on his body that I sometimes asked him about, only to be given a different answer each time. Also the fear and hatred of having no money, from which I wanted to protect him—that was the one thing I could do for him. I did feel very protective of him, sitting with him in the taxi; I put my arms around him and held him as though he were not Crishi but the little boy his mother had loved. And he murmured in my arms like a little boy dropping off to sleep, secure, loving, and grateful.

Later I told Barbara and Manton some lie about why I hadn't come to meet them; and after that, although I continued to join them on some of their outings, it was more out of duty than for pleasure. Secretly I wished they would go back to New York and leave me to my own life in London. There was no way I could draw them into that—how to explain about the upstairs and downstairs flats, or about Bari Rani's household, and what could I tell them about Anna, or the gallery, or our weekends at Babaji's house? More and more, as I accompanied them on their shopping tours, or to museums and matinees (I was never free for them in the evenings because of waiting for Crishi to call and tell me where to come), I found that I was looking forward to the time when I could leave them and go back home. They noticed, and it made them sad but I couldn't help it. I mean, I loved them but not in that deep, and often deeply painful, way I had loved others.

Barbara and I spoke about it one day in a museum. She and I spent quite a bit of time in museums, for Barbara was in the process of educating herself. She admitted that she didn't have much education—she was sent to some fancy schools but pulled out of them quite soon because of her mother either quarreling with the teachers or wanting Barbara to be with her on location in Egypt or somewhere. Her mother had absolutely no respect for education, and how could she have, Barbara said, never having had any herself beyond ninth grade and afterward working in a laundromat and marrying at fifteen? Barbara was determined to stock up on the treasures of civilization as fast as possible, to have something to hand on to her family and not be just this dumb blonde, mashing baby food or whatever. Manton, who didn't feel in need of any further education, would leave us at the portals and, kissing us both, hurry off to his own London pursuits. We tramped around till Barbara got tired, and with being pregnant, this happened quite soon. We would find a painting we both liked and sit there and talk. That day we were in front of a Veronese or someone from his school. We were on the round velvet-covered seats in the center of the gallery, under a lofty glass roof grimy with rain and among soaring marble pillars with gold capitals. The picture was a huge high one, with a huge bearded father and huge white-bosomed mother, both in pearls and velvet and making energetic lunging motions toward a very large naked baby. It was this latter that had attracted Barbara and was the reason why we sat there. It was a male baby, and Barbara said "Manton hopes it'll be a girl."

I said "He likes girls."

"Yes he does, but it's also because he's so disappointed about his relationship with Michael. . . . Manton really cares for Michael—he'd like to get really close to him, but you know how Michael is." There was a silence; we both looked at the picture. It struck me that, in spite of their size, their mythological proportions, they were really a very ordinary, bourgeois sort of family—mother, father, and baby.

Barbara said "Manton feels very strongly about family— our family, that's you and Michael and me and the baby."

"I know. He talked to us."

"I feel strongly about it too. I do love you, Harriet. Isn't it funny, I'm going to be your mother." We squeezed each other's hands and giggled. It *was* funny. I knew Barbara was coming around to say what Manton had said—about the properties and the money. I saw she felt shy about it for fear of being misinterpreted; so I helped her. I said "Michael and I explained to Manton, about being committed and all of that. To the movement. It's got a new name, Barbara—Transcendental Internationalism." I don't know why I told her that; maybe to impress her, or at least to have her take it more seriously. But I did not succeed. She said "Manton wants to call the baby Elisabeth, after his mother; and if it's a boy, after your grandfather of course." She looked at the picture, and I could see she was getting herself together to say what she felt but was too embarrassed to come out with.

She had always been like that—shy, fond, and reticent. But feeling she had to speak, for everyone's sake, she overcame her own sense of inadequacy; being pregnant helped her— I mean, it was not only her but two of them speaking; and there was the picture to look at for inspiration. She said "Manton says he hates not being a family—everyone not caring and letting everything go and fall apart. He says it's taken him till now to realize that it's more important than *any*thing—the family, and everything that's been built up; holding it all together. I think so too," she said, looking at me in appeal. "That we should all—be together. Hold together." And she took my hand and kept it in hers.

I said "What about Crishi?" and went right on: "I'm married to him, Barbara, just like you and Manton are going to be married. And like those two are," I indicated the gigantic couple in the picture. What could she say to that? Our hands were still intertwined but not our feelings. I knew she wanted to contradict me, and she was right. It wasn't like that at all! There was no resemblance in these marriages, any more than there might be in our lovemaking. I knew that Barbara loved Manton; and perhaps also how she loved him, in her soft voluptuous way. But she couldn't know—she could have no conception of the way I felt for Crishi: the sick hunger that gnawed at me. Dear good plump pregnant Barbara—I kissed her for her innocence; and melting and tender, she said "You'll come for our wedding, won't you darling, we want you there so very much." I promised I would and meant it —provided of course I wasn't needed here.

I HATE to say it, but I was relieved when they returned to the States. Although Crishi never again tried to stop me from seeing them, I still felt split between two opposite sides. But I never for a second doubted which one I belonged to, even though I was not always happy—far from it. There was no change in our circumstances: Anna remained with us, waiting for Crishi as I was; and Renée continued to come upstairs in the dark—not often, but from time to time, sort of establishing her right. It is strange how you can get used to something and make compromises and accept what is presented as inevitable. I suppose that was how the Bari Rani had got used to her situation and adjusted to it, so that our two households had grown together.

Sometimes I wondered about the Rawul, how he was taking these developments in his family; but I don't think he was too much aware of them. He lived on another plane. He was there to change the world. Anna said he was crazy, and while it was true that there was a strange light in his eyes, I still believed that it was the light of the skies he had gazed into so much, and everything he had seen there and dreamed. While the rest of us revolved around him, immersed in our preoccupations, he stood alone—or would have, if it hadn't been for the Bari Rani. For her he wasn't this almost symbolic figure, but a husband who often enraged her, whom she fussed over and fought with and said was getting too fat. And in return he shouted right back at her and became

enmeshed in the petty quarrels she started with him. And
when he rose to her that way, although she pretended to be
indignant, she also appeared satisfied—as though she had
been testing him, to see if he was still as he had been.

Around this time, Crishi began to have a lot of business
troubles. He became more cheerful than ever and bustled
around and whistled between his teeth—anything not to let
anyone know he was worried, least of all me. But of course
Renée shared every secret with him, and whenever I came
in on them unawares, they were in some deep confabulation;
but the moment he saw me, he would draw away from her
and become the most lighthearted person in the world. For
Renée it was more difficult to pretend there was nothing the
matter. A heavy weight made her sigh frequently, and her
eyes were veiled with melancholy. She was particularly sweet
with me during these days but very short-tempered with Anna.
She complained about Anna to me, said that her pretense of
writing a book about the Rawul was only an excuse to hang
around and freeload. She warned me never to give her any
money. I didn't tell her that I had been doing so—at first
nervously, because I knew Crishi would be going through
my checkbook; but he never said anything about the amounts
I lent to Anna, so I guess he didn't disapprove of them.

Anna told me that the reason everyone was so worried was
that a huge amount of bail had had to be found for Rupert;
and it was an especially bad time because there had been
some arrests among the followers and what they were carrying had been confiscated and lost. "Naturally she's in a bad
mood," Anna said, referring to Renée; she added "Never
mind, it's only a little while longer and their troubles will be
over." I knew she was referring to when Michael and I would
come of age; I had got used to it being generally assumed
that everyone was waiting for that time, and I guess Michael
had too. He and I never spoke about it to each other.

Then Lindsay and Jean appeared on the scene. I can't say
I was really pleased to see them, but Crishi seemed to be. He
made quite a fuss of them. They went through the same
routine as Manton and Barbara had—that is, they were ceremonially received by the Rawul in the downstairs flat and
met both households at the Indian restaurant. They were as

stiff and out of place as Manton and Barbara had been; I
decided there and then it was hopeless to bring everyone
together. Michael cared neither one way nor the other; he
sat there with his head bent over his plate, eating. But Crishi
and Renée really put themselves out; and when Lindsay and
Jean asked me to accompany them on a tour of England,
Crishi insisted I go, though I didn't want to.

That was a strange trip. Lindsay and Jean were very, very
loving with each other, with their differences apparently resolved: It was the same as with Manton and Barbara, who
had also, since my marriage, drawn closer together. And like
Manton and Barbara, they loved being in England. Lindsay
often said she felt more at home here than anywhere else,
or rather, she didn't say, she asked—"Why do I feel so at
home here?" The answer you were supposed to give her, and
if you didn't she supplied it herself, was that it was where
her roots were. Technically this was true, for both sets of her
great-great-grandparents had emigrated from here in the
1850s; but all the same, she appeared exotic and trans-
planted—more so than, for instance, the Rawul, Renée, and
Crishi, who somehow belonged. While in London, Lindsay
and Jean stayed at the Ritz, but once in the country, they
booked themselves into what they liked to think of as inns.
They *had* been inns, often dating back as far as the fifteenth
century, although converted into hotels with modern baths
and central heating that was never on high enough. After
English breakfasts in hotel dining rooms with wooden beams
and Tudor fireplaces, Lindsay and Jean went out to visit
churches, abbeys, and manor houses. With me in the back-
seat, they drove from one old village and market town to
another, content with everything they saw, soothed and lulled
by the green fields, the riverbanks, the low clouds spilling
alternately soft rain and watery sunshine. Looking very
American in the Scottish country clothes they had bought in
London, they walked sturdily in brogues, while I trailed behind them. Mostly I was on the lookout for pay phones from
which to call Crishi. I tried every place he might be—in the
upstairs flat, the downstairs one, the gallery, the office, the
Earl's Court house, at Babaji's—but he either had just left
or was expected any minute. When I did get him, he was

loving and happy to hear me but there was someone waiting
for him in a car outside or on hold on another line. I would
say "I think I'll come home," and he'd say "Oh I miss you
ever so—I have to go, they're waiting—" "Crishi, I *want* to
come home!" He had hung up. Sometimes I got Michael,
who was more sympathetic. "It must be a drag for you," he
said when I told him I was tired of touring with Lindsay and
Jean. But when I said I wanted to come home, he too became
evasive—not as evasive as Crishi, but more embarrassed as
he advised me to stick it out a bit longer.

The high point of the trip was our visit to what Lindsay
liked to think of as her ancestral village. Actually, the
Macrorys had come from Ireland, and Lindsay had visited
there. But she hadn't liked it—it depressed her, she said, it
was too primitive—and much preferred this English place
where one of the Macrorys had come to be the vicar and
where the great-great-grandfather who had emigrated to
America was born. We went into the church, which was very
old, the oldest part dating from Norman times. Between the
stone buttresses, the walls were plainly whitewashed; the pews
were no more than wooden benches; the stone floor was
scrubbed to the bone; but the outside light, refracted through
stained-glass windows, made this simple interior glimmer like
a semiprecious stone. There was a register of the vicars in
an unbroken line from 1176 to the present day. They included Lindsay's ancestor, the Reverend James Macrory, with
the dates of his vicarage, 1837–1850. He lay buried in the
graveyard adjoining the church with his wife, Margaret Jane,
beside him. Lindsay, who had been here before, led us to
these graves, wending her way between ancient tombstones,
some of them half sunk into the ground. Oh, Lindsay was
so proud here, queenly; she strode with her head held high,
her golden hair and designer scarf blowing in the wind. When
we reached the Macrory graves, she and Jean held hands
and read the inscriptions out loud to each other. Neither of
them seemed to feel the rain-cold wind that swept through
the grass and the yew trees and through me, making me
shiver. Their imperviousness may have been partly due to
the warm, woven new clothes they wore; but mostly to the
reverence they felt as they stood hand in hand by the ancestral

grave, like two pilgrims at the culmination of their destined journey. I was not only cold but impatient—because I knew that when at last we could turn from this sacred place, we would have to retrace our steps through the graveyard, past the church, along a brook, over a stile, around a haystack, and not a telephone in sight till we got back to the hotel.

When Jean asked me that night at dinner in the hotel dining room, "Aren't you proud?" I knew she meant proud of my ancestry. What could I say? It didn't seem such a big deal to me to belong to any one place, even if it was old. But Lindsay said it gave her a very special feeling to think of the Reverend James Macrory and Margaret Jane his wife mingled in this earth. There was an old, old waiter serving us, a shuffling and surly old man who couldn't manage all the tables; everyone had to wait a long time and sometimes got the wrong orders. Lindsay, who at home tended to be short with waiters and salespeople so that it got embarrassing to be with her, was very patient with him. Lindsay was in a mellow mood; mellow and thoughtful. "Jean and I've been thinking," she said, during one of the long waits between courses. "About Propinquity."

They outlined their plan to me. They said they wanted to turn it into a historic house—"Historic," I said, "it was only built in 1906." "We want to show how people lived. How it was in Grandfather's time. We'll restore everything the way it was—we'll lay the table in the dining room with all the things so it'll look as if the family was just sitting down to eat. And we'll hang the pictures back—you wouldn't remember but we used to have Father's Uncle Gerald on the stairs till someone wrote that book implicating him in some awful murder on St. Kitts, which Father said was all lies, though he did take the picture down. But every family has something in it; I mean, that's what history *is*."

I said "What about the Rawul and the movement?"

"Oh Jesus," Lindsay said, hiding her face in her hands. I had spoiled her mood.

Jean said gently, "Lindsay thinks it's wrong."

"What is?" I asked; and when they didn't answer, I said to Lindsay, "You used to think it was all right. You wanted to give the place; you yourself wanted it."

"I've been thinking lately," Lindsay said. "We both have—haven't we, Jean?"

"What about?" I asked.

"Oh well, many things." She glanced up suspiciously: "I suppose only you and Michael are allowed to think. You two are the great intellectuals and I'm the dumbbell."

"Now dear," Jean said warningly, "we're here to have a sensible talk and not to pick on Harriet."

"I'm not." She made a visible effort to be sensible and continued: "It's been helpful having those people at Propinquity—the Rawul's people—they work hard and they've done a good job on the grounds and they're not bad in the kitchen either, though nothing very special, not like when Else was there."

"What, Else's gone?"

"Didn't I tell you? It was getting too difficult, Harriet. She had too many personal problems. And just when Jean and I were trying to work out our relationship, which is what we've been doing, haven't we, Jean, so that we know a little better where we're going."

It was clear where they were going with each other. Jean's sad-dog air had given way to one of happy fulfillment. They appeared to have reached a plateau of accord that was not unlike Manton and Barbara's; and judging by what they went on to say, they had also reached the same conclusions as my other set of parents.

This was that I had made an unfortunate marriage. They had had time to think about it, and to discuss it with each other, and they knew a mistake had been made. Lindsay even blamed herself, which was unprecedented for her, saying that she should have warned me—"Against what?" I asked.

She stared at me, with her beautiful though rather blank blue-gray eyes: "Don't you know? Isn't it perfectly obvious? What he married you for? But of course he did," she said when Jean tried to hold her back. "They might dress it up under all sorts of fancy names, but that's what it comes down to: your money. Our money. Our properties. Propinquity."

"It isn't true," I lied.

"No? Then why has he been pestering me to mortgage the property? He's in such a hurry to get his hands on everything, he can't even decently wait till you're twenty-one. But I've disappointed him, I'm afraid, and I'm going to disappoint him even more—him and Michael both. Oh yes, we've been hearing from Michael too, didn't you know?"

"Yes I did know. Of course I know," I lied some more.

"And you think it's quite all right? That I should mortgage Father's house, the Macrory house, our property—throw away our property—" At that moment the waiter came with our dessert, and she felt compelled to be charming and grateful to him the way she was with people in England. We ate in silence, even taking care, as did the other guests in that well-bred dining room, not to make too much clatter with our cutlery. I took the opportunity to think out what to say, now that I knew why Crishi and Michael had sent me on this trip; what it was they wanted me to say.

"It's only a mortgage. We'll be able to repay it when we get the house on the Island and all the rest. . . . And it's just temporary: I mean, we're just in temporary difficulties."

"Who's we?" Lindsay said. That was too obvious for me to answer. She and Jean might think I had made an unfortunate marriage, but that wasn't my opinion.

For the rest of our trip, they said more or less what Manton had said: about family, tradition, holding together. It must have been maddening for them, the way I was so impervious to everything they said—as well as to the sights we saw, the well-kept castles, mansions, gardens. Wherever we were, all I thought about was getting home.

WHEN at last I did, Crishi wasn't there, so I
went to look for him. First I went to the
gallery, where Nicholas was now in sole charge. Ever since
the trouble with the stolen paintings had started, Rupert
didn't come there any more; it was thought that, with all the
bad publicity attached to him, his presence might undermine
the prestige of the place. As usual, the haughty girl assistants
tried to discourage me from staying, and not finding Crishi,
I was ready to leave when I heard Michael's voice from the
little office downstairs—and that was how I came in on the
scene between him and Nicholas. Nicholas, who was quite
short, had drawn himself up to his full height and was being
very cocky with Michael. He said in his sneering, drawly
accent—"You surely don't imagine that I run this place in
order to act as your fence." Michael said "You're here to do
what you're told." Nicholas twitched his nose in an uppity
little sniff: "I might have my own ideas about that"—but had
hardly got it out when Michael caught hold of his elegant
lapels and drew him up close: "You do what you're told."
Nicholas maintained his dignity awhile longer: "Would you
mind taking your hands off me?" he said, trying to keep
his voice steady but sounding fussy and frightened. "You
do what you're told," Michael repeated, more threatening,
and tightening his grip. Nicholas looked down at his own
lapels—he seemed as nervous about any damage to his very
smart suit as to himself, or perhaps made no distinction

between the two. His eyes roved around for rescue, but he saw only me. Michael, too, glanced at me for a moment but had no time for me. His fury was rising, fueled perhaps by Nicholas's fright, or the sensation of having caught hold of him. Nicholas tried to be defiant. "I have no business with you," he said. "But I have with you," Michael replied; Nicholas's voice rose to a rabbit's shriek: "Get out of my gallery, you and that sister of yours, before I call the police!"

"Yes why don't you," said Michael, and at the same time he struck the other's face so hard that blood gushed out of his nose. Nicholas cried out, "My glasses!" for these had fallen to the floor. Michael said "Pick them up," and struck him again; Nicholas fell to the ground, where he began to crawl around in search of them. Blood came from his nose, tears from his eyes; he groped for his glasses, but they had fallen some way off and I went and picked them up for him. This seemed to infuriate Nicholas and he screeched "Get out of my gallery, both of you!" By this time the haughty girls had arrived and Nicholas cried out to them, "Call the police!" Then Michael did something really horrible: He kicked Nicholas where he was on the floor, not once but several times, and Nicholas crawled away to get out of his reach. "Go on, call the police, why don't you," Michael told the girls. "And let me give you something more to call them for— assault and battery," he said. "Isn't that what you call it?" and he followed Nicholas and kicked him again, and again, just the way I had seen Crishi kick Paul, and with the same expression on his face.

But there was this difference between Michael and Crishi, or used to be: Whereas Crishi accepted everything he himself did as right and never thought about it again, Michael had to go through a long course of self-justification. As we walked away from the gallery, Michael reflected on what he had done. But, unlike in the past, he didn't have to justify himself to himself—he was absolutely certain that he was right. "What's the matter with him?" he said angrily. "Does he think we go through all that so he can play it big in his crappy little gallery?" "Go through all what?" I asked, though I knew perfectly well. Naturally, he didn't answer my unnecessary question, and I asked another: "Where's Crishi?" "Risking his neck so that creep in there can wag his ass at duchesses."

"When's he coming back?"

"When he is back. . . . Don't fuss, H."

"I only want to know when. I miss him." Yes that was true, but it wasn't that I was worried about the hour of his return: I was worried about him, as I was each time he or Michael went on a trip, each time fearing what would happen, what I might expect to hear.

And I wasn't the only one who felt that way. When we got back home and were walking up the marble stairs, the door of the downstairs flat opened and Renée came out. She said "I thought you were Crishi." Then: "Is he back?" When Michael said no, she tried to sound casual: "Oh well, I'm sure he will be, any moment." Michael and I went on upstairs. The flat was empty, Anna wasn't home; Michael and I were alone. This happened so rarely nowadays that I felt I had to take advantage of it. I faced him and asked straight out: "Why do you have to do it? Why do you have to go, you and Crishi?"

"What a question," he brushed me aside, but I insisted: "Why you and he, when there are all the others?" I meant all the followers—I meant, quite frankly, Let them take the risk, not you.

"Oh they panic," Michael said. "They get scared. That's how they're caught."

"And you?"

"Shall I tell you something? I like it." His eyes, cold and clear as water, narrowed with pleasure. "If you're not scared—if you make yourself not be—you just walk through; no one can touch you. It's almost *they*'re scared, if you're not. You should see Crishi—it's like he's daring them to stop him, always hanging around to ask some damn fool question about where's the men's room or what's the local time. Well I can't do that, not being naturally gabby like him, but I can be not scared—you know? Keep my head up, walk through any place I want, at any pace I want, in a hurry or with plenty of time to spare. God, it makes me feel good. Better than anything I've ever done." And really, there was a sort of glow about him I hadn't seen before, as if he had truly found, fulfilled himself the way he had always wanted to.

I said "Lindsay says you want a mortgage on Propinquity?"

"We need it, only she's being her usual dumb stupid bitch self. . . . I tell you, I'm counting the days till we're twenty-one and can do what we want and get rid of everything."

"Is that what you want?"

"Well don't you?" he said and continued at once. "Of course you do. You don't want to be tied up with all that junk."

"Lindsay and Manton have gone into a big thing about the family. Families: the Wishwells and the Macrorys. They've both developed strong feelings on the subject."

"Too bad we've got different plans."

"A different family too, I guess."

But Michael frowned. He said to hell with all that. And he went off into what I can only call an impassioned speech. It would have surprised anyone who didn't know him well—which I guess was practically everyone, since he wouldn't let himself be known well. His manner made people think he was made of ice whereas really he was very fiery—in his ideals, that is; and it was only because he had been afraid of having them disappointed that he had kept himself so aloof, had played it so cool. But now, with the Rawul's movement, he felt he could let himself go because at last he had found something in which to pour his whole self.

He said I knew how he felt about the concept of family—and I did know, and to some extent, though not entirely, I shared it. Michael and I didn't have that much of what is always thought of as family, not with Manton and Lindsay as parents. Grandfather's embassies couldn't take the place of a conventional family; as for Sonya—we had always been very fond of her, and in her last year Grandmother too had learned to appreciate her, but there were those years when everyone had to pretend Sonya wasn't there, and that we weren't visiting her in the hotel suite or sublet apartment she had taken near the embassy. Many people who don't have a conventional family—and I suppose that is almost everyone nowadays—make up for it by getting very enamored of their ancestors, but that never happened to Michael and me; on the contrary. Everything Grandfather had said to us about the Wishwells, and everything Lindsay had tried to say to me about the Macrorys, had passed right over us. Michael said all that was played out. And not only family and family tra-

ditions, but also countries and the patriotism one was supposed to feel for them—humanity had passed beyond the
stage of what Michael called tribal loyalties into a much higher
concept of worldwide unity. It was the inevitable outcome of
the scientific transcending of spatial limitations: No one was
expected anymore to stay in the village where they were born,
nor in the town, the city, the country, the nation, the
continent—why, the very planet on which we live had been
transcended! Ridiculous, said Michael, in such a world to
remain imprisoned within the tiny concepts, geographical or
other, of an earlier humanity. He said he had long felt that
way—bound and imprisoned—and before the Rawul he had
tried to free himself by means of philosophical ideas, which
was what his studies of Eastern religions had been about. But
it had been too abstract—he understood intellectually but as
an existent being, as the everyday Michael, he remained bound
to his own conditioning. It was only with the arrival of the
Rawul that he was given an absolutely practical way of transcending his human bonds and boundaries. Moreover, here
was an organization to perform this function—for the individual as well as for all peoples, all nations, all humanity.
True, so far it was only an embryonic organization: but wasn't
that part of the excitement, to be in on the beginnings of
such a movement, to be among its, if you like, apostles, and
to have the privilege of day-to-day contact with the founder?
All this Michael said to me, his gaunt face irradiated by a joy
and passion that would make anyone, let alone me, forget
that participation in this grand and heroic mission involved
participation in what were I guess some rather sleazy smuggling activities.

The privilege of day-to-day contact with our founder could
sometimes be disconcerting. I was prepared to admit that the
Rawul lived on a higher plane than the rest of us, but then
I would see him emerge from his bedroom, completely con-
founded because there was a button missing on the sleeve of
the shirt he had just put on: He held his arms out and looked
piteously at Renée or anyone else who might be able to help
him. He was very fond of drinking tea, and it was brought
to him on a tray with the milk and sugar separate so he could
stir them in to his own taste; he would do so very carefully

and with relish, in the middle of dictating something or speaking into Anna's tape recorder, sitting there stout and handsome in his velvet smoking jacket. One day I saw Bari Rani tie a bow tie on him, and having got him captive in that way, she took the opportunity to complain to him about one of the girls, who was going out with an unsuitable boy. "I think he's on—you know—" Bari Rani said. He didn't know and anyway wasn't listening; he wanted her to hurry with his bow tie, he had a lunch appointment at the Savoy.

"D-r-u-g-s," Bari Rani spelled out for him. "Not that I think for a moment that Daisy would be silly and take anything. Although you might think she's a scatterbrain sometimes, and certainly very untidy, God bless her, basically she's a very sensible, good child and we've had a talk about it too. I've told her—if you don't stand still I can't do this—I've told her, Daisy, you know that at home only coolies at the railway station take that sort of stuff."

"My grandfather died of an overdose."

"Oh well, your grandfather. But you know how young people are. If one of them does something all the others have to do it too, and quite apart from anything else, I don't like the boy."

"Finished? I do have an appointment, I'm afraid, and a very important one at that."

"He's not the sort of boy you would want your daughter to be going with, and though she swears that 'We're just friends, Mummy, that's all,' we know how one thing leads to another. He is not an educated boy or even a nice boy and one is not supposed to say this but I don't think he comes from a nice family, his father is a—oh I don't know—something not very nice. . . . Oh well, if you're happy if she marries a coal man or something of that sort, then what more can I say."

"Good Lord," the Rawul said, really struck now, for he did care—he cared as a father, and he cared dynastically as a ruler, and most important, he cared as a world leader whose image had to remain unblemished.

He thought a lot about the image of his movement. He liked to devise new emblems for it, and new celebrations and rituals like the flag-hoisting ceremony at Propinquity, and my wedding. His own birthday was coming around, and he was planning to make a sort of Founder's Day out of it. He had never mentioned any particular day as the one on which he had founded the movement, but his own birthday appeared appropriate, and he could be heard rehearsing a speech that began: "Not only was I born on this day but also reborn . . ." While he was completely involved in planning for the great day, all sorts of other things were going on that he knew nothing about—that were being kept secret from him the way our crises usually were, especially the financial ones.

The reason Crishi needed a mortgage on Propinquity was that the movement had had "losses" lately. He said "losses" vaguely, but through hints from Anna, and also some rest-lessness among the followers, I gathered that there had been more arrests at certain borders. Each arrest meant—besides the disappearance of the arrested person into some foreign jail—a considerable financial setback with the impounding of whatever it was that was being carried from one place to another. While the ranks of the followers could be filled in without much difficulty, the other loss caused embarrass-ment. A mortgage on Propinquity would at this point have been helpful. It was impossible to get at Grandfather's prop-erty, which was solely in our name and unavailable to us till next June; but since Lindsay was both co-owner and trustee of Propinquity, she could have easily raised some useful cash on it for the movement. The fact that she refused drove Michael mad. He had gone to the Ritz to try to reason with her, and when she gave him the same argument she had given me—about family and tradition—he stormed out and said he never wanted to see or hear from her again. I came in soon afterward and found Lindsay and Jean packing. Or rather, Jean was packing—she usually did that, anyway—while Lindsay was working herself up against Michael. When I arrived, she let go about him to me. I had already heard a lot about her from him, and the only conclusion I could come to was that they were two people who had better not meet. I had come to the same conclusion about Manton and Mi-chael. I suppose it is something that often happens between parents and their children, although in this case it went a lot further than the generation gap. It was a pity that both Lindsay and Manton had developed such strong feelings about family, since the only family they had was Michael and me —at least in the sense that they meant, as a continuation of their line and as inheritors of ancestral money and property.

UNLIKE Michael, Crishi didn't seem in the least put out by Lindsay's refusal. He even very politely came to say good-bye to her and Jean before they sailed (both loved the fun to be had on an ocean liner). That was his way—never to waste regret on a scheme that didn't come off but to be busy planning another. What he planned next was to use the old guru's house as a collateral, but here he came up against other difficulties. Since he had not yet managed to raise the full price on the house, Babaji and the Devis were still its part-owners besides living up on the top story. The arrangement was loose and friendly, and the Devis might have consented to the mortgage if in the meantime they hadn't had their own troubles. These were to do with Babaji's failing health. I had never known him anything but bedridden, but now there was a change; the top floor took on a sickroom atmosphere, and the Devis constantly went in and out of Babaji's room with his bedpan or drink of pomegranate juice. None of them believed in modern medicine, so there was never a doctor but only little packets of powder, which they tried to coax him to take. He was weak but cheerful—I could hear him singing in a reedy voice, and whenever he caught a glimpse of me passing his door, he would call "Bring her in, let me see her," and the Devis would usher me to his bedside. He laughed and nodded at me, and the most he would ask was for me to bring my face close so he could pinch my cheek. I was glad to do this for him. It seemed to give him pleasure and made him cackle and cough and laughingly wave away the Devis, who tried to calm him down. At other times he would tell me about India—at least I presumed it was India; it was always some hut by a river where he said he was born.

I think he wished to die by this river, and the Devis were very keen to take him there. They wanted to dissolve their last asset in England, which was this house, and so it happened that when Crishi needed to raise a mortgage on it, they needed the final payments he owed them. Nina Devi had a long business talk with him, in which he agreed to everything she asked; but after that she could never get hold of him, and whenever she wanted to renew their talk and settle the terms with him, he was in a terrible rush to get to a meeting or catch a plane. I had noticed this about him— when people wanted something from him, whether it was money or, as in my own case, anything else, he tended to disappear.

One day there was a conversation between Renée and Rupert concerning Crishi. While awaiting trial, Rupert was out on bail and had taken Robi back to live with him. He continued to stay away from the gallery but visited us at home. I say us, but it was Renée he came to see. Although they were no longer husband and wife, two strong links remained between them—one was Robi, and the other must have been Rupert's feelings for her, for he couldn't keep away, although when he was there, she was irritable and impatient with him. She was the same with Robi, and he usually got away from her and came upstairs to be with me. I missed him now that he was back with his father, and made a big fuss of him whenever he came to visit. He sat very still when I combed his hair and even let me kiss him sometimes—he pretended he was doing me a favor, but I think he wanted me to. We played the games we used to play when he was living here, hide-and-seek around the flat or catch, not caring how much noise we made even when Anna was in the flat and said we were giving her a headache. We played forfeits and tickling games—these latter with him squirming and screaming around on the bed. In these abandoned moments he looked much more like Crishi than when he was his usual staid, shy self.

But if being with Robi was sometimes reminiscent of being with Crishi, at other times it was as if he were Michael—not that he looked like Michael but it was as it had been when Michael and I were children together. Whenever Robi came it was very satisfactory for me, and when he had left, I wanted more than ever that Crishi would let me get pregnant, but he kept saying "Wait," or "Not now," though in a nice way, as if he wanted it very much as soon as it would be convenient.

On this day, when it was time for Robi to leave and I took him downstairs, Renée and Rupert were in the middle of an argument. When I say argument, I mean that it was as usual between them—Renée irritated with him, and he doing his best to placate her. Only this time she was more than irritated, she was really upset, and I guess it was an indication of the progress of our relationship that she at once told me what it was about. Perhaps I hated Renée and she hated me—and how else could we possibly feel about each other, as how else could she and Bari Rani feel about each other? But just as in many ways she and Bari Rani were closer to each other than to anyone else, in so far as they shared the same close concern—that is, in their case, the Rawul—Renée and I too were united, even tied together through our concern, if that is the word, for Crishi.

Rupert had come to warn Renée that, in the course of the inquiry against him, he had begun to realize that the police were well informed about Crishi and his activities and those of the followers, including Michael. The recent spate of arrests should have been a warning, but Crishi either was not ready to listen to warnings or enjoyed carrying on in spite of them, or both. Taking risks put him in a good mood. Even in things like swimming—if there was a rock to dive from, if the Coast Guard had the red flag out, that was his best time; or just crossing a city street, he seemed deliberately to wait for the "Don't Walk" sign. As for Renée, I think she didn't want to know about the police—both because she wanted to shut her eyes and depend on Crishi completely, and because she couldn't deal with the idea of any danger threatening him. When Rupert gave her this information to warn her, she turned on him. It was at that point that I came in with Robi. Robi must have witnessed fights between his par-

ents before and didn't want to see any more; he pretended
nothing was happening and got behind a sofa, where he
played a game I had taught him, of making animals out of
a combination of your fingers and a handkerchief. I would
have liked to join him but couldn't; and if I had had any
doubts about being fully adult, Renée settled them at once
by drawing me in and telling me about the information Rupert had given her. She made it sound like Rupert was
responsible—she accused him of giving this information to
the police. It was useless for him to try to defend himself;
she insisted that was what must have happened.

"I'm not even blaming you," she told Rupert, though her
eyes flamed with fury. "I blame myself for getting you involved at all. I should have known—I did know—you couldn't
handle it. You couldn't even sell your own house, even a
simple little thing like that I had to come and do for you, so
how to expect you to get anything else right."

Rupert stood very upright and said "I did my best."

"Oh your best." She turned to me: "Rupert's best isn't up
to much. As you can see, all it's done is land us in trouble."

There was plenty he could have said in reply but he only
stood there and watched her pace up and down, working
herself up against him. He had tried to sacrifice himself—to
divert all blame and punishment on himself so that they could
carry on their work—but had failed even in that. And maybe
that was why he didn't defend himself more—because he did
feel guilty in general, for not being the strong and able personality she required him to be.

The Rawul came in, with the speech he was writing for his
birthday celebration. He had been working on it for many
days in his study, and every now and again he emerged to
try it out on his household. He saw at once that the moment
was not right—there was Rupert standing like an accused
person in the middle of the room, and Renée had thrown
herself into an armchair in a movement of despair. Her despair appeared to include the Rawul. She glowered at both
of them as they greeted each other with the cordial courtesy
of two English gentlemen, as if she were asking herself what
good were they to her—her two husbands—how could she
depend on them.

"Is something wrong?" the Rawul spoke into this con-
strained atmosphere. "Can I help in any way?"

He looked around at us, genuinely concerned to participate
in any difficulty there might be. But there was the understanding that the Rawul was not to participate in these aspects
of the work: that as the founder and figurehead of the movement he was not to know what had to be done to keep him
afloat.

It was Rupert who reassured him: "No," he said, with his
deprecating smile, "there's nothing wrong except that I've
been a fool again and Renée is quite rightly telling me off."

"My dear fellow," smiled the Rawul in return. "I can't believe that. We all have utter trust in you—don't we, Rani?—
we know you to be an utterly splendid chap, and we also
know—don't we," he said coyly, "that our Rani can sometimes
be a little bit—impatient? Just a little bit?" He smiled at her,
and went on quickly, "But where would we be without her?
Where would I be without her? Yes, I have these ideas, but
without her I would still be up there in my mountains dreaming of my new world—while thanks to her, here I am, making
that world. We have to hand it to her, absolutely," he said
and began to pat his palms softly together at her, in applause.

"Absolutely," agreed Rupert, looking down at the floor.

"You'd better go," Renée told Rupert; she was still sprawled
sullenly in her chair. He hesitated, wanting so much to stay,
maybe even try to improve her mood toward him, but when
he took a step in her direction, she turned her head away.
"And take the boy with you," she said. Rupert got Robi from
behind the sofa, and they went out in the rain together. I
watched them from the window, walking in the street below—rather slowly and sedately, tall Rupert holding his umbrella protectively over Robi.

Renée didn't stir from her chair but continued to stare
ahead of her in moody silence. The Rawul glanced at her,
and at the sheets of paper in his hand he had come in to
read to anyone who might be there to listen. He proceeded
to do so; it was a good speech. Renée wasn't listening, but
he didn't notice, he so much enjoyed his own words; he smiled
and glowed as he read. It was a shock to him, and to me,
when suddenly she shouted: "Oh be quiet, can't you, I can't

stand it another minute!" She had flung back her head and let her hands sink down to the sides of the chair, in weariness. The Rawul appeared not to know what to do; he looked at me, helplessly, the way he did when there was a button missing on his shirt. He approached her very slowly, very carefully—there was always that air about her, of a tigress who might do something terrible and entirely unexpected. He put his hand on hers, gingerly, fearing she might claw him. But she left his hand there as though she didn't feel it. She said to him as she had said to Rupert, "You'd better go," only in a less hostile way.

"Are you all right? You're sure?" he said—wanting to go but making himself inquire soliticiously. "No headache? You're not sick? Tell me. Rani." "No no," she said. "Go and write your birthday speech." His round face lit up with pleasure: "I've found such a good quote—shall I read it to you? . . . No not now, later," he answered himself, smiling at her, and at me, "when she's feeling herself again. We have to look after her. Such a precious person," he said and lifted her hand to his lips, dropping it quite soon; he hurried away, on tiptoe as if in deference to an invalid. I said to her, "Are you sick?" "Sick to death, that's all," she answered.

She came upstairs that night—I guess I had expected her to—and she sat on the end of our bed and told Crishi what Rupert had warned her about. Obviously it was a great relief to her to tell him; she was like a person laying down a heavy burden for someone else to pick up. He listened to her and was completely calm; in fact, he made out he knew about it and had planned what to do. When she finished, he said "Is that all? Is that what's been bugging you?" She burst into tears; it was as sudden as her outburst with the Rawul had been. She buried her head against Crishi's chest and sobbed—heavy, heavy sobs, of relief more than pain. And Crishi held and comforted her, and at the same time he smiled and shrugged the tiniest little bit at me. It took a long time before she had finished; in fact, she never really quite finished. When he laid her on the bed and put a pillow under her head, her sobs continued intermittently and new tears came trickling from under her closed lids. This continued even after she fell asleep; the passion inside her was inexhaustible. She slept there alone, for Crishi had gone to sit by the window, and I was squatting on the end of the bed, where I could watch his face in profile. It was lit up only by whatever light came from outside, so that it was mostly in shadow; and this may have accounted for the gloomy, brooding look I saw there, so different from the carefree, sunny aspect of himself he had shown only a moment before.

IT may have been that night that the decision was taken to begin the next phase of the movement. I tried to remember how it had been when we had passed into the present phase—that is, had come from America to England—but could remember only what a shock it had been to realize that everyone was leaving. Now I lived much more intimately at the center of the movement and was in on the earliest stages of planning. Or was I? Crishi made out that he was working to an absolutely preconceived program and that the decision to begin on the next phase— that is, to go to India—had been taken long before and had absolutely nothing to do with Rupert's warning. Renée, entirely herself again and not in the least like the Renée who had sobbed herself to sleep, also acted as if it were a long-standing decision. She began to be very busy with the arrangements for our departure, and for the consolidation of the English chapter. And by the following day the Rawul too seemed to think that we had been planning all along to leave for India, and that the coming celebration had been intended both as Founder's Day and as a valedictory occasion.

Only the Bari Rani had not anticipated our departure and had made all sorts of plans in England for the coming year. Daisy had started a typing course, and the other two girls were learning I think it was French; the Bari Rani herself was taking lessons in ikebana, and she had also found the most wonderful girl for her hair—no one had ever understood it so well. All the same, she did not seem displeased by our plans for departure; on the contrary. But she continued to warn me about the Rawul's kingdom of Dhoka—"oh my God, that dump," is how she referred to it—and advised me to take every kind of necessity, like Tampax and ballpoints; she said you couldn't get one single thing there, except of course for diseases you had never heard of and thought had been wiped out since the Middle Ages.

The kingdom of Dhoka: Up till now I had thought of it as sort of mythical, even though I knew it to be a real place. That was because of the way the Rawul spoke of it. It was his home—the place where his eyes had absorbed the color of the sky; where the gods had come down to be men; the country not only of his own birth but that of all humanity; the cradle of civilization. Well, naturally, hearing all that, anyone would want to go there: but now that we actually were going, I couldn't quite believe it was there and I would see it. And that was how it must have been with the followers who were being left behind—they envied those of us who were going but accepted that they themselves weren't worthy or at any rate ready to go there yet, like people feel themselves not ready for paradise or some such higher sphere. But there was also Renée's view of it—and to her it wasn't a bit mythical but a very definite place, even a place of business like the other ex–royal kingdoms where she had gone for art objects and antiques to smuggle out and sell.

I'm not sure how Crishi saw it. Sometimes he would repeat the story he had told Anna and make it sound like a place of miraculous happenings; but at other times he would look grave and say "I don't know how you're going to cope with it, Harriet—it's so primitive and you're used to such a nice standard of living." It was no use scanning his face to see if he was serious—he would start out looking very serious but next moment his lips twitched in amusement. I didn't always like it that he should be laughing at me—I was beginning to feel that I should be taken seriously sometimes, treated like an adult the way he treated Renée, like an equal, like a wife. When I said that, he did become serious, even sad; he said "See, you're getting tired of me—you don't laugh at my jokes anymore. I knew it would be like this, and why shouldn't it;

a person like me with such a bad record. And what will
happen next June when you come into your money—"

"What will happen?" I took him up, quite annoyed.

"You'll take off. You won't want anything more to do with
me. You'll leave me up there in Dhoka without a dime and
go back to Propinquity and never even answer my letters.
It's going to happen."

His eyes danced over my face; I knew it was as easy for
him to read my thoughts as it was impossible for me to guess
his. And on this subject of next June I didn't want him to
read my thoughts. I knew what most other people said, and
there was a part of me that shared their opinion. This didn't
change my feelings for him, but it did make me afraid. I
wanted a way to fasten him to me apart from the money and
real estate.

Michael was so busy nowadays that we hardly met, and
when we did, he didn't seem to see me at all. Michael never
really *saw* other people, but with me, even if he didn't physically perceive me—if anyone had asked him does Harriet
have long hair or short, he would have had to think about
it—all the same, he used to have this inner vision of or communion with me. But now—when his cold sailor's eye fell on
me, it was as blank as though he saw nothing. Perhaps that
was my imagination. Anyway, I could hardly during those
days have expected him to spare much time for me, since he
had to both prepare for Founder's Day and wind up our
activities here. This included deciding which followers were
dispensable—not an easy task, for naturally none of them
wanted to be thought dispensable after pouring their devo-
tion and energy into the movement. They had accepted the
fact that they would not be accompanying us to India. It had
been presented to them as a political decision, but the truth
was we couldn't afford their fares, and besides they would
be superfluous in India, where there was enough cheap labor
already. A skeleton force was to be left behind to keep the
movement going—or rather, keep the houses going, for in
the same way we had Propinquity and the house on the Island
in America, in England there were the Bari Rani's properties
and the old guru's house.

I watched Crishi and Michael one evening at home, going

over the list of followers and deciding who was to be part of
the caretaking force and who was to be got rid of. They
looked like a couple of Roman tribunes—Michael had the
list and a pencil, and when Crishi said "No, she won't do,"
Michael struck that name off in one firm exterminating stroke.
I noticed that the people struck off were the most idealistic
ones, all those who were waiting to immolate themselves for
the movement, whereas the ones to stay were more hard-
headed and practical. That made sense, I suppose, since their
job was a practical, caretaking one. Michael was to carry out
the task of informing the others that they were no longer
wanted. No doubt he was the right person for the job since
he would hand down the decision without giving anyone the
chance to argue with him. For the people's own sake, I wished
it had been Crishi, who would at least have let them say
something in their own defense—not that it would have made
any difference, but it might have relieved their feelings. Unlike Michael, Crishi would also have gone to the trouble of
telling some lie to make them feel better.

Anna was one of the people who was to be let go. She
didn't fall into the category of followers, but I can't define
where she did fall. A change had come over Anna, and also
our perception of her. We were hardly aware of her anymore—there were days when she didn't emerge from the
flat, not even to go downstairs, although she was supposed
to be taping the Rawul and writing this book about him. She
had sometime ago stopped waiting for Crishi or trying to
attract our attention, and we tended to forget about her; only
Renée sometimes said "Can't you tell her to turn that thing
down," and Crishi would rap on the wall for her to lessen
the volume of her TV or cassette player. He went in there
only when he wanted to know about the progress she was
making on her book. At first she must have taken the trouble
to lie to him, but as time went on and no progress was made,
he would get very impatient with her and once I heard him
say "Then what use are you to us?" She laughed—not bitterly,
a matter-of-fact sort of laugh.

What had happened to her? It seemed to be the opposite
of what happened to other people caught up in the movement. When I thought of Debbie and other followers, it was

clear to me that, whatever the conditions under which they were living—and in the Earl's Court house they were pretty dreadful—and however hard they had to work for the organization or as personal body servants, they found it more than worthwhile: They found it fulfilling. The same was true of Michael, for whom the movement had become the higher objective he had been seeking all his life. But Anna hadn't been seeking anything. Of course she was older—no one knew how old, for she was the type to keep very quiet about her age, and she could get away with it, for she was petite and in a good light could have passed for young. And Anna had a career, was a successful journalist, whereas everyone else didn't have anything—for instance, Debbie, though a college graduate, took on jobs waiting tables or selling door to door or anything she could get by with: So naturally Debbie was looking for something better, something else. But although all Anna had been looking for was a place to live, she too had got attached to us in the same way—or rather, Crishi had attached her to us. When she had first come to Propinquity, I didn't let myself look too closely at the situation, but it must have been clear to everyone that she was having an affair with Crishi. Probably for Anna any assignment meant a love relationship with someone, it was almost part of the deal for her; everyone knew how she had slept with the Lebanese guerrilla leader who was later executed, and how she had become so involved with a member of a terrorist group that she had become part of their gang for a while. But once her story was finished, so was the affair that went with it, and maybe this was what she had intended to happen with Crishi. He didn't see it that way. For one thing, he needed her as a publicist for the movement; and for another, and I had noticed this with him before, he didn't like to let people go. Once they were involved with him, he felt they had to belong to him; that his brand was on them.

Maybe if she had met him in earlier years, Anna could have passed on from him as easily as from everyone else. She used to take it for granted that she would always be a top journalist, in demand for her in-depth political-plus-human-interest stories. But these magazine stories were being replaced more and more by television profiles; and lately she had not been picking the right kind of subjects—that is, her instinct for what was central in the public interest was no longer as sure as it had been. She herself said that choosing our movement as a topic was a mistake. "I must have been crazy," she told me one time. "Who would want to know about a cheap little crank outfit like that?" I wasn't used to hearing the Rawul's movement referred to in those terms, but I put it down to her general disappointment. It couldn't have been pleasant for her to be left to rot in the upstairs flat; or the way Renée did nothing to disguise her contempt for her; and, worst, Crishi's neglect. I had seen him treat her very differently before, doing everything to attach her to us, making her feel wanted for herself and not only because she was writing a book about the Rawul. Now he made no secret that all he wanted out of her was the book, and if she wasn't going to deliver it, she was no use to him. So it happened that when he and Michael came to Anna's name on the list of followers, Crishi negligently waved his hand and Michael crossed it out.

Anna didn't drink or smoke or take anything else to blunt the edge of her very sharp mind, and that made her more aware than people usually are of what happens to them. I mean, most others, and that includes myself, when something bad happens to them and they suffer, they don't so much analyze the causes as tend to blur them. But Anna faced up to the truth absolutely. She said she had been used—by Crishi—and at first she blamed herself more than him, for letting this be done to her. It must have been particularly humiliating for her because she herself had made a career of using people—literally a career, getting them to throw themselves open to her so she could throw them open to her readers. She felt outwitted, and brooded in the way someone who has played a bad game of chess goes back to analyzing the causes of why he lost. It was strange to me, how she could do that when the stakes were herself; but she was a very cool, strong person, not unlike Crishi. She said he had got her at a bad moment, when everything was going wrong for her: but of course, she said, that was just when someone like him did get hold of people, when he knew that they were in need. "Like you and your brother," she said. I objected to, I denied her view of us, but she laughed at me and said Michael and

I were the neediest people she had ever met. "The young always are," she said. "They need a future, like the middle-aged need to recover the past that didn't come up to expectations." But she wanted to talk about herself, not us; she said several times, "He got me wrong," narrowing her eyes, determined to set him right and show him what she was really like.

The Bari Rani was finding tenants for the flats falling vacant when we left for India—that is, her own flat as well as the downstairs and upstairs ones in our house. She didn't believe in going through agents and paying them what she called some ridiculous percentage, but she personally took people around. She came upstairs several times and barged in and out of our bedrooms and bathrooms and opened closets to show them to prospective tenants. These were mostly foreign businessmen and their wives, and they trailed behind her and appeared intimidated, as well they might be, for the Bari Rani was regal and at the same time a sharp business-woman; if the client, or usually his wife, plucked up courage to object to some feature of the accommodation, she over-ruled them at once and moved firmly to the next room. She didn't care who was inside—once Michael was squatting in the tub holding the sprayer over his head and she didn't even apologize. When she opened Anna's door without knocking, she just said "Oh are you still here"; Anna could be seen crouching inside as in a lair and she stared out at the intruders with very bright eyes, so that even Bari Rani thought it best to close that door again right away.

In the past, Anna's presence had made me uneasy because she was waiting for Crishi in the same way I was. She was still waiting for him, but in a different way. Crishi didn't seem to give her a thought and acted as if she weren't there, while we could hear her playing TV or her tapes in the next room. When he was tired, he turned around and went to sleep. I kept on listening to the mechanical sounds from her room. Behind them, I felt I could hear her sharp thoughts clicking, her hard heart beating, and I leaned over Crishi as if I had to protect him. He looked very young sleeping, though I knew by this time he wasn't. He slept naked, which made him seem particularly vulnerable. One night I crept to the door to lock it so no one would be able to get in. I did it very softly, for I knew how lightly he slept, alert to every sound or movement. But when I returned to the bed, he was lying there with his eyes wide open and watching. He looked ready to spring, or any other action that might be necessary. He asked "Why did you do that?" I wouldn't tell him at first, knowing he would laugh at me, and when he got it out of me, of course he did. "Oh you're scared she's going to use her little pearl-handled pistol on me? . . . You don't by any chance think she hasn't got one? Someone like Anna? Are you kidding? She wouldn't be seen dead without it."

It was one more thing to deal with in my mind. I looked back at myself as I used to be—at Propinquity, or in Grand-father's embassies—Michael and I both. We used to think we had to deal with such a lot: our parents, Lindsay and Manton, and going from country to country and being in international schools and not belonging anywhere, not wanting to settle anywhere, not wanting to go to any more schools, and not knowing what to do next; and the way we would discuss it and try to think out our values in absolute truth and purity. But now all that seemed so childish and unreal, blank some-how; as though we were blank pages no one had ever written on. That was not the right image—I had heard it used but it was not the right one for what I felt was happening to me. It was more like having my consciousness made deeper as more and more things—of which Anna's little pearl-handled pistol was one—were dropped into it. Things I didn't know about, which people did or had; the way other people were or lived. Now I was not only learning about all that but par-ticipating in it.

I began to wait for Anna to go out, so that I could get in her room and search for her gun. It is strange to go secretly into someone's room—this was my first experience of it— for they seem to be as much in it as when they are actually there; or even more so, maybe because you are thinking of them so intensely, and afraid they might come back and catch you. This inhibited me from searching very thoroughly; be-sides, I didn't know where to search, where people might hide guns. I opened her closet and chest of drawers, stuffed with clothes; she had an immensely large wardrobe, so many little dresses and shoes to match them, and silk shirts and cashmere sweaters. Otherwise there was nothing—no photographs, no letters she had kept, or any object or memento: just clothes, and her dressing table full of cosmetics. I must have gone in there two or three times, in fact every time she went out, which wasn't very often. I never stayed long, always thinking I heard her coming back. But the thought of that gun had got wedged in my mind, and I imagined every sort of situation, especially at night when Crishi was sleeping.

One day when Anna had gone out, Michael was home—this was rare too—I could hear him showering, and I went in the bathroom and sat waiting for him to finish. It was a long time since I had seen him without his clothes. We didn't avoid it but it didn't happen, probably because we were no longer together as much as we had been. I had forgotten how very white he was—peeled—or maybe it hadn't struck me so much before I got used to Crishi's color. When he turned off the shower, I told him about Anna's gun, and he wrapped a towel around himself and went straight in her room with me. He searched much more thoroughly than I, more skillfully too; and he wasn't a bit nervous that she might come back. There was something nice about being there with him on this secret search—not the actual search but the two of us doing something together after such a long time. He didn't find a gun but he did find a folder with her passport—or rather, passports. She had three—he showed them to me—one British, one French, one Iraqi.

Something else that was happening at this time was that Babaji's health was really going down. He still spoke of returning to India, and the two Devis told him they would take him there, but I could see they were not as hopeful about him as they pretended. He remained cheerful—he kept trying to sing and some very high, cracked notes came out, driving Crishi crazy when he was there so he would tell me to go and shut the old man's door; but I wouldn't do it because I knew he liked to have it open to see everyone passing. Whenever he saw me, he would call me in—it got so that when I was busy I crouched down to get past without his seeing me. Once when I went in, he said to me, "Do you know where I'm going?" I said "Yes, to India." "Right," he said and beckoned me closer, closer, closer; he had always done that, so he could pat my cheek or whatever, but now it was so I could put my ear near his mouth because his voice had become very weak.

"I'm going home," he said. "Do you know where that is? It's by a river and I shall swim in it; bathe and sing sing, pray pray, all day long. When the sun goes down, all the birds fly home and they sit in a tree and make a lot of noise and then they're asleep. I'm asleep too, in my little hut. Yes, I have a little hut by the river, and when I get up at night to relieve myself, the moon is shining on the river and also on the water I'm making, and my water is a clear pure shining silver stream. . . . This is what I cook and eat: a handful of rice, a turnip and an onion, and one piece of pickle—do you like pickle? It burns but it tastes good, hm hm, hot. I wish I had it right now—just now—call the Devis—tell them Babaji wants his pickle. Run! Quick!" But when I ran to Nina Diva, she said "Oh no he mustn't. Poor Babaji." She returned with me, but he was talking about something else then: "They gave me a watch—a big big watch, I never took it off, I could tell the time and the day and the month; and then they gave me a radio and the radio was as small as the watch was big—tiny tiny tiny—and then they said you have to have an airplane. I said all right. They all came with me in the plane, all singing, and we landed on the mountain and they built a big beautiful place with air-conditioned Meditation Hall. They came from everywhere to be with me—Germany—all the countries. I taught them everything. I had to, because they didn't know anything—nothing at all—only eat, sleep, fuck, that's all. I taught them. I taught you," he told Nina Devi. "You didn't know anything."

"Nothing," she confirmed. She grasped his hands—"Dear Babaji, everything has come from you"—but he pulled them away and said "Don't touch me! You're old. I want her—let her do it to me." I knew he meant me, though I wasn't sure what he wanted me to do to him. When I looked inquiringly at Nina Devi, she said "Babaji has to rest now. For the journey. You want to be nice and fresh for the journey, don't you Babaji?" "What journey? I'm not going anywhere." "Why Babaji—we're going home to India." He waved her away— "You don't know anything about that place." He turned his face away from us and didn't try to stop us when we left.

Of course the two Devis were tremendously sad to see him sinking but, like him, they remained happy and cheerful. And they too kept harking back to the past—they couldn't tell me enough about it, how nice it had been. The Devis were always dressed in white cotton saris with Jesus sandals on their bare feet, and they wore their hair Indian-style and that red mark on the forehead; but they looked and spoke and were as English as you could be. Nina Devi was short, sturdy, and apple-cheeked; a wonderful manager, a wonderful gardener, full of common sense, calm, pleasant, affectionate. Before joining Babaji's movement, she had taught English and geography in a girls' school, and she was the sort of person you would want to be your teacher. Maya Devi had also been a teacher, but only for a very short time because she said she found it too consuming. I could imagine how she would get very involved with some of the girls and have these very strong favorites and care nothing for the rest of the class at all except for disliking some of them. She was herself like some English girls I had gone to school with; she had the same gawky figure and columnar legs and big hands and feet she didn't know where to put. She was always starting up with pleasure or anger, but having been so long with Babaji, she had learned to curb herself more—at least she tried to; you could see her doing it, rearing up and then making herself get down again as if she were both horse and rider; and if she didn't manage it herself, there was Nina Devi to gently warn "Maya Maya," whereupon Maya Devi would strike herself about the face with her fist and say "I know I know I *know*," in an absolute passion with herself.

They had both been among Babaji's earliest followers and remained part of his most inner circle right through his high tide of public success when he had had many rich followers and a few famous ones. It was never those years the Devis dwelled on, but the beginning, when there had been just a handful of them living in old army huts on vegetables and goat milk. It did sound very beautiful—the river Babaji had spoken of, where they had bathed and prayed, and the sunrise and sunset reflected in it, and the trees, birds, and hymn singing—everything was pure and bright and so were they when they spoke of it. They were middle-aged, old even, but their eyes shone and their voices skipped a bit and they tripped each other up with laughter when they told how it had been.

Unfortunately, at this time the house was very noisy. Led by Michael, the followers had their usual arms drill and other martial exercises; they ran and marched around Nina Devi's flower beds, and they pinned a board for air-pistol target practice on the shower curtain in one of the bathrooms. In addition, there were the preparations for Founder's Day, involving a lot of hammering and moving of furniture, so Babaji certainly couldn't get the silence and rest required for a sick man. Nina Devi decided she would have to appeal to the Rawul, and one day she came to call on him in the downstairs flat. I was surprised to see her and the way she was dressed—not in her usual sari but in a baggy brown skirt and jacket, which must have dated back to when she was teaching school. She sat on the black-and-gold sofa in the drawing room with her flat-heeled shoes dangling over the Persian carpet, very patient and determined as she waited to be admitted to the Rawul's presence. There was always something of being "admitted to a presence" with the Rawul, but Nina Devi was one of the people who met him with an equal dignity. She was small and shabby, had come to him as a supplicant, yet with the air of an ambassador representing a power as important as the Rawul himself. The Rawul was silent for a long time after she had made her plea to postpone the celebration. His eyes were downcast, looking at the floor, and when he raised them again, they were full of sorrow to have to refuse her. He explained how utterly it lay beyond his, beyond any person's power to change a date that lay within the rotation of the movement's calendar. I felt that it wasn't up to me to point out that it *had* in fact been changed—that when it was thought better to leave the country because of the police inquiries, the date of both his birthday and Founder's Day had been moved forward. Nina Devi listened as patiently as he explained; and when he had finished, he got up and moved in his stately way to the door, which he opened for her. He bent down toward her and took her small hand in his and kept it there, while assuring her of his concern for Babaji and sending heartfelt wishes for a full and speedy recovery.

But Babaji died before Founder's Day. Michael was in the

house at the time, together with other followers, working very hard to get the downstairs rooms ready for the celebrations. The Devis had to come down several times to ask them to make less noise, but it was impossible to be quiet in the process of such a major job. Anyway, Babaji died in the middle of it all, and when Michael came home at dawn he either forget to mention the fact, or was too tired from working. I didn't get to know till one of the Devis called to tell me. Even then, it was some time before I could take her news in, for she told me in a bright happy voice that Babaji had attained *samadhi*. At first I thought she was telling me he was better, and it was only when she gave me the time and place of the cremation that I understood. Of course I said I would go. I dressed up for it—I didn't actually have anything black, but I did have a sort of suit Lindsay had once got for me. I had assumed we were all going, only it turned out everyone else was much too busy with preparations for Founder's Day.

But when he saw me dressed up, Crishi said he would go with me. I was grateful, especially as he too made the effort of changing into a dark suit and sober tie. I thought we both looked very, very respectable, but Crishi wasn't satisfied and made me change into high-heeled shoes and tie my hair up. I was glad to do it, to be at my most presentable for Babaji's cremation; only it turned out we weren't going to the cremation, although I failed to realize that until our taxi drove up to one of those big stone buildings with symbolic sculptures in the city. When I protested, Crishi said it was all right, that he had to see someone about the interest payments on some loan he had taken and that there would be plenty of time to go on to the funeral afterward. I wasn't too surprised—we had done this before, dressed up in very presentable clothes and gone together to some creditor where Crishi introduced me as his wife. I guess we made a good impression together, for these interviews went off very cordially and the problem, whatever it was, was either settled or postponed. That was what happened this time too—Crishi was very charming, and frank and open, and I was demure with my little purse and gloves. Sherry was called for and brought in by a butler, and afterward there was a lot of handshaking and goodwill, and the whole thing took so long that it was too late to get to the cremation in time.

The Devis brought the ashes back in an urn, and they were very eager to travel to India and immerse them in some sacred river there. To defray their expenses, and maybe also to keep them going in general, they urgently needed the rest of the payments on the house, and Crishi too was anxious to be in undisputed possession before our departure. He had payments to make on the gallery as well, and the rent of the Mayfair office had to be kept up in our absence, and there were many other financial settlements he had to take care of, not to speak of the cost of getting us to India: so there was a lot of wheeling and dealing going on, and I had to make calls to Sonya in New York to ask her for various loans. She was very willing to make them—she always was; asking her for money was the biggest favor you could do her, and she would bring you the check herself as fast as she could. But these were pretty big amounts we needed, which she couldn't get at without Mr. Pritchett's knowing. He must have said the usual sort of things to her, I mean, issued the same warnings he did to us: because she rang me back very embarrassed and said was I sure I needed quite so much—not that she wasn't happy to let me have it, but she didn't want me to make a mistake. I said what sort of a mistake, knowing all this came from Mr. Pritchett, and that as far as he was concerned, I had already made it, in marrying Crishi. I went on to tell her in a breathless little-girl voice I was surprised to hear from myself—Crishi was sitting there listening and nodding to me in encouragement—about what a great time we were having, Michael and I, and how much we were looking forward to going to India and having an even greater one there. Sonya was so moved and happy with our being so happy she could hardly wait to hurry away to Mr. Pritchett and overrule him: Money and the caution it should engender were to her as foreign as they were at that time to me.

A few days before Founder's Day, Barbara and Manton called to tell me the date of their wedding. Barbara said it was the last possible week—as it was, she had to go to the maternity department to have her wedding dress made; she asked for my measurements so she could order my matron-of-honor outfit from the regular bridal department. The date they gave me was when we would be in India, but I didn't tell them that because they so absolutely expected me to be present. And later, when I told Crishi, he said that I would just have to fly back from India to New York for it. I didn't like that idea. When I thought of India, and in particular of Dhoka, it was as a sort of absolute destination from which there was no looking back, let alone taking a plane back for a wedding. But Crishi said "Your old dad's wedding" in a shocked and sacred voice; then he said "Doesn't Manton have some sort of trust fund?" Although I protested that he was usually horribly overdrawn on it, Crishi said that surely he could raise a loan for a daughter in difficulties, good heavens. When I called New York, I was tearful and Manton said "What is it, baby?" in his new voice of concern and responsibility. But when he had coaxed it out of me that I needed a loan, he went off the deep end in the old Manton way and said my God, didn't I know what sort of a hand-to-mouth existence he led anyway, and now with Barbara having got herself pregnant—I heard Barbara on the other line burst into sobs at this reproach, and I too began to sob but managed to say "It's only till next June, Daddy," in between *my* sobs; till Manton grumbled, Well he would have to speak to his accountant and I hung up and smiled at Crishi, who said "Okay, every little bit helps," in an offhand way but seemed pleased with me.

FOUNDER'S DAY started off as an ordinary family birthday. Bari Rani and the girls came for breakfast, bearing gifts. The Rawul was in his family-man aspect, extending his plump, shaved cheek to each girl in turn to come up and kiss. He was wearing his brocade dressing gown over his undershirt and the white leggings he had got on for later in the day. He smelled fresh and nice of after-shave and eau de cologne and beamed all around in radiant goodwill. It was a big and happy day for him. The girls had made birthday cards and wrapped their gifts very artistically, and he accepted them graciously and put them aside. But the Bari Rani insisted he open them there and then, and she also made him try on the contents because, if they didn't fit, she was going to take them back right away to change them. He didn't want to but she insisted, and this ruffled him a bit—in his mood, as well as literally, because of having to pull a sweater over his smoothly brushed hair. But everyone was determined that no cloud should mar this perfect day. Renée and Bari Rani were on their best behavior with each other, and they even joined in protest when the Rawul began to make a little impromptu speech at the breakfast table. "We're going to hear enough of that all day," said Bari Rani, and Renée agreed he should be saving his voice. "Only a few words," he pleaded, looking around the table. "A few special words to those of you who have made my dream yours." The girls groaned, and the Rawul defended himself: "It's not a speech—it's a declaration of love. For my family," he said. "Because at heart that is what I am—a family man, in the deepest sense of that term. That is the instinct prompting me—driving me—to make a family of the whole world, to make everyone sit down together in peace and love as we are sitting here around this table—" "It's a *speech!*" cried the girls accusingly—"No no no," said the Rawul, but he laughed and good-naturedly allowed Daisy to stop his mouth with a piece of croissant.

But what he was saying was true, and I too looked around the table at all of us sitting if not in unalloyed peace and love, at any rate in some sort of harmony, which was in itself an achievement. The Rawul sat across from me, partly hidden by the big Georgian coffeepot; beside him sat the Bari Rani and beside her their three daughters. The five of them appeared as the solidly Indian phalanx of our family—not that they were very dark; on the contrary, they were light-skinned, Aryans, Parthians; yet in the timbre of their voices, their deportment, their physical aura, there was something that spoke of different landscapes from those we knew, with strange mountains and rivers springing out of them and flowing over pastures where strange cattle grazed. On the other side of the Rawul sat Renée, and although her skin had an ivory tint to it and her hair was as dark as that of the girls and flashing with the same dark auburn lights, there were other countries and climates compounded in her, nearer home, and not only because she wore Parisian clothes (Bari Rani wore those, too, sometimes, but they only made her look more Oriental). Crishi sat next to Renée—if he had been younger or she older he could have been her son, for he also had an Oriental basis underlying his many other characteristics: but in his case the mixture was even more indefinable, for it seemed to include everywhere he had been, the many places where he had lived and traveled in every hemisphere, and all the things he had done there. And next to Crishi there was Rupert—yes, also a member of the family, tall calm courteous noble English Rupert; and next to Rupert, Michael with his pale craggy visionary's face and his hair shaved to a bristle; and me, his twin; and next to me Robi—completing the circle and somehow belonging to Bari Rani's side of it, for he looked as

Indian as that side: as though the Oriental quality, which in his mother—and in Crishi—had been overlaid with other strains, had come out pure and strong in him.

The only one who was not there as a member of the family was Anna. In fact, she was packing upstairs, for she was moving out that day. I had heard her during the whole of last week making phone calls to find a place to live. She spoke in a soft low cajoling voice, which wasn't part of her personality and which she took off the moment she replaced the receiver, looking disgusted, like one who had done this before and was sick of it. But she tried to make her own arrangements and never complained or confided in anyone. She and Crishi were no longer on speaking terms—she never came out when he was there, and he never went in to her. There was something still, self-contained, and brooding about her. I found it impossible to put her out of my mind; and when, during the Rawul's birthday breakfast, the doorbell rang in a very short, sharp way, I knew at once it was she. I went to open the door before anyone else could, and there was Anna wearing a hat and coat. She asked me to go and call Crishi; something in my expression made her laugh and she said "I only want him to help me carry down my luggage." I said "I'll do it"; she said "No, you don't have to do all his work for him." She was not looking at but past me, alert for an opportunity to push her way in. I was determined not to let her. I put the chain on the door and we stood on either side of it, both of us waiting. I was afraid Crishi would come to see what was happening, so I held on to the dining-room door from outside. She said "One day you'll want to do the same thing yourself." I didn't argue with her, just held on to the dining-room door. When someone tried to open it from inside, I threw my whole weight against it.

But it wasn't Crishi, it was Michael. It was his voice I heard say "What's the matter?" I let him come out; he went to the front door and took the chain off, for now there were two of us to stand guard, facing Anna. We were very unevenly matched; he and I were not tall, but we towered over her small figure. On the other hand there was the possibility that she had a gun, and this was in his and my mind, and maybe it was what made her so tense and determined as she faced us in her hat and coat and clutching her handbag. I could feel Michael beside me revving himself up—getting himself to that pitch of precision that all his exercising was about— and next moment he put out his hand to grab her bag; but she was as quick as he was and swung it aside and he grabbed hold of her wrist instead. They were locked together in an impasse, with her not letting him get hold of her bag but he, with his grip on her wrist, preventing her from opening it and taking out whatever was in there. Clearly it was now up to me, and I caught hold of her bag. I was surprised by the fierceness of her struggle, but obviously she didn't have a chance with him holding her, and I soon had the bag. I opened it and found the gun I had been searching for all these days. The moment Michael let her go, she pounced on me to try to get the purse back; he pulled her off me and threw her down on the floor and, taking the handbag from me, he extracted the gun. He tested the safety catch, and he put the gun in his pocket. Anna was lying on the floor with her skirt half hitched up and one leg bent in an awkward way under her; her hat was still in place, and she looked up at us from under it with the eyes of a fierce, hurt little animal. Now that we safely had her gun, I wanted to help her get up, but Michael said "Let's go," and flung her handbag down on the floor beside her so that the harmless contents scattered, some on the landing and some on the stairs. We didn't wait to see her retrieve them but returned to the breakfast table. Crishi looked up at us and said "Where have you been, you two?" rather casually, as if he weren't expecting much of an answer.

It was the second time I had seen Michael in action—the first time had been with Nicholas in the gallery—and I was impressed with him. I mean, the way he was so decisive and in a completely unreflecting way, although he was by nature such a deeply reflective person. And that same day I saw him again in this new aspect—or maybe it wasn't new, maybe it was the same Michael, my Michael, completed, fulfilled. An important part of that day's festivities was the ceremonial march in the back garden, followed by a display of martial exercises. Michael was sort of the commanding officer of the squad of followers, and they filed past the Rawul, who, standing under an umbrella, took the salute from the stone-flagged terrace at the back of the house. Of course it was raining and of course they got wet, but that had been expected—in fact, in his inaugural address the Rawul had made a little joke about it, how they were now in that part of his dominions where he had to contend for his title with the god of rain. But as with all his jokes, he lifted the theme into a higher sphere: saying that it was an essential part of his movement, and of his inspiration, that all landscapes, all climates as well as all peoples and nations, should be comprised within it. Anyway, there they were, now marching, now displaying their martial skills of judo and karate in the rain. I don't know if it was an inspiring scene for everyone, but it was for me. Unlike the front yard, laid out with flower beds and bordering the main road, where commuting cars whizzed past, the back had been left more untended to give some impression of a rural retreat. It stretched for quite a way, and beyond it there was an open field with a horse or two in it from the neighboring riding school. Although beyond that there was a new housing development and a glassware factory, these were blotted out by the rain so that the mists and vapors enveloping them might as well have been enveloping a lovely English landscape of fences and stiles and yellow-and-green fields with haystacks in them and brown cows. That was the background; and in the foreground there were Michael and the followers—I must admit I didn't take much notice of the latter, except for being impressed by their eagerness, which made them absolutely impervious to the rain. This eagerness, so it seemed to me, reached its highest pitch in Michael as he shouted his words of command and wheeled and turned and threw up his knees. He radiated pride and joy and certitude, and these were also there in the Rawul watching from under his umbrella—I don't know if they flowed from him to Michael or from Michael to him but I suppose it was a sort of two-way traffic between them, each inspiring the other, each believing with an ardent soul in the high destiny of the Rawul's mission.

I don't think the others were watching as intently as I was. They were all there, ranged behind the Rawul, everyone who had been at breakfast that morning; but they were

fidgety and Bari Rani and the girls were whispering together
till Renée shot them an angry look. But Renée herself appeared to be restless and looked as often at her watch as did
Bari Rani. And afterward, when the audience filed into the
drawing room for the Rawul's speech, several of our family
members lingered around the house with other matters than
the Fourth World on their minds. The Rawul carried on
undeterred, speaking with the same fervor as always and
saying the same sort of things: about his dream, and looking
up at the sky, and one world for one mankind. It was wonderful how consistent he was, and how it didn't make any
difference to him whether he was under the tree at Propinquity, with the lake and the sun setting in it, or here in this
cramped, genteel house in a London suburb, and the electric
light shining dully against the windows, where the day was
dying without ever having come alive.

I didn't see Crishi in the room, nor Renée, so I knew they
were together somewhere and went to look for them. They
were in one of the upstairs bedrooms and I went straight in
there as unhesitatingly as Renée came in when Crishi and I
were together. They didn't challenge my right to do so, nor
did they try to disguise their intimacy. Renée was lying on
the bed, on her back and with her arms flung out; and Crishi
was exasperated with her and at the same time trying to
comfort her, trying to make things sound better than they
were. He pointed to me as a good example, how willing and
happy I was to pack up and leave and go along to wherever
we were going. "Aren't you?" he said, and I said yes I was.
He smiled at me warmly—and when she wasn't looking, he
cast his eyes up in comic exasperation for my benefit. She
said "I'm sick of running here and there to raise money, and
then more money, and what's it all for? . . . Has he started
down there yet?" I said "Yes the Rawul has started his speech
and we'd better go." "Oh we've heard it before, so often it's
coming out of our ears," she said. Crishi sat down beside her
on the bed and said "How you carry on"; and when he was
close to her, she flung herself across his lap in one compulsive
movement and clung to him. He looked so slight and she so
large, I thought she must be awfully heavy for him to support.
He didn't appear to be overwhelmed but was lightly stroking

her back to comfort her; it was a son comforting his mother more than anything else, and I felt nothing except maybe sorry for her.

After a while she sat up. She said "And what for? What's it all been for? I don't care for anything except that you and I should be together."

She said this quite openly before me; and it seemed all right to me—or he made it seem all right by being turned toward me even while he was holding her. She was like the mother he had to humor and I the wife he wanted to be with.

"It'll work out," he promised her. "Rupert's here, and when we want to come back it'll have blown over."

"And then you'll start again."

"No I won't. Why should I? I won't have to. I'll be such a good boy, you'll see. Just wait till June."

"Yes," I said, "in June I'll get my money."

She looked at me; and I back at her, quite calm and reassuring. It did seem a very good thing to me that in June everyone's financial problems would be solved, and they wouldn't have to continue what they had been doing. My assurance calmed her; and Crishi said "Surely you can wait till June?" in a sort of coaxing way, playing with her large ringed hand in his, but at the same time looking at me and appearing to promise me something different from what he was promising her, as to what it would be like after June.

I didn't mind leaving them alone—she wanted it so much —while I went down to join the Rawul's audience. But on the way I met Rupert. He was sitting on the bottom stair, with his elbows on his big knees and supporting his head between his hands in a despairing attitude that was quite uncharacteristic of him. I mean, he was usually so upright and invincible, whatever happened to him, through all the ugly things that he had taken on himself. I sat beside him on the stairs, and he said "You'll look after Robi, won't you?" I knew Rupert was staying behind—he had to, because of his case—but this was the first I had heard about Robi coming with us. "It'll be easier for him with you there," Rupert said. "He's rather nervous with everyone else. I suppose he's nervous generally—we've been together alone too much. My fault. I gave him to understand I'd always be there." After a while he said "I have to let him down." And glancing up at the bedroom door where we both knew Renée was with Crishi, "I promised her the earth too and didn't deliver."

Rupert wasn't the type to talk freely about anything, least of all himself; but I guess there was a bond between us. He may even have thought that our situations were alike—only there he was wrong, even though the stairs on which we were sitting led up to the door where my husband was with Renée. We could hear the Rawul from inside the drawing room —his voice sounded high and bright as he proclaimed his new world order. He probably didn't notice that we weren't there; maybe he didn't even glance toward his scanty audience of earnest English people. I think the Rawul was never much concerned about who was physically present, carrying as he did the cheering crowds of the future inside him.

Rupert said "She was bored from the first day she married me—bored with me and everything I thought I could offer her. Such as my freezing house which I loved, but all I ever saw her do there was walk around shivering and rubbing her arms. She couldn't get rid of it fast enough; and to keep her, I let it go and sold whatever she wanted me to sell. I couldn't have loved it so very much, after all, could I? Finally it was nothing to me, compared to her. It still isn't; and all I regret is—you know—not coming up to standard. To her standard." He looked at the door again and said matter-of-factly, "I suppose only Crishi does that."

Crishi came out of the bedroom upstairs just then, glanced around, glanced down, saw me—"There you are, Harriet." He had been looking for me! He had come out of that room, leaving Renée behind, to look for me! I forgot about Rupert that instant, rose from the step where I had been sitting with him, and walked straight up to the landing where Crishi was. He took my hand, and instead of going downstairs to the Rawul's lecture as we should have done, we went up to the little attic room next to Babaji's. Of course Babaji was gone; only the urn with his ashes was there on his bed, waiting to be taken to India. Crishi locked our door and we fell on the bed, laughing like runaways, escaped from somewhere or someone. We started kissing and never had his lips tasted so soft and sweet, like sweet soft berries, and when we took off our clothes, his skin was smooth as honey except for the places where it was puckered by his scars. With his clothes he had thrown off everything else, whatever worries he had, and his deals, even his own past and whatever might have gone wrong in it. "Isn't this nice," he kept saying as he kissed me again and again with those lips like berries. We clung together—it was wonderful the way our two bodies fitted into each other.

He started making plans. I don't know for when, but the point of them was that they didn't include anyone except him and me. We were going to get a two-seater convertible and keep driving till we were tired. If there was a big hotel, preferably by the ocean, we'd stay in that and dress up and dance in its discotheque, or if it was just some motel, we wouldn't dress at all but stay lying around in bed eating fried chicken we'd sent out for. I assumed this trip was taking place at home in the States, but next moment he was talking about crossing the Alps, and then we were driving from Marseilles to . . . to . . . Istanbul; across every European border where they might search us and our car as much as they pleased and wouldn't find anything because we wouldn't be carrying anything. Perhaps we would get a dog, a German shepherd or golden retriever, and it would come with us in the car everywhere, except in some countries there would be trouble about quarantine so we'd better forget about the dog.

Then I made a mistake; I said "But we're going to Dhoka." As soon as I said it, I felt a shadow pass over his bright and happy spirit. I didn't know why that should be but wanted above everything to get rid of it and went on quickly, "I guess you mean when we come back." "Yes," he agreed as quickly, "when we come back." But the shadow remained.

Trying to return to our earlier mood, I said "All we need do is wait till June." He agreed heartily and I went on, "We could go to Hong Kong if you like."

"Hong Kong!"

"Your mother. Don't you want me to meet your mother?"

He groaned, though it was partly in amusement. "Leave it, Harriet. Leave all that. It's too much. . . . Isn't it enough that you know Rani? That we have Rani?"

"She's not your mother."

"She's adopted me." And he invited me to gaze into his

eyes, which he made very serious; but his mouth corners were twitching and next moment he was laughing and so was I and we rolled around a bit.

I couldn't leave it alone. I said "I want to know everything about you and everyone who's ever known you and everything you've ever done."

Crishi groaned again and shut his eyes. When he opened them, they had a very young puzzled look in them; and when he spoke, he sounded genuinely aggrieved: "Why can't we take it easy? Why does everyone want something all the time? Nothing is ever enough—whatever they've got, it's never enough. Rani is like that, you are, Michael of course; what is it? What's the matter with all of you? I can understand it with people who don't have anything—who are sort of hungry, like my mother, and me, I guess, when I started out. My mother was so pretty, in her little pink negligee with swansdown on it. But there were weeks we lived on packet soups and pizza till she found someone who liked her enough to take care of us. Her and me that is. They weren't always very nice people, but what could she do? She didn't like to go out to work—she tried it, she took a job in one of the big stores in the makeup department, but her feet hurt from having to stand all day. Well, now she's got her Chinese wrestler, she's okay and can just sit and eat and grow fat and read palms and tea leaves or whatever. Kiss me, Harriet," he ended up. When I did, he shut his eyes again and sort of sank down in what was bliss or relief—as if he didn't want anything else ever except to be in bed with me. Of course that suited me too, better than anything.

It was Michael who disturbed us. He came up the stairs, calling for us. He said we had to go downstairs now because the weighing ceremony was about to begin. It was the climax of the celebrations, so we had to go, though I think Crishi was as reluctant as I was. Before going down, I called in on the Devis in the next room to invite them to join us, but they declined. They were busy packing, which they did very expertly, like people who are used to going from place to place and know exactly what to take. They had old-fashioned luggage, the kind there used to be before air travel, bound with heavy leather straps. Some of the open suitcases were on the floor and some on the bed along with the urn of Babaji's ashes. Although they themselves had no time to come down, they urged me to hurry so as not to miss a second of the occasion. They beamed with joy for me that I had this wonderful festivity to go to; probably they remembered similar events in their own past when they had celebrated Babaji's birthday or other big days in their movement's calendar.

But when I went down, I didn't find the atmosphere very festive, especially compared with earlier celebrations, like the flag-raising ceremony at Propinquity, or my own wedding. By this time in the history of the movement—or in our own history—a guiding hand seemed to be missing. I guess it was Renée's, for she and Crishi had taken no part in these preparations. Everything was left to Michael and the followers, and although they had spent days trying to get the house ready, their efforts didn't add up to much more than the tacky decorations pinned up for a school's annual day. The rainy midseason twilight did not enhance the effect; and neither did the audience—our usual one here, of very serious people who thought and studied hard in whatever spare time their jobs left them and took for granted such inconveniences as sitting in wet clothes in a not-too-well-heated room.

Having spent time with the Devis upstairs, I came in too late to join the rest of our party in the front row. I stood to one side at the back, together with Michael, who was there to oversee the arrangements. He didn't want anything to go wrong, and I could feel him tense and concentrated beside me. I must admit that I wasn't paying too much attention to the ceremony but was mostly looking at our people in the front row. All the glamour that was missing from the rest of the room was concentrated in them: Renée, Crishi, Bari Rani and the girls—they shimmered in their gorgeous clothes and were exotic, so that even the earnest listeners to the Rawul's lecture were diverted into throwing glances in their direction. But perhaps the effect was not unintentional—it struck me for the first time that the Rawul's family were an integral, a physical part of his movement, their presence giving body to his ideas, like a pantheon of gods embody a pantheon of Ideas, or Ideals, or Virtues; and it doesn't seem to matter that sometimes these gods don't behave too well, Venus running off with Mars, Krishna cheating on Radha—they still remain gods whom others can look up to, worship if they want to, for their divine qualities. In the same way, it wasn't important that none of our family in the front row paid attention to what was going on. Renée was fidgeting with her bracelets, and I saw her yawn without even bothering to put her hand in front of her mouth except perfunctorily at the end of the yawn; and the girls were whispering among themselves, and when Bari Rani shushed them, she got drawn into an argument with them; and Crishi was looking everywhere except where he should be, and sometimes he was amused by the Bari Rani and the girls whispering and sometimes he turned around to wink at me. But still, they were there, they were with us, and this seemed to satisfy some need in most of the people present, including, I guess, myself.

The climax of the ceremony consisted of the Rawul being weighed against a pile of books. He explained that in Dhoka it was the custom on the royal birthday to weigh the ruler against gold, which was then distributed among the poor; a beautiful custom, he said, as were so many prevalent in his country, and one he wanted to preserve and adapt to the conditions of his modern world-state. And so it was not gold that this modern ruler had himself weighed against but wisdom—the Wisdom of all ages and all cultures; the Wisdom of Mankind. The Rawul had the ability to say such things absolutely straight because he so absolutely believed in them. And to him it wasn't a bit ridiculous to have this huge pair of scales carried in by four followers and to seat himself in one of the balance pans. Stout and majestic as he was, it wasn't easy for him to get into it and there was a bit of heaving to do before he smilingly sat there, like some giant exotic produce, pomegranate or pineapple—no, not one bit ridiculous but meaningful, solemn, and satisfying. Because he believed in himself so utterly, everyone else was willing to go along with him, even the family in the front row. The girls tittered at first, but Bari Rani soon had them in line and looking as respectful as the rest of the audience.

The books were piled into the other pan: truly the Wisdom of the ages. There had been some discussion about these books, not about what they were to be—Michael settled that;

I suppose he was the only one who had actually read most of them—but about their purchase. Michael had wanted to buy whole sets of beautifully bound editions, but Crishi said we couldn't afford it and why not get them from the library; and when that was unacceptable, he had suggested paperbacks, except that these would not have weighed enough against the Rawul. In the end there was a compromise, and Michael bought whatever he could secondhand or in cheap standard editions; so that it was a somewhat tattered assortment that was piled onto the weighing pan. But only physically—in content they were top class: They included the Bible, the Koran, Plato, the Dhammapada, the Questions of King Milinda, the Tibetan Book of the Dead, the Tao Teh Ching, Carlos Castaneda, St. Augustine, Plotinus, Kierkegaard—it was at Kierkegaard that the Rawul started to swing up so that a few volumes had to be taken off to get him even and then put on again, with some fine adjustment to get it right. And when that happened, at that moment of perfect balance, the little band of musician followers struck up—flute, *tabla,* and guitar, and including a pianist, since there was a piano in the room left over from the stockbroker's day and bought by Babaji along with the rest of the furniture. This truly cross-cultural group of instruments played their cross-cultural synthesis of sounds: and everyone applauded as the Rawul swayed there in midair, balanced against the wisdom of past ages. Calm and self-possessed, he was equal in weight and value with the knowledge and philosophy of the whole world, and therefore its natural ruler, the ruler of the modern world. He believed it, and I don't know who else did in that room except I was sure about Michael. I stood next to him and felt him draw in his breath, holding himself totally still in total conviction. It was a sort of climax for him, this weighing of the Rawul, of everything he had thought and read and experienced up to this point. It was all summed up for him in the pile of books on the one hand, and the Rawul, smiling and spotless in white silk, on the other.

3
IN THE RAWUL'S KINGDOM

OUR arrival in India was not what I had expected. I had thought that we would go right off to Dhoka, but we stayed on in Delhi. We took suites of rooms on one floor of a high, huge luxury hotel—it wasn't quite finished yet and maybe never would be, like some great cathedral or palace complex to which something always remains to be added over the centuries. The unfinished sections of the hotel were barricaded off, but the constant thuds of a building site penetrated to our suites through the silvered paneling on the walls. We all had suites; they varied in size from the Rawul's, which was the biggest in the hotel and was called the Shah Jehan suite, to the one where I was with Robi, and with Crishi when he wasn't somewhere else. Michael stayed with us when he was in the hotel, but that wasn't often. Robi and I were mostly alone together, during the day and the night. I can't say I was bored because I thought of it as an interim time in which we were waiting to go on to Dhoka; and though Robi sometimes got querulous with nothing to do, he had periods of furious activity going up and down in the elevator or chugging along the corridors as train or plane. We took tickets on a tourist bus and were driven to all the interesting historical places in and around Old and New Delhi. They *were* interesting, and I thought I got a lot out of that trip but it couldn't have been all that much, because, looking back on this period, what I remember principally is the hotel room with its exotic decor and the view from the picture window when I drew back the raw-silk drapes. This view was very extensive, for we were high up in the hotel, which was so tall that it dwarfed the rest of the city. From my room, I looked over a great expanse of new neighborhoods with identical one-story cement structures and what appeared to be a bridge spanning an empty riverbed, though it may have been a bypass built across barren land. It was a very flat expanse with here and there a high-rise office building or apartment block sticking up out of it, and then some domes of a tomb or mosque, and an occasional royal or presidential palace, looking very small; the only buildings on a par with ours were other luxury hotels. Everything appeared dry, white, parched by the sun like skeletons, although it was the coldest season, with a sharp, frosty tang in the air at night. Inside the hotel the temperature was carefully controlled, creating the stifled, pampered atmosphere of a place closed off not only against heat and cold but everything else coming in from outside.

Crishi seemed to know as many or even more people here than in London, and he was out for most of the time—at least I thought he was out, but it happened more than once that I came across him inside the hotel. A lot went on in the hotel; in many ways it was a city in itself with enough to do in it to keep everyone occupied. There was the arcade with all the fancy shops, or boutiques, as they were called on account of their high prices. Once I came across Crishi in the jeweler's shop, which was as tiny as all the others and appeared even tinier because it was so crammed with both junk and treasures of jewelry and miniature paintings, scimitars, incense holders, silver idols, even a complete suit of Moghul court dress of tattered silk splayed out on the wall like the dissected corpse of a frog. There was the jeweler himself: He greatly resembled and may have been one of the men who used to bring paintings to Crishi in London, with the same oiled hair and skin and shiny rings. He wasn't pleased to see Robi and me, for he only had enough space in his shop for serious customers, which we obviously weren't.

The small shop had an even smaller back room, and it was from out of there I heard Crishi's voice. Before the jeweler could stop me, I dodged behind his counter to look into that back room. The moment I appeared in the doorway, the

three men in there, one of whom was Crishi, looked up at
me with startled expressions. They were sitting on the floor
on mattresses with white bolsters behind them, and they had
been looking at a picture, which one of them quickly con-
cealed under his hand. And the way they looked up at me
was like a flash photo of three guilty men caught in some
illicit act—and caught not for the first time, so that they lived
in dread of it. Yes, Crishi too: For once I saw fear in his face.
But only for a moment, and then he laughed and said "It's
Harriet." They relaxed instantly, and the jeweler said from
behind me, "Who is she?" I expected Crishi to say "My wife,"
but I don't think he did—he spoke in Hindi to them, and
whatever he said made them laugh and look at me in a certain
manner that was very different from the way they had looked
when I first came in. They kept on laughing, maybe partly
in relief.

I left them and went upstairs to my room, waiting for Crishi
to join me there and say something about what had been
going on. When several hours went by and he had not come,
I went down again and back to the jeweler's shop. The jeweler
was standing outside, looking up and down the arcade, perhaps for customers, or only to watch what was going on and
pass the time; anyway it was an idle moment and he began
to talk to me. He said that he had known Crishi a very, very
long time. He suggested he knew him very well, and then he
smiled as one who knew more than he was going to say. But
because there was nothing else to do at the moment, and no
one else to talk to except me standing there, he did go on
talking about Crishi, smiling more and more: "He likes girls,"
he said and looked me up and down as one of them. "Many
girls. Many many many girls. English girls." He wasn't telling
me anything new; still, I went on standing there—it was
irresistible to me to hear about Crishi, anything about him
at all. "His wife was English. Two little children—" He showed
how little, and that moved him to pity; he clicked his tongue,
shook his head—"He was running here and there, having
good time, and the wife and children left alone with no food
in the house. What could she do? It was all in the newspapers,
everyone knows the story, you know the story." He looked
at me and I said yes, I did.

It was Renée I asked about it, and she was willing to talk. There was a change in Renée nowadays—the way to describe it is that she seemed more vulnerable. I guess the process had been going on for some time—I only had to think of the last days in England—but by the time we got to this hotel in India she was like a different person. She was startled at first when I asked her about Crishi's wife, but it didn't take her long to come out with the full story; she was glad to let me know all she could, which was by no means everything. There were areas of Crishi's life that were as unknown to her as they were to me, and his first marriage was one of them. It had happened long before he met Renée, when he was young and poor. Presumably the girl was the same; she had been traveling around on the usual penniless Kath- mandu and Goa trail. A nice young middle-class English girl in revolt against her parents—temporary revolt it should have been, adolescent restlessness, only her marriage with Crishi took her much farther. Renée didn't meet her till later when she was worn out by misery and poverty. Renée sighed and said she had done what she could for her. She had even sent money as soon as she learned of her existence and that of her and Crishi's children—and this was by no means as soon as she met Crishi himself; he kept quiet about his family for a long time. He had left them behind in Delhi, in a little room on the roof of a house belonging to a municipal build- ing inspector who lived in the downstairs part with his family They were kind people, Renée said, didn't press the girl too much for rent and sent up little sweet dishes for her and the children on festive days. It was they who had found her on one such festive day, and it had all been very embarrassing and awful and totally unnecessary, Renée said. "But she was a depressive," Renée explained, "and there is nothing you can do for such people."

I was listening in silence and made no comment, but she went on as though I had: "What do you expect of him," she defended Crishi with energy, "what could he do? The only thing you could blame him for was that he got tied up with her in the first place, and even that—he was so young, what did he know, he hadn't found himself yet; he hadn't found me." She smiled for a moment, thinking of that time when he found her or she him. "You can have no idea, Harriet," she went on, "what he was like then. Young! Young! And hungry like a young wolf—for everything he could get. I really had to teach him to be a little more discriminate; and I must say this for him—he learned fast." She gave another smile before growing serious again: "That's the trouble with him—he learns so fast—gobbles everything up so fast—and then gets tired of it and starts looking around for something new. Don't you feel that about him?" she asked, looking at me keenly as if she thought I might know something she didn't. I shook my head, remained deadpan; I had got in the habit with her of not showing what I thought or felt. She frowned, dissatisfied with me. "He's restless, don't you think?" she tried to draw me out; "like he's getting tired of something." "Tired? But we've only just come." "Not of the place but of—" "People?" "Maybe," she said. We looked at, into each other: testing each other out—did she mean herself or me, which one of us was he getting tired of? She looked away first, probably not wanting me to read what was in her eyes.

In contrast to Renée, Bari Rani appeared not weakened but strengthened by our move to India. She belonged to the place, I could see, and was quite at home in this palace hotel where the staff was more deferential to her than to anyone else—certainly much more than to Renée, who was treated with the scant courtesy of an ordinary hotel guest. Here Bari Rani was the true queen; and here also it was she who was the Rawul's official consort. She lived in a suite adjoining his with a connecting door through which he kept coming in to try out his speeches on her; they were in high Hindi, so she was the only one who could understand them. She accompanied the Rawul everywhere—it was he and she who were invited to dine at a presidential banquet, not he and Renée, and he and she who sat in specially reserved seats at the Republic Day Parade. The girls attended some of these functions—not without protest, for they preferred to be with their own friends in the latest hot spot or driving out for moonlight picnics. It was considered a duty for them to be seen on occasion with their parents, for here they were not just girls but princesses, descendants of a royal figure.

I'm not saying that the Rawul wasn't a royal figure wher-

ever he went—that was after all the strongest impression he
gave; but here it was more than a personal impression, it was
supported by his whole background, his whole dynasty, which
everyone knew about and could place him in. He was a king
come home to his own country. And here the movement
wasn't eccentric or odd or fantastic: You believed in it as you
did in him, that it could be and would be real; that it could
and would happen. He was forming an independent political
party in opposition to the ruling party, which he intended
one day to defeat, and from this base, with real political power
in his hands, he could work outward toward his great ideal
—that is, from ruling India he could advance to uniting the
world. There was an absolutely practical first step to be taken,
and that was to have himself elected to a seat in the upper
assembly—not all that difficult, with his contacts, and the
votes he could count on from his own district. But it needed
organizational work and that was the reason we lingered in
Delhi instead of going to Dhoka, as I had expected. Bari Rani
worked tirelessly, and also tirelessly poured in her considerable inheritance. I think she was looking forward to mine,
to pour that in too. She organized lavish entertainments for
the politicians, journalists, government officers, and big businessmen who were going to help the Rawul to a seat in Par-
liament. She hired banquet and conference halls and the best
caterers, and she mingled among the guests and was charming to them, though privately she confided to me that they
were very uncultured people whom she was only treating as
equals for the sake of her husband's career.

All this policy making belonged to the upper echelons; but
there were the lower echelons—that is, the followers who
were organized as usual by Crishi and Michael. At least I
thought that was what Crishi and Michael were doing when
they were away the whole day. I soon discovered that it was
only Michael who was doing it—when he came into my hotel
room and said "Where's Crishi?" I said "I thought he was
with you," and he said "I haven't seen him in two days." He
sat down, looking dispirited, tired, and also I thought sick,
or anyway drained. Since our arrival in India, Michael only
wore Indian clothes, a loose white pajama with a loose white
shirt over it. They did not suit him at all. These clothes need
a sinuous physique to wear them, and Michael was bony and

rigid; his neck stuck out of the collarless shirt like a scraggy, angry bird.

He began to complain about Crishi. I'm not used to Michael complaining, so it sounded strange to me, and his voice sounded strange too, almost whiny. He said it wasn't fair to leave him alone with this new group of followers, who understood him no more than he did them—he meant literally; they spoke no English at all. And besides language, they were very different from the other followers, who had all been—Michael swallowed, his Adam's apple labored up and down while he tried to bring out a word he didn't like: He forced himself to say it—"idealistic," he said. They had been true believers whereas these people here . . . He didn't go any further, he was never quick with judgments; instead he continued complaining about Crishi. "It's not fair,' he said again, "he has to give me some help, some support—where is he?" "I don't know." "No, no one knows, he disappears and leaves me to deal with all of it." Again he sounded whiny and I asked "Are you all right? I mean, healthwise?" "Of course I'm all right," he said in his old impatient way with me, but then admitted grudgingly, "except for the stomach things one expects to get in India. Who cares about that—but to leave me alone this way—throw it all on me and take off—" The corner of his mouth turned down disagreeably; there was a sore on one of them; he touched it irritably with his finger.

Crishi came in, burst in—like a flame, bringing (depending on your point of view) light or danger; saying impatiently before he was even quite in the room, "There you are, Michael, I've been looking for you all *over*." But as always hypersensitive to every nuance between people, he looked at us both, from one to the other—"What's up?"

I said "Michael's been complaining about you."

"About *me*?" cried Crishi, pointing to himself, utterly absolutely incredulous but making sure I saw the smile flitting around his lips; and of course I did and responded to it, disregarding Michael. "What have I done, what's wrong?" said Crishi, putting his hand on Michael's shoulder; but Michael twitched his shoulder to remove that hand and, taking a step away from Crishi, he said "You leave me to deal with that bunch and disappear."

"Can you believe it," said Crishi in outrage. He took a deep

breath before he was able to go on: "And what do you think
I've been doing? Playing around? Having a good time? Amusing myself? Is that what you think, Michael? Is it really?" He
took a step forward to stand right by him and to touch him
on the shoulder again; and this time Michael didn't move
away but stood there silently and even cast down his eyes,
making him look coy for a moment, girlish, womanish even,
ready for submission.

For a few seconds Crishi kept him like that, before taking
his hand away. He went on talking to him in a gentle, understanding way: "I know it's tough for you being on your
own with them but you'll get used to them. I'll come along
with you now, shall I, and give them a little talking to; set
them right, like. Okay? Okay, Mike?"

"I'll come too," I ventured, and Crishi laughed and said
"Why not." It was Michael who said "Why? Why should she?"
Crishi shrugged, leaving it to the two of us to settle. I could
see Michael didn't want me to come, and in the past that
would have been enough to make me not want to. But I
doubted his motives; without quite admitting it to myself, I
felt that Michael was trying to guard something that was
between him and Crishi and excluded me—that is, their work
with the movement. In other words, Michael was jealous of
me! Perhaps he suspected this of himself the same moment
I did, and it was as inadmissible to him as to me, for he too
shrugged and said "Well why not, if you want to," trying to
sound as indifferent as Crishi but not succeeding.

The Indian followers, who were known as the Bhais, had
been installed in a house on the other side of the river. To
get there we had to drive over an old pontoon bridge. The
lane they lived on was too narrow to admit our car, so we
got out and walked along some planks laid across a miry
path. Their house was as new as our luxury hotel and as
unfinished. The outside walls had been whitewashed but the
window frames were still raw wood, and a pile of bricks and
a ladder on the roof may have meant that another story either
had been abandoned or was being completed. The Bhais all
lived in the three little downstairs rooms and the courtyard
leading off them. They *were* different from the other followers. Those others may have burned with a fierce flame from

within, but from without they were mostly meek, pale, and mild. These Indian followers were a tough, burly crew, hairy and dark within their loose white clothes, which suited them so much better than they did Michael. They had been brought from Dhoka—I thought that they might be family retainers but Crishi said no, he had recruited them from that desert state, where they had been hanging around in the bazaars, all of them penniless and some in trouble with the police. I felt something violent and threatening about them, partly because of the weapons they so openly displayed around the house. Several hunting rifles were hung up on the walls, and one Bhai was sitting there digging at his toenail with quite a dangerous-looking knife.

As soon as we came in, they surrounded Crishi. They were mostly taller than he was, and certainly all of them more muscular; they seemed to be demanding something in their loud, harsh voices. But Crishi kept calm, reassuring them in a soft, even tone. He spoke to them in their own dialect— he always said that he didn't speak any Indian language well, just what he had picked up here and there, and that he couldn't sustain much of a conversation. But he communicated perfectly with them, and after a time he had them laughing—that is, when he opened the money belt he wore under his shirt and started distributing rupees to them. They were happy, they shouted and joked, and dispersed, satisfied, each counting the notes he had received.

There was another group of followers for us to visit. The place they stayed seemed familiar—not that I had actually seen it but it was the hotel near the railway station Michael had described where he had first met Crishi. There was the tea stall outside and the Hindu temple opposite with the bells ringing from it and making the house shake The followers who lived here, five or six of them in one little blue-plastered room, were European or American and had the usual pale drained look about them. One of them greeted me as if he knew me, but it took me some time to recognize him, because I hadn't expected to see him or because our last meeting seemed so long ago and far away. It was Paul. When I looked surprised, he said laconically, "I got out"; he jerked his head toward Crishi: "He got me out." He laughed and made a grim joke of it: "He got me in and he got me out."

I lowered my eyes, I didn't want to know too much about any of that. I felt ashamed, as though I were responsible— I mean, for Paul's suffering. And in a way I was; if Crishi was, so was I. It was like that now.

But I don't think Paul held anyone responsible. None of them did—they seemed weary and fatalistic, but also cheerful, unlike the followers at home, who were mostly rather glum. After my first visit, I often went to see Paul and his companions, taking Robi with me: It was somewhere to go and they were nice to be with. They had a lot of time and the air of people used to killing it. They sat crowded together in their little hotel room, doing personal things like trimming their beards or their nails. They were ready to talk, though not necessarily to any other person—sometimes I heard them muttering to themselves and cursing not anyone in particular but life in general, in an almost good-natured way. They liked it when I brought Robi; they showed him magic tricks and made puppets out of handkerchiefs for him. What they didn't like was when Michael came. They seemed to dislike him intensely, I don't know why; and he had absolutely no use for them.

I heard him argue with Crishi about keeping them. Crishi said they were useful because they knew their way around; had done this so long that they were like trained and experienced soldiers. Michael said yes, but on the other hand they were known to every customs officer between here and San Francisco; Crishi argued that could work both ways because it made the couriers aware of who was to be avoided and where the weak links were. No, Michael said, they weren't aware of anything, their minds were too far gone; all they were fit to do was scheme for their own survival. "That's good," urged Crishi; "it makes them more careful." "They're more than careful," Michael said. "They're afraid. They smell of fear," he said with contempt. I too had noticed that about them.

These followers stayed in their own bazaar hotel and never came to ours, and they had nothing directly to do with or for the Rawul. That was left to the Bhais, and there were several of them on duty during the day, and at night two of

them slept outside his door. They also acted as guards at the
Rawul's political meetings, and it was they who recruited
people and paid them and brought them in truckloads to
cheer for the Rawul. Bari Rani always sat on the platform
with the Rawul at these meetings, and when they could be
wooed away from their friends and discotheques, the girls
sat with them too. The rest of us could be there or not, and
most of the time I must admit I preferred not to. If someone
had asked me if I believed in the movement, of course I
would have said yes—I mean, one world where everyone is
united and no more wars, what could be better? But I couldn't
say that it was my whole life the way it was for Michael, who
never missed a meeting if he could help it, or an opportunity
of being near the Rawul, or doing something to promote the
movement. Even if he wasn't feeling well or had to deal with
people he didn't like and who didn't like him, such as the
Bhais and the other followers—he never let his personal
feelings stand in the way of what he saw not only as his duty
but his whole existence and self-fulfillment.

I don't think Crishi felt that way. Maybe he never had—I
can't say; but because he was still bustling around as usual,
full of eagerness and energy, I thought it was in the service
of the Rawul. It wasn't until Michael had several times come
to ask "Where's Crishi?" that I realized there was a change.
And more and more I heard Michael nag at him, pick fights
with him for not working hard enough for the movement;
although the way he fought with him was the way you fight
with someone you love and feel slipping away from you.

There was the night of the party in the Bhais' house. The
Bhais liked to eat and drink and make a lot of noise, and
they loved having a party. On that night they had lit a bonfire
in their courtyard; whole chickens were being roasted on a
spit, and there was singing to the accompaniment of one of
those drums that are banged from both ends. The Bhais were
wrapped in blankets and their faces lit up by the flames. I
was there by special invitation, as was Robi, and we sat with
Crishi by the fire on cushions placed there for the three of
us. Crishi was enjoying himself. I could see that he liked being
with the Bhais and that he belonged with them in a way he
didn't with the pale foreign followers. Robi sat between us

and did his best to have a good time, but he was a bit frightened; and when someone picked him up and he was exu-
berantly passed from hand to hand around the fire, he was
ready to cry, and would have if he hadn't caught Crishi's
frown on him. Like Renée, Crishi could stand no sign of
weakness in Robi.

Michael arrived, not to join the party but on business. The
Rawul was holding one of his meetings next day, and Michael
had worked out a duty roster for the Bhais to act as ushers
and bodyguards. When Michael came, austere and pale in
white, the Bhais had started dancing—a parody of a dance,
with one of them pretending to be a girl in a veil eluding the
attentions of another. It made all of them laugh a lot, and
some joined in, dancing by themselves or around an imagi-
nary love-partner, with fingers snapping and eyes ecstatically
closed. They made Crishi get up, and he didn't need much
persuading; he danced around with the others and knew how
to do it too. I enjoyed watching him but I could see Michael
looked disgusted, as well as impatient at not being able to get
on with his business. And when someone pulled his arm to
make him join in, he snatched it away and gave a push to
the person who had touched him. He shouted something but
couldn't be heard—at least no one took any notice of him—
and that made him more furious; and next thing he did, he
strode into the circle, and roughly pushing the dancers aside,
went straight for Crishi and caught him by both arms to make
him stop dancing. Crishi did stop; everyone did; the drum-
mer went on banging for a while before he too fell silent with
a last embarrassed little bang. Only the flames roared and
someone was washing dishes in the kitchen, clattering the
plates.

Michael and Crishi stood confronting each other while
everyone watched them. Now that he had Crishi's attention
completely, Michael calmed down; he tried to speak reasonably: "Can't you see that I've come for some work? There's
a meeting tomorrow." "There is?" said Crishi. "Poor Michael.
Always working; slaving away for everyone. Poor old Mike."
And he held Michael's chin and fondled it, and Michael, who
so hated being touched, didn't jerk away but looked back at
Crishi with steady eyes. They stood there, face to face, daring

each other; and Crishi took his hand away but went on talking in the same sweet and taunting tone: "Shall I tell you something, Michael? You might not like it; you *won't* like it." Crishi ran his tongue over his lips: "I don't care one fuck for your meeting. Not this much: not one fuck." Crishi was rather drunk, or I don't think he would have done what he did next—he snatched Michael's duty sheet, which was clipped to a board, and he held it up high and started to fling it in the fire. Michael, who was of course very sober, easily prevented him; and besides retrieving his board, he gave Crishi a push that sent him sprawling against the people standing around watching. "You belong with the rest of these swine," Michael said and turned and went out without glancing back: except for one look at me, which under normal circumstances—I guess I mean in the past—would have made me follow him. But all my attention was on Crishi, lying half sprawled in the arms of the people who had caught him; and he had that smile of his, which might also have been a snarl. Next moment he released himself and said "Is this a party or what is it," and at once it became one again, with drumming and dancing.

AND then suddenly one day Sonya arrived. She had flown straight from New York and was suffering from jet lag but otherwise was entirely her old, her usual self; in fact, a familiar apparition, for we were used to Sonya turning up wherever we were, at whatever embassy Grandfather had been posted to—whether it was London or Beirut, sooner or later she arrived with all her matching luggage and her jewel case. So after the first amazement at her unexpected arrival, it was really quite natural for me to go into the suite where she had already made herself comfortable, having unpacked and set out the things she needed most urgently, such as her makeup and her pills. She was propped up in her nightgown and lace jacket and hairnet, pursing her lips and saying "Give Sonya a kiss, darling." Oh but I was glad to do so; I rushed over to the bed, and while she pressed her mouth to mine, I hugged her so hard I half-lifted her out of bed. She cried aloud and laughed and then she said "Let me look at you." She tried to study my face—but I got up and walked away from her, at the same time assuring her that I was as happy as she had hoped and prayed for me on the night of my wedding. We were laughing together at my happiness when Michael came in—rushed in, rather, and he didn't have to be invited over to kiss Sonya, he was by her side in no time, and it was he who held her. I think Sonya was as amazed as I was: This was not Michael at all, Michael, who, however happy he was to see anyone,

wouldn't do more than give a cool, indifferent nod. But he
didn't let go of Sonya for a long time, though he wouldn't
let her look into his face any more than I had; and when she
at last managed to do so, he turned it away and he released
her and got up. I watched him and saw what she saw—only
I looked away again at once because it didn't seem becoming
for me, for anyone, to see Michael dash tears out of his eyes,
even if they were tears of joy at Sonya's arrival.

Sonya made a big splash—I mean, she was a presence. To
the hotel staff, for one; she was the type of hotel guest who
was forever calling for room service and the housekeeper
and the laundry and whatever else there was to ask and tip
for; she knew everyone's name and, quite soon, personal
history. But besides the hotel staff, her arrival was a big event
for our family, including the Rawul and Bari Rani, who both
paid her every courtesy. She was invited to his meetings, and
he was also available to her for private audience whenever
she might desire it; and the Bari Rani entertained her to
lunch and took her shopping and sightseeing, treating her
as a close and dear member of the family. Both she and the
Rawul let her into their plans for the movement and gave
her details of the present state of its development. Well, Sonya
listened to them but not, anyone who knew her could see,
with the rapt attention with which she had received such
communications before. The movement was not apparently
what she had come for and not what she wanted to hear
about, nor was it the subject she had traveled all this way to
discuss—if, that is, she had come to discuss anything.

"What's she want?"

"Crishi! To see us of course."

"You and me?"

"And Michael."

Crishi made no comment, but not as if he had nothing to
say but as if he weren't saying it till more was known.

Although Sonya appeared to be as fond of, and doting on,
Crishi as before—even more, because he had made me so
happy—what she liked best was to be alone with Michael and
me. Michael too seemed to like that best—any free time he
had from the organization, he would be with her in her hotel
suite, where she spent most of her time. She had no interest

in going out and seeing anything, however much Bari Rani urged her and put herself at her disposal. Sonya told us she hadn't come here for the sights, and in any case she had already seen them. She had seen everything, she said—this was when the three of us were in her room, in fact all three of us on her bed, she inside the covers and Michael and I lying on top of them—everything there was to see and do in life she had seen and done, so now all she wanted was to be with those she loved; that is, with Michael and me. "Am I hurting you?" said Michael, who was lying on her feet—his voice was gruff, his intention tender. "No, no, darling, perfectly comfortable, perfectly happy." She went on to say that she knew it was wrong of her, since we had our own lives to lead, but she did miss us terribly at home—everyone did, she said, prompting Michael to ask "Like who?" "Everyone," she said. "And especially at darling Manton and dearest Barbara's wedding—" "Oh they've had it, have they?" said Michael. She was brought up short—"Didn't you know? They said they called and called and sent cables—" Michael looked at me and I felt embarrassed for a moment—it was true, after calling me in England, they had repeatedly called me in India and I had promised to come, but it had gone completely out of my mind, especially after I spoke to Crishi again and he said "Oh leave it, forget it."

Sensing an awkward moment and wanting to cover it up, Sonya went on to describe the wedding. It had been in a side chapel of the same cathedral where Manton and Lindsay had been married twenty-three years earlier; many of the guests were the same, though now including Lindsay accompanied by Jean. Everyone was very moved by the ceremony—Barbara had wept copiously; so had Sonya and all her friends who had come in full force, except for the Princess, who had gone into a coma and was no longer taken out. The archdeacon had spoken beautifully—he was an old friend of Manton's, had been to school with him, knew about him and the whole family, and wasn't in the least put out by the fact that Barbara was so hugely pregnant. No one was, Sonya assured us; on the contrary, it was a heightening of the occasion to see the bride at the altar so beautifully bearing the fruit of the love they were there to consecrate; and then the pride with which Manton carried himself as bridegroom and father-to-be. He was even more handsome than at his last wedding, for he was more mature, more ample, amply filling his superbly tailored cutaway and striped trousers, his belly straining against the latter, the four-in-hand curving over his thrust-out chest, the white carnation in his button-hole blooming in a maturity as full as his own. And when he turned from the altar and walked down the aisle, his bursting bride on his arm, leading her in slow measure to the notes swelling out from the organ—if only, Sonya said, we could have been there to see him; but of course she knew we couldn't. And Grandfather, if only it had been possible for him to see his son at that moment—it would have been the end of all those superficial little differences between them: not that they had ever counted for anything—what were they in face of the great fact that the two of them *were* father and son, just as Michael and Manton were son and father, and now another son would come. It was so wonderful, a matter of such gratitude, she said, squeezing one hand of Michael's and one of mine, that we were one family, all of us belonging together; including, she said, Lindsay and dear Jean too, and also, she ended up for good measure, Else Schwamm, who had been there at the wedding, crying as much as everyone else.

"Looks like we missed a big event," said Michael at the end of this recital. He glanced at me: "You didn't even mention it."

"As if you'd have cared."

"It doesn't matter at all," said Sonya quickly. "Not one bit. Sometimes it isn't possible for people to be where they most want to be, but all the same they're there in their feelings. Just as long as you have those, and Manton knows you do and Barbara too—they know you'll love your little brother when he arrives, in the same way as you love each other."

"When's he due?" said Michael—surprising me again by his interest in such a subject.

"Any day soon." Sonya was silent; I could see her reflecting on how to start on her next theme. To save her the trouble, I said "Manton wants you to talk to us about the money."

Sonya blushed as if I had caught her out in something. She did look sweet, very girlish with her round face and wrinkled, pampered skin. Grandfather had always been touched by her blushes, and now Michael was too—he went up closer to her so he could put his arms around her in a protective way; and since it was I who had caused her embarrassment, he seemed to be challenging me when he said "Well why not—it's a perfectly natural subject for a family to talk about."

"Of course it is," I agreed, not reminding him that it was he who had up till now imposed silence on it.

Whenever she and I were alone, Sonya spoke to me of Michael. She said she was worried about his health. I reassured her the way he had me—"It's just the usual stomach things everyone gets." "And what's this on his mouth?" "Just a sore, it's nothing." "He's changed, he's not Michael." I pretended to laugh: "Of course he's Michael!" She shook her head: "Our Michael was—he was—" "What?" "Strong. A rock. You couldn't change him this much, not from here to there. Like his Grandfather." "He's still like that," I tried to maintain. It hurt me to have to lie—disguise my own feelings—to Sonya, but I couldn't very well tell her that there was trouble between Michael and Crishi. Anyway, I thought, it was temporary, it would blow over when we moved away from this place and went to what was our real destination: that is, to Dhoka, to the Rawul's kingdom, the source and fountainhead of our movement, where everything would be refreshed and restored.

I discovered that it wasn't only his deteriorating relationship with Crishi that was making Michael unhappy. One evening there was an important function to which some big shots were invited. Bari Rani was as usual in charge. She rented a house and put up a spacious tent on its front lawn for the general meeting, and afterward there was a grand feast inside the house arranged by the leading caterer after detailed consultation with Bari Rani. Usually these parties went off very well—the Rawul would be very pleased, and the next morning he would discuss the event with Bari Rani while she helped him dress. They would talk about the important people who had been there and what effect the function had on them and consequently what the Rawul's chances were of being nominated. Apparently each time they had a big party these were enhanced, and the Rawul and Bari Rani were satisfied. But that evening something had gone wrong, and next day Bari Rani was in a state. She called for Michael, who was having breakfast with Sonya, me, and Robi. When he had gone, Sonya said "Why is he so upset?" I said "Is he?" I hadn't noticed; he was always pale and silent anyway. But after she had said it, I became uneasy, especially when he didn't return; and Sonya said "Yes, why don't you go and see." I left her and Robi to entertain each other, which they always did very well, and went to the Rawul's suite.

I could hear raised voices from the corridor, and when I went in, I found the Rawul and Bari Rani in the middle of an argument. I couldn't make out at first what it was about and Michael gave me no help. He didn't even look at me but stood there all clenched up. The Rawul was saying to Bari Rani, "You're exaggerating, as usual," which made her address herself to me as a new person to take her side. She said that nothing was closer to her heart than her husband's career, and everything that it was possible for a human being to do, she unstintingly did: but unfortunately she was born neither with four pairs of hands nor with eyes at the back of her head, and she did have to rely to some extent, in some little ways, on the help and vigilance of others; and if these others let her down, then all her work and efforts were in vain. As, for instance, last night—and here she turned to Michael: Surely, she told him, he was not so overburdened with duties that he could not have checked up on the dietary laws of their most important guest and provided the unpolished rice and onionless vegetables these demanded. But no, this detail was omitted, thereby giving grave offense to the most influential person there—defeating the entire purpose of her efforts and instead of promoting the Rawul's career setting it back by months, years even—"Years and years!" she cried, working herself up, so that I couldn't help being amused at the thought of the unpolished rice and onionless vegetables. But Michael was getting to the point where he had difficulty holding himself in. I knew this point in him so well—rarely reached, but when it was, his anger would burst through all the controls he had imposed on it. And as if afraid of this himself, he turned and went out of the room, leaving

Bari Rani in indignant midsentence and the Rawul looking after him with concern.

"Well madam," said the Rawul, "I hope you feel you've said enough and are fully satisfied with the result."

"I? What have I done? Except of course as usual kill myself with work for your sake."

I left them and followed Michael. He hadn't gone back to Sonya's room but to his own. I understood completely how he felt—Michael had not come all this way to get himself mixed up in local politics! I could see that everything that had exasperated him about our parents and our whole life and everyone's expectations—everything that was "neti, neti"— was coming back on him. But I said "Michael, you have to be a little bit practical."

"Well what do you think I've been doing?" he said. He lay on his bed like a knight on his tomb; his face was white, his eyes shut. "Who's been booking everyone's tickets and arranging every kind of practical shit—food and beds and guns and you name it, down to getting the Rawul's clothes from the dry cleaner's. I'm not complaining," he said. "I don't mind. I like to do it, so long as I know what we're doing. Aiming at. As long as I'm sure of that." He paused—I guess it was a natural place for me to ask "Well aren't you?" I didn't ask, and there was a silence; Michael opened his eyes and shifted them sideways to look at me—"What'll you do? . . . When we're twenty-one," he added when he saw me hesitate.

"Same as you," I said, looking back at him in surprise.

"Same as me," he repeated as if he weren't sure what that might be. Again, I didn't want to get into it. There was nothing to discuss; it had all been settled long ago—when Grandfather was still alive and he had said three times to Michael "Are you sure?" and three times Michael had replied yes.

I was relieved when the Rawul came in—knocking timidly before entering and asking "May I? I'm not in the way?"— all tact and delicacy. Dear, good Rawul: He knew that Michael had been upset by Bari Rani and had come to make things better. "No absolutely not, my dear fellow," he said when Michael tried to get up. He pressed him down gently, also pressed Michael's forehead and then looked at me with an expression of concern. "He's all right," I said, and Michael confirmed this, but the Rawul shook his head regretfully: "It's our climate," he said. "Our climate and our wretched conditions. My poor squalid country," he smiled. He wasn't serious, and how could he be—in this air-conditioned hotel room on the latest modular plan and with a picture window framing and rendering innocuous whatever lay outside.

The Rawul had come to apologize not only for his country but for Bari Rani. He said he knew how Michael felt—goodness, smiled the Rawul, he felt the same himself; because he was like Michael—fiery, impatient. "Yes yes, my dear fellow, that's the way we are—we want to shoot ahead, straight up to the stars, forgetting of course that human beings can't fly, that there are certain practical steps—yes very dull, very plodding, but unfortunately very necessary to get us where we want to go. Isn't it a bore," said the Rawul, smiling down at Michael and squeezing his shoulder in a comradely way. Although so stout and sleek and middle-aged, the Rawul did give an impression of youth and idealism. And what he said was true—he and Michael were the same: They were the only two among us who still cared for the world movement, for Transcendental Internationalism, with a passion that the rest of us had dissipated on other, more personal ends of our own. Only those two continued to live in high, pure regions—though in different ways; for whereas the Rawul bloomed and flourished up there in that altitude, Michael was hollowed out, exhausted with effort and strain.

The person who had changed the most toward the movement was Renée. She carried on as if it didn't exist, never attending any of the Rawul's meetings or social entertainments. She rarely emerged from her suite but often sent for one or other of us to come to see her in there. These interviews were never easy, for she would ask a lot of questions but was too intent on something she was brooding on inside herself to listen or wait for any answers. She had violent mood swings, especially toward Robi. She might be passionately loving to start off with, crushing him in her embrace, gazing into his face in longing; and suddenly she would change utterly, pounce on him for some fault, that he hadn't cleaned out his ears properly, or was shrinking from her embrace— which I'm afraid was true; the most he would do was endure

it. She would push him away, strike at him, order him out
of her sight. And how quickly he got out the door—relieved
to get away but also terribly upset, as he ran down the carpeted hotel corridors sobbing out loud. When I wanted to
follow him, she said "No, stay with me." She forgot about
Robi and started in on me. And with me too she was at first
very sweet and loving, taking my hand in hers, turning it
over and over, tracing her finger along the lines of my palm
as if she were reading them; only the next moment to turn
on me violently, to say I was jealous, selfish, possessive, and
didn't care if I killed her or not as long as I had what I
wanted. And like Robi, I was glad to get out of her sight
when she told me to and went running down the hotel
corridor—not sobbing, in my case, but lighthearted the way
I was most of the time now, and completely forgetting everything she had said to me and even that she existed.

Crishi too had changed, with regard to the movement and
in other ways. Just as Renée left everything to Bari Rani,
Crishi left it to Michael; but unlike Renée, he didn't stay
brooding in the hotel but was out and about all day long. He
had so many places to go to, some of which I knew about
and others not. There was the back room of the jeweler in
the hotel lobby, where he sat with cronies or business partners
or whatever or whoever they were; and there must have been
other back rooms, all over the city, where he was familiar
and known and where secret business was transacted. And
there was the house of the Bhais and the bazaar hotel where
the European followers lived—each entirely different from
the other and only Crishi at home in both. I think he had a
good time roaming around the city all day and half the night;
he usually came home the other half of the night—that is,
back to the hotel where I was waiting for him, though I must
admit I didn't always manage to keep awake because it was
near dawn when he came in. Renée too was waiting for him;
I think she was a complete insomniac nowadays. She called
several times in the night to ask if he had come home; sometimes she came in to check for herself. Half-asleep, I watched
her moving around the suite, her reflection ghostlike in the
mirror as she leaned over Robi, who slept in the dressing
room. After she returned to her own suite, she phoned again

an hour later to ask if he had come in; I said no, even if he had, because he told me to. He didn't want her disturbing us. He locked the door after he came in, and we heard her rattle it but never for long, because once the door was locked, she knew he was home. Then she returned to her own room to brood on God knows what. I might have felt sorry for her—the way I used to for Anna—except that there was no time to think of her. However late it was when he came in, Crishi was wide awake and ready to talk and make love, though when he went to sleep at last, he slept till midday.

During these nights—or early mornings—I could ask him about anything I liked and he would answer me. For instance, when I asked him about his first wife, he was absolutely free and open about that chapter in his life and seemed to want me to know about it. He even offered to take me to the place where she had lived with their two children. It turned out to be in a very ordinary middleclass district, with a lot of run-down two-story houses and a municipal milk booth and washermen pressing clothes on the sidewalk. The house too was ordinary, just like all the others, with the whitewash flaking off and bars on the windows. He took me right inside—there were people living there, but he asked them so nicely if we could come in; he told them some story in Hindi, which I couldn't understand but it made them very friendly toward us and offer us tea and send out for sweets. It was the upstairs flat, two little rooms and a veranda; everything was painted pink and with fluorescent tube lighting and calendars of saints and film stars and not much furniture except for string cots and steel trunks. Several children stood around, staring at us with their fingers in their mouths. It was so domestic and ordinary—maybe that was why he had brought me here, wanting me to see how they had lived.

After that we often talked about his first marriage, and I was eager to know everything about it because I was eager to know everything about him. And he was entirely frank with me, even admitting his own fault in getting married so young and to such a young girl—she was seventeen—and both of them without any money. "But what could I do?" he appealed to me. "I was crazy about her, I had to be with her all the time—just like I have to be with you. Nothing wrong in that, is there?" I shook my head; I agreed with him all the way. Still he went on blaming himself—he said maybe he shouldn't have left her here by herself; she was only a girl just out of school, from Romford, Essex. But his work at that time was here; and as a matter of fact he had been getting on quite well when unfortunately he had a setback and was forced to be away for some time (I guess he meant in jail). It was very tough on her, being left alone with two little children and no money and too proud to ask anyone, not even her parents. "Stupid little girl," he smiled affectionately, and I too felt affectionate toward her, thinking of her in those little pink rooms and too proud to tell anyone she had a husband in jail. He said "When she came to see me there, she was always crying. She had been so pretty when we got married, like one of those English flowers, what are they called, but with all that crying—I *told* her everything would be fine and of course it was. I got out much sooner than anyone expected and started doing very well but by that time she had done that silly thing. I'll never know why, Harriet," he said, looking at me with honest and innocent eyes. "Except she did have a bit of a tendency toward depression and she never could take the heat, especially when she was pregnant." "And was she—?" "Yes," he said regretfully; "I told her it would be okay—if you can look after two, what's three, but she wouldn't listen, wouldn't wait." "Where are they?" "The children? With her parents. I send money whenever I can." "Well thank God," I said. "What?" he asked, kissing me in some nice spot; we were back in bed; it was dawn. I said "Soon there'll be plenty for everyone." "Of money? Yes, thank God," he echoed, though his voice was muffled as he was kissing me again in the same spot.

It may have been because of my knowledge of his two previous children—or because we had Robi with us—or just because he himself, Crishi, was so very much more with me—but my desire to get pregnant had completely disappeared. In fact, I took every precaution against it. My attitude did not change after we lost Robi, which happened around this time and in the following way. One morning Renée called for Robi and me to come to her suite. When we got there, we found someone was with her—a tall gaunt priest in a cassock that had been washed too often to come anywhere near white again. "Ah here he is," he said to Robi, in an accent as English as Rupert's; and at once, in spite of their very different appearance, or very different aura, I knew him to be Rupert's brother. Robi must have had the same feeling, for he went to the visitor immediately and stood before him and raised his face to be studied; which the visitor did very earnestly, with his finger under Robi's chin.

"He's come to take you away," said Renée.

Robi didn't react to this but continued to stand between the other's big knees; and still studying Robi's face, turning it this way and that, the priest said "Don't you want to? Go to school and all that, hm? Don't you think you ought to?"

"Where's my father?" Robi said.

It was the first time Robi had asked after Rupert. He had never mentioned him any more than the rest of us had. On our part, the silence was deliberate, for the subject of Rupert, who had been sentenced, was embarrassing; now, from the promptness of his question, I realized that Robi had been afraid to ask what he was longing to know.

"Your father's written to me," said the priest. "It's he who wants you to go to school."

"Why doesn't he write to me?"

"Because he wanted me to speak to you for him. Because he wanted us to get to know each other and be friends. Because I'm his brother—which makes you what? . . . Hm, what?" he said, turning Robi's face again, and answering himself: "my nephew."

Did he—could he—really believe that? There was a suppressed smile on Renée's face, mocking his assumption. Certainly, Robi, with his creamy skin, his dark curls, and the embroidered silk shirt we had bought him in one of the fancy tourist shops downstairs, did not appear to bear any more relation to this tall bald pale man than did Renée herself, lounging on a velvet sofa in her satin negligee.

Nevertheless, undaunted, "I'll take you with me," said our visitor, taking charge as though his study of Robi's face had fully satisfied him as to his rights as a blood relative. "I'm leaving in a few days. We'll go on a train and then on a bus up to the mountains; to the school, in the mountains. You'll like it there. My name is Tom," he said and held out his hand for Robi to shake; and when Robi did so, his uncle smiled with such a real, such a radiant pleasure that one couldn't help returning this smile; at least I couldn't.

And as I did so, he seemed to see me for the first time and said "Hello?" half in query as to who are you, and what are you doing here?

This was not a question I felt I had to answer. I dropped my eyes away from him; and I looked at Renée, who slightly raised her eyebrows at me, in a signal that united her and me against the stranger. But Robi said "Can she come too?" indicating me, and after looking in my direction for a moment, his uncle answered "Surely, if she wants to."

I laughed; I said "Robi, I'm too big to go to school." Straightaway I felt the stranger—Tom—studying me, assessing me, as if he weren't convinced by my statement but, on the contrary, was deciding what class I should be sent to. It was partly his cassock that gave him his authority, but there was something else about him too, something schoolmasterly, which made it right for him to be in charge.

"Well," he said, "I'm not leaving for another week so you have time to decide."

"You're not that big," Robi answered me.

"I'm twenty-one," I quickly made it known; finding Tom's strange clear gaze on me, I felt compelled to add "nearly."

"Very nearly," Renée said. To the visitor she said "We'll let you know about the boy." She spoke both irritably and dismissively.

Robi said to me, "You said you never finished school."

"Never finished college," I corrected him but found myself blushing as at something I didn't want to admit before his uncle.

"I'll come and see you every day," this uncle promised. "We'll get to know each other." The first part of the promise seemed addressed only to Robi but the second to both of us; and he shook hands with both of us warmly in farewell, though Renée he acknowledged only from a distance, which somehow left her out. She said again, "We'll let you know," sounding even more irritated than before. And after he was gone, she was really angry. She said "I'd hoped never to see

him again; but he always turns up again with some piece of
unwanted advice. . . . You should have heard him when Rupert was— Go in the other room," she told Robi. "Go and
play; do you always have to listen to everyone's conversation. . . . As if I had wanted to marry his precious brother
instead of doing everything possible to run away from him.
But Father Tom carried on as if I were this terrible *femme
fatale* he had to rescue his brother from. There's something
eerie about him, don't you think? He makes me—" and she
did genuinely shudder. "I just hate men who don't have sex,
there's something dry and rotten—some dry rotten smell—
he has it—or do I mean no smell at all? Anyway it makes me
sick. I've always hated to be in the same room with him."

"He's my uncle," said Robi, reappearing in the doorway.

"Didn't I tell you to go and play and not hang around here
listening?"

"He came to see me."

"Yes to take you to school where they might teach you
some sense. . . . Perhaps he's not so wrong for once. Come
here. Closer. No I won't hurt you, what do you think I'll do
to you?" But she must have been hurting his arm where she
clutched him to draw him closer. "Do you want to go?" she
asked, scanning his scared face. "Do you want to go away
with this uncle whom you don't even know and leave all of
us who love you so much—so much," she said and drew him
very close and stifled him against her bosom. When she released him, there were tears in his eyes and it made her mad
to see them; and yet at the same time she was sorry to have
caused them. "What's the matter with you, can't you even
stand a little love from your own mother? He *is* right; you
should go to school, to learn something and to get away. I
suppose you want to get away? Do you? Answer me!" she
said and shook him by both arms.

"I don't know," he was sobbing openly.

She let him go and sank back against her cushions. "I don't
know either," she said and was as unhappy as he was. "What
to do. About you. About anything. I just don't know anymore." She leaned back like an exhausted creature.

Tom kept his word and came to see us the next day; and
the next; and the next. It wasn't only Robi he got to know

but all of us—all, that is, except Renée, whom he knew already. And Crishi—I guess he had met him before too, in the course of Renée and Rupert's marriage; anyway, he certainly didn't try to pursue his acquaintance with him. But he made a point of dropping in on Sonya, who had a very high regard for him. Like Renée, Sonya rarely left her hotel suite—I don't know what it was about that hotel—sometimes I thought of it as an upholstered prison but sometimes as a giant carapace protecting us from whatever lay outside. We rarely went to the unfinished parts of the hotel, where walls and windows gaped open to the dusty desert air; only drilling and, faintly, the shouts of workmen reached us through our splendid padded walls. Sonya sat in the inner sitting room of her suite engaged in one of her favorite occupations, which was reading the future from cards. She was a bit shamefaced at being caught doing that the first time I brought Tom in to see her, but he didn't think anything of it and even asked her about the system she followed. When he came the next day, she was doing it again, and this time he asked her what it was she saw in her cards. At once she swept them up and said "Forgive a stupid superstitious old woman, Father— what must you think of me?" She tried to shake off whatever it was that was oppressing her and became her usual animated self; she made him sit close to her and began to ask him all sorts of questions. I didn't stay to listen because I knew it wouldn't be interesting for me. I was used to seeing her sitting in conclave with clergymen and other divines; whatever their denomination, she was forever catching hold of them to discuss spiritual matters. These were very important to her. In spite of her worldly tastes, of *haute cuisine* and *haute couture*, what mattered more to her than anything was the higher mystical element.

There were also discussions between Tom and the Rawul. These started off on the subject of Robi's schooling—as head of the family, the Rawul had to be consulted—but from there they branched out into other areas. This always happened with the Rawul; sooner or later he got back to the movement and his ideas. He particularly enjoyed his sessions with Tom because he could regard him not as an individual but as the representative of an equal power, and their talks became a dialogue between Transcendental Internationalism and the traditional church. Not that there was much of the traditional church about Tom, or of a potentate, and yet on the whole he did not hold his own badly with the Rawul. Anyway, he soon had the Rawul agreeing that Robi should be taken away to school and from there to go on to another subject of his own choosing, which was me. The way I knew it was that the Rawul sent for me during one of his sessions with Tom. I found them seated face to face, both on chairs as upright as any the hotel could furnish—not unlike the way I had seen the Rawul and Grandfather in conference at Propinquity. Like Grandfather, Tom looked tall, austere, and uncompromising; and like him he appeared skeptical of whatever it was the Rawul was saying. The Rawul invited me to sit with them. There wasn't another chair, only a velvet ottoman on which I perched between them, wondering what they wanted of me. The Rawul looked at me in his kindest manner (which was *very* kind): "Father Tom seems to think you're not happy with us."

"What!"

"No no no," laughed Tom. "I didn't say that. Quite the opposite."

I speculated on what was the opposite of not being happy: Did he mean that I was *too* happy? If so, it was the first time I had heard that this might be considered bad. With these thoughts, I must have been looking at him defiantly, for he went on as though defending himself: "All I said was I didn't think you had had enough choices yet. Like Robi really. . . . You said yourself," he stopped short my protests, "you didn't finish college. Well it's not too late yet."

I flushed with anger, but before I could say anything, the Rawul came between us in a conciliatory way: "Father thinks you should go home for a while. Go back to your family."

"*You*'re my family."

The Rawul made a gesture toward Tom, signifying, You see, I'm helpless. It also appeared to me to be a signal that I had to make my position clear to Tom, and I was glad to do so. "It's the first real family I've ever had, my own family having split up ages ago."

"And you don't care for them at all," Tom said—as a statement, so that I felt I had to modify it a bit: "We're not all that close anymore. My father has remarried and my mother has other interests and Grandfather died and Michael is here of course."

"Yes Michael is here," Tom said, and again in such a way that I felt he needed clarification: "It was Michael who started it in the first place—brought me into the movement and arranged for us to—" I was going to talk about the money but felt reluctant, so I ended up: "You should talk to Michael, he'll explain everything to you."

"I have talked to Michael."

"It's always the same with these young people," said the Rawul, making another helpless gesture, though this time with a tolerant smile. "They won't listen to reason, to anything sensible that we can say to them. Yes, we must blame them for that, we must be severe with them; but at the same time, my dear sir," he appealed to Tom, "shouldn't we be a little bit indulgent with them—even perhaps admire, even envy them the tiniest little bit for being—ah!—such idealists; such pure uncompromising spirits."

Tom was amused—I don't know whether it was at the Rawul or at me, but it was me he smilingly asked: "Is that what you are?"

Without thinking, and not even knowing this was what I was going to say, I said: "And I'm married."

"So you are," said Tom. The smile went from his face. He got up, and while the Rawul tried to detain him to continue their conversation, Tom seemed to feel there was nothing more to say, at least not to the Rawul. Putting his arm across my shoulders, he made me come to the door and outside with him; and there he said, smiling again and looking down at me from his great height: "Not all marriages are made in heaven, you know."

I dropped my eyes to his white feet in Jesus sandals. I was furious and was thinking what to answer him, but he strode off—down the deep-pile carpeted corridor with "Don't Disturb" signs on the closed doors and trays of dirty dishes waiting to be collected; he returned the respectful greetings of the hotel bearers and sweepers, all in uniforms much cleaner and smarter than his cassock.

The Rawul must have mentioned his conversation with

Tom to the Bari Rani, for she sent for me that same day and made me repeat everything to her. She was extremely indignant—"It's always that way with these missionaries. They think they have the right to interfere in everything that's no concern of theirs." I could see she wanted to have an extremely long and intimate talk with me, but this was even more difficult here than it had been in London. Besides the girls and Teresa running in and out to consult her about their program and problems, her hotel room had taken on the air of a party headquarters: The phone rang constantly, and people stood around waiting for her orders. She took everything in her stride, was flushed with activity and importance, and had time also to respond to the Rawul, who wandered in sometimes to try out a speech on her or have her do up the top button of his long silk coat. It was not the most convenient place to have the long talk she wanted, but she did her best She said "All right, let him take the boy. He needs to go to school and he is (they say) his nephew. . . . But you? What has he to do with you?"

"No nothing," I agreed.

Here there was another interruption, and when she came back to me, Bari Rani began to interrogate me: "What did he say to you? How has he been trying to get at you? . . . Oh I know how it is; didn't everyone try with me in the same way, first not to marry the Rawul, then not to let him get at the money. My own family, the lawyers, every busybody there ever was, even after the girls were born—all everyone was waiting for was for me to say it was all a mistake, help me, don't let him get at my money. That's all they're interested in really—the money. These wonderful Christians just like everyone else. *Tom,*" she said, pronouncing his name as something ridiculous. "I suppose he pretended great concern for you, tried to make you say you were unhappy. You're not, are you?" she suddenly shot at me.

"Of course not," I answered her at once, indignantly.

She patted my cheek and smiled: "I know you're not. Not now. But if ever—no, wait: Every marriage has its ups and downs, and one day we'll talk about it in *detail*—but whatever happens, you won't forget, will you: that you're ours; our child; just as much as the girls, you belong to us."

"Oh absolutely," I agreed with enthusiasm.

ONE morning Sonya came rattling at our door in excitement. It was Robi who let her in—he got up hours before we did and went down to forage for his breakfast in the twenty-four-hour coffee shop. Sonya had great news—there had just been a phone call from Manton; she had tried to call Michael and me to speak to him but the connection went off: The news was that Barbara had had her baby, a boy! "Just think, darling," cried Sonya, clasping her hands, "another sweet little darling baby boy!" "How wonderful," I said, wishing she wouldn't shout so loud. I gave a quick look at Crishi, lying on his stomach, one cheek pressed into the pillows; he appeared not to have woken up. "What's the time?" I asked. "Darling, it's *noon*," said Sonya. "Oh is it"; I failed to stifle a yawn; we hadn't been asleep all that long —it was three or four o'clock in the morning by the time Crishi had come home and there had been a lot to talk about and do. But Sonya felt everyone had to participate in her news, and she tried to shake Crishi awake—"It's a boy!" she cried to him. It was strange the way he went on sleeping, he who sat up awake and alert at every sound. "No he must get up, we must tell him," she insisted when I got between him and her. "He'll never forgive us if we let him sleep through our great news. Our boy! Our baby!"

"What's his name?" asked Robi.

"Darling, of course he'll be called after Grandfather; his grandfather. Oh my darling, my heart will burst," she said to me. "Another Samuel Wishwell." She stretched up to kiss me on the mouth in her usual way; she was wearing little high-heeled mules and a high turban around her curlers, but she remained considerably shorter than I. Stretched up on tiptoe, she whispered into my ear: "Perhaps it *is* Grandfather. I have a feeling, darling." Her secret tickled my ear; I knew she believed in transmigration of souls—I had heard her discuss it with her friends, many of whom had had proof of it.

"We must get back," she said with decision. "I told Manton we'll be there for the christening. We have to see him. Aren't you dying to see him?"

"Yes," I said. "Have you told Michael?"

"I can't find him. I must find him! My goodness, a sweet little brother has come—"

I asked Robi to go with Sonya to help her find Michael. She was a bit reluctant to leave, having so much more to say, but I persuaded her that Michael must be found and told at once. When they left, I locked the door, and by the time I returned to the bed, Crishi had rolled over on his back and was lying there, looking up at me, wide awake. "So there's another Wishwell," he said. I leaned over to kiss him; when I released him, he said "Another brother."

"Stepbrother." I tried to kiss him again, but he held me off.

"Are you going?" he asked.

"Going where?"

"With Sonya. To see him."

"Are you crazy: leave you?" I fell on top of him and kissed his face and hair. He kept still; and when I left off at last, he said "What about your baby? We haven't heard about that for a while."

I didn't bother to answer. Not only would a baby have been superfluous now that I had Crishi, but it would have been a hindrance between us and everything we did together and were going to do together—in the future, that is, when we had the money.

I was surprised at the way Michael got excited about Manton's baby. It was totally uncharacteristic of him. Then Lindsay called—that was strange too—I mean, why should *she* be so happy about Manton's baby? She kept on and on over the phone from New York—she and Jean had driven there straightaway from Propinquity to visit the baby. Michael listened to her, and I heard him ask "Who's he look like?"— what a question, from Michael! I stared at him, and he thought I wanted the phone and offered it to me. I wasn't all that keen but I took it, and there was Lindsay echoing from outer space in her girlish girl-of-good-family voice: ". . . the cutest little nose, just like you two, and the same funny pointy ears Michael has. . . . Oh isn't it just too—to have a baby in the family again—I've absolutely decided that Thanksgiving every year has to be at Propinquity, and Christmas—well we'll think about it—Manton and Barbara have bought this place which might turn out all right, though personally I think they paid too much for it. . . . Who's that? Michael? Harriet? He's a very very blond baby like you were, Michael, with the tiniest bit of downy fluff on his head—"

"What's she saying?" Michael said. He went in the other room to get to Sonya's other phone; but in the meantime I wiggled the receiver a bit and Michael called "What happened?"

"She got cut off."

"Well we were lucky to have her so long; Manton was only on for a few minutes," Sonya said. "Get me the airline, Michael!" she called to him in the other room. "Ask when we can have three seats."

I went into the bedroom where Michael was already dialing. I took the receiver from him and said "You're not really seriously thinking of going, are you?"

Michael thought this over, and having done so, having given the question respectful consideration, he said "Why not"; and after a while, "Going to New York isn't that big a deal."

From an absolutely practical point of view, he was right. Airplanes flew between New Delhi and New York every day, constantly, and one sat on them and got off at the other end and did what one had to do and came back; not a big deal at all. Except that I wanted it to be: wanting to be as far as possible from everything that lay behind me, not in space as much as in orientation. Hadn't Michael felt the same during the years he was traveling in all those different places—not for the sake of the places but for himself, his own fulfillment, his own happiness, rejecting everything that was a hindrance to that.

I said "And your work here?" But knowing this was no longer the ultimate question it had been, I went on, "It's only temporary, Michael, I mean being here in this hotel and all the political stuff of the Bari Rani's, it's only till we go—you know—up there, to Dhoka."

"Oh are we going?"

"Why, Michael, what do you mean, what do you think it s all about? Haven't you heard the Rawul say a million times how it's the pure source we have to get back to? Without that, it just wouldn't be worth it, would it?"

He was still sitting by the telephone on Sonya's big hotel bed. I got up there too and into a cross-legged position, just behind him. We were as close as we could be without quite touching; we could feel each other intimately, physically and otherwise. My mouth was so close to his ear that my breath must have tickled it as I whispered to him: "I don't like it any more than you do here. But I know it's all right because we'll be leaving soon, going on—you know, up there." All I could see was the back of his head, until he turned and I saw him in profile. His expression had lightened, waiting for me to say more: "Once we're there it'll be like the Rawul said— not neti but high and pure—oh you know it all much better than I do. . . . Only what I can't understand, Michael, how at this stage you would want to turn back—go *back*—when we've got this far, that's just completely incomprehensible to me. It's not like you; it's not like us." I felt the good impact I was having on him—by what I said and, more, by being so close to him. It was as if at that moment he felt himself again.

Sonya came in to ask if he had got through to the airline —but when she saw us, she stopped short. She stood in the doorway and regarded us with her head on one side. She must have been happy to see us the way we were at that moment. "Did you get them?" she said again but absently— preferring to stand there and see us together on her bed. But this being Michael, she got an answer, and a bald and truthful one: "I didn't call them," he said. She appeared satisfied, pressing no further but retreating to leave us alone to decide whatever we wanted to.

And when we did decide—that is, to stay—she showed no disappointment but said she would ask them to postpone the christening till she could be there. I felt there had been a great misunderstanding and said at once, "Oh no, Sonya, you must go, of course you must, they're waiting for you." She shook her head, she said no, she would stay with us, what else had she come for. I tried to catch Michael's eye to make him help me persuade her, but he avoided me; I realized he wanted her to stay. But I felt more like Crishi, who had said several times, "Shouldn't she be pushing off now?"

I was impatient to be alone with Michael so I could present this point of view to him; but when we were and I did, he wouldn't see it. He said "Why shouldn't she stay? She wants to be with us." "It's bad for her here—cooped up in her room all day, doing all that stuff with cards. . . . And when we leave to go up there? She can't go with us then?" "Why can't she? Of course she can. She's always gone with us everywhere, wherever Grandfather went she came too. Wherever it was." "Oh Michael." But there was no point in arguing; he wouldn't listen. He wanted her there; He was clinging to her. He said "You don't want her here." It was no use my saying that I was thinking of her, that for her own sake it was better she should leave. He knew that wasn't true—he knew it as clearly as if he had been listening to Crishi and me talking.

For only the night before Crishi had said to me, "You'd better get rid of her now. She's a bad influence."

"On me?"

He laughed at that—and it was ridiculous, to suggest that anyone but he could have any influence over me now. "No but on Michael," he said. He didn't elaborate—he didn't have to. It was funny, what was happening between him and me, the way I knew exactly what he meant, just as it used to be between Michael and me.

Crishi and I were also, without having to talk about it, in agreement about Tom: that he should leave, taking Robi with him. I hardly liked to admit it, but I wanted Robi to be gone, and not only because it was time he was sent to school. Although Robi had learned long ago to keep very quiet—especially when Crishi was there—his presence in our dressing room did have an inhibiting effect on me, and I kept listening for any movement from him, in case he was awake. I never did hear any, but that wasn't necessarily because he was asleep; unfortunately he had learned to be canny and watchful. But more than Robi, it was Tom we wanted to be gone, for he made absolutely no bones about being a disturbing influence; in fact, he deliberately set out to be one. I knew he often talked to Michael, as well as to Sonya, and though it was never when I was there, I don't think he was interested in keeping what he said a secret from me. I had the strong impression that he was trying to talk to me on the same subject, and I took care to avoid him. But he was a difficult person to avoid for he had no inhibitions about stalking you down. He could be seen purposefully striding around the hotel, and it didn't bother him that he was such an incongruous figure there.

He caught up with me one morning in the hotel lobby, which was a very public place for the kind of conversation I knew he wanted to have with me. He more or less maneuvered me—I must say, for a man of God he was pretty forward—into one of the deep damask-covered sofas in which hotel visitors were encouraged to relax. The place was as busy as an airport, with guests checking in and out and mounds of luggage everywhere and boys in uniform carrying them. In the center of the lobby was a huge marble fountain with little jets of colored water playing.

Tom came out with an apology—for what he had said the other day, about not all marriages. . . . He didn't finish the sentence this time, but went straight on to explain it: "It's because I've been through this before, with Rupert; with my brother."

"I know you didn't want him to be married to Renée." I looked at him, defiantly; I felt I had to be defiant with him. "But it was what *he* wanted, so who was anyone else to say." I went on: "If anything bad happens to me, I'm not going to be sorry—not at all! I'll still be glad that I did what I did: that all of it happened. And I think Rupert feels the same way."

"But I," said Tom grimly, "would give my right arm for it

not to have happened; that I had been strong and clever enough to prevent it. He's my younger brother," he said, and saying this, softened. "I was quite a practical sort of chap always but Rupert's a dreamer; full of ideals—Beauty and Truth and all the rest. I admired him for it: for thinking all that was available here and now. . . . I know they're very different types, but *your* brother reminds me of him. Don't you think so? No? But surely you agree that Michael too has a purity that one could not bear to see besmirched."

I don't know whether Tom had arranged it—for Michael to meet us here in the lobby—but at that moment I saw him come toward us. Among the tourists in pastel-colored summer playclothes, the Arabs in robes, the rich Indians in shiny brand-new suits and ties, the smartly uniformed hotel staff, Michael looked as out of place as Tom. He was, as usual, in white cotton clothes; but these were not very clean, and in all I have to admit Michael did not look clean—no longer the spare stern upright ascetic Michael but more like one of those sick kids who drag themselves around the bazaars and beaches of the poorest countries in the world. When he came closer, this impression was confirmed; he did look—not exactly sick, but unhealthy; his complexion, always very pale, was blotchy, and the sore on his mouth had not gone away. The word "besmirched," which Tom had pronounced, was still in my ears, but I dismissed it as being entirely wrong, unacceptable when applied to Michael.

Tom said to him, "I've been telling Harriet how you want to go home."

This was a lie; it was not what he had been telling me, and Michael too contradicted him—"You mean, how *you* want me to go home."

Tom grinned in a good-natured way and shrugged as though it didn't much matter. Michael was looking at me: "You and I talked about it," he said, as if defending himself against having done anything behind my back.

"Of course we did," I answered Tom more than him. "And decided how stupid and weak it would be to turn back now."

"Stupid and weak," Tom repeated, weighing these two words as if he weren't quite sure how or to whom they were to be applied. He asked: "Do you mean turn back from the movement or from your marriage?"

"Both, of course," I answered.

"And are you speaking for Michael or yourself?"

And again I answered without hesitation: "Both, of course."

Michael didn't say anything; he stared straight ahead, absenting himself from the scene. But even when he did that —gazed into the far distance the way he used to—his eyes no longer had their seafarer's look but were blank, like those of people who don't want to, or are unable to think.

"Are you sure?" Tom asked me then.

I wasn't even sure what he meant—did he mean sure of myself, of Michael, of the movement, of my marriage? But on all counts I answered in the ringing way Michael had once answered Grandfather's same question: "Absolutely sure." I glanced at Michael, expecting him to second me, but his eyes didn't unfocus from the distance, nor did any expression enter into them. Tom also waited for confirmation from Michael, and when there wasn't any, I felt it was up to me to repeat "Absolutely," in the same absolutely unwavering way.

Tom had no alternative but to accept our answer and let us go; no alternative really except to take Robi and leave with him. But there was a new complication, for by this time Renée had decided that she didn't want to let Robi go. She must have come to this decision during a restless night, for it was early in the morning when she came to our room to announce it. Only Robi was awake and he let her in. It was the morning of the day he was supposed to leave, and he had got dressed and was waiting for us to wake up. But what woke us up was Renée standing over us and announcing in a loud voice, "*I* care if the child leaves or stays, even if no one else does." We were forced to wake up, though Crishi made a great business of yawning and rubbing his eyes. When Renée said "Even his father doesn't care," he was too engrossed in his own yawn to hear her.

But she couldn't be ignored. She loomed over us in our double bed, and it was as if we could hear her heart beating in a fury and passion that menaced herself from within more than it did us. I could feel Crishi beside me tense up to deal with the situation; and next moment he was utterly relaxed and tried to make her so too. He caught her hand and swung it: "What's it all about? Sit down." She swayed over us a moment longer, before letting him pull her gently down. But she said in a threatening voice, "I'm not letting him go."

Robi stood there looking at them; he was dressed and his
bags and new bedroll were packed for departure—I had
done it myself the night before. But he knew he didn't matter
much at that moment, and I knew the same about myself.
In fact, I got out of bed, and this being the only occupation
that occurred to me, I sat at the dressing table and started
brushing my hair. I had my back to them but could see them
in the mirror.

They were sitting side by side on the bed, and Crishi had
his arm around her in a comradely way. He said "I don't
know why everything is such a big thing with you"; but he
said it tolerantly, tolerant of her temperament. "If you don't
want him to go—if you've changed your mind—you only
have to say. We'll tell him—Tom, that is. *Father* Tom."

Robi whispered to me, "He's coming to get me. He says
we're going on the eleven o'clock train."

I whispered back, "Do you want to go?" He didn't answer
me; maybe he was awaiting developments on the bed, as
I was.

"What'll we do then?" Renée was saying.

"With the boy? . . . Do we have to do anything?" Crishi's
relaxed, smiling manner would have had a soothing effect
on anyone, let alone on anyone who loved him. I was glad
he was being that way with her.

"We could go back," Renée said, soothed enough to sound
wistful.

"What, all of us? The Rawul and Bari Rani wouldn't like
that."

"I don't mean them." He didn't ask who or what she did
mean. He was doing up a button on her dress, solicitous, as
with a little girl disheveled and in distress. "I mean—just—"
She may have been tempted to say "you and me," but recognizing the impossible, she said "the rest of us."

Then Crishi called to me to ask me what I thought. I hesitated—perhaps I wasn't supposed to be listening in but on
the other hand it did concern me. Renée said in her old impatient way, "Harriet doesn't care—she'll go where you go."

"Yes?" asked Crishi, smiling at me, pleased it was that way
and wanting to hear me admit it.

But at that moment I couldn't. There *were* other considerations. Robi was one—he was standing there waiting to hear what was to happen to him; Michael another; and the Rawul—and the whole movement—everything I thought was important to everyone! I said "I thought we were going to Dhoka."

Renée exclaimed impatiently. "Whoever put that in your head—did you?" she turned to Crishi, and back to me: "I suppose you think you'll have him to yourself up there." It was Crishi who began to protest—I kept quiet—but she cut him short: "Oh I don't blame her, I know how it feels to have a horde of people hanging around when you want to be alone with someone. But what to do," she said to me as to an ally or someone very close. "We have to put up with one another, there's no other way."

Deep in my mind I thought, Oh isn't there? And at the same moment I caught Crishi's eye and he seemed to be signaling some similar thought to me. I felt safe, reassured; and that I could leave her to him and it would come out all right for me. They were still sitting side by side, lovingly, on our bed; she was fondling his face as if he were a little boy and she his doting mother: "All because of him," she said. He lowered his eyes, so sweetly, bashfully, I couldn't help smiling and neither could she.

There was a rap on the door—it was Tom come for Robi. We had almost forgotten about Robi; but he was still standing there, waiting to see what was going to be decided about him. "Well—ready?" Tom asked him, in his cheery way; he himself seemed to be ready for his journey with only an old cloth pouch slung across his cassock.

I think Renée was about to speak—to tell him of a change of plan—but Crishi prevented her. He tried to get up but there she prevented *him*—if he was embarrassed to be seen sitting so close beside her, she was not; on the contrary, she caught his hand and held it tight, flaunting their close proximity. Tom didn't look at them but only at Robi: "Ready?" he said again. He saw the bags I had packed and hoisted one, encouraging Robi to try with the other. No one stopped them—I don't know what secret communication Crishi made to Renée beside him, but she said nothing about a change of

plan and only watched the preparation for departure. Tom
continued to take no notice of them, but he did of me; with
Robi's suitcase on his shoulder, he looked down and said quite
wistfully: "And I can't persuade you to change your mind?"

"Look out for him!" cried Renée in a merry mood from
the bed. "He's forever trying to make people change their
minds to what he thinks is good for them."

"But I don't succeed very often," Tom said, speaking
to me and not to her, and lingering for my answer to his
question.

"And he never gives up!" Renée continued to taunt him;
she seemed to be challenging an old adversary whom she had
once defeated so that she felt safe and victorious with him.

To get away from Tom looming over me, I went to help
Robi carry his luggage. But Tom followed me and said "If
you leave, Michael will too; he'll do what you do."

"Why should I leave?" I said, busying myself with the luggage to avoid looking at him, or at the couple on the bed.
Not that *I* minded looking at them but I knew he did; I knew
he was misinterpreting our whole situation and there was
nothing I could do to set him right. I just wanted him to
go—take Robi and *go!*

But instead of doing that, he put down the suitcase he had
hoisted and, pretending to rearrange the luggage, he knelt
on the floor and unbuckled the strap I had fastened around
Robi's sleeping bag. I don't know whether it was the effort
of doing that which made his face and balding head flush,
or whether it was the effort of staying here where obviously
he didn't want to be. Because if I was impatient for him to
take Robi and go, he was perhaps no less so; but being what
he was—that is, vowed, I suppose, to duty and sacrifice—he
stuck it out with us, on the off-chance of—what? What? Why
should he care for me and Michael or what happened to us
when he already had Robi, who was at least something to
him, since he had accepted him as his brother's son?

It was Renée who asked that question: "What is it to you
what they do? What any of us do? Why have you selected us
for your missionary activities?" Crishi murmured to her, to
calm her down; she was seething with excitement. Tom hadn't
yet glanced at her but had his head lowered over the strap

he was retightening. Robi stood by him, watching him, as if there were no one else in the room and nothing else were happening here.

But "Come here!" Renée called to her son. Her voice and its tone of command made him start. Never very quick, he didn't move at first but kept on standing there; and worse, he didn't look at Renée but at Tom, as though asking him what he should do.

"Oh my God can't you hear me!" cried Renée. "Or has he trained you already to do nothing without his permission?"

"Come on now, Rani, leave it," said Crishi and grasped her arm. She shook him off and said "Because he couldn't turn his brother against me, he's started in on my son, to get him away from me. And for what, why? What are we to him that he's so concerned with us?"

"Obviously," Crishi said, "since Robi's his nephew—"

"Oh obviously," said Renée; "obviously, obviously." She made it out to be the best joke she had heard in a long time; she flung back her head and burst out laughing. But it sounded desperate, despairing—was it because of letting go of Robi? Or whatever it was that had happened in the past between her and Rupert and Tom? Or was it something new, some new turn, new fear in her life?

Crishi was irritated; he hated hysteria above everything. He got up from beside her, and turning his back on all of us, went to the window and pulled the curtains aside. The room had been in the soothing twilight in which we had been asleep—Crishi and I—since dawn. But now everything, including our rumpled bed, was exposed to harsh daylight blaring in through the picture window. The hotel, towering like a ruler's palace over the surrounding newly built flats, and stalls, and straw huts where the construction workers lived, stood in a very exposed position in that raw, treeless land: so that the light coming through the window, unmediated by anything green or pleasant, seemed to strike straight in from the desert, and was white and laden with dust. We blinked from its impact, and Renée put up her arm to shield her eyes; or was it her whole face she was trying to shield, its beginning signs of age so unfairly exposed? Crishi kept on standing by the window as though he saw something out there more interesting to him than were the rest of us in the room. Renée was half turned toward him, and there was something imploring in her attitude. He never glanced behind, and, intent only on him, Renée didn't notice that Tom's gaze was for the first time fixed on her. Like the light striking in through the window, this gaze was unmediated and so perhaps could be interpreted as unmitigated; he had pale, colorless eyes that reflected no judgment of any kind but looked very steadily out of his narrow, hollowed face. Whatever it was they saw in Renée, it made him want to finish this scene and not provoke her anymore by his presence. He said to Robi, standing tiny beside him and holding on to his cassock, "Say good-bye to your mother." But he had to say it again before Robi let go of him to approach the disheveled figure squatting on the disheveled bed.

She still had her arm up to shield her from the light and was half turned toward Crishi: and it was some time before she noticed Robi standing before her. When she did, she looked at him as if she had never really seen him before. She cupped his face between her hands; of course this face was very much like Crishi's—triangular, delicate, with slightly slanted eyes. She said "So you're going, you're leaving us, are you?" As usual with her, he held himself rigid, as with an unpredictable animal. She smoothed the hair from his forehead with her large palm; her scarlet nails lingered in his dark hair. "And are you going to be a good boy and do everything your teachers tell you?" she said. Her voice, husky with tenderness, was unfamiliar to him, and not knowing how to respond, he continued to stare at her. This must have irritated her, and though she tried to continue to speak tenderly, there was a sharper edge to her voice: "I hope you're going to write long letters home and tell us everything you're doing." He said "I want to write to my father." After this declaration, he looked around him, maybe for protection; and finding that Tom had come up very close, he clung to him.

Renée let him go. Tom began to bustle with the luggage again, picking up most of it himself, and letting Robi carry what he could. Quickly getting into my jeans and shirt, I followed them down the hotel corridor and to the elevator.

I was a bit hurt by the way Robi never glanced back for me, any more than for Renée or Crishi, but stuck close to Tom; maybe he was afraid of being left behind. A party of Japanese businessmen got in the elevator with us, separating us, I on one side and Tom with Robi clinging to him on the other. It wasn't only Robi who had nothing to say to me; Tom didn't either. I went right out in the street with them, and helped them get into the auto rickshaw that Tom hailed to take them to the station. By this time Robi was quite excited, and when they took off, he waved to me cheerfully, and so did Tom, though both soon turned away. I went back slowly into the hotel, through the revolving door into the artificially cooled and freshened lobby. I had a slight feeling of having been abandoned but it didn't last long—no longer than it took to get upstairs, back to our room, where Crishi was again on the bed with Renée, holding her in his arms, though not so engrossed in her that he couldn't acknowledge me over her shoulder, in the amused conspiratorial way he nowadays had with me.

"YOU can't do it," Michael said to me. This was just before the Bari Rani's biggest party yet, and maybe that is why his words have stayed with me so clearly through the years, though at the time I was too preoccupied to be listening to them very carefully. He went on, "You can't let another person take you over that way. Even if it's a good person, and not—" I don't remember his finishing the sentence. Then he said "Self-surrender is okay, but it has to be to something—" his Adam's apple worked up and down—"something higher—" he flushed fiercely— "nobler"—he swallowed as if in pain—"of a different quality altogether from what we are." I didn't know what he was talking about, or didn't want to know. Because on the subject of self-surrender—at that time I loved Crishi in such a way that I wasn't capable of keeping back one ounce of myself but wanted to give myself completely for him: my will, my intelligence, my understanding, everything I was. I'm not saying I'm not guilty but only stating the reason why.

And so I come to Bari Rani's big party. It was a very important event, she impressed on all of us—important, that is, for the Rawul's career. By this time we had got used to the word *career*, and it no longer sounded odd to us in conjunction with the Rawul. There was a conference of the chief ministers of all the states of India, and Bari Rani wanted to take advantage of the presence of so many VIPs. She hired one of the lawns at the back of the hotel and had a big orange tent put up with carpets and bolsters inside it, and rows of lights, long buffet tables, musicians, and armchairs for the guests who found it difficult to get down on the carpets. These turned out to be more than expected—some were grossly overweight, some suffered from piles, and there were those who didn't want to be put in an inferior position to the ones favored with armchairs. Bari Rani had gauged the problem almost before it arose and more armchairs were quickly carried down from the hotel. There were plenty of helpers, for besides the hotel staff, Bari Rani had engaged an outside caterer; and the Bhais were there in full force—they had to be, for the Rawul could not fall short of his guests, who had all come with a large retinue of personal assistants and general hangers-on.

To keep the events of that night straight, I had better record them one by one. The center of activity was inside the tent, where the Rawul was receiving his guests. He stood resplendently by the entrance, and as each VIP came in, he greeted him with that formal, stylized courtesy he had worked up to such perfection—one world power meeting another, making an event that went far beyond the personal to where the fate of nations hung in balance. How ofen I had seen and admired the Rawul in this role—with Grandfather, with Babaji, even with Tom: but never had the scene been as impressive as it was now. This may have been due to the guests, who, for one thing, were *physically* as weighty as the Rawul. They wore various forms of national dress—pajamas, *kurtas, lungis, dhotis;* the thin muslim cloth, starched to perfection by Indian washermen who had done nothing else for generations, showed off the full weight and volume of each chief minister. And besides the physical weight, there was also the moral one—I mean, they were very important, each in his state literally ruling over millions; they had in reality what the Rawul so far had only in his thoughts and dreams.

The tent was filled to capacity, for besides the chief ministers with their retinue, there were other dignitaries with theirs, and local politicians, and whoever else Bari Rani considered useful to her cause. The serving staff circulated with trays of fruit juice and hors d'oeuvres and carried in the dishes to be placed on the long buffet tables, behind which

more attendants stood ready to serve. The tent had begun
to heat up, and the electric fans, hanging down among the
lights, had been set in motion; along with the air, they circulated the smell of spicy foods and hot breads and pickles,
and of heavy bodies lubricated in perfumed oils. The wives
sat to one side, and it was the task of Bari Rani and the girls
to make what conversation they could with them. I could see
them working hard at it—even the girls, who had had to be
primed for several days before, were rallying nobly to their
parents' cause. It couldn't have been easy for them, not even
for Bari Rani, for their guests were mostly peasant women
with plain manners and plain speech, some of it in a dialect
no one could understand. Since there was such a crowd, Bari
Rani had given orders that those of us who had no duties
inside the tent should stay in attendance outside; I took this
to apply to myself, as did Michael. The Bhais squatted at the
back of the tent, where they had got up a game of throwing
dice among themselves.

I enjoyed lingering outside and watching the goings-on
inside the tent. I ought to say that the weather had changed
since our arrival—the crisp North Indian winter had gone,
and the air, no longer tangy with the breath of Himalayan
snow, was soft and warm and shot through with desert dust,
also with waves of some exotic perfume. "What is it?" I had
asked Crishi, and he had said "Oh some Oriental creeper the
hotel people have planted." "What's it called?" "How should
I know?" (How indeed? Nothing was further from Crishi's
interests than any kind of flowering natural thing.) The sky
shone with more constellations than I had ever seen. It lit up
the lawn where the tent was, eclipsing the rows of lights and
paper lanterns strung from skinny, newly planted saplings.
Beyond the lawn loomed the hulk of the main building, and
here the sky was itself eclipsed: for inside all sorts of parties
and receptions were going on, and the hotel was afloat like
an ocean liner with lights and music streaming from it. Although I was watching the proceedings in the tent, some of
my thoughts lay in the direction of the hotel, for Renée was
in there, as was Sonya, and maybe Crishi too: For some reason
he hadn't come down for the Rawul's party.

I made the mistake of asking Michael why Crishi wasn't

there. I knew it was a mistake as soon as I said it, for as always nowadays with Crishi, even at the mention of his name, Michael shrugged and turned away his face; and next moment he burst out, "Never mind why he's not here. Why am I? Or you?"

A new phalanx of heaped and steaming dishes was carried past us by uniformed hotel bearers, and the Bari Rani appeared at the door of the tent to hurry them up. Before she could go back inside, Michael blocked her way: "What's the program? What's going to happen next?" She stared at him blankly, too preoccupied as hostess to quite connect with him. "When's he going to speak?" Michael went on; and when she still said nothing but tried to push past him to get back to her guests: "Don't say he's not going to speak—that this is all- -that it's just an eating and drinking party?"

She had re-collected herself and tried to soothe him— "Michael dear, not now—this is not the time—"

"Not the time for him to speak?" Michael took her up. Soft and insinuating, she was stroking his chest; it must have felt like a rock under her hands. "He's got to speak," Michael said "They're all here, they have to listen to him. He's been silent too long; bowing and smiling too long."

Looking into the tent, I saw that was exactly what the Rawul was doing. He was standing among a group of the chiefest of all the chief ministers. Anyway, they were the most massive—vast men in thin drapery shoveling food into their mouths. Whenever a bearer passed with a dish, the Rawul stopped him and insisted on serving the guests himself, ladling food onto their already overflowing plates, bowing low over them as he did so, coaxing and smiling and putting everyone in a good mood so that bursts of fat laughter rose from that group.

"See that?" Michael turned to me; and then he said "It's disgusting," bringing out the word like a lump from his chest.

Bari Rani also turned to me—she looked worried, as if she thought he was sick in his mind. Well he wasn't—I knew that—but he was suffering in both his body and his mind, the way he did when something deeply, deeply affected him. He breathed heavily, the disgust he spoke of suffocating him; his face was contorted with it. It may have been a trivial cause to set him off that way—just a bunch of fat men eating—but I could see how for him it was the culmination of his disappointment.

"Listen," he told Bari Rani. He was still barring her way. "If he won't do it—if he's not going to speak to them about our movement—and why we're here—why we're *here!*" he repeated, choking on his fury—"if he won't, I'm going in there and I'll break it up. I will," he said. "Don't think for a moment I wouldn't."

Again she put both her hands on his chest, and now *she* was barring *his* way: for he did seem ready to rush in there, maybe to make a speech, or in his fury to brandish his Swiss army knife, snatch dishes and plates, scourge away the guests—Christ among the money changers—both Bari Rani and I knew he might do that; to me he looked stern and ascetic, to her I guess mad.

At that moment two of the Bhais who had been gambling at the back of the tent came around to ask Michael when their meal was going to be sent to them; and so that no mistake could be made as to their meaning, they made eating motions by stretching their mouths wide open and pointing inside them. Michael's fury turned on them—in any case, he hated them, ever since he'd come. It may have been these feelings, festering inside him, which were responsible for his sick look and the sore on his mouth that didn't heal. That was how it was with Michael—he turned everything inward on himself; but it had never harmed him before, perhaps because up till now all his deeper feelings had been good and noble.

Bari Rani spoke across him to the Bhais in the language he and I didn't understand. Whatever it was she said, it made them draw closer together as if they were getting ready for attack or defense. Advancing toward Michael, they stood and looked at him. "Michael dear," said Bari Rani in a sweet, subtle, insinuating tone, "you're not very well, why don't you go and rest. Don't you think he ought to?" she said to me, but I wasn't about to be drawn to her side against Michael.

"That's all anyone can ever think of," said Michael. "When someone's serious, they're sick. . . . Yes I know," he said when she was about to speak again, "it's the climate. But there's

nothing wrong with the climate, it's everything else. Every
rotten thing else," he said, and in a way that made her turn
again to me and, getting no response, to the Bhais, who stood
there in readiness.

But Michael laughed: "You can call them off. I'm not crazy";
and to them he said "Don't panic, you'll get your food." They
waited for Bari Rani's command, and when she hesitated,
Michael laughed again. "It's all right, I'm telling you—I'm
not dangerous."

She didn't seem at all sure of that, and to see her dubious
about him got me mad. I told her, "Get your watchdogs away
from us." She communicated with them again. Though I
couldn't understand the words, I sensed some other secret
exchange hidden inside them. The Bhais withdrew, leaving
Bari Rani facing the two of us. She was in a dilemma, I could
see. She wanted to get back in the tent to the hostess duties
she performed so well; but she didn't want to leave us on a
note of hostility. It was not so much that she was afraid
Michael would rush in there but that she might lose us—that
is, our allegiance, or rather, our money. What power this
money gave us—without it, what were we but a couple of
American kids who were getting in her way and whom it was
just the easiest thing in the world to have thrown out. But
there we stood, and had to be cajoled.

We both wanted to save her the trouble; and anyway what
could she say to allay his doubts, when these were only too
visibly confirmed by the goings-on inside the tent. We both
told her not to worry but to go and help the Rawul entertain
his guests. She said she wasn't worried about anything except
Michael's health; that she felt he had been working too hard,
had had to bear too many responsibilities by himself—"Where's
Crishi?" she interrupted herself at this point, and she couldn't
have said anything that so diverted our attention from the
party inside.

Michael said "Don't ask about him—he has a lot of things
of his own to do, a lot of other interests."

Bari Rani said to me, "Is he in the hotel? Why don't you
go and find him? He ought to be helping Michael and all of
us down here."

When I promised her I would, she was partly satisfied to

leave us, though not without first trying to make me understand that Michael needed watching. "He's been working so hard," she said, once more passing her hands over his chest so that he stiffened against her. With a last half-warning, half-pleading look at me, she went inside. I was glad to be alone with Michael. And he with me—he must have been waiting for this moment and said at once: "Sonya's right. Tom's right. We should go."

My heart leaped up in shock; at the same time my mind began to work furiously, getting together reasons to refute him. As though he knew them already, he said "Sometimes you just have to admit you've made a mistake."

He was still standing at the open door of the tent and could look inside at the feasting. I felt it to be important to turn him away from that sight, for anything I said would be at once contradicted by it. I took his arm and pulled him into the semidarkness of this newly planted garden, between the tent and the looming ship of the hotel. "The Rawul told you," I said urgently. "How we have to be practical and do things we don't care for if we want to get even halfway to our ideals. He's *told* you. Do you think he likes all this any better than you do? No he doesn't!" I at once answered myself, not giving Michael a chance to say yes.

"It's not only that," he said, gritting his teeth. "It's not only negative that I don't want any of this. I'm positive too—absolutely positive what I do want: Sonya and I've been talking. Don't think she's tried to change me or anything. But I've changed myself, by myself. It's like you think and think and think—about what you want and don't want; about what you're going to do and not going to do: and all the time something quite different is preparing inside you, so suddenly you *know:* not what you want to do but what you have to."

I said "You mean go back to Propinquity; take back the house on the Island; you mean go on fighting with Mother and despising Manton and everything else you've always run away from. All that damn neti." I looked at him sideways: In half-darkness, his pale face illumined only by the glow of the lanterns strung up around us, he appeared most beautiful to me. By which I mean he was like the old Michael before we came here. No, from long before that—what seemed long,

long before that—I guess I mean before he ever met Crishi and the Rawul and Renée. But you can't go back like that in time even if you want to. I felt I had to think fast, talk fast, hold on to him, get him on my side; I said, in a half-complaining voice: "And whatever you did, I followed you. Whatever it was; wherever you went; you never had to ask me or explain anything. I was right behind you." Thinking or maybe only hoping that I saw a shadow of doubt pass over his face, I went on more directly: "It was you who met Crishi first; and liked him—very very much. You liked him very much. It was your fault," I said like an accusation.

But he wouldn't take that; he said dryly, "I never asked you to follow me there. I've liked other people before—in that way—but I didn't ask *you* to fall for them."

"Is that all it was then? Just falling for him—and when it's over, it's over? Is that all it was?"

I was really shaken, and he was too and said "No. That's not all." But I knew he meant the Rawul and the movement—everything that was at this very moment being dissipated for him in a vulgar feast. If he had said, about the Rawul and his movement, "It's all a fraud. Let's go home," I wouldn't have made a fuss; I would have followed him as usual. But he was saying it about my marriage—about me and Crishi—and there I couldn't, wouldn't, wouldn't ever agree with him.

He said "I told you, you have to admit sometimes when it's a mistake."

"Yes when it's something small that doesn't matter very much—"

"Is that what you think it was for me?" he answered. I took him up at once and said "No it wasn't and that's why you can't walk away from it, any more than I can . . ." I failed to conclude the sentence, not caring to point out that it was two different things we were committed to. But I felt he was eluding, slipping away from me—that I wasn't making enough impact on him. After all I didn't have much practice at it because it had been always he who thought and decided for both of us, not the other way around.

But he was fair-minded, with me as with everyone. He went his way and asked no one to follow him—no, not even me;

he never had; it was out of my own free will and feelings for him. So he could now say "Well you know, H., you don't have to come with me if you don't want to," and say it calmly, as though it were a possibility. But for me to admit that it was, that it could be, was like breaking off a part of myself. I was so shaken, I could only speak in a hushed voice; I said "You mean you go, and I stay."

We looked at each other. Although there was no physical resemblance between us, this act of being face to face had always been and still was at this moment like facing a mirror. The possibility of our parting may have been open—but how do you tear yourself apart from your own image or reflection?

"You're so impatient," I said. "We've spoken about this. It's only here that it's—you know—" I made an impatient gesture toward the tent behind me. "But once we get to the Rawul's kingdom and can really work—devote ourselves— once we get up there—"

"You mean where they come from?" His gaze had shifted from my face over my shoulder. I turned around. Some Bhais—four of them—had approached us. I must say, they looked like terrible brigands standing there. One of them was repeating that eating motion into his open mouth, the others were grinning; nevertheless, there was something menacing about them.

"They're all right," I said. "It's just we can't understand what they say."

"Oh no, I understand," he said. "Food. Drink. Money. Hold on!" he called to them. "I'll get it for you."

"You needn't be doing this," I said.

"Who else then?"

Not wanting an answer, he went away to where a makeshift kitchen had been set up behind some shrubbery. I followed him and heard him give orders to the cooks there, doing his best to make himself understood. It was wrong to leave him with these menial tasks he hated, and nothing else. But where was Crishi? I went toward the hotel to search for him.

The nearer I approached the hotel, the louder it became. All the lights were blazing and the sound of several bands came blaring out. Many strains of music were mixed up— there were ballroom-dance tunes, some disco music, some

South Indian sort of toneless throbbing rhythms, and one of those festive instruments they play at weddings. Somehow all this did not result in hideous cacophany but blended into festive noise. The whole huge hulk of the hotel, rearing up into and eclipsing the night sky, seemed to be shaking and vibrating with this noise; it was really like some big liner sailing by with parties of revelers on board. And inside it was packed with people in their shiniest clothes and jewels, for several wedding and other receptions were going on simultaneously in the various banquet halls. The inside of the hotel was of white marble and it was flooded by a light so bright that it appeared almost supernatural. There must have been hidden lamps and tube lighting, but the entire illumination seemed to be concentrated in, to stream down from the gigantic crystal chandelier that reached right from the highest point of this tall building to the white marble fountain in the center of the lobby.

To take advantage of the many guests and visitors that night, the shops in the arcade were wide open for business and had hung their most tempting carpets, shawls, and brocades outside their doorways. I stopped by the jeweler's, to see if maybe Crishi was there; the jeweler's assistant was in the front of the shop, displaying some very good fakes to a couple of American customers who were making knowledgeable comments about them. I peered past them into the back room, and there I saw the jeweler himself. He was crouching on a stool over a little white-covered table and displaying some jewels to a customer who turned out to be Sonya. From the confidential way he was talking to her, I suspected it wasn't about the jewels. When I entered and she looked up at me, my impression was confirmed, for her eyes were full of tears, so I knew he had been telling her all sorts of things about Crishi. All those old past things!

I said "What are you buying?" and sat down next to her on another little stool. I didn't want to leave them alone any longer. But I knew it was already too late, and he had told her more than I would have wanted her to know.

"Oh darling," she said; she was sobbing and I pretended not to know what about. I looked at the jeweler, who was concentrating on his stones and arranging them for her inspection. I said to him, "Why don't you go and see to your customers outside." When he hesitated, I laughed. "We won't make off with your stuff," I said, so he had to go though I could see he didn't really trust us.

The moment he went into the front of the shop, I put my arm around her and said "You mustn't cry about it." I went on, "How do you know what he told you is true? . . . And anyway, you knew some of it—about being in jail and all that—"

"But the rest! The rest!"

She drew away from me; she was so horror-stricken, I wondered exactly what he had told her. Probably about the English wife and who knows what else, true or false, but I didn't want to go into it. I said "You're willing to listen to anyone—any stranger—who'll say anything about my husband. . . . How do you know it's true?" I urged her again. "Any more than you know if these stones he's selling you are true or fake—" I picked one of them up, a little black stone that didn't look like anything, but she quickly took it from me. She said it was a very unlucky stone for me, the sort that would have a baleful influence over my destiny. I said "But if what he told you is true, isn't it too late to worry about my destiny?"

"Oh my darling, don't laugh about it. Your grandfather always laughed—all of you did—so I kept quiet. But if I had only spoken—as long ago as your wedding night—"

"Why? What happened that night?"

Instead of answering, she seized my hands and said "Let's go home, darling, everyone wants it."

She was pleading, but I withdrew my hands and said "Not everyone. Not me. . . . No nor Michael either!" I cried, more stubbornly than necessary since she hadn't mentioned him.

I don't think she believed me, but she changed her plea to: "Then for my sake. Only for me. Please, darling, for Sonya." She desperately patted her little stout bosom in floral silk and looked at me with faded blue eyes brimming. "What if something were to happen—" She became desperate and didn't even hear me when I laughed at her and asked "Such as what?" "I'd never forgive myself," she said, wringing her hands and went on: "And what would I tell him, what would I say to Grandfather?"

There was a pause. In the front of the shop, separated from us by a curtain, we could hear the jeweler trying to sell his clients his fake pictures; but Sonya went on talking as if she and I were alone and in a very private place. "Yes darling," she said, "I talk to him. You might as well know it—how Grandfather comes to me at night and says 'Well, Sonya?' and I tell him what's happening, what I've been doing and about you two children. He wants to know everything there is to know about you and Michael, he asks me the most searching questions, you know how he does so that you have to tell him even if you'd rather not. . . . I know you don't believe me, darling, but it's true, and if it weren't I wouldn't want to go on living." She dried her tears.

No I didn't believe her—how could I—and yet I wished I could because I thought it was so beautiful, such a wonderful thing to hope for. I mean, if you love a person that much in your life, then you can't be separated from him afterward. I wanted to ask her more—sort of detailed questions about Grandfather—but she went back to her first theme and the tears she had been drying welled up again: "And now what can I say to him—if something happens—"

"But what could happen?" I cried. Instead of answering me, she put up her hands to ward off something—it might have been a blow or it might have been a vision. At that moment the jeweler stuck his head through the curtain, I waved him away in anger, and though it was his shop, he obeyed me. Maybe he felt guilty—he *was* guilty, for it was he who had filled her with this fear: by telling her about Crishi's first wife, I suspected, and what she had done to herself. I made Sonya look at me and said "Do you really think I would ever—" She wouldn't let me get any further; she put her hand over my mouth but I took it away and went on speaking: "It's not the same at all—for one thing, she was very young—"

"Yes and you're fifty years old," Sonya said, not humorously.

"And she was pregnant—no I'm *not*—and he was away and there was no money—which you can't say about me, can you, and besides," I said firmly, "I'm happy. I'm very very happy."

"And Michael?" she came back at once.

"You know perfectly well how it is between me and Michael.

Whatever one of us feels the other one is the same."

"Not now," she said in sadness.

"How do you know that? Shouldn't *I* know better than you?"

"Not now."

I was silent. I was getting annoyed with her. She was coming between Michael and me, influencing him to feel and want in a different way from me. "What's he said to you?" I asked her.

"Does he have to say anything for me to know? Or you, darling—don't you think I know about you too without your having to tell me?"

I was too fond of her to contradict her; but it had never been true. Although she so deeply cared for us, she had never understood us in the way she thought she did. And now she knew even less—now she had absolutely no idea!

"And we did talk," she went on. "You were there too. We discussed it and Michael thinks—"

"What?"

"Michael wants to see his little baby brother. Don't you? Don't you want to see him?"

I said "You know how much Michael cares about babies and such. All right! Supposing he has for the moment got sentimental—or whatever you want to call it," I conceded. "How long do you think it'll last? And you know how it is once he gets together with Manton, how he can't stand him for five minutes—"

Sonya was pained by the way I spoke and she interrupted me: "They've both changed."

"They'll never change." I spoke with confidence, and I did know better than she did. She never really saw people but wrapped them in her own romantic ideas about them.

"Michael has," she said. She looked at me sideways, shyly but speculatively, wondering how I would react. I tried to hide it but I didn't react well. She and Michael had talked together too much—she had encouraged him, thinking she was helping him by making him talk about himself. She was wrong. I remembered how Crishi had asked "When's she leaving?" He had known before I did that it was better she should.

The jeweler came back through the curtain, and the irri-

tation I felt with her turned into fury against him, who had
wrought her up with all his slander. I saw him cast a quick
look over his tray of jewels and that gave me an excuse to
let go—I shouted "Why don't you count them and make sure
we haven't made off with any"—and I went further and
tipped the tray so that the jewels rolled to the floor. He cried
out, as did Sonya; he got down on the carpet at once and
began to pick them up, making distressed little noises. It gave
me a sort of pleasure to see him on his hands and knees. I
wanted to kick him while he was down there, the way Crishi
had kicked Paul, and Michael had Nicholas in the gallery. I
understood now what had compelled both of them to do it.
And I think I might have done it myself—I was standing
over him—if it hadn't been for Sonya looking so aghast at
me, staring at me as if she didn't know me. I said "Why doesn't
he say we've stolen his jewels, why doesn't he? He's said everything else he possibly can!"

That made him stop for a moment and look up from the
carpet: "I've said nothing—if I were to speak out what I
know, he would be in there again tomorrow." I made no
move toward him but something in my face and attitude
made him put up his hand to shield himself. I laughed, but
Sonya was clinging to me to hold me; she too didn't know
what I would do next. I asked her, "Do you believe him?"
and when she didn't answer at once, "Do you believe this
creature against me?" "I told her the truth! The truth about
him! You don't know!" he cried. The curtain behind him
shook a little—I could imagine his assistant and the two customers standing there petrified, listening—well let them. I
said, very calm and sure, "If I tell him to, he'd come in here
and kill you." It gave me satisfaction to say that; nor did it
seem to me such a very big deal if Crishi did it, or had it
done. The man was still on the floor and staring up at me
with his dark eyes; it was funny about his eyes, that they were
so beautiful and dreamy, not at all the mean shrewd merchant
eyes you'd expect. On the wall there was a picture of one of
those fearful-looking holy men, and smoldering in a corner
of the frame, a stick of incense. Sonya had let go of me by
now and was standing in a peculiar way with eyes downcast,
like one ashamed.

"Let's go," I said to her. "I can't stand being in here with this liar and cheat."

She didn't answer me; instead she got down on the floor and started crawling around, helping him search for the scattered stones. Her action seemed to me very undignified, and when at my urging she wouldn't get up, I left her to it and passed through the shop, brushing carelessly past the assistant and the two customers who moved out of my way. I resumed my search for Crishi.

He liked dancing but he wasn't in either of the two discotheques; nor in the twenty-four-hour coffee shop, where he sometimes entertained acquaintances whom he may have known for a long time or happened to pick up around the hotel; nor in the health spa, where the masseur was a special friend of his. I went upstairs to our room, though not too hopefully, for it was very rare for him to go there before he was ready to sleep around dawn. From there I went down to the next floor, to Renée's suite. I knocked on her door once, and louder a second time. There was no answer, but I was sure she was inside. In fact, I felt a sort of potent force straining at me from in there—and then I had a foreboding. I thought what she might have done to herself to give herself relief from the pressure of her passion, on the same principle that they used to let blood. I rattled the door; I called her name. Voices came from inside—they were kept low but that didn't prevent me from recognizing Crishi's. I rattled the door louder, and banged on it with both hands. Again the voices spoke, nearer the door, there was the click of a lock, and the door opened. Renée stood there, and behind her was Crishi. He spread out his arms in a helpless gesture and said "What can I do—she locked me in." He looked at her with amusement as if it were a joke she had played, but she was deadly serious.

Apparently they were at the end of whatever scene it was they had had between them. Although I didn't know what the scene was about nor its result, I could see how it had left her exhausted but him absolutely fresh, untouched. Also how he was dying to get away—was glad to be rescued by me— while she hadn't finished yet. She locked the door again, with the three of us inside, and Crishi and I just had time to exchange glances before she whirled around at us and looked keenly from one to the other as though suspecting some conspiracy between us. "Well tell her," she said to Crishi; but without giving him time to tell me anything: "What's the use of hanging around here?" she said to me. "There's nothing more for us to do." By us I guess she meant the three of us.

Above all, I wanted guidance from Crishi. But it was impossible for us to talk in front of her; she even continued to watch us to make sure that no secret signs passed between us. I realized that I would have to feel my way, and to guess what it was he wanted me to reply to her. I began with "Aren't we going up there—to Dhoka—"

"That's all nonsense," she interrupted me. "There s nothing more to be got from there, or any of those places. Whatever's left, the museums are snapping up and we can hardly hope to compete with them."

I realized she was talking about her business—what she used to make her living by, she and Crishi both. I was surprised—all that seemed so far behind us. She went on: "There are some pictures in The Hague—they're not entirely safe but we might make a deal and get them for the gallery."

"She means they're stolen," Crishi said, giving me the sweetest smile, which I couldn't help returning. This incensed Renée and she turned on him: "You used to be interested in the business and everything I taught you about it. You didn't know anything before, did you? You were just peddling rubbish It's I who gave you your eye for the real stuff—not that you didn't learn fast—you always have learned fast when it was for your own advantage."

"Oh don't start again," Crishi said, ruefully pleading. To me he explained "She's been at me for hours, even locked me in as you saw to tell me what a nasty selfish swine I am. Did I ever say I wasn't?" he ended up mildly.

"He's so slippery," she said to me, as to a referee between them. "It's impossible to get hold of him. He won't say yes and he won't say no."

"But to what?" I asked.

"To going home. To going back. To starting our business again and running the gallery and everything as it used to be. . . . Of course," she said quickly, "you're with us now,

Harriet, I know that, and I'm glad that it's the three of us—
we need one another."

She didn't explain who needed whom, but obviously she
needed Crishi so badly that she was willing to put up with
me. I felt sorry for her—especially as Crishi wasn't paying
much attention to her but was wandering around the room.
He sat down and started leafing through the telephone directory as though he had just remembered an urgent call he
had to make. She was forced to address herself mainly to me,
and something even more desperate began to appear in her:
"Who was it anyway," she said, "who started the whole
thing—who was it in the first place," she challenged me, or
was it him through me, "who asked you to marry him?"

"Jesus Christ, Rani, what's got into you," said Crishi, looking up from the directory with calm eyes. "Digging up all
these old stories, all that's been and gone—"

"Oh yes, old stories. Been and gone," she repeated bitterly.
"That's how he feels about everyone who's been of use to
him till he found someone to be of more use to him—whether
it's his mother, his wife, God knows how many others before
he got to me. And then to you," she said to me, and was
silent for a while and brooding; and Crishi, his lips moving,
ran his finger along the names in one column, utterly absorbed.

"Except you might last a bit longer," she went on to tell
me. "Because he hasn't had a prize like you before, or as you
will be soon."

Crishi burst out laughing and, snapping the directory shut,
he said: "She's on again about your money."

I said "As if that mattered."

"Oh no not at all," she said. "No one cares about your
money. All he cares about is you. Is that what you believe,
really and truly? You poor child!" she cried, flinging back
her head in what was meant to be laughter.

Again I tried to guess how Crishi wanted me to react. He
himself was so utterly untouched by what she said, and by
her general air of hysteria, that I thought it best to follow
his example. And it was easy for me, because what she said
couldn't touch me in the least; *she* couldn't touch me in the
least, nor stir up any strong emotions in me, though she
herself was tormented by them.

I spoke to her very calmly and in a sort of naïve voice "No," I said, "I don't believe that. I believe he cares for us equally but most of all for the movement, and he's looking forward to the money coming to help the Rawul and the movement."

She stared at me as if she thought I was crazy. When she looked at Crishi, he turned away from her, trying to suppress the twitching of his lips. I continued as I had started: "And that's why I'm glad I'll soon be twenty-one and can do what I want."

"And what do you want?" she asked.

I looked at her steadily and I answered her steadily: "To help the movement, of course. Don't you? Isn't it what's most important to you?" I waited, daring her to say no, and continued, addressing both of them now: "There's this party going on down there and I don't know why you're not there—the Rawul's looking for you, he needs you—so does Michael. He's on his own and it's difficult for him." This was meant for Crishi and he acted on it at once: "If she'll let me out, I'll go down. I'd have been there hours ago if she hadn't locked me in." He held out his hand, smiling, cajoling: "Give me the key, Rani; that's enough." His tender voice made her suddenly fling her arms around his neck—she was so ample, he so slender, but he caught her around her big hips and made a laughing sound like someone who has caught a heavy ball thrown at him in a game. "Promise and I'll let you go. Promise, promise," she said. She was laughing and crying at the same time. "I'm not saying just you and me—I'm not asking for that—Harriet'll come too—"

"How do you know she'll come?"

"She'll go where you go."

He stood holding her and she clinging to him; and without looking at me, he said "She won't leave without Michael."

"Michael wants to go home with Sonya." I delivered this as a warning, and I could see he took it as such. "Come on, Rani," he murmured, "let me go, let me go, let me go"; and with each repetition he kissed her inside her neck, pleasing and tickling her so that she laughed; and he unwound her arms very gently and very gently he took the key from inside her clenched palm, not forgetting to kiss that palm. She became soft and yielding and made no difficulty about his letting himself out—and I couldn't help wondering why he hadn't done this hours ago, if he had really wanted to go. But I didn't have much time to wonder, for he shot me a look—a glint of his quick eyes—and next moment I was by his side. He let both of us out, and we went hurrying down the corridor. As we went, I told him everything that was happening—about Michael and Bari Rani and the Bhais, Sonya and the jeweler.

Inside, the hotel was impossibly loud and bright, but outside, in the space between the building and the tent, there was a soothing darkness. The air was balmy and saturated by a honeyed fragrance. Here he stopped and held me; he said "I didn't promise her anything." He ran his hands down my back to my thighs, and as always at his touch. I became a flame of desire. I pressed myself against him, wanting to burn him up with me, and I shut my eyes and I clung to him and clung to him and clung to him. "Oh my," he whispered, "where's Aunt Harriet now." Some bearers were coming toward us, carrying empty dishes out of the tent to the make-shift kitchen behind the hedge. I didn't care who saw us, I wanted to go on standing there with him; and when he wouldn't, I said "Let's go in." "We can't—you said Michael needs me." "He's all right. Let's go. Now, Crishi. Now." So we went back inside.

NEXT morning I was woken up by the phone ringing by the bed. It was Sonya. She was very apologetic—she said she hoped she hadn't woken me up, she knew that we slept late—as she talked, my eyes fell on the empty pillow next to me: Crishi had gone! At the same time Sonya was saying "Where's Michael?" I assumed at once that he and Crishi had gone out on some mission together, and I was glad that Crishi was helping Michael. Sonya was saying "I know I'm an old fusspot but Michael comes every morning to breakfast with me, sharp at eight, bless him, every single morning till today." I had a sort of twinge—that they did this every day and I hadn't even known. I reassured her; I said Crishi had gone out too, and that they were together.

Several hours passed, and she called again. "Have you seen him?" she said at once as if she hadn't been thinking of anything else the whole time. Her unease transmitted itself to me—about Michael; not about Crishi. I was sure there was no need to worry about him, wherever he was and whatever he was doing. I told myself that it was equally unnecessary to worry about Michael, who sometimes disappeared for several days—at least from my sight, though it turned out that he and Sonya had been meeting every morning. I called her back and she must have been sitting right by the phone, for she snatched it up immediately. I asked her whether she had seen Michael last night; she said no, that she had gone straight back to her room after—after I had left her, she concluded

the sentence. There was something shamed in her voice and
I knew she was thinking of what had happened in the jeweler's shop. But I was thinking only of Michael. I tried to
recall exactly when I had last seen him: It was when he had
gone to order the Bhais' food. I also recalled how the Bhais
had stood there waiting for him outside the tent.

I went to Bari Rani's suite to find out what had happened
at the end of the party. I got as far as her sitting room, where
Teresa, her maid, sat stitching the hem of some bright-yellow
silk skirt. Yes, she said, Bari Rani was in the bedroom but
had a terrible headache and had given orders not to be disturbed; no, the girls were not there; they had gone out shopping. She didn't look up from her sewing while giving me
this information. I lingered and asked more questions: Why
did Bari Rani have a headache? Had she gone to sleep very
late? Had the party lasted very long? Teresa knew nothing;
she hadn't been there; she had gone to sleep at her usual
hour of ten o'clock. That was her habit, she said, lowering
her face to bite off her thread, and if she didn't stick by it,
she was a wreck the next day, unfit for anything. It had
happened to her hundreds of times before, so now she knew
better. She was still biting at the thread, which appeared to
be rather tough.

The Rawul's suite was next to the Bari Rani's and with a
connecting door to it. But I went around to the main door
in the corridor and was let in by one of the European
followers—which surprised me, for since our arrival it had
been the Bhais who were in attendance. The Rawul was mag-
nificently dressed, in white silk with jeweled buttons, ready
to welcome an important delegation. Even though I wasn't
one, he received me graciously—of course I had never seen
him as anything but the soul of graciousness and courtesy,
lightened for my benefit by a dash of fatherly affection. But
there was something impersonal in those qualities, as there
was in everything he said. It was because he was concerned
with the universal and couldn't stoop to the particular; but
it made it difficult to ask him a direct personal question—
like what had happened at the end of the party. I couldn't
even mention the party, his thoughts were so far beyond it.
That was another thing about him; he never looked back—

not even to last night—but only forward, forward, to new plans and triumphs.

This might have gone on for some time—my standing there growing every minute more anxious about Michael, and his giving me a speech on how he was going to mobilize the potential dynamic of the youth of his country—but we were interrupted by Renée coming in. He trailed off, and lowered his eyes, extinguishing the vision in them. She, however, faced him aggressively—I had never seen them together this way; but of course I hadn't seen them together since our arrival in India. She said at once, "Do you have it?" and he murmured "Dearest Rani, where should I get it from?" At the same time he looked warningly toward me, not wanting her to speak before me of whatever it was she was speaking.

But she waved him away: "It's too late to have secrets in front of her—and especially that sort of secret. We're talking about money," she told me. "I'm sure you've heard that talked about often enough by these people. It's all they ever think of. All they ever want from anyone." Ignoring the Rawul's small cry of pain at this utterly unfair accusation, she said to me: "Is that why you're here? Did he call you to get some more out of you?"

I hated her coarse directness as much as he did but made use of it by answering truthfully: "I came to ask him about Michael. . . . I haven't seen him since last night. Since the party." I looked at the Rawul to see if there was any change of expression at the mention of the party, but there wasn't. I said "Michael hated the party."

"And he's right," said the Rawul. "Right from his point of view—and from mine. Don't you think I feel the same way about these things? But alas I have had to learn to bow to necessity." He literally bowed his head and neck as one submitting to a yoke. "Naturally for a young person it's more difficult. Impossible! Don't I know it? Wasn't I the same at his age? Fire and flame; fire and flame; shooting—whoosh!—up."

"Don't let him fool you," Renée said. "He knows very well what's going on."

"Rani, Rani," he implored.

"Of course you do! You always do! You're only pretending you don't know about her brother."

I wasn't sure if she was hitting out at him blindly, or if she really knew of something that might have happened to Michael. I could see she was frantic on her own account and capable of saying anything.

"Ask him!" she cried. "Or his Bari Rani, why don't you ask her—call her, she's listening to every word anyway!" She took a few steps toward the connecting door, ready to fling it open and expose the Bari Rani listening at the keyhole.

The Rawul prevented her: not for his own sake, not for Bari Rani's, but for Renée's, to bring her back to herself. For it was painful to see her in this state. He grasped her hands; he begged her to be calm: "We'll talk about everything," he promised her. "We'll try to satisfy you in every way. We'll do whatever you say."

"Just give me my money and let me go! Give me all those thousands and thousands and hundreds of thousands you made me get for you!"

"What hundreds of thousands?"

This was Bari Rani, who evidently *had* been listening at the door and now appeared on our side of it. At the sight of her, Renée pulled her hands out of the Rawul's tender grasp and turned toward her. The two women faced each other, and although Bari Rani was by far the smaller, rounder, softer, she appeared the stronger. She said "It's we who've given everything, and without looking for anything in return."

"And what have I had in return?" said Renée.

"In return for what? You were only carrying on your business. You cared nothing for us—no she didn't," she said to the Rawul, who had made a movement to interrupt, "and the only reason she stayed—well, we know what it was." Bari Rani looked at me and said: "Of course that's all changed now."

"Nothing has changed," said Renée. "We're clearing out —this girl too, and he and I. That's what they're afraid of," she said to me. "That you'll leave. The same way they were afraid with Michael."

Bari Rani came between us; she said "Don't listen to her rubbish and lies."

Renée ignored her and went on talking to me: "Wasn't he getting wise to them?" she said. "Wasn't he planning to leave—and before his twenty-first birthday?"

I said to Bari Rani: "What happened last night?" When she didn't answer but stood there not looking at me, I said it again and louder.

"Nothing at all," she said. "Nothing worth mentioning—a little scuffle between the young men—"

"What happened!" I cried to the Rawul.

"He doesn't know!" cried Bari Rani. "He was inside the tent with his guests."

"Then what happened outside?"

"You saw yourself what a state Michael was in. He was ready to pick a quarrel even with me—of course I knew he was not well, I was concerned only for him, not for myself. But between young men it's different—they're hotheaded and ready to flare up at a word—"

"Was there something between the Bhais and Michael?"

"I don't know—after all, I did have three hundred guests to see to—I couldn't take care of everything that went on last night."

"She's lying," said Renée. "She's lying to both of us."

"Where is he?" I said to Bari Rani. But I knew I could get nothing from her; she would continue to plead ignorance for herself and the Rawul. I turned to him—I felt that if he knew something he would tell me—but was met by his visionary eyes looking back at me out of his baby-plump face. I ran out of the room. All I cared about was to find Michael.

In the street, I jumped into one of those bone-shaking auto rickshaws and had myself driven over the pontoon bridge to the new colony where the Bhais lived. We were stuck on the bridge for a while, together with a host of cycles and a bullock cart loaded with cauliflowers that kept rolling off. It was hot, the season had changed, we had got into the Delhi summer, and its heat and dust blew through the open rickshaw in which I sat. There was no cooling water under the bridge, for the river was in its dry stage and had contracted to a few wet patches seeping into acres of mud flats from which flies arose. I waved them off me absently—my thoughts were elsewhere—I was thinking of where Michael could be, and

where Crishi was, and I was hoping I would find them together. In fact, by this time I was expecting them to be together, and that I would find them at the Bhais' house. And
I thought, I must keep them together, reconcile whatever
small differences there were between them; for it was
unthinkable—unbearable—that the two people closest and
dearest to me, the two tenants of my heart, should not be at
peace with each other.

When I reached the Bhais' house, it was empty. They had
moved out, leaving nothing whatsoever behind—not even a
beer bottle or one of their film magazines. There was absolutely nothing and the doors were wide open from the front
to the back of the house. Even their cooking grate was empty.
Except for a little pile of ash, they had taken away the last
piece of coal, but the ash was still warm. From the workshop
next door there was the usual noise of people shouting to
each other and machines whirring and a dog barking, but
the house was completely silent and deserted, with no breeze
to stir the desert dust, which had already begun to settle on
the floors and window ledges.

I returned to the main road and found another auto rickshaw, which took me back over the pontoon bridge and into
the bazaar streets near the railway station. Here it was even
hotter, for the dense city streets had stored up the day's heat,
along with the smells that had accumulated in the gutters
and from the day-old produce of the vegetable and meat
stalls. When I arrived at the hotel where the European followers stayed, I had braced myself to hear that they too had
left; but the hotel clerk, smoking foreign cigarettes and with
his feet on the counter, only told me that they were out.
"What, all of them?" I asked. He said someone might be in
and shouted to the hotel boy to go and see, but though he
called him some bad names, the boy did not appear. He told
me to go up myself and came around from the desk to watch
me walk upstairs. When I knocked and got no answer, he
encouraged me to go in. I did, and found Paul alone. There
were as many of those string cots people sleep on as the room
would hold, as well as everyone's baggage and bedrolls, leaving no space on the floor. Paul was lying on one of the string
cots, the one right under the fan, and to get to him I had to

crawl across several other beds. He was sleeping but opened his eyes when I leaned over him. He said he had a fever.

He was certainly very hot, and eagerly drank the water I gave him out of the mud jar. When he had finished and I had tried to make him a bit more comfortable by settling his pillow and straightening the dirty sheet on which he lay, I asked him if he had seen Crishi or Michael. Maybe he didn't hear me; maybe his mind was wandering with the fever. Another possibility was that he didn't want to hear me. He took advantage of his weakened state to lie back with his eyes shut and ramble on about his own thoughts. He said this was the hotel in which they had first met Michael—the same blue distempered walls, he said, waving at them, except that they were more flaking and stained and scrawled with messages and phone numbers. After all, many, many travelers must have been here in the two years that had passed (only two years!). Paul remembered Michael distinctly, the way he had been. Michael had lived in a room of his own on the floor underneath this one; he didn't join them upstairs very often but kept mostly to himself. Paul had envied him—Michael came and went where he pleased and did what he pleased; he wasn't bound by anyone. Paul himself had been that way once upon a time—it was why he had come here in the first place: to get away, from home, from his family, from himself, his own personality as it had been formed by these outward circumstances; not to be bound by anything. But by the time he had met Michael, he had been more bound by circumstances than he would have ever thought possible. They all were, all the group around Crishi. Some of them, like Paul himself, had been in jail and, expelled as undesirable, were waiting for new travel documents: these documents were being got for them by Crishi, and it was he who was paying their bills in the hotel and doling out money to them. It wasn't only that they were materially dependent on him—most of them couldn't live any longer without him telling them what to do and arranging everything for them; and with some of them it was even worse—they needed him emotionally—like the German girl Ursula, who had been pregnant by someone or other, and when she couldn't get into Crishi's room, she had slept on the stairs outside it.

But Michael had been completely free. He might sit in their room with them and accept some hashish, but if he didn't care for the atmosphere—if it got too tense for him, or someone went berserk from having taken too much—he left them and went off on his own. Sometimes Paul sat at the window to look out for him; it gave him pleasure to see Michael walking down the street by himself. It was a very crowded street full of tourist hotels and the eating stalls catering to them, with homeless animals as well as some people hanging around for something to be thrown to them; and there were also stalls selling garlands and incense and offerings of candy to be taken into the Hindu temple opposite. For the sake of coolness and convenience, Michael was dressed like everyone else in muslin *kurta* and pajamas; but he walked there apart and alone, as if nothing and no one could touch him. And somehow people were careful to walk around him, and even when someone in a great hurry bumped against him, Michael went on undisturbed—gaunt, fair, self-sufficient, with his light eyes fixed on some far horizon

"Do you know where he is?" I interrupted Paul. "Have you seen him since last night?"

"Why are you crying?"

I hadn't realized I was, but now I brushed the tears away. I was angry with myself, and with Paul, for saying all that and bringing up Michael as he used to be. I had to get going, I had to find out where Michael was—and Crishi—instead of sitting here listening to Paul. But he hadn't finished yet.

"I'm going to be like him, you watch," he said. "Just let me have my papers and get out of here—I know a girl, Monica, she lives on a farm in Yorkshire; it's not much of a farm but it's near a river where you can swim and there's masses of yellow flowers growing on the bank. She says I can stay with her, she wants me there. Just let him get me my papers and my fare home. That's all I want from him."

"But where is he? Can't you tell me? Hasn't he been here?"

"Oh he's been here all right—I said have you got my passport—he hadn't but he said he was getting it, soon, tonight, not to worry, he said. Not to worry: how many thousands of times I've heard that from him. And then he said, If Harriet comes here—"

"Yes yes, what?"

"Tell her Michael's okay. He was here too."

"Who, Michael?"

"Yes they brought him here. Carried him in and put him on the bed there. That doctor came—the little Bengali, the same one they brought for the German girl after she took the pills—he fixed him up and then they took him away."

"Away where? Where, Paul? Can't you tell me any more? *Paul?*"

"I suppose the Bhais' house."

Here the bells started ringing from the Hindu temple, completely filling the room the way Michael had once described to me. Michael had said that it was a very loud sound and got even louder when the devotees started singing, as if trying to outshout the bells and vie with them in fervor. This was happening now.

"He was as white as a sheet, but he was always pale, wasn't he? It used to strike me, that very white skin of his. A bit unnatural I thought it was."

"Did he speak to you?"

"He didn't speak to anyone. I think he was unconscious. They said it was only a flesh wound. Not to worry, they said. Not to worry," he repeated, twisting his face.

I asked him question after question—I begged him to tell me every detail he could remember, but they were few. Michael had been carried in by Crishi and some Bhais, the doctor came, then they carried him out again: probably to the Bhais' house. "Harriet," he said, "if you see Crishi, tell him I'm waiting. Tell him he promised me for tonight. . . . Oh don't carry on, Harriet. I wish I hadn't told you. These things happen all the time. It's those damn Bhais—they're just animals, and they have these knives they can't wait to get out. I've told Michael before, he shouldn't be carrying his dumb Swiss army knife—it only makes them mad to think someone might get at them first. Give me some more water before you go, and don't forget to tell Crishi about tonight. Go to the Bhais' house, that's where they are, I bet you."

I went back to our palace hotel, running along the street —people laughed at me, pointing at this mad girl—till I found a rickshaw. At the hotel, they were taking down last night's tent from the back lawn—the tent people were there to take it down, and some of the hotel staff were helping

them. These usually greeted me, but today they kept their
eyes strenuously on their task though I hovered around,
hoping someone would tell me something about last night.
They did not; and when I spoke to the one I knew best—he
had often been sent up by room service when Crishi and I
called—his quite-fluent English failed him and he couldn't
understand a word I said. The same happened with others
I approached—they either couldn't understand or hadn't
been on duty last night; in any case, they were exceedingly
busy, shouting instructions to one another as they cleared
away all traces of last night's feast. Kites came swooping down
continually to a particular spot on the lawn and pecked at
something there; and although they flew off when the bearers
descended on them with flapping arms and dust cloths, next
moment they were back. They didn't bother to fly off when
I came to see what it was that had attracted them. I found it
was just a mess of what I presumed to be gnawed chicken
bones, flung there by careless guests. There were more kites
behind the hedge where the makeshift clay ovens had been
set up last night, and where Michael had gone to get food
for the Bhais after our conversation together. This place was
being disassembled, but the people on the job were also too
busy to talk to me.

Was it my imagination, or was it the same inside the hotel
lobby? Did the clerks behind the desk, the porters and the
elevator boys, all know something they wouldn't tell me? As
I passed through the shopping arcade, it seemed to me that
the shopkeepers were peering out at me with the same secret
knowledge as everyone else. I stopped outside the jeweler's
shop and hesitated only a moment before going in—he *had*
to tell me, whatever his feelings about me after our scene
yesterday. His assistant was in the front part of the shop. I
didn't believe him when he said his boss had gone out—I
went past him and pushed aside the curtain leading to the
back room: but it was as empty and seemingly innocent as
everyone's stare at me. This stare was also in the assistant's
eyes when I asked him directly if Crishi had been there, or
when he had last seen Michael. He appeared not to know
who these people were.

I had hoped to have more information before facing Sonya;
but it was she who knew. When I went to her suite, I found

the jeweler there, and whatever it was he had told her, had made her both frantic and resolute. She was dressed to go out. She had on a frock and little white hat that I had seen her wear to lunches and matinees in New York. She said both of us had to go immediately to the embassy, we couldn't delay another minute. "Why, what have you heard?" I asked her. I looked down at the jeweler sitting there—he avoided my eyes, but Sonya said "He's trying to help us." Then she asked "Have you heard anything?"

I sensed she was trying to hide something that *she* had heard; I was doing the same with her, so there we were, sparing each other. I stalled: "Why do you want to go to the embassy?"

"Who else will help us, who else will do anything!"

"Do what?"

"Find Michael! We have to find Michael!"

I turned on the jeweler—"Do you know anything?" He wouldn't answer me—he looked at Sonya; she was nervously running her tongue over her lips. I could see her little plump hands trembling. She did know something and was trying to prepare both herself and me to tell me. I thought I had better come out cautiously with what I knew: "Michael's been hurt a little bit. It's nothing much and in a way it's his fault, for playing around with that knife of his."

Sonya looked at me with round eyes: "Then why did they—" she began; I intercepted an exchange of glances between her and the jeweler and got in there promptly—"Why did they what? What did you tell her?" I challenged him. Still he wouldn't look at me; his eyes were lowered. "What do you know?" I went on. "Or is it all just rumor again, just things you've heard and like to whisper around."

"I don't know anything."

"You must know something or why are you here?"

"Darling, he's trying to help us!"

"Then why doesn't he speak! If you know anything, why don't you speak!" Actually, I was shouting at both of them: my God, if they did know anything about Michael, what a time to keep quiet; what a time to spare me!

Sonya begged him: "Please be so kind—tell her what you told me."

He still wouldn't look up, his face was sullen and closed

I was so desperate, I was ready to assault him again. Sonya begged me: "Darling, he's the only person who's told us anything at all—"

I controlled myself; I spoke to him in the calmest voice I could, asking him for information. At last he consented to speak, though he remained sullen: "I don't know anything about this hotel. When my shop is shut, I go home to my place in Shakti Nagar. I eat my food and go to sleep. When I return in the morning, I open my shop and attend to my business. Yes, sometimes someone may come and say this and that has happened. I may listen but I don't ask, Is it true? It may be true, it may not be. I don't call that person a liar. I listen."

After this cautious and cautionary preamble, he repeated what he had told Sonya. There had been some sort of scuffle between Michael and the Bhais. The cause was not known —it may have been that Michael had wanted to go into the tent and make a scene; or it may have been about their food, or some personal quarrel. The Bhais were always quick to draw—it was well known that they never lost a chance to use the knives they carried; and in the present case, with Michael, they had probably been waiting to use them for a long time; and so maybe had he. Anyway, whatever the cause, Michael had been wounded—here, said the jeweler, pointing to a place on his chest. I quickly said that I knew it to be only a superficial flesh wound; I spoke with confidence, for Sonya's sake, though I felt very little of it myself. The jeweler had heard otherwise but did not commit himself to any details; and I beat down my fears with the thought that in the telling everything tends to grow much bigger and worse than it is. They had wanted to carry Michael into the hotel but had been prevented by the hotel staff; the manager himself had come down to bar their way. He had explained that with their kind of clientele—wealthy Indians and international travelers—they could not afford a scandal, especially since it was a case where the police might be involved. In fact, he couldn't wait to get Michael off the premises, and taking no chances, had had him carried out by the back way, by the block of servant quarters.

"What time was all this?" I asked.

The jeweler's report was not clear. Two in the morning, he said at first—it was a time when Crishi was with me in our room upstairs; next he said it may have been four—we were still having a good time with each other at that hour; or it may have been five, he said—by then I had been asleep and presumed Crishi was too. I asked "Who directed all this operation?" "He did of course." said the jeweler—off the top of his head, I could see, and I took some melancholy pleasure in contradicting him: "Crishi was with me." The jeweler shrugged; he didn't believe me.

It was not known where they had carried Michael. Sonya had tried to call various hospitals, but the jeweler doubted that they had taken him to one, for fear of a police report. I lied quickly: "They probably took him to the Bhais' house. That's where he is." Sonya said "We must tell the embassy to send their doctor." She wanted us to leave at once and take an embassy official and their doctor to the Bhais' house. She told me to hurry, she said the chargé d'affaires himself was waiting for us—"What, you've spoken to him?" I asked. "Did you tell him anything?" "Anything! Of course I told him—I've reported Michael missing—"

"Ah," I said, sitting down instead of hurrying as she wanted me to, "I wish you hadn't."

Sonya began to defend herself, but she was not sure of her ground. She was used to making mistakes. Always trying to do her best, she was quick and impulsive to rush into action—too quick and impulsive, as Grandfather had known. But in the past he had been there to shield her from the consequences. "I was so frightened, darling," she said to me, "and I couldn't find you. I felt so alone. I had to speak to someone, get someone to help. There was no one."

"The hotel is full of our people," I said. "All my family is here—the Rawul, the Bari Rani, Renée—why didn't you go to them instead of to strangers at the embassy?"

Sonya was silent. I felt sorry for her—especially to see her dressed up in her fringed and floral silk frock and with her slightly swollen ankles bulging above her high-heeled pumps. She was as frightened as I was, for Michael; and for her there was another fear: of the place, and the strangers among whom she found herself. But who had asked her to come in the first place—and, having come, to stay?

I said "You'd better call and say it's okay, we know where he is. . . . We do know!" I insisted. "He's at the Bhais' house and I'm just going there to see him."

"I'm coming with you."

"No. No. You call the embassy and tell them it's okay. And someone has to wait here, in case there's a message. Crishi might try to call. He will try, and if he doesn't get me in my room, he's sure to try here."

The jeweler got up to leave. He and Sonya began to exchange courtesies—she thanking him profusely, he protesting that he had done nothing but was ready for any service. I think he was glad to retreat without further involvement. Just as he reached the door, the phone rang. Stung by curiosity, he hesitated for a moment, but on the whole felt it safer to know nothing more. He even hastened his departure, as if afraid that whoever it was on the phone might discover his presence.

Sonya said "If it's the embassy, what shall I say?"

I said "I'll do it." I went into the bedroom and shut the door. There was no need for her to hear what lies I told them.

It wasn't the embassy, but it was Crishi. I had to sit on the side of Sonya's bed because my legs wouldn't support me, between the relief of hearing his voice and the fear of what he had to tell me. Of course his voice was absolutely cheerful and normal and he went on the offensive at once: "Harriet, where have you *been*? I've been trying to ring you all *day*!" It was the way he had rung me from Holland or Basel or the States, when he had taken off without telling me and I had been going crazy for two days wondering what had happened. But there was this difference now—he sounded far far far away, so far his voice seemed to be disembodied, coming to me like a spirit across untold worlds of mountains, rivers, deserts. I kept shouting "Where *are* you? Where *are* you? Can you hear me?" Sonya came and stood in the doorway, her hand on her heart. I asked "Where's Michael?"

"Michael's right here!" cried the disembodied Crishi. "Right beside me! He'll talk in a minute! But first listen to me, Harriet: very carefully. What you have to do."

Well I did want to listen very carefully, but there was Sonya, plucking at my sleeve, and I had to tell her hastily, "Michael's okay. He's with Crishi," before I could concentrate on that voice from far away.

What he wanted me to do was come where he was—"But where are you?" "Here of course in Dhoka." "But how did you get there?" "Oh for Christ's sake, Harriet. By plane." "You and Michael?" "Listen to me—operator, operator, operator!—okay, listen: The planes have been canceled, because of the weather—you'll have to come by train."

It was very difficult for me, concentrating so hard on what he was communicating and at the same time having to give reassuring glances at Sonya, who stuck close beside me, eating my face up with her anxiety. Giving up on Sonya for a while, I threw my whole being toward him. "I want you to come alone," he went on. "Don't tell anyone where you're going." "No one?" I asked and flung another reassuring glance at Sonya. He said "This is what you tell Rani: to go to London and wait there for a consignment." "What consignment?" "Are you stupid or something? . . . Tell her we'll be joining her soon—tell her in a few days, a week at the most—can you hear me?" "Yes yes yes—" Sonya imploringly touched my arm and I said: "Can I talk to Michael?" He said "You should be here day after tomorrow—can you hear me? Operator—ah well—"

He was cut off. I too began to scream for the operator and to bang the cradle up and down. Sonya was clutching my arm: "Did you speak to him?" In my agitation I yelled at her— "Didn't you hear? We were cut off!" She snatched the receiver from me and listened into its blank interior. "Better put it down," I said, "so they can ring back." She did so. We waited. Nothing came.

"But didn't he tell you where they are? Can't we try to get through to them?"

"Michael's all right," I said. "I was just going to speak to him when we were cut off."

The phone rang again—both of us snatched for it—I got there first: But it was the embassy. A very polite young man with a nice New England sort of voice—I kept him talking for a while, not letting on I wasn't Sonya. I wanted time to think; and also to readjust myself to the difference between that mild voice—the things that were in it! the ski lodge in the winter, the carved pumpkins at Halloween, the drive to Vermont to see the leaves turn—and the distant disembodied dearly beloved Crishi still tingling in my ear. Finally I asked the young man to wait and I laid aside the receiver; I took Sonya's arm and led her some distance away from the phone. She looked up at me expectantly.

"Tell him we've found Michael"; and at the shadow that crossed her face, I said more intensely, "He's all right. Tell him." She didn't move. "Sonya, Michael's all right. I was just going to speak to him when we were cut off. Be quick," I urged her. "Michael and Crishi must be trying to get through now. We have to hang up. Go on, Sonya, hurry."

She didn't hurry but walked with slow steps toward the phone, slowly picked it up, and was silent for a moment while she threw me a doubting look. I nodded to her in impatient encouragement. She had to speak. I listened. She said Michael was found; she apologized for troubling the embassy; she thanked them for their efforts; she hung up, not looking at me, and not happy with what she had done.

I had no more time for her. I had to get started. I told her I was going to my room, in case Crishi and Michael tried to call there, and asked her not to move from hers, so as to answer the phone from hers. When I approached my room, I saw someone standing outside it and was surprised to find it was Paul. I said "I thought you were sick." "I am sick. Bloody sick. But I have to take you to the train." As I let us both in, I asked "Did Crishi call you from Dhoka?" Paul said "Get your things together; we have to go. The train leaves in two hours, and if you miss the connection, there won't be another one for three days."

I decided to pack only a small overnight bag. Someone else could send the rest after me, or whatever had to be done with it. I asked Paul if Crishi had said anything about bringing some of Michael's things. He didn't hear me. He was lying back in a chair with his eyes shut, his hair damp on his forehead. I was very quick with my packing, for I still had to go and see Renée. I left Paul in the room, promising him I would be back very soon; he nodded—I think he wished I wouldn't come back at all and he could stay there resting forever. Although the room was air-conditioned, I turned on the ceiling fan so that a breeze blew refreshingly over his wasted face.

Renée overwhelmed me with questions—or rather, first, with reproaches: She asked where we had been all day, said that she had been trying and trying to reach us, that she hadn't dared leave the room in case we called. The room did seem as if someone had been shut up in it too long. The feral quality that was part of Renée's personality was strong in the air, no longer that of a wild youthful tigress but of one who had grown desperate from restless pacing in a cage. Desperate and maybe a bit mangy too—I don't think Renée had had her bath for some time; one could tell with her because she perspired so strongly that her odor overcame even the potent scents she used. The room was littered with her underclothes, which she had taken off and left lying where they were, and she had also pulled out everything she possessed in an attempt to pack up.

"I thought we were leaving," she explained. "I was getting ready. But instead you disappeared and I hear all sorts of rumors from the bearers—where is he, for God's sake?" For a moment I wondered if she meant Michael or Crishi, but of course it was Crishi. I said "He called—this minute. Actually he called for you. He tried to get you here, and then with great difficulty he got through to me instead. He just had time to give me a message for you before we were cut off. What rumors did you hear?"

"Not about him, about Michael: how he got in a fight with the Bhais. What message did he give you?"

I told her first where he was, and before she could protest at his taking off without warning, I said how I hadn't known either but had woken up in the morning to find him gone. Well, that was true, at any rate. I gave her the message—I said I didn't know what he meant about the consignment but that Crishi seemed to think she would? She nodded gloomily, she paced up and down in her usual way, her arms crossed over her bosom; she was sunk in thought, and I let her think for a while, though I took a quick glance at my watch because of not wanting to miss the train.

At last she stopped pacing and stood in front of me and said "All right, I'll do it, but it has to be for the last time. Absolutely the last time, Harriet." She had forgotten I had told her I didn't know what it was about but took it for granted that I did: that I was in with them on everything. She asked me if I was coming with her, but I said no, he had told me to stay in Delhi and wait for further messages here. As I said this, I looked at her with the same direct and serious gaze Crishi had when he told lies.

She put her hands on my shoulders and looked back into my eyes. Yes, she trusted me, we were comrades now, we were united forever. She said "I promise you, it'll be the last time. I'll never let him take these sort of risks again. And he won't need to, will he? It's all changed now, isn't it?"

"Oh yes," I said. "It's only a few more days before we're twenty-one."

Suddenly, impulsively—in a great access of maybe affection, maybe gratitude, maybe some fear of what might happen—she took me in her arms. This was entirely unexpected from Renée, who was not demonstrative by nature, and certainly had never been so to me. But now she loved me very much and drew me very close.

I felt uncomfortable—for one thing, I couldn't return her ardor. I'm afraid I held myself as rigid as a broomstick within her embrace; and I kept thinking about the time and having to wait three days if I missed the connection! She didn't notice—she was whispering into my neck, "I'm so glad it's you, Harriet, and that we can be together, the three of us."

But when she let me go, she said in quite a different voice, "I couldn't live without him, you know. I wouldn't. I wouldn't consider it for a moment." She put her hand in the pocket of her negligee, and there was a little bottle of pills in there. She held it in the palm of her hand and invited me to look at it as at a precious object. "It's nothing to me," she said. "I wouldn't care a damn. I'd just take a handful—" She cupped her other hand, threw back her head and made the gesture of throwing a handful of pills into her mouth.

I uttered a shocked sound, then closed her hand over the bottle in her palm and said "Oh no, Renée, you mustn't think of such a thing—and why should you, ever?" I pressed my own hand affectionately over her closed fist.

"He knows," she said in a warning voice. "He knows I'll do it."

"You'll never have to," I promised—and got out as fast as I could: no time to stand on ceremony, I had a train to catch.

My plan was to pick up the bag I had packed, rouse Paul, and get going. I had forgotten Sonya; or had edged her out of my mind. But when I returned to my room, she was there. All she said was "I'm coming too." I began to protest, but she was absolutely adamant. Paul said "You'll miss your train." I picked up my bag hurriedly and tried to kiss Sonya good-bye. "I'll be back in a day or two, with Michael," I promised She repeated "I'm coming too." When I went out with Paul, she followed us. She came with us in the taxi we took to the station; she was wearing the clothes she had put on to go to the embassy. She had no baggage of any kind, not having had time to pack anything, only her white purse.

At the station she gave Paul money to buy a ticket for her as well as for me. I had given up arguing with her, hoping to lose her in the crowd. But she clung to me while I pushed my way through and went up and down stairs and across a bridge, in search of the right platform. Paul explained that the train we were taking didn't have an air-conditioned section so we would have to go in an ordinary first-class compartment. He installed us in a coupé and stood outside the barred window, waiting for the train to leave. Everyone stared at us—I guess we made a strange threesome, Paul and I in old jeans, and Sonya in her floral dress, with white hat, shoes, and purse. Paul was urging me through the window to remind Crishi about his passport; I only half-listened to him, for I was making a last-minute attempt to persuade Sonya to go back to the hotel. Vendors tried to sell us oranges and magazines, and in fact were successful with Sonya, who felt sorry for them. Other vendors came, selling tea and buns and plastic dolls. She bought from everyone. Paul explained where we were to change trains; he said he would leave us now, because he felt so rotten. He didn't go far—I saw him stretch himself out on a stone bench on the platform. He lay between a fat peasant in a *dhoti* and with Shiva marks on his forehead and a very thin poor woman who may have been a beggar and was eating something messy from a leaf. People pushed and snouted and spat all around him, and skeletal red-clad porters, balancing huge metal trunks on their heads, screamed for passage way. Paul didn't stir; he lay in the middle of it all, utterly spent and gaunt, his eyes shut, stubble on his face, the soles of his feet as black as any beggar's or holy man's. And like any holy man, he appeared beyond everything, beyond every desire except for rest and peace.

OUR compartment or coupé for two, had only two bunks in it, one on top of the other. I climbed up the ladder to the top bunk, where my head was very close to the fierce little black ceiling fan. A door led to our bathroom with a brown-stained washbasin and WC and immemorial sewage smells seeping through the disinfectant. Before the train started, a sweeper went in there to give a last officious wipe around, and was rewarded by Sonya; and also a bearer in a frayed and food-stained uniform came to make up our beds and take our orders for meals. We were entirely self-sufficient in this little box of a compartment; and for the next twenty-four hours the two of us might as well have been sealed in a capsule and hurtling through uncharted regions. First it was day, then night, then day again; it didn't make much difference except that our box got hotter and grimier. Although we kept the window tightly shut, soot and cinders came through the cracks. There was nothing to see outside beyond an immense flat space wrapped in a pall of dust; at night the dim blue-colored bulb cast a ghostly light around the compartment. The train stopped several times at little wayside stations; both by day and by night, it seemed to be the same men who came up to our window with pitchers of tea, and the same raucous, incomprehensible cries of hawkers and railway officials were heard along the platforms.

Within our neutral space, Sonya spoke of matters close to her heart. I fitfully slept while we chugged on and on and on; I don't think Sonya slept at all. She didn't lie down but sat up on the seat in her elegant silk dress, which had got very crumpled, and there were smudges of soot across her face where she had wiped off the perspiration; her coiffure was blown apart by the fan directly over her head. Was she talking to me? I guess she was, since no one else was there, though I couldn't hear her too well from the top bunk. She spoke about Grandfather, and about Manton and Lindsay and the new baby. She spoke about Michael—a lot about Michael, not as he was now but as he had been when he was little, as far back as when he was a baby. She spoke of him entirely in the past tense. She said that as soon as she had seen him at a few months old, she had known that he was a very old soul who had come to us from far back, having passed through many births in many strange and wonderful countries.

The small station at which we had to change trains was like the other ones where we had stopped along the way. We had to wait there a long time—so many hours we lost count of them. At first we sat in the waiting room, but it got very hot and the atmosphere was fetid because of the crowd of poor people waiting with their babies and bundles of food. Then we sat on the platform, under an asbestos roof, hoping that some fresh air would blow in from the open sides. Here too there were a lot of people, some of them passengers and others come to pass the time or with nowhere else to go. A beggar had got in, a crazy woman in a strange assortment of rags, who didn't ask for alms but shuffled along with a guttural chant that may have been an invocation or a curse. The passengers were sitting or lying asleep on their luggage laid out on the platform. Sonya and I didn't have any luggage except for my overnight bag, so we squatted on that and on a shirt of mine, with our backs propped against a pillar that held up the roof. Flies and hot air came in from the flat empty space beyond the station; far in the distance, across the vacant landscape, a line of hills or undulations shimmered. Sonya's white hat had slipped down over her eyes; she wiped flies or drops of perspiration from her face. She didn't complain of the discomfort but went on talking in the same way as in the compartment, and on the same subjects

As for me, I was only impatient for our train to arrive and
for the next—the last—stage of our journey to begin.

It was the middle of the night when we arrived, and two
Bhais were there to meet us. This station too appeared to be
identical to the others we had passed—a roof over a platform,
set in surrounding wilderness. The Bhais had brought a very
old Daimler, with torn leather seats, and they put Sonya and
me in the back while the two of them sat in front with the
driver. They didn't talk to us and couldn't understand what
we asked them, like where Michael and Crishi were; they
didn't talk to each other either. We drove through utter
darkness—it was as though the entire landscape, or country,
had been blotted out. It seemed to me that our whole journey
had been like that, ever since we had left the hotel: in darkness, in a country shrouded in dust, a region of invisibility,
which we had traversed encapsulated within our own thoughts
and fears.

I had no particular expectations of the place where they
were taking us—if I thought anything, it was that it would
be the Rawul's palace. But when we finally arrived at our
destination, it wasn't a palace but a comfortable sort of family
house, with some good pieces of furniture and carpets, and
at the foot of the staircase a marble statue holding up a lamp.
Here the Bhais handed us over to some exceedingly ancient
men in exceedingly ancient uniforms, who were so polite that
they walked backward before us, saluting all the way, with
Sonya saluting back at them, in appreciation of their nice
old-fashioned manners. If they were surprised to see two of
us instead of one, they didn't show it. First they ushered me
into the room designated for me—I took a quick look around
and was utterly reassured, seeing Crishi's pajamas laid out
on the bed and his silver dressing set (given by Renée) on
the dressing table. I followed Sonya to see where they were
taking her, and this turned out to be an equally comfortable
bedroom with everything in it that anyone could want. One
of the old men was hastily making up the bed, and another
was spraying DDT in the bathroom. I felt reassured for Sonya
too, and that we were both safely at our journey's end. But
she—still in her white hat and floral dress, both bearing every
mark of our journey—didn't seem in the least reassured.

There was something wild in her look around the room that was being made comfortable for her (another old man came by with a set of matching towels); and while I was cheerfully kissing her good-night, she clutched me and said "But where are they?" I laughed at her: "Where would they be this time of night? You didn't expect them to wait up for us till three A.M.?" "You're right, darling," she said, not at all happily. "We'll see them in the morning," I said. She nodded.

I slept very soundly—naturally, after such a journey—and when I woke up, Crishi was sitting on the side of my bed. I was so happy and relieved, I threw my arms around his neck, and it was some time before I asked him, "Is Michael all right?"

"All right? Why shouldn't he be? . . . Oh you mean that scrap he had with the Bhais? That was nothing." He stroked my face and kissed it; he smelled so fresh and sweet, newly bathed and in a clean shirt of fine Egyptian cotton. But the bed next to mine hadn't been slept in, so maybe he had been up all night.

"I don't know who's been telling you what in Delhi, what sort of rumors they've scared you with. I had a job calming down Sonya too." When I began to apologize for bringing her along in spite of his express orders to come alone, he kissed me again: "I can see how you couldn't get rid of her. But don't you think you ought to have a bath? Pfoo, sweetheart, you stink—well, anyone would after that journey. Rotten luck about the plane; but it's all right now—they've started flying again, so Sonya can go back nice and comfortable. It only takes three hours; that's why we got here so quick. Michael and I," he said. "Come on, I'll run your bath."

He went into the adjoining bathroom and continued talking to me from there. I got out of bed and opened the curtains, but all there was to see was what I had been seeing for the past two days from the train window. I drew the curtains shut again; it was so much nicer that way, the two of us in the room together, with the air-conditioner on. He called me into the bathroom; it had a big old-fashioned bathtub and all sorts of ancient fittings, which looked as if they belonged in a much bigger, older place. He confirmed this: He said they had been brought in from the palace. "Where are we?" I asked him. "Oh it's where everyone stays when they come here." "But don't they stay in the palace?" He laughed at that: "Wait till you see it."

Well, I had a very nice bath—he made it a playful occasion—and when I went back in the room, someone had brought a lot of breakfast with juice and eggs, just like in a hotel. "What about Sonya?" I asked him. "She had her breakfast hours ago, sweetheart; now it's just you and me." There was a table at which we could have eaten, but we preferred to sit on the bed, one on each side of the tray and feeding morsels to each other. After such a good night's sleep, clean and fed, in this pleasant air-conditioned room and with him beside me, I was absolutely contented and peaceful; so, it seemed was he. We were happy, as always when we were together.

Then he said "Now, Harriet," and at once my heart lurched, and I said in fear, "Michael."

He frowned: "Oh yes, do think the worst straightaway, go on, think that Michael's dead. . . . I told you, didn't I, he was all right? What's the matter with you, why do you have to have this morbid imagination? Just like an old woman; just like Sonya. By the way, she'll have to leave today, I've got a seat for her on the plane. Because I'm telling you straight— I'm not having two hysterical women on my hands; one is quite enough for me."

"I'm not hysterical."

"Oh no? Then what's that—'oh Michael'?" He imitated the start I had given. "And if you're like that now, what are you going to say when I tell you Michael's not here? There, you see."

I made every effort to be completely unhysterical because the most important thing was not to irritate Crishi any further. I said in a calm and steady voice: "Then where is he?"

But Crishi *was* irritated—not with me, but with Michael. "Packed up and gone, that's where he is. It's always the same story with you people—you play around with something and when you get tired, you quit. No consideration for anyone else of course—oh no, why should you? The rest of us are just there for your amusement."

He sounded so bitter that I felt I had to defend myself. He did have to admit that it wasn't fair to include me in this accusation because never once, not for a second, had I thought of leaving. "Well all right," he conceded, qualifying with a frown: "so *far*. But who can tell with you people? I'd have thought—anyone would—that Michael was absolutely one hundred percent with us, but no, suddenly it turns out it wasn't the right thing after all—that it was your goddamn neti, neti, and all that crap—so next thing we know he's climbing on a bus to God knows where."

"Michael left on a *bus*?"

Crishi couldn't help smiling a bit: "You should have seen him, wedged in with all the peasants and their chickens, making his tight-ass face like he was much too superior to notice any of those nasty smells creeping up his aristocratic nostrils."

I had seen enough of the public transport system to get the picture of Michael accommodating himself to it in his aloof way; but what about the other picture, the one Paul had given me—of Michael being carried unconscious into the hotel room? Crishi must have guessed my thoughts, for he said at once, "I told you all he had was a scratch on his arm—you don't think anyone who's got anything more than that would let himself be rattled on one of those Indian buses across the Thar Desert?"

"Is that where's he gone?"

"Or wherever. . . . Gave me one of his lectures too before taking off—about how the Rawul was all bunk—"

"He said that?"

"Should I tell you something, Harriet: I think Michael's so selfish, such a complete egotist, that he doesn't care for anyone else in the world—not only not for the Rawul or me or any of us, but not for his own people either, for Sonya and the rest of you, and that, sweetheart, includes you. . . . All right!" he anticipated my protest. "If he did care, wouldn't he have stayed? I told him, Harriet's on her way, she's on a train this very minute, can't you at least wait till she gets here—oh no, he had to go, the bus was leaving, on no account was he going to miss it, so good-bye, nice knowing you."

Crishi was silent, and so was I. In a way, I was relieved that Michael was well enough to set off on a journey by himself; and I was used to his going off like that, without warning, on some quest of his own. Crishi had opened the front of my shirt and was burying his face into my very modest cleft; he murmured from out of there, "Anyway, I'm still here, if that's any good to you." I pressed him closer to me, so close he could surely feel my heart beating for him.

We stayed like that for a while, very much satisfied with each other. After a last shower of kisses, he raised his head and said to me: "You'll have to tell Sonya. That Michael's gone," he explained. I nodded; it wouldn't be difficult, for Sonya too was used to Michael setting off suddenly on strange journeys. "And get rid of her," Crishi went on. "There's absolutely no point her hanging around here, getting in our way. She should never have come—no, I'm not blaming you, I can see how you couldn't shake her off—but she'll have to go. Because I want to be alone with you, and that's all there is to it." I felt the same, needless to say.

I found Sonya downstairs with some ancient retainers hovering around to anticipate her wishes. She was peering into the rooms there—perfectly ordinary, comfortable family rooms with nothing sinister about them; yet she asked me in a whisper, "Where *are* we?" Before I had time to explain, she whispered again, "Have you seen Michael? I've looked for him everywhere." I made her sit down on one of the fat settees in the living room (it had colored studio portraits of the Rawul, Bari Rani and the girls, and a Bechstein grand with a pile of beginners' piano pieces on it). She looked at me with scared eyes, anticipating the bad news I was about to give her; it must have been in this way that I had looked at Crishi, irritating him as Sonya did me now. I told her, as quickly as possible, "Michael's left. . . . He walked out, that's all; on all of us."

"Darling, how could he? When he was—"

"He wasn't," I said. "He was nothing of the sort. That just goes to show how you shouldn't listen to rumors from people who don't know what they're talking about. It's really ridiculous—the way you jumped on the train with me and came all this way because some idiot told you how he'd heard something had happened to Michael."

My indignation made her hang her head; I began to feel sorry for her. And she looked so terrible—she must have slept in her little silk dress (if she slept at all); she had brought nothing else to wear, and though she had put on her usual makeup, it was no more than a layer of color daubed on an ancient, ancient face.

I took her hands in mine; I said "It's my fault. I shouldn't have let you come. . . . But I couldn't have stopped you, could I?" She shook her head with a shy smile. "No, I know how you'd run from one end of the earth to the other for Michael and me." I kissed her hands I was holding. When I felt her tears fall on me, I said "I told you—it's all right; Michael's all right. It was all a false alarm."

"Did you see him?"

"How could I see him? He was off and gone away before we ever got here. And not so much as a note for us, not one single line. Isn't that just like him?" I said, laughing and encouraging her to laugh with me. But she didn't, and I went on: "Of course it is! He's done it hundreds of times—don't you remember when we were supposed to be on the Island for Grandfather's birthday, only Michael was in Iran? Don't you remember how worried we were because of what was going on there, and Grandfather had to call people in the State Department? And no one could find him till he turned up in some monastery in Ladakh. That was when he shaved his hair off—it never really grew after that," I suddenly remembered. "He used to have nice soft floppy hair but after that it was always sort of stubbly."

Sonya said "My baby, my sweet baby"; I guess she meant Michael, though she was hugging me. I laughed at her: "You see, that's the trouble with you—you think we're still babies who can't look after ourselves."

She admitted it; she apologized for it. I said "It's lucky you've got a new baby to fuss over. Aren't you dying to see him? Manton's baby? Oh I am."

"Let's go, darling," she said.

"Yes, you must go," I said. "They're waiting for you—they can't christen him without you, can they? Not without his godmother, they can't." I was stroking her head with its ruined coiffure. When she reached up to kiss me on the lips, I let her: how familiar the taste of her lipstick, which, as a child, I had wiped off as soon as she wasn't looking. "You'll be so proud holding him, won't you, in his christening robe.

Do you think he'll be wearing Michael's? I'm sure he'll be
blond like Michael, what with Barbara being so blond—oh
they told you he was? There, you see, it'll be just like holding
Michael."

"The two of you, I can't tell you—you were two little angels
come down from heaven, one fair, one dark. I couldn't see
you during the christening—there were too many people in
front of me—but I sneaked a look when you were being
carried out of the chapel—oh, what sweetness, what sweetness, I could have died." At that time, when we were born,
Sonya was still "unofficial," and the nearest she could get to
a Wishwell christening was to lurk somewhere in the last row.
But now she would be there right in front, holding the principal personage.

"Watch out you don't drop him—he's probably a huge big
fellow, with those two parents how could he not be, and look
at you, you tiny thing." I kissed a tiny plump hand of hers:
"And you must send me lots of photos—I want to see you
in all your glory with the latest Wishwell in your arms."

"But you'll be there, darling."

I had been talking to her as to a child who had to be
humored, but as with a child, it was time to be firm: "It can't
be, Sonya." I went on: "If Grandfather was here, wouldn't
you want to be where he is, and nowhere else in the world?
. . . There, you see; that's how I feel, with Crishi."

She was silent. I knew she was struggling to respect my
feelings and to accept the, for her, unacceptable comparison
of Crishi with Grandfather. But that was her problem, not
mine in the least.

"And your birthday," she said at last, somewhat shifting
her ground. "Your twenty-first, darling—don't you want to
be at home for that?"

"I am at home. Yes I am—yes even in this weird place that
we don't even know where it is except it's somewhere in the
desert, and in this weird house with someone else's family
photographs and piano music. Crishi's here, so it's okay; it's
home for me. Don't say any more, Sonya. You ought to know
how I feel—you of all people," I said, ending up with the
reminder that it was she who had taught us to live for love.

But from this point Crishi took over: "What are you doing?"

he came bustling in on us. "Do you realize you'll miss it if you don't get a move on?" There was no arguing with him, for he made out that a decision—to catch the plane—had already been fixed, and that it was up to him to hurry Sonya to the airport. He had a car outside, with the motor running and a Bhai at the wheel. It was impossible to talk inside the car, because whenever Sonya began to say something, Crishi would be shouting at the Bhai to ask him was this the fastest he could drive. We traversed the already familiar dust-enveloped desert landscape with a line of undulations, but these were closer and turned out to be jagged rocks. We drove through a very ramshackle little town huddled at the foot of one such rock; it had low buildings, some of which were very old and some very new, but all looked as if about to tumble down. There was a cinema and rows of tea stalls with long-distance trucks parked outside them, and some commercial activity like grain and planks of wood being transported on bullock carts. With Crishi shouting at him to hurry, the Bhai at the wheel maneuvered his way through a battalion of beat-up old bicycles, hand carts, rickshaws, children, goats, and dogs, keeping his finger pressed on the horn. Sonya gave up any attempt at conversation—one moment she was screaming "Look out!" as we skirted a naked child with a black thread around its extended stomach, and next moment leaning back against the car seat with her eyes shut and her hands over her ears.

We left the town behind and were back in some more desert landscape, and after a while it turned out we were at the airport. It was only a bit of desert land with a very small old-fashioned airplane standing on it. "Hurry up, hurry up, they're just leaving!" cried Crishi, leaping out of the car and getting us out of it and making us run across the stony soil. Actually, we were the only people running; the other passengers—several stout traders in stiffly starched *dhotis*—were boarding in a very leisurely way, and the pilot was leaning against the plane drinking a Coke. Sonya hardly had time to kiss me good-bye and no time at all to say anything, let alone ask any questions, for Crishi had her up and settled in the plane, and he relieved the pilot of his Coke bottle and told him to get in the cockpit.

We ran off the field, waving good-bye, and were back in the car before the plane had properly ascended. We even raced it for a while. This time we skirted the town and drove around to the other side of the rock rising above it. We went up as far as a plateau cut into the bare gray stone, then had to get out and walk up some steps to the next plateau. Our destination was the Rawul's palace.

I had often thought of this palace, of which I had heard a great deal, but it turned out entirely different from my conception. It was not very old—late Victorian perhaps, built around the same time as Propinquity—and was a mixture of Indian temple and English "bungalow," with arched verandas running all the way around it and a dome on top. It was huge—truly a palace—and lay in a wasted garden. But if the garden appeared wasted—dried and dead—that was nothing compared to the palace itself. From a distance, that is, when we first came in through the gates, it looked imposing and intact, but as we drew nearer, I could see that it was entirely derelict. And when we entered—I've never seen anything like it. The encircling verandas had high rounded ceilings from which lamps must have once hung down. These had been removed, and most of the ceiling had come off with them, so that rain had poured through and rotted the floors. We passed into halls and courtyards, one leading off from another until we seemed to be wandering through a succession of mirrors: and everywhere it was the same, complete and utter ruin, emptiness, and desolation. There wasn't a stick of furniture to be seen, nothing except this empty waste—as empty as the landscape we had traversed in the train. The marble floors were stained and worn from previous monsoons, for the roof, though nobly arched, was leaking. Many of the windows were empty of glass and all of them had had their latches removed; whatever doors there had been were gone, presumably for their wood and hardware. The same with every fitting a palace could have, in all its halls, and rooms, and bathrooms: everywhere only gaps and wounds, where some salable object had been. We heard bats, sometimes saw one, always smelled them, for their droppings were everywhere; and besides theirs, those of other animals too, probably including humans. However, these smells were not overpowering because there were so many places where roof and windows gaped and let in wind and air. I marveled at the speed with which this must have happened, for it couldn't have been too long ago that the place was fully furnished, fully inhabited by family and retainers. It was here the Rawul had grown up; from here he had left for Harrow and returned for his vacations; and it couldn't have been more than ten years ago that Renée had first arrived to survey the place and see what business deals she could make with the Rawul for his pictures and possessions.

At last, as we penetrated farther into these empty regions, we heard sounds of human voices, and some radio music; and in one of the halls toward the back of the palace we found the Bhais. They were busy preparing for some sort of celebration and had propped up a ladder to hang decorations. Some of them were in costume—very old, dusty, tinsely ones, the sort that for generations are packed away in trunks and unpacked for special occasions. Several Bhais were dressed up as women, and these minced about and coquetted with their veils and chased each other with shrill cries. The radio was playing the sort of film music they listened to, but one of them was practicing on the harmonium. Beer bottles were strewn about, and there was the usual raucous atmosphere that surrounded the Bhais; but here it was overlaid by something older and more—I wouldn't say refined, but more cultured, in the sense that at some point here they fitted into an old culture. I thought it was an ancient folk drama they were acting out for a ritual connected with a local festival; but when I asked Crishi he said no, it was in honor of my birthday. "Don't say you've forgotten it's your birthday tomorrow!" I said I hadn't forgotten, but that I didn't feel like celebrating it without Michael: because that was one thing we always did together—celebrate our birthday—wherever he was, he had come back for that. "Except this year," Crishi said. Yes, this year Michael had left me. But, in fact, I didn't feel too bad about it. Crishi was here now, and I realized that was the reason Michael had gone—to leave me entirely free to be with Crishi. Only someone as noble as Michael could have stepped back that way, surrendering the part of me that had been his. It was as if he had given me the total freedom he had always claimed for himself.

The Bhais dressed up in costume began to clash around with swords. The costumes may have been tinsel, but the swords were real. I asked Crishi if they were practicing martial exercises, but he said no, they were enacting an ancient battle that had been fought in this kingdom. Over a woman, Crishi said—one local chieftain having snatched her away from another to whom she had been betrothed; but their marriage party had been waylaid by the enraged rival and a terrible combat had taken place in the desert. "That's the bride—that beauty over there," said Crishi, pointing to a Bhai with an empty sleeve. He obligingly came over and dangled it in my face, laughing and thereby releasing a garlic-and-beer smell that didn't go well with his costume. I was told what had happened was that, when her newly wedded lord was killed in the fight, she took a sword and struck off her arm. "Why?" I asked. "Just to show off," Crishi said. "They were a nasty violent lot. Then she got up on the funeral pyre and called for someone to cut off the other arm, seeing as how she couldn't do it herself. Both arms were full of bangles and bracelets—all her wedding jewelry—and someone had the good sense to take them off and save them, and a couple of years ago Rani put them up for sale at Sotheby's." He wouldn't let me watch any more—he said I could see it at midnight, when the birthday celebrations were scheduled to start.

We went up an open winding staircase, which led straight to the roof terrace, most of which was taken up by an enormous cracked dome of flaking plaster. We stood in its shadow and looked over the crenellations at what I presumed to be the Rawul's entire state, dribbling away farther and farther until it disappeared into the horizon. Was it from up here that the Rawul had looked at and absorbed the sky until it entered his eyes and made his mind soar? Or was it from the top of another of these rocks, which rose in an irregular range from the flat soil? They were entirely bare, except for one at some distance into the desert. Crishi told me that the fragments of walls and battlements I could see on it were what remained of the old fort—it had been from there that the Rawul's ancestors had stormed down to die heroes' deaths, leaving behind them the burning pyres in which their women had immolated themselves. This fort must have been incredibly old, but when I asked Crishi how old, he answered irritably. 'Who knows and who cares."

There were two string cots set up in the space between the dome and the crenellated parapet; also a rickety little table with a chimney lamp on it. Crishi asked me to sit with him on one of these string cots; we both tucked our legs under us the way Indians do. Although the sounds from the Bhais and their radio and harmonium floated up to us from the open staircase, they came as from a long way off. Otherwise it seemed to me that we were more private up here than we had ever been anywhere—really and truly at last the two of us were alone, above the Rawul's land and under his sky. I liked being here very much, but Crishi said we were leaving the day after tomorrow, at the end of my birthday celebrations. If that was what he wanted, it was all right by me; and all I asked was—idly and not caring much, "Where are we going?"

"Where do you think we're going!" said Crishi with the mock exasperation he put on whenever he thought I was being particularly stupid. "Don't you think you have some responsibilities now that you're twenty-one—don't you think there'll be papers to sign and stuff like that—not to speak of the pleasure of telling old fool Pritchett what he can do with himself. Well, you needn't worry about any of that—I'll be looking after things from now on." He spoke with a sort of grim resolution, really ready to shoulder all these responsibilities. I pressed his hand; I felt it was lucky that I was married to such a practical person, for left to ourselves Michael and I would probably have messed up everything.

I said "I'll sign whatever I have to, but I guess we can't really do much till Michael gets back. Isn't it dumb of him to walk off right at this time; typical of course, but dumb all the same." I smiled a bit, thinking of Michael, without a thought in his head for anything practical, disappearing into the desert on some abstract quest of his own.

Crishi's hand that I had pressed still lay in mine; he took my other hand as well and said "Now, Harriet." So I knew he had something difficult to tell me; but remembering how exasperated he had been in the morning when I had said "Michael" in fear, I kept the expression on my face as placid as I could; placid and attentive.

Crishi told me Michael was dead. When he had said it, he tightened his grip on my hands, so I wouldn't fall over or anything. But I remained sitting cross-legged on the cot with my back very straight as in a meditation pose. I kept my eyes fixed on the drained expanse of sky beyond the cement dome. The only sound was from the Bhais shouting and making music way below, and Crishi's voice close to me, telling me that Michael had killed himself. Here for the first time I gave a start, and this made Crishi speak a little bit defensively: "I don't know why you believed all that about him getting hurt in a fight—he was perfectly okay, I tell you, and why he had to go and do what he did is an absolute mystery to me. Or it would be if I didn't know Michael and how—well, I have to say it—how crazy he could be." He was silent after that. I waited. When he went on talking, it was very gently, in a gently sympathetic way, trying to make it as easy for me as possible. He told me that Michael had taken pills. I said "What pills?" Even then I knew it couldn't be because Michael never had any pills, not as much as an aspirin; he wouldn't touch them on principle. Crishi said he didn't know the exact details, but it would all be explained to me by the coroner and the doctor who had made the report. "Yes it's all done, everything's been taken care of, sweetheart," he said. "That's one advantage of a dump like this—you know everyone and can get things done without the usual hassle. I did want to spare you all that, sweetheart, because it can be very nasty. That's why I made you come by train—so it would be over by the time you got here. The plane was flying—I told you a lie there, and I'm sorry." He kissed my cheek most sweetly.

I said "But why? Why?" really wanting to know why this should have happened to Michael. I wasn't hysterical, not in the least, but Crishi knew how much I needed his help in this most terrible moment of my whole life. He said "Let's sit quiet for a bit," and we did that. He was holding my hands, and from time to time he kissed me, as before, very chastely on the cheek. We must have sat for a long time because the colorless sky began to change—first it faded even more, then it began to flush with a changeable light, now dazzling gold, now orange melting into pink.

At last I said "Didn't he leave a letter or anything? Nothing at all? Not one word for me?"

"Yes he did. Of course he did, sweetheart. If you'll let me go a minute, I'll get it. Just one second," he pleaded, for I was reluctant to let go his hands. I felt they were the one anchor I still had, and had to cling to.

He went around to the other side of the dome and came back with a file of papers he must have kept hidden there. He opened it and took out Michael's letter—or rather, a photocopy of it; the original he said was with the coroner. Photocopies always look sort of official and impersonal, and what it said was too: It was only two lines—"No one is to blame. I don't want to live anymore. I apoint my sister Harriet sole heir of our joint inheritence." It was signed Michael Wishwell and was undated.

The sky was in full flood of sunset—and a desert sunset at that, compensating for the dun day—and the Bhais down below had got louder with their chanting and music. Crishi said it was at just this hour, and with just this sort of flamboyant sunset, that they had cremated Michael. "We had to," he apologized. "I wish we could have waited for you, but you know how it is with the heat in India; it has to be done the same day." He tried his best to make it up to me by describing the ceremony to me—and it did sound beautiful, with this glorious sky and the flames leaping up in it, and they had got a priest to chant some very ancient Sanskrit verses; Crishi himself had performed a brother's office, which was only right since he *was* his brother.

I didn't want to hear any more. Of course one day I would want to know everything, every detail of what had happened, over and over again, but now at this time I wanted only to be silent; to rest. Yes, rest and recuperate, as you have to when you have received a blow that has shattered and stunned you till you can't even get up on your legs and move, let alone think or anything. Crishi completely understood my need and was prepared for us to sit there for as long as I wanted. He continued to hold my hands and sometimes to kiss me with his cool, sweet lips. The color had gone from the sky and it was that sort of dim, translucent light there is at dawn as well as dusk, for it seems that light dying is the same as light being born. There was a slight segment of moon and this too was dim and pale.

When it was almost completely dark, Crishi said "What about this?" He indicated the photocopy still lying in my lap. He took it up and looked at it, turning it over back and front although he could hardly have read anything in the dark. "It doesn't look much like Michael's writing, does it? No," he answered himself, pursing his lips. "What's friend Pritchett and all those clever lawyers of yours going to say when they see it? We can tell them till we're blue in the face that people under stress don't write the same as normal, they still won't believe us. They might even say we forged it, you and I— you know how they are."

I was hardly up to these considerations, but I think Crishi was deliberately trying to fix my mind on something practical. Usually people get over the immediate shock of loss by thinking about funeral arrangements, but since here all that had been taken care of, he wanted to get me going in some other way. He took out his cigarette lighter and lit the candle in the chimney lamp. He could do this easily since there was no breeze; and the flame hardly flickered within the glass chimney but was as still as in a still room. The light shone through the colored glass and it wasn't very bright, but with good eyesight, which I had, it was possible to write by it. Crishi took a blank sheet of paper out of the file in which Michael's note had been and he gave me his ballpoint to write with.

Michael's handwriting and mine were similar, though not the same. His was bigger and more scrawly, so that was how I tried to make mine now. It wasn't difficult and I almost enjoyed it. It was as though I were entering him, becoming him; and that was what I tried to do with my thoughts—to make them Michael's thoughts; what *he* would have written. I said that I—that is, I, Michael—was going away because there was nothing in this world that was good enough for me; that I had tried everything and had looked in every direction and there was just absolutely nothing that came up to my expectations. I said that if once you have these expectations—that is, of Beauty, Truth, and Justice—then you feel cheated by everything that falls short of them; and everything here—that is, here in this world—does fall short of them. It is all neti, neti. I wrote with ease—I mean, it came easily to me because I knew it was what Michael felt; but at the same time I was writing I was crying because it wasn't what I—I, Harriet—believed at all; how could I, and especially with Crishi sitting there beside me. At one point he told me to copy the end part of Michael's note and I did so, correcting "apoint" and "inheritence," for Michael's spelling was always perfect. In order to see to write, I had to bend my head close to the lamp, which made my hair fall over either side of my face like a curtain. Every now and again Crishi lifted the strands on one side to kiss my cheek, murmuring to encourage and comfort me; and to please him and also in gratitude for his concern, I tried to smile, though I was crying too. My tears fell on the paper, and when I wiped them off they smudged the writing, but Crishi said that was all right, for they appeared to be not mine but Michael's tears.